D0009297

Berkley titles by Nalini Singh

Psy-Changeling Series

SLAVE TO SENSATION
VISIONS OF HEAT
CARESSED BY ICE
MINE TO POSSESS
HOSTAGE TO PLEASURE
BRANDED BY FIRE
BLAZE OF MEMORY
BONDS OF JUSTICE

PLAY OF PASSION
KISS OF SNOW
TANGLE OF NEED
HEART OF OBSIDIAN
SHIELD OF WINTER
SHARDS OF HOPE
ALLEGIANCE OF HONOR

Psy-Changeling Trinity Series

SILVER SILENCE

OCEAN LIGHT

Guild Hunter Series

ANGELS' BLOOD
ARCHANGEL'S KISS
ARCHANGEL'S CONSORT
ARCHANGEL'S BLADE
ARCHANGEL'S STORM
ARCHANGEL'S LEGION

ARCHANGEL'S SHADOWS
ARCHANGEL'S ENIGMA
ARCHANGEL'S HEART
ARCHANGEL'S VIPER
ARCHANGEL'S PROPHECY

Anthologies

AN ENCHANTED SEASON
(with Maggie Shayne, Erin McCarthy, and Jean Johnson)
THE MAGICAL CHRISTMAS CAT
(with Lora Leigh, Erin McCarthy, and Linda Winstead Jones)
MUST LOVE HELLHOUNDS
(with Charlaine Harris, Ilona Andrews, and Meljean Brook)
BURNING UP
(with Angela Knight, Virginia Kantra, and Meljean Brook)
ANGELS OF DARKNESS
(with Ilona Andrews, Meljean Brook, and Sharon Shinn)
ANGELS' FLIGHT
WILD INVITATION
NIGHT SHIFT
(with Ilona Andrews, Lisa Shearin, and Milla Vane)
WILD EMBRACE

Specials

ANGELS' PAWN
ANGELS' DANCE
TEXTURE OF INTIMACY

DECLARATION OF COURTSHIP
WHISPER OF SIN
SECRETS AT MIDNIGHT

Archangel's Prophecy

Nalini Singh

JOVE
New York

A JOVE BOOK
Published by Berkley
An imprint of Penguin Random House LLC
375 Hudson Street, New York, New York 10014

ISBN: 9780451491640

First Edition: November 2018

Printed in the United States of America
1   3   5   7   9   10   8   6   4   2

Cover art by Tony Mauro

A time of death
A time of life
The drinker of blood lost
The agony of rebirth
The last feather to fall
Such eyes of wild fire, Such broken dreams
One must die for one to live
And the birds, ah, the birds always know

—ARCHANGEL CASSANDRA, ANCIENT AMONG ANCIENTS,
LOST TO AN EONS-LONG SLEEP

1

Elena noticed the sparrows with the periphery of her mind.

The small birds were dipping and dancing beyond the Tower windows, their wings nearly brushing the glass. For a second, she felt a chill on the back of her neck, but then the sparrows flew off to do sparrow business and she realized she was being paranoid. Just because the city's birds had gone all creepy and otherworldly once didn't mean every sparrow was a harbinger.

Sometimes a bird was just a bird.

She returned to her Scrabble death match with Vivek.

Ten minutes later, the two of them were taking an insane amount of pleasure in arguing over a word when Sara called to ask her to track a young vampire who thought he could skip out on his Contract. "Why?" she said to both Sara and Vivek, after putting the conversation on speaker.

"Because you're a Guild Hunter, and we find and haul back runaway vampires," was Sara's dry response. "If you don't know that by now, Ellie, there's no hope for you."

"No." Elena leaned back in her chair across from Vivek.

"Why do a certain percentage of baby vamps think that (a) all the nasty, terrible things they've heard about the old angels aren't true, and (b)—after discovering that, in fact, all the previous knowledge they had *is* true, why do they think they'll be the one wet-behind-the-ears idiot who'll make it to freedom?"

Both of those things made zero sense to Elena. You'd have to be blind, deaf, and mentally unhinged not to realize that angelkind was not human in any way, shape, or form. To a being who had lived a thousand years, what were mortals and new-Made vampires but bugs to be crushed? Nothing but fragile fireflies. Pretty perhaps, if your tastes ran that way, but gone and forgotten in mere heartbeats.

That Elena was now the consort of the most powerful immortal in North America didn't change her bone-deep understanding of that searing truth. Raphael was learning to act with more humanity because of the bond of love that tied them together, but he *wasn't* human, and he never would be; it'd be like asking a ferocious tiger to turn tame. An impossibility—and a destruction.

Raphael was a glorious fury, a *power.*

Elena was a newborn angel with a heart that would always be mortal, even should she live ten thousand years.

"I have an answer." Vivek raised his hand, his sharply handsome face bearing a cheek-creasing grin, and the rich brown of his skin lit with good humor.

It had been a long time since Elena had seen any sign of the petulance and pettiness that had once been as much a part of him as his striking intellect. Then, Vivek had controlled the Cellars, the hidey-hole the Guild kept for hunters who needed to lie low for a while—such as a wayward hunter who might've slit the throat of a vampire so brutally powerful he was an archangel's second.

Elena still wasn't sorry about that. Dmitri had deserved to feel the lethal edge of her knife and more. And it wasn't as if he'd been at any risk of dying. The arrogant fuck had blown her a kiss while his shirt was wet with darkest crimson, the blood loss nothing to a vampire that strong.

Not that his lack of injuries and twisted delight in the violent interaction had stopped him from stalking Elena—hence her need to disappear into the Cellars. In that underground world, Vivek had been king, and he'd relished his power. Piss him off and you'd say good-bye to air-conditioning, your room a sauna—and forget about fresh coffee. These days, however, the Cellars were someone else's domain; and, like her, Vivek was growing into a strange new skin.

In the five years since he'd been Made a vampire, the formerly tetraplegic guild hunter had regained the use of his arms and most of his upper body. Even though his lower body remained numb to sensation and offered no way for him to get out of the wheelchair he'd been in since childhood, Vivek wasn't complaining.

The healers had predicted it would take *decades* for him to regain even basic movement.

"Enlighten us," Sara said in response to Vivek's declaration, her tone distinctly amused. Whispers coming through the line told Elena her best friend was clearing paperwork while she spoke to them; the Guild director's job was never finished.

"The transition to vampirism," Vivek said in an ostentatiously pompous tone, "causes a reaction in a small percentage of vampires that turns on the idiot gene." He held up a finger in a "pay attention" stance. "Said gene is located on chromosome pair twenty-four, colloquially known as the vampire chromosome."

Elena nodded with equal solemnity. "An intriguing hypothesis, Professor Kapur. Perhaps you should apply for a VPA research grant."

As Vivek cracked up at her reference to the Vampire Protection Authority—which seemed to exist to slap guild hunters with "excessive force" violations, usually while the hunters were still bleeding from vampire bites and clawings—Sara said, "If you two comedians are finished, I need you to haul ass, Ellie. Angel involved is very senior and very angry. Name's Imani."

Elena could've resigned from the Guild years ago. Being

Consort to the Archangel of New York tended to tie up a woman's time. But she'd clung to the Guild with her fingernails, being a hunter as much a part of her psyche as breathing. Even more so because she was hunter-born: a bloodhound with the capacity to track vampires by scent.

Rusted oak, champagne, sugar mixed with camphor, a cascade of flowers.

Just four scents among the millions in the world. Her brain had the capacity to narrow down a particular scent to a particular vampire. Vivek, for example, was cold and fresh river water and a vivid burst of aquamarine shards. She knew the latter wasn't a scent, but it was the only way she'd found to describe what she picked up around her friend.

As for the angel-tracking ability she'd begun to develop after waking as an angel, that remained erratic at best and nonexistent at worst.

"I know Imani," she said to Sara.

"I was hoping you'd say that. She's . . . touchy."

That was one word for the angel in question. "I'll calm her down."

"I've sent the details to your phone. You want a necklet?"

"No, I'll be fine." No point detouring to Guild HQ for the vampire immobilization device when she already had the advantage of wings as well as a droplet of immortal strength. Not much. Laughable when compared to angelkind, but she was now much harder to hurt than any other hunter in the Guild. "If I can't haul back a runner on my own, I need to be put in Guild remedial school."

As Vivek grinned, Sara said, "Come by tonight for a coffee. I want to talk to you about something."

"I'll be there." Hanging up, Elena pointed a finger at Vivek. "I do not withdraw my challenge about your most recently *created* word."

"Your funeral." Vivek had on his Scrabble poker face. "I'll save the game to continue the next time you're in." A beep sounded behind him in the surveillance control center.

Turning his wheelchair around using his hands, he went

to check on the alert. After much anguish, he'd retired his previous high-tech and networked electronic chair—the manual chair gave him a way to exercise his upper body without having to spend even longer with the physiotherapists. He'd bulked up considerably in the past couple of years, his shoulders strong and his arm muscles defined.

"Ellie, hey, wait." He flicked up an image onto one of his many screens. "Signs of seismic activity out by the Catskills."

"Shit." She stared at the jagged lines that danced across the screen, her stomach suddenly in knots and images of the sparrows blazing to the forefront of her mind. One word loomed large in her thoughts: *Cascade*.

A confluence of time and unknown critical events that had ignited a power surge in the archangels who ruled the world, with a side-helping of random cataclysmic occurrences, the Cascade had demonstrated a tendency to spike then flatline as it built toward an endgame none of them could predict. It had been two and a half years since the last resurgence—back during her and Raphael's trip to Morocco—and she'd been hoping the damn thing would go from dormant to stone dead.

Elena was sick of fucking *zombies*, impossible diseases that struck angels from the sky, and storms and quakes that left scars in the earth. Oh, and let's not forget the Hudson turning crimson, as if the city was bleeding. That had been just lovely. "How bad?"

"Too deep and too weak for humans to feel. And it looks like I have a report from the seismic people at the university." He read the e-mail. "Movement tagged as standard settling of the land. Only picked up because they're testing the super-sensitive new equipment the Tower helped finance."

Stomach unknotting, Elena blew out a quiet breath. No Cascade-linked insanity, then. No need to put on her tinfoil hat and start yelling about the end of the world. Just a tiny—*normal*—tremor deep in the earth. "Ping me if you get any more alerts, and make sure Dmitri knows too. I better get going on this hunt."

Vivek swiveled his wheelchair around. "Happy hunting." In his eyes, dark and intense, lived a feral hunger. It was as if his transition to vampirism had splintered more than two decades of grim-willed control.

Because Vivek, too, was hunter-born, the hunt in his blood.

That he hadn't gone mad long ago was a testament to his incredible resolve. Elena had used him as backup on two recent jobs where he could situate himself on a rooftop and cover her using a sniper's rifle. A number of other hunters had pulled him in the same way. For now, that seemed to be enough to take the edge off. "You, too," she said with a nod at his control center. "Say hi to your man-crush for me."

A raised middle finger before he turned back to the screens that flowed with data. "Come back when you're ready to get massacred on the Scrabble board."

Leaving the Tower's tech hub with a final "You made up that word!"—to which Vivek called out, "Illiterate Luddite!"—she read the details of the job on her way to her and Raphael's Tower suite. All she had on her were knives, and she liked to take a weapon with distance reach when on a retrieval.

Droplet of immortal strength or not, arrogance was a good way to get dead.

Just last week, Ransom had barely escaped being disemboweled by an aggressive vampire's disgusting dirty claws. Some people had no sense of good hygiene. As it was, Ransom's treasured leather jacket hadn't escaped the attempted mauling unscathed.

He'd still be sulking over it if his wife hadn't managed to source a near-identical jacket from who-knew-where: Librarians obviously had stellar research skills. And librarians married to guild hunters had nerves of steel. Per Ransom, his wife had told him to hose himself clean of the vampire blood before he set foot in their home.

Demarco had snorted when Ransom relayed that story, the shaggy blond of his hair in serious need of a cut. "I wouldn't obey my wife's orders like that—you gotta be the man in the relationship, wear the pants."

"Sure," Ransom had drawled, unperturbed. "I'll pass your words of wisdom on to Nyree the next time she talks about inviting your sorry ass over for dinner. Enjoy the moldy bread in your fridge."

Laughing at the memory of how Demarco had clutched at his heart and fallen off his chair, Elena entered the suite. She grabbed her crossbow first and strapped it to her left thigh. Lightweight, with the extra bolts carried in a new flat quiver she would strap to her other thigh, she treasured and babied it like it was "her precious."

Ransom's words.

Also true.

She decided against a gun; she kept up her training, but the crossbow combined with blades was more her thing. Today, she slid a long blade into the sheath that ran down her back. The near-white of her hair was already in a tight braid, and she had her heavy-duty hunting knife in her boot, so all that was left for her to do was check that the knives she wore in her forearm sheaths were all snugly slotted in, and she was done.

Striding across the thick carpet of the living area, she opened the doors that led out to a railingless balcony and stepped into the crisp white of a winter's day.

The cold slapped her. Hard.

She gritted her teeth, grateful for her long-sleeved thermal black top. It had been designed especially for her, to provide a measure of protection at high altitudes. She had nowhere near ordinary angelic levels of cold toleration. The squadron with whom Raphael had gone out in the predawn darkness were probably in sleeveless tunics.

Her teeth threatened to chatter.

"Screw looking tough," she said to the disinterested pigeon that had stopped on the balcony. "I'd rather be warm." Going back inside, she pulled on a form-fitting black jacket designed with slits for her wings, and fancy straps that held it tight to her body. Then she tugged on gloves for good measure—after first moving the forearm knife sheaths on top of the jacket sleeves.

"Okay, *now* I'm ready."

Shutting the balcony doors behind herself, because she had no desire to return to an arctic environment, she took a moment to enjoy the glittering spectacle of New York gearing up for the day after a long, cold night, then fell off the edge of the balcony, her wings spreading behind her in a snap of strength. Those wings were an extraordinary blend of colors, beginning as pure black on the inner curve, then flowing into indigo, deepest blue, and the whispered shade of dawn.

Her primaries were a shimmering white-gold.

Beautiful wings, but they could've been dishwater brown and she'd have loved them as much, for they took her to the skies.

The air was razored glass in her lungs, it was so cold, but a cool yellow sun rode the sky today. The distant star wasn't strong enough to melt the snow that blanketed the city, but it made that snow ignite with light and turned the ice that dripped off the edges of buildings into iridescent diamonds.

Beneath her, the Legion building lay draped in pristine white.

The greenery that covered its outsides in spring and summer slept under winter's kiss, but Elena knew that should she fly inside, she'd be met with a blast of heat and the rich, earthy humidity of growing things. Green was the color of the Legion building on the inside—living green.

The beings who'd risen from the sea in response to the turbulence of the Cascade, their age unknown and their origins lost in time, had worked with two of the Tower engineers to create a method of heating for their building that didn't put undue pressure on the city's systems, but that kept their plants alive through the coldest months. At least ten of the Legion sat with gargoyle-perfect immobility on the roof, their bat-like wings folded to their backs.

Snow had collected on their motionless bodies, a coat they didn't shrug off and never seemed to feel.

Elena. Elena. Elena.

No movement from the gargoyles, but their whispers echoed inside her head, the Legion's voice both singular and a multitude.

Waving a quick hello, she carried on toward the Hudson River. It had begun to freeze at the edges, shards of ice spearing across its surface in a jagged painting, but that ice was an illusion. It wouldn't hold if she landed on it—a frigid truth two younger angels had learned yesterday.

Regardless, the beauty of it stole her breath.

Maybe that was why it took her a second to notice the sparrows.

2

Elena wasn't strong enough to hold a proper hover, but she could do a short approximation using delicate wing movements. What she saw had her throat going dry. *Raphael?* It was instinct to reach out to her archangel even though she knew he was probably out of range—after completing a set of training maneuvers with the squadron, he'd left to meet with a senior angel in another state.

But the wind and the salt-lashed rain, it crashed into her mind in a welcome storm. *Hunter-mine.*

The birds are being weird again.

Describe it for me.

Elena swept around to watch the hypnotic mass movement again. *They're dancing all together. Thousands and thousands of them. This giant spiral that moves and sways and sweeps like a choreographed chorus line.*

Storm winds in her mind, the scent of ozone sharp and unmistakable, Raphael's presence powerful even at so far a distance. *You are witnessing a murmuration. Are you close enough to recognize the birds?*

Elena went to say "sparrows" then realized she was wrong. *Starlings.* She slapped a hand on her forehead. *A starling murmuration. Unusual but a natural phenomenon.* Blowing out a breath, she said, *Go back to flying to your meeting. My paranoia and I are going to continue heading to the Enclave to track a rogue vamp—and if you tell anyone I nearly lost my mind over a bunch of birds doing bird things, I will spike your cognac with chili peppers.*

His laughter was a feeling more than a sound. *I will see you tonight,* hbeebti.

Shaking her head at her jumpiness this morning—next, she'd start imagining heavily armed enemy angels in the sky—she reached the other side of the perfectly *normal*-colored Hudson River to sweep over her and Raphael's home. No footsteps broke up the glimmering layer of fresh snow that had fallen after she left, but she knew that, inside, the house would be humming with quiet efficiency.

Montgomery, butler beyond compare, would permit nothing less.

Angling inward from the cliffs and trying not to listen to her yet-elevated heartbeat, she flew deeper into the exclusive neighborhood populated almost entirely with angelic homes. The only exceptions were a rare few old vampires—and Janvier. The comparatively young Cajun vampire had been given the house by an angel in thanks for a task where Janvier had gone above and beyond.

He'd never lived in it until Ashwini and he became a pair.

No mortal called the Enclave home, and as an ex-mortal, Elena figured that was probably better for their health. Old immortals weren't always rational in their behavior—they might be sorry for decapitating an annoying neighbor, but said neighbor would still be deader than dead.

Flying on, she considered the facts of this job. Vampire concerned was one Damian Hale. The easiest place to start would be his room at Imani's residence; that he was suspected to have run the previous night, his disappearance not noticed until this morning, shouldn't matter to her bloodhound nose.

Neither was the weather a problem.

After many winter hunts since she'd first joined the Guild, Elena could scent-track through snow so long as the scent wasn't buried too deep. Since it had snowed only a little this morning, she should be fine.

Spotting the correct home—though "mansion" was the better word for the stately edifice that occupied its surroundings like a grand dame who had no time for anyone's bullshit—Elena winged down to land on the snow-covered lawn.

It had been churned up by multiple pairs of feet.

Elena winced, her nose assaulted by a chaos of scents tangled together in a great big knot; if Damian Hale's was in there, it'd be a pain in the posterior to dig it out.

"Consort." The vampire waiting in the doorway wore a white bow tie and old-fashioned black tails over a pristine white shirt, his pants pressed to razor sharpness and his shoes polished to a shine. He bowed his stilt-tall body in her direction, the action as precise as the stiffly combed and pomaded strands of his black hair.

Elena nearly expected him to creak.

"Good morning, Taizaki," she managed to say while squirming inside. This deference, it wasn't earned; the old vampires and angels did it out of respect for Raphael while waiting for the former mortal to fall on her face.

It was enough to give any sensible woman a complex.

Since Elena had fallen madly in love with an archangel who could snap her spine without straining his pinky finger, she was clearly in no danger of being hit with the sensible stick.

"I need Damian Hale's scent," she said the instant Imani's majordomo rose to his full height. "A piece of his clothing that hasn't yet been washed would be best, but I can also pick it up from his living quarters."

"I have prepared such an item of clothing." Taizaki's face was Japanese but his accent unbendingly French, as if he didn't often lower himself to speak the barbaric language of English. "My mistress awaits you in the conservatory."

Raphael, this is how much I love you, she muttered inside her mind.

The sea crashed into her again, the storm winds distant but present. *How much?*

Elena nearly jumped. *You're still in range?*

Is that why you are muttering at me? Because you thought I would not hear? I am heartbroken.

Now the man was messing with her. *Just pointing out hunting was faster when I was a nobody,* she said darkly. *None of this making nice with your angels.*

Try not to stab anyone. It would be most difficult to attempt to explain that as an accident—especially given your stellar aim.

Her lips threatened to twitch. *No promises.*

Nodding at the majordomo to lead her inside, she stepped in behind him with a crisp stride. Taizaki picked up speed when he realized she wasn't interested in strolling; she was sure she saw his spine go even stiffer in affront.

He was probably waiting for her uncivilized self to pee on the furniture.

Biting back a snort of laughter at the image, Elena walked on.

The conservatory was a large room at the very end of the building and to the right. Elena had been inside the crisply formal chamber with floor-to-ceiling windows once before, during an evening Imani had hosted to welcome Elena to her new position. The angel might be prickly and about as much fun as an undertaker at a funeral, but she was also scrupulous in following angelic social etiquette.

"Imani," Elena said as she walked in, the majordomo fading away to leave them in privacy.

An angel who bore wings of white with scattered feathers of bronze and had glowing skin of tawny brown glanced over from her position at the window. "Consort." Her hair was a mass of black curls braided fine and tight against the left side of her skull but otherwise left to fall in glossy perfection to her shoulders.

"I was not expecting the Guild to send you." Imani's gown of deep blue velvet moved like dark water as she shifted to fully face Elena.

"I like to keep my hand in, make sure my hunter skills don't get rusty."

Imani's lush lips pressed into a thin line. She was stunning even for an angel: those lips that had no doubt spawned countless male fantasies, high cheekbones, skin so flawless it was ridiculous, that incredible hair, and eyes of cinnamon brown with a darker burst around the pupil. Add in her tall hourglass form, and the woman looked like an artist's fever dream of regal but sensual angelic beauty.

The illusion held until she opened her mouth. Oh, her voice was as lovely as the rest of her—but like her mansion, Imani was a grande dame who had no time for anyone's bullshit. She also had zero time for people who did not color between the lines. Needless to say, Elena was not her favorite person.

"I *see*," she said now, in the tone of a woman who didn't see at all. "It is most irregular to have to deal with a consort on such a matter." A *very* pointed look. "However, I assume the Guild director has given you the details? I made certain to speak to her rather than her underlings—she is a most competent mortal."

Making a note to pass on the compliment to Sara, Elena told herself to behave and act professionally—even though tweaking the noses of stuffy old angels by upending their expectations of how a consort should behave gave her a wicked kind of satisfaction. "I have everything but Damian's scent," she said with commendable cool.

"My majordomo has that for you." Imani opened then shut her wings with unusual sharpness before beginning to pace the room.

Elena shifted to keep the angel in her line of sight, the snow-draped gardens beyond the conservatory windows now at her back.

"I cannot believe the boy was foolish enough to do this."

Damian Hale was thirty-four years old—or that was the age he'd been at his Making. He'd now stay thirty-four for hundreds upon hundreds of years. The one thing he wouldn't do was become a boy. Of course, Imani was somewhere around eight thousand years old and had the "crotchety grand-mother" thing down pat.

She'd probably needed smelling salts after learning that Raphael had chosen a mortal as his consort. Though, to be fair to Imani, she was trying in her own way. Discreetly gifting Elena a book on angelic protocol that she'd written herself had probably been meant as a gesture of kindness.

Raphael, the fiend, had taken great pleasure in reading the text aloud to her every night for a week, as she attempted to hide her head under a pillow while calling down curses on his head. But he'd also said, "Be patient with Imani, Guild Hunter. She is not cruel or unkind. What she is, is a very old angel who finds modern existence jarring—and you do not fit any of the neat boxes she uses to make sense of the world."

With that in mind, Elena said, "Do you have any idea why Damian ran?"

Imani pursed her lips again. "He chafes at the bit." She flicked a hand devoid of rings, though a thin diamond bracelet glittered around her wrist. "He was a leader among men before his Making—a thing called a CEO—and he is aggrieved at not being permitted to run my home."

Elena raised an eyebrow. "Arrogant?"

"A foolish child who believes himself a big man." Imani compressed her lips until her mouth was a flattened prune. "I wished to talk to you prior to the hunt because we have just discovered that he took weapons."

Snapping to full attention, Elena said, "Which ones?"

"Walk with me. I will have my majordomo report to us." Despite her words, Imani paused in place. "How strange," she said softly in a voice that was suddenly full of the dark and haunting potency that was *age*.

Elena didn't want to follow Imani's gaze out the window. Her blood was suddenly cold, her pulse staccato. And in her ears thundered a roar of sound.

Birds, she thought, she'd see birds out there doing inexplicable, unearthly things.

It wasn't birds. It was worse.

3

Imani's roses were blooming.

Roses that had been buried under two feet of snow when Elena walked into the conservatory.

Roses that should've stayed asleep until the green breath of spring.

Roses that were a fucking harbinger of fucking doom.

Elena cleared her throat. "Do you always only plant red roses?" An endless sea of crimson, like a certain river had once become.

What the hell was it with the Cascade and the shade of blood?

"A small indulgence," Imani said softly. "More important, it appears change is coming once more." A sigh. "I do so dislike change."

Staring out at the roses, Elena decided not to bother Raphael again. It wasn't as if the roses were going to grow legs and attack New York. It was only the Cascade screwing with the natural order of things. "You know, Imani," she muttered, "I agree with you on the change thing."

For once in harmony, the two of them turned their backs to the blooming that should not be and met Taizaki in Damian Hale's room. It turned out the ex-CEO had taken two guns and a crossbow. Imani confirmed Hale had enough of a facility with both types of weapons that Elena would have to take care.

That done, the angel left to walk in her creepy rose garden. "Change is disruptive," she said when Elena arched her eyebrows. "But such dark beauty will not long survive the ice. Not even an immortal can stop the rot of time."

Elena stared after the angel for long moments. A shiver rippled down her spine.

Shaking it off, she called Vivek and got him to remotely hack into Damian Hale's computer—which the vampire had left passcode-protected. Vivek discovered evidence of multiple international airline tickets all booked for the same time and day. The most interesting find, however, was that Hale had managed to gain access to the household account and siphon off a significant cushion of money.

"He's no ordinary runner." Elena's blood heated, her pulse faster. "I don't think he'll be on the planes, either. He left this trail for us to find."

"I'm on it." An exhilaration in Vivek's voice that justified her decision to call him rather than the Guild's own tech team.

She was by the mansion's front door with Taizaki when Vivek confirmed her hunch. Damian Hale hadn't boarded any of the ticketed flights. "I've set up a notification alert across every possible system. Anything else pops up, I'll let you know."

"Thanks, V." Elena secured her phone in a zippered pocket, then opened the bag that held the exemplar of Hale's scent and took a deep breath. "The brush of aspen trees entwined with a hint of ripe peach."

Taizaki blanched at her murmur.

Elena shrugged. "Vampiric scents often have nothing to do with the strength or dangerousness of a vampire." She decided not to tell the snooty majordomo that he smelled of burnt sugar candy and curdled milk.

See, she was being all political and nice even though Taizaki had curled his lip the first time she'd ever met him. As if mortality was catching. Montgomery would've never been so tacky as to betray his personal feelings. The first time she'd met Raphael's butler, she'd been a rough-and-tumble mortal hunter, but he'd offered her tea or coffee with utmost politeness.

But, she admitted, Montgomery was the gold standard. Every other butler—or majordomo—was going to suffer by comparison. Poor Imani would be mortified if she ever realized Taizaki's lapse.

Handing the exemplar back to the majordomo, she turned to begin the hunt in earnest.

Roses, opulent and intoxicating and hella-creeptastic.

Elena gritted her teeth against the overwhelming perfume that stained the air and shouted omen, omen, omen! She began to walk out from the mansion in increasingly large semicircles and finally caught Hale's scent about fifty yards out from the front door, heading into the trees that surrounded the property.

Twenty minutes later, the scent came to an abrupt halt. When she crouched down to dig lightly through the dirty snow that had been protected from the light morning snowfall by a heavy tree canopy, she spotted a drip of oil. "Smart guy." She rose, walked out from under the canopy.

Bunching up her wings, she went to go airborne to see if the oil leak had left a trail . . . and felt an excruciating wrenching in her muscles.

Breathless, she froze then tried again.

She got airborne, but her shoulders and inner wing muscles hurt as they hadn't since she'd first become strong enough to pull off vertical takeoffs. The pain throbbed through her like an infected tooth.

Damn it.

She must've inadvertently moved the wrong way and twisted or torn a tendon or muscle. Hopefully it was small enough that her body would heal on its own. Angelkind's healers were gifted, but while they could help the healing process, they couldn't magic away major injuries.

As for Elena's own capacity to heal, it was more than she'd had as a mortal but nothing in comparison to even baby angels. No one knew how long her journey from post-mortal to immortal would take. Keir, a gifted healer respected by immortals, and Jessamy, their trusted historian and librarian, had been digging for information about the previous angels-Made, but so far all they had to show for their efforts were a lot of dust sneezes and reddened eyes.

The frustration was even worse because everyone knew those once-mortals *had* existed. They were the flesh and blood reality behind the legend that when an archangel loved true, his body would spontaneously produce a sweet, erotic golden substance called ambrosia. Raphael had kissed her with ambrosia as she fell, her back broken and the rest of her wounded beyond repair, and now she soared in the sky.

Ambrosia was accepted as a given among immortals. Researchers had even attempted to study it. Unfortunately, they were hampered by the lack of records—or an actual sample. It wasn't as if Raphael had been in any condition to save them a drop; he'd given it all to Elena.

You must live.

Elena's heart stretched on the echo of memory—of the raw determination in her archangel's voice, of the piercing love that had marked them both. But what of the other lovers true who'd come before them? Where had they gone?

The prevailing theory was that the last angel-Made had been born so very long ago that the angel-Made *and* all those who knew his or her name were lost to deepest Sleep. Elena wondered at times about what it would be like to meet one of her predecessors, uncertain if she wanted the opportunity or not. What if those predecessors had lost their humanity after an eon of existence? What if she recognized nothing of mortality in them?

Today, she felt mortal down to the bone, but the pain in her wing had faded from pulsating abscess to throbbing bruise, so she decided to continue the hunt and swing by the infirmary when she got back.

There were no visible oil stains on the road, anything once there long erased by the passage of other cars. This hunt would have to be more technical. But when she asked Vivek to locate Damian Hale's phone, he told her it was back in the general area of Imani's mansion. "He probably hid it on the grounds, hoping to send everyone on a wild-goose chase."

A flock of starlings flew off the trees right in front of Elena. Hundreds of tiny bodies and sharp beaks and un-blinking dark eyes. Thousands of wings hitting her skin. Endless shrills of sound bursting against her eardrums.

She dropped on a bitten-off imprecation, barely managing to catch herself before she fell too far.

"Ellie!"

"I'm fine, I'm fine," she muttered into the phone while the birds flew in a spiral around her before scattering to the winds. "Have there been any other seismic events since I left?"

"No, all calm." Vivek's voice was sharp. "You're really okay?"

"Yes." The Cascade might be stretching awake again after this latest bout of dormancy, but Elena wasn't planning to dance to its tune. No one knew how long the power surge and accompanying chaos would last. It could be decades for all they knew. None of them could stop living their lives.

Today, Elena's life included finding Damian Hale. "How about his car?"

"Guy's got no vehicle registered to him," Vivek replied without pause. "I called and talked to Imani's majordomo vamp—he confirms none of their vehicles are missing." A sudden pause. "Hold on. Our clever rabbit might've for-gotten something."

Elena stayed aloft while Vivek worked, her eyes sweep-ing the ground.

"A lot of the angelic homes have surveillance directed out to the road," Vivek said in her ear, "and the Tower's got access to those eyes in case of enemy threats. I picked up your runner's face in a red sedan, and I'm tracking him using various cameras and toll points. Hacked those years ago, so it doesn't even count."

"Point me in the right direction, partner," she said, her skin going burning hot then searingly cold. Every hair on her head felt electrified. "V," she said before he could answer. "Is there a lightning storm on the horizon?"

"No, weather report says clear skies with limited chance of weirdness." Shifting focus, he began to give her directions; he stayed with her all the way to a small cabin-style hotel at the foot of the Catskills. She ate three energy bars in the air as lunch, drank water from the slim water packet she kept in a lower pants pocket.

"I've got nothing beyond the cabi—" A quiet exhale on the other end of the line. "You know that small chance of weirdness?"

"Yeah?"

"Seismic report came from a sensor located near those cabins."

"Of course it did," Elena muttered even as her skin tingled as if a current were arcing through her cells. "I'm about to land. Call you after I have something."

It took her two tries to zip up her phone in her pocket again, the sensation of electricity was so distracting and disorienting on her fingertips. Her cheeks felt burned with ice, the tips of her ears red-hot.

"Normal thoughts," she ordered herself. "Normal thoughts."

When the starlings surrounded her as she looked for the best spot to land, she ignored them . . . even when she could swear the birds were whispering to her. She couldn't hear the words, the shape of them *just* out of hearing range, but the tone was a warning.

The birds flew up higher now and then to dance in intricate patterns that kept her airbound as she looked on in fascination, but they never went far from her side. A strange, murmuring escort.

That winged escort stayed in the sky when she did finally land—in the large area in front of the hotel that was probably full of wild grasses and flowers in summer; today, it was a sheet of white barely marked by life. A single draw of the bitingly cold air and vampiric scents touched her nose, each line clean and unentangled with others.

There, a brush of aspen and the juicy extravagance of ripe peaches.

Strong. Rich. Not just a residue. Damian Hale was here.

Taking another breath while trying not to notice the electric prickling on her face, Elena triangulated the source of the scent to a particular cabin. She'd just stepped foot in that direction when the electricity vanished. The birds stopped singing. The air froze.

And the earth trembled under her feet.

She came to a halt. An unknown sound made her look up. The starlings were circling in a constant wheel as they whispered their frantic and incomprehensible warning inside her skull.

The earth jolted violently.

Bunching her wings and gritting her teeth against the renewed pulse of pain, she rose up off the shaking ground. Cabin doors flew open below her, people spilling out like disoriented ants to run in the direction of the lawn.

The ground under the cabins began to crumble.

Elena swept down to grab a young woman who was a frightening half step ahead of the disappearing earth. Elena wasn't strong enough to carry a full-grown adult any real distance, but she managed to haul the woman to where the other guests could grab her, then yelled at everyone to go farther.

A scream split the air.

Elena twisted back . . . to see Damian Hale, his arms and legs flailing, disappear into nothingness. The ground had opened up under his feet in a rushing crash of dirt and rock. She flew toward him as fast as she could, but it was a futile effort.

Even as she reached the spot where he'd disappeared

into the stygian maw of the earth, the sprawling and chillingly deep hole began to fill with a golden-red flow of magma. There was no sign of Damian, no sign of any of the cabins. Not even a smear of flesh or a splinter of wood.

The ground stopped shaking.

The earth stopped crumbling.

The birds danced.

Below Elena glowed a wound in the earth that pulsed with scalding heat.

The drinker of blood was meant to die. That was his destiny. To be the first mark in time.

Elena rubbed her hands over her upper arms as the words appeared full-fledged in her mind. As if she'd thought them up. Except she *hadn't*. That had been someone else's thought, and it had been inside her head.

She raised her eyes to the whispering starlings, wondering if they were the source of the words. But the small birds began to disperse under her gaze, moving to sit in the trees or to land around the lava sinkhole. A few flew close to the heat in movements that felt like a dance, only to sweep back up just when she worried they'd fly too close and be burned.

All at once, there were no more starlings in the sunlit winter sky. Only screaming, sobbing people on the snow-heavy ground safely distant from a lava pit that shouldn't exist . . . and Elena's left wing was beginning to drag. It was only when sweat dripped down her temple that she realized she was hovering directly above the lava. Far too close to the core.

She looked down at the viscous cauldron of it . . . and an invisible hand *pushed* her with murderous force.

4

Elena's instincts screamed.

Her first and most overwhelming reaction was to fight—then she realized her wing was dragging even more heavily, and the unknown force was pushing her *out* of the danger zone. After landing safely not far from the sobbing or preternaturally silent clumps of survivors, she turned to walk to the very edge of the tear in the fabric of the earth.

Thick liquid moved ponderously below, the color a glowing orange-red. Despite the movement, it seemed quiescent now, the land on which Elena stood stable. The heat that emanated from the sinkhole to hit her face, however, was a scorching burn that made it clear nothing and no one would survive contact with the molten magma.

Liquid bones, skin turned into crackling, burst eyeballs . . . Damian Hale hadn't deserved such a fate for the crime of arrogance and conceit. "Rest in peace, Damian," she murmured as she crouched down to examine the edges of the sinkhole, deeply conscious that Imani would mourn his loss. As Raphael had said, the angel might be a stuffy old stick, but she wasn't unkind.

Elena. Salt and the sea, a crashing wave of violent power as familiar to her as her own breath. *The ocean is turbulent and rising as a result of the recent earth tremor. Get away from the coast if you're near it.*

So, the quake hadn't been localized to this region. *I'm at the foot of the Catskills—and there's a sinkhole filled with lovely bubbling lava in front of me.*

The minutest pause. *Guild Hunter, we must discuss your penchant for finding danger. I am on my way.*

Any damage in the city? It was full of people she loved.

Wait. Thirty seconds later. *Dmitri says no damage reported. The tremor was widespread but minor except by the mountains near where you stand.*

The tightness in her chest easing, Elena rose from her crouch and had to fight back a wince—damn, she must've hurt her wing more than she'd realized. She took care to make sure she was holding it in the right position before she walked over to the survivors.

No point exacerbating the injury with messy muscle control.

Among the huddle of mortals and young vampires on vacation was a sandy-haired vamp with a laptop under his arm; he wore a brown polo shirt with a graphic logo on one side that looked vaguely like a set of cabins against a mountain backdrop. "You're staff?" Elena asked the man who smelled like torn paper and crushed mint.

"Manager," he said, the whites of his eyes yet showing and his glazed attention on the spot where the cabins had once taken center stage. His freckles stood out like islands against the bloodless hue of his tanned skin.

"I don't suppose you have the guest list on that laptop?"

He stared blankly at her for a long second before blinking and jerking his head up and down like a broken marionette. But the action seemed to jolt him out of his shock, and he opened up the laptop without further nudging on her part. While he did a roll call, she responded to Vivek's message asking if she was all right, then returned her attention to the roll call.

The only person who didn't reply to their name was "John Smith." Not rocket science to figure that had been Damian Hale, but Elena got a description out of the manager to be certain. It didn't take much prompting—Hale had only recently checked in, and the manager even remembered the small scar on his eyebrow that Elena had noticed in the images she'd been sent of her target.

The marker in time.

Shaking off a shiver that threatened to crawl over her at the memory of that otherworldly voice in her head, Elena spread then tightened her wings to her back. It was an automatic action, one she often did when on the ground for long periods. It felt good to stretch out her wings.

Not today.

Stabbing twinges through her back. Razors shaped into long needles.

She sucked in a breath, breathed past the pain. At least she had no trouble keeping the survivors away from the lava sinkhole. No one wanted to end up with their flesh melted from their bones, the aural stain of Damian Hale's chilling screams too recent to be ignored. When the manager offered to organize a bus to take his guests to temporary lodgings in the city, no one hesitated in agreeing.

Raphael arrived before the transport.

Elena heard a whimper from the knot of survivors as the magnificent spread of his wings came into view. Sunlight sparked off the white-gold filaments within his feathers, the midnight of his hair blowing back in the wind generated by his landing to reveal the clean lines of a face brutal in its masculine beauty.

"Archangel." A soft whisper, an equally soft hand slipping into Elena's.

Startled, she looked down to find a boy of maybe five standing there with a rapturous smile on his face. His coppery brown skin glowed, the wide and high cheekbones beneath the baby fat of his face reminding her of a photo Ransom had shown her of his Cherokee great-grandfather. Of course it would be a child who wasn't afraid; children never were of Raphael. *You have an admirer, Archangel.*

Raphael closed his wings to his back with warrior efficiency before turning to nod in greeting at the child. His eyes were a blue so pure that it nearly hurt to look at him, his skin sun-golden. He wore leathers today, a beaten-down brown that bore the nicks of past battles and sparring sessions. The tunic left his arms bare, revealing the sculptured muscle of his biceps. He had been a warrior before he became an archangel and a warrior he'd always stay.

On his left ring finger was a chunky platinum ring with a square piece of dark amber that had a heart of pure white fire. Her mark. Worn always by a being who'd lived a thousand five hundred years before she ever existed.

If the heat coming off the sinkhole was a pulse, Raphael's power was a throb that beat deep in her bones.

He was deadly and he was beautiful.

Most of all, he was hers.

And he had enough heart in him not to crush that of a small boy.

Beside Elena, the boy's eyes widened at being acknowledged, the silent connection more than enough to bring joy to his childish world. Beaming ear to ear, he ran back to his parents—who'd only belatedly realized he'd slipped away.

Elena walked over to join Raphael at the edge of the sinkhole, aware of the deathly quiet that had fallen behind them. People trying not to attract the attention of a lethal predator. All except for a small and bright-eyed little boy who was ignoring his desperate parents' attempts to hush him; he wanted to tell them all about how the archangel had *seen* him!

"He is a strong one," Raphael murmured, though his attention was on the lava, hypnotic in its luxuriantly slow movements. "I will tell Dmitri to keep an eye on him as he grows."

"Already thinking of recruiting him for the Tower?"

"An archangel's work is never done." He stretched his wings. One brushed across her back in a caress between lovers, between an archangel and his consort. "You are holding your wings with unusual rigidity." Those piercing blue eyes formed of crushed sapphires and light caught the much more prosaic gray of her own gaze—prosaic but for the rim of silver that had appeared as she grew deeper into her immortality.

"I've wrenched the left one." She made a face, reaching up with one hand to manipulate her shoulder in an effort to ease the discomfort. "I must've taken off at the wrong angle or something." From the feel of it, she'd done a number on her poor wing. Hopefully the healers wouldn't ground her while the wound healed.

But when Raphael frowned and began to raise his hand to her back, she shook her head. "Don't waste your healing energy on me. I don't want you at anything but full strength with all this going on." She gestured to the deadly beauty of the hot, jeweled chasm in front of them. "Tower healers will fix me up."

Frown not fading, Raphael nonetheless lowered his hand and returned his attention to the sinkhole. "I sense no aberrant energy from it."

"Thank God." She put her hands on her hips. "I can live with random lava, but I'd rather pass on zombies or other nasties crawling out."

A whispering rustle, leaves shaking. The starlings rose en masse from the trees behind where the cabins had once stood, their tiny bodies a black cloud in the sky that swirled for a heartstopping moment into the shape of huge angelic wings. Then they were gone, scattering to all corners.

Elena looked to Raphael, saw his gaze remained skyward. Her own, however, locked onto the Legion mark on his right temple. The lines were complex, forming into the shape of a stylized dragon with no softness to it. It blazed a dangerous blue lit with searing white fire, an artifact of an ancient power that lived in Raphael.

Elena lifted her fingers to brush the mark. "It's afire."

The Cascade awakens again. I wonder how long this cycle will last, and if it will be the final one before the cataclysmic crescendo the Legion warn us is coming. Raphael's voice was the sea at its calmest while treacherous currents swirled underneath. "Look up."

Elena shivered, not wanting to see whatever it was that had captured an archangel's attention. Not wanting to know why Raphael's skin was suddenly brushed with a light that held edges of crimson. At the same time, she had to see, had to know the threat looming on the horizon.

She looked up.

The sky boiled as red and angry as the lava at their feet.

And the rain, when it fell, was almost hot enough to burn. Minuscule bullets fired into the snow, creating tens of thousands of tiny tunnels and causing the survivors to run for the shade of the trees.

None of that, however, was as bad as the haunting and old, *old* voice in Elena's head that wasn't her own: *Child of mortals, your time comes. For one must die for one to live.* A sigh drenched with a terrible sadness. *You must die.*

5

Chilled to the bone in more ways than one, Elena barely made it to the Enclave house as night began to fall in a cold curtain bright with starlight that cut. Her wing was no worse than when she'd first injured it, but she was exhausted. Her muscles ached. Her back felt as if it had been pummeled by a prizefighter. And her boots had turned into heavy cement blocks while she hadn't been looking.

"I think I'm getting the flu," she said to Sara on the phone, after collapsing on her back on the enormous bed in her and Raphael's bedroom.

"Immortals don't get the flu."

"I'm only a fledgling immortal." She could swear her bones had begun to ache too; maybe it was growing pains, a kind of immortal puberty.

She made a face at the horrifying thought. Puberty had been bad enough the first time around—she didn't need a redo. "Was the rain hot in the city?"

"Melted the snow right down. Which means it's now

turned to ice—I almost brained myself three times on the walk home from the subway."

A higher-pitched voice in the background, excited and fast.

"Come on, then"—Sara's tone held a love intense enough to burn—"say night-night to Auntie Ellie."

"Hi, Auntie Ellie! I gotta go to bed." Words heavy with disappointment. "I made you a crossbow. I'm gonna paint it red for *danger*."

Elena grinned despite her fluey exhaustion. "I can't wait to see it." Zoe Elena might be a girl of barely seven and a half, but she'd been "helping" Sara's husband, Deacon, in his workshop since before she could walk. Six months ago, she'd graduated from plastic toy tools to miniature actual tools. "Give your mom extra kisses for me tonight."

"Mwah! Mwah! Mwah!" Each word was accompanied by a loud smacking sound and Sara's delighted laughter.

"Good night, cuddle bug," Elena heard through the line, followed by a deeper voice responding to Zoe's animated tones. Then Sara said, "Ellie, give me a minute to go tuck her in with Deacon."

A knock sounded on Elena's door at almost the same instant.

Levering herself up into a seated position with a small groan, her wings spread out on the bed behind her, Elena said, "Come in."

Montgomery—handsome and precise in his black suit, his black hair newly cut, and his white shirt spotless—entered with a tray. "The sire asked Sivya to prepare a high-energy bite for you," he said in his English-accented voice.

Elena's heart did that mushy thing it only ever did for Raphael. The first time they'd met, he'd forced her to close her hand over a knife blade, cut herself until her blood dripped to create a dark splatter at her feet. Life and love had changed them both, until she could barely remember the cold and pitiless archangel who'd once hired her for a hunt unlike any other.

"Thanks, Montgomery. It looks like I've turned into an

eating machine again." Her stomach rumbled on cue as he put the tray onto a small table, then moved the entire thing closer to the bed. "Can you ask Sivya to make her special energy bars?" Elena's immortal development surged and ebbed like the Cascade, with her body demanding enormous amounts of fuel during each surge phase.

"She begins even now," Montgomery assured her.

Mouth already full of a delicious cheesy thing, Elena mumbled her appreciation. Montgomery's eyes were smiling when he withdrew, closing the door behind himself. Elena put her phone on speaker then dug in.

"Ellie, you there?" Sara's voice.

"Uh-huh," Elena got out past the bite she'd just taken.

"Zoe will stretch things out for another half hour," Elena's best friend said affectionately. "Extra bedtime stories, bathroom visit, a glass of water—our little scam artist's got every trick in the book down pat."

"That's my girl." Elena took a drink of the vitamin-infused water on the tray. "I actually called to say I won't make it for coffee tonight."

"I figured that after I heard about the sinkhole. Is it bad?"

"One fatality." She'd made the notification personally on her way home, hurt wing or not. Imani's sadness had been all the more affecting for being so contained.

"Foolish boy," she'd said quietly as the two of them stood in the midst of the eerily blooming rose garden. "Now he will never have a chance to gain wisdom." Her lovely, sad eyes had met Elena's. "You are tired and yet you offer me the respect of words spoken from your own lips." An incline of her head. "I will not forget, Consort."

Behind her, the roses stirred in a cold wind, petals falling to the snow.

Drops of bloodred against pristine white.

Elena had left unsettled, the roses as unnerving as the unearthly voice in her head. That voice hadn't spoken again after telling her she was going to die, and she hoped it'd stay silent forever. No one sane heard predictions of her own death from inside her own skull.

Talking to Sara was exactly the antidote she needed. After bringing her friend up to speed on the sinkhole, she said, "I managed to tear a muscle in my wing." The increasing pain was why she'd returned ahead of Raphael—there was no point being in the field if she became a liability. "Senior healer did some work on it, slathered my shoulder in ointment then grounded me for the night."

"How did you injure it?" Sara demanded, her tone curt in that way it got when she was worried. "Shouldn't you be beyond that?"

Scowling, Elena told her best friend the worst of it. "Nisia said she'd only seen this injury on baby angels—*actual babies*—who were trying to do tricks before their bones hardened enough." Needless to say, being compared to angelic infants who flew like drunk bumblebees had been excellent for Elena's ego. "She thinks I must've been 'too enthusiastic' with my vertical takeoff this morning."

"So it'll heal?"

Elena swallowed her current mouthful before replying. "Within the week, but good news is I'm allowed to fly again come morning." To lose the sky after gaining the beauty of flight would be a nightmare. "No verticals, but glides and low-speed wing movements are fine."

Sara chuckled. "Remember that time you tore your hamstring jumping off a building on your first hunt?"

"Jeez, Jameisha tore a strip off me." The now-retired Guild medic had been ancient even then, but they'd all been petrified of her wrath. "What's she up to these days?"

"According to her last message, whatever the hell she damn well feels like," Sara said in an excellent approximation of Jameisha's croaky chain-smoker's voice. "You should go rest," she added afterward. "We can talk later."

"No, I could use the company." Grounded as she was, she'd just be eating and waiting for Raphael to get home otherwise. "What did you want to talk about?"

Sara took a long time to speak. "Archer," she said at last.

Elena's muscles bunched. Putting down the savory muffin she'd picked up, she leaned forward with her forearms on her thighs. "I'm still having trouble getting my head around it." Hunters lived dangerous lives, but for Archer to have gone out the way he had, it just seemed *wrong*. "I half expect to find a message from him in my e-mail even though I went to the funeral, even though I know he'll never message me again."

Quinton Archer had been the Guild's Slayer, the hunter charged with tracking down and executing those of their own kind who'd turned murderous. Hunters were trained killers after all, and had the expertise to avoid or eliminate anyone who stood in their path.

It took a hunter to track a hunter. It took the Slayer.

Archer had been so good at remaining unseen by skilled hunters that they'd called him the phantom. He'd been the Guild's Slayer since Deacon stepped down from the position, but Elena had only met him about two years ago—at a dinner at Sara's. The two of them had stayed in touch since; Elena knew he'd only given himself permission to begin the friendship because she existed outside the Guild. He'd never be called upon to track and execute her.

"It was seven months ago today that he died," Sara shared softly. "I think about what his final moments might've been like each night when I close my eyes."

Elena's fingers clenched on the phone. "Do you think . . . ?"

"I don't know." Her best friend's voice held the weight of what it meant to be director. "Losing his wife one year then his daughter the next messed him up—especially after he'd managed to get her into rehab, but he was upbeat the last time I saw him, said he had plans for the future. And the police confirmed skid marks on the road. It was just an accident on a rainy night."

Elena nodded; better to believe that than to think strong, dangerous Archer had suicided by crashing his car into a closed gas station one dark, desolate night. The resulting fireball had lit up the entire surrounding town. "You need to fill his position," she said, realizing it wasn't only Archer's death that haunted Sara but what it meant.

"Deacon stepped in on an interim basis," her friend said.

"But he can't keep on carrying the load. There's a reason he stopped being Slayer when we got together."

"Yes." Deacon wasn't the kind of man who was threatened by female power; he and Sara would've never lasted had that been the case. But Sara desperately needed Deacon to be her husband and lover, never her subordinate. With him, she could lay down the mantle of Guild director and just be Sara as he was Deacon.

Deacon had also forged a new career path for himself; he was now a weapons-maker whose work was coveted by mortals and immortals both—to ask him to abandon that work would be to ask a gifted artist to lay down his tools. "Who are you thinking of?"

"That's just it, Ellie." Sara sounded as if she was moving, pacing. "Who do I ask to take this on? It's a lonely, heartbreaking role. You saw how Archer was. The Guild is family to the rest of us, but the Slayer has to live in the shadows outside it."

Elena thought of how Archer had never accepted an invitation that included other mortal hunters, how he'd only ever had a drink with her when it was just her and Ashwini or Honor. All hunters now associated with the Tower and thus beyond the Slayer's purview. "The new Slayer will have me, Ash, Honor, and of course you and Deacon."

"I just . . . I worry about him, too." Sara lowered her voice. "He left that life behind years ago, but he's stepped back into the darkness for me."

Elena would never know all of Deacon's demons, but she could imagine the toll being Slayer took on a man. "I could act as his backup once my wing heals," she offered.

"*Ellie*. That's not why I wanted to talk—I just need to vent, and Deacon's already handling so much." A sense of Sara pausing. "I'd never ask you to go after another hunter."

History was a whisper of evil and a race against time between them.

"It's all right, Sara. I did what was needed." Or Bill James would've gone on killing young boys. "I've made my peace with it—and if you appoint me Slayer, the Guild will never have to worry about appointing another one."

The idea of executing rogue hunters through time had her stomach twisting violently, but evil had to be stopped. Even when it came from your own family. "I'm stronger than anyone else in the Guild," she pointed out. "Less liable to get wounded during the hunt."

But Sara wasn't open to accepting her offer. What she wanted was Elena's input on creating a shortlist. Elena gave it without withdrawing her candidacy for the difficult position. She also forced herself to continue eating. Her pants were already loose—if she kept losing weight at this rate, one of these days she'd flash all of New York when her pants fell right off.

She'd just ended the conversation with Sara when a hint of movement made her glance toward the windows. Snow had begun to fall again, soft and light, Manhattan a shimmering mirage through it. A snow globe world sparkling with tiny stars. But that wasn't what caught Elena's attention.

Rising, she walked to the doors that led out onto their balcony, wonder unfurling inside her. *Raphael, do we have white owls in New York?*

What do you see?

Owls gliding through the falling snow. She opened the doors, walking out to stand in the freezing cold just so she could watch the exquisite, unearthly creatures move silently through the air. *A hundred of them, maybe more. They're like living ghosts.*

Graceful beyond compare, their feathers sleek and perfect, and their eyes huge orbs that burned a luminous gold. Her fingers curled into her palms, but she felt no fear, only endless wonder that such beauty could exist in the world. *Their eyes are glowing golden.* She reached out a hand to touch one that seemed a bare hairsbreadth away, but her fingers met only the snow.

And the cold, it was searing her bones.

The sea crashed violently against her senses. *ELENA.*

Shuddering, she stepped back from the snow, from the night, from the fucking voice in her head that had held her captive with musical words about the owls, and slammed shut the balcony doors. *There are no owls, Raphael.* She stared at the falling snow from behind the glass, her heart thunder inside her chest. *Someone is messing with my mind.*

That was when she noticed the owl sitting quietly on her vanity, watching her with eyes so haunting in their clarity and beauty that her soul ached.

6

Raphael scythed through the snow-laden blackness of the skies above his territory, his jaw a grim line and his mind only on getting to his hunter. When he neared their home, however, he was drawn not to the house but to the greenhouse that sat a short distance from it.

It glowed from within, a beacon through the falling strokes of white.

Landing outside the glass structure, he saw her silhouette within, his dangerous warrior mate who was so gentle with the plants she nurtured. When he walked in, he brought with him a breath of winter air, but it was soon overwhelmed by the warmth that held sway here.

"Archangel." There was a tightness around her eyes as his consort walked, tall and strong, toward him. She'd taken off her jacket and her larger weapons as well as her forearm sheaths but was otherwise dressed as she'd been earlier, her garments sleek and black. Sliding one hand around the back of his neck, her other on his chest, she kissed him in welcome, her warm lips thawing his cold

ones and her fingers on his face a caress. "Am I glad to
see you."

Raphael curved his wings around her. "Any other incur-
sions into your mind?"

A shake of her head. "Not after the owl on the vanity
flew through the balcony doors." She paused before adding,
"I keep telling myself there was nothing scary or threatening about the experience—the owls were astonishingly
beautiful, and I actually felt privileged to have seen them."
The rim of silver around her eyes glittered. "And aside from
the whole predicting-my-death thing, the voice hasn't
harmed me."

"Do not joke about your death." He cupped the side of
her face, felt the life of her burn him with its fire. "I have
spoken to the Legion." The last time the birds had begun to
act strangely, the voices had been in Raphael's head; it had
turned out the birds had been acting as the Legion's eyes
and ears.

"I don't suppose they sent the owls?"

"No." *The Primary says they remember white owls with
golden eyes from long ago, but they do not know why they
remember.*

Elena ran her fingers through his hair, dusting off stubborn
particles of snow. "No point wasting our time obsessing about
it." Words that held a resolute decisiveness. "We'll find out
when the Cascade is ready to let us know."

I do not do well with such a lack of control, hbeebti.
Especially when it involved her. His hunter whose mortal
heart had permanently altered his own and in so doing,
saved him from an eternity of numbness and ice.

She patted his chest. "We all have crosses to bear. My
most annoying one right now isn't the voice that waxes
rhapsodical about owls, but this." She pointed to the wing
she continued to hold stiffly. "Nisia says it's a toddler's injury." A sulky look to her that would've made him smile at
any other time. "She did what healers do, but she couldn't
repair the entire tear."

Raphael ran his hand down the wing, sending healing

energy into her before she could stop him. That energy was more potent than anything possessed by even angelkind's most senior healer, but it remained stuck at a frustratingly low level in terms of capacity. Raphael's body only ever contained a trivial amount, and once utilized, it took time to rebuild it.

But it was enough to further Nisia's work and ease his consort's pain.

She sighed, moving her wing more naturally after he was done. "Next time I get all noble and turn down your ability to heal"—she pointed a finger at him—"ignore me and do that."

"Next time you will not have a chance to argue with me. I will do what must be done to care for my consort."

"Come, Your Archangelness." Laughter in the curve of her lips as she teased him, a fading of the lines around her eyes. "Montgomery brought me more goodies to feed my bottomless pit of a stomach." Scrunching up her nose at the demands her body placed on her as it grew deeper into immortality, she said, "I haven't got any alcohol out here, so I'll fix you a coffee and you can tell me about what's happening at the sinkhole."

"As in the old movie we saw where the wife waits for her husband with a hot meal and perfectly groomed hair?"

"Don't forget the pink frilly apron," said the woman whose hair was escaping her braid in curling tendrils around a face that bore a smudge of dirt—and whose body generally bristled with knives.

Far more at home with such a welcome, Raphael ran his hand down the glory of her wing as she moved to the part of her workbench that held the trays of food and drink. "We've finished erecting the fence around the sinkhole." Raphael had assisted in shifting the necessary building materials—an archangel could fly with considerably more than the strongest angel.

The construction itself had been done by a mix of human and vampiric firms. The line between mortals and vampires and angels remained, *must* remain, but Raphael's city functioned a great deal more cohesively than most. The battle with Lijuan followed by the rebuilding process had forged certain ties of loyalty and cooperation.

"You built in the windows I suggested?"

"Do not worry, Elena, your curious cats will not pay a fatal price." Smash-proof, the viewing panels had been placed at a number of points around the fence. "Angelic guards will prevent others from overflying the lava." While the furious burst of unknown energy had pushed Elena out of danger, that could've been nothing but luck.

And the idea of her life hanging on such a slim thread was enough to freeze Raphael's breath in his lungs. "Honor spoke with a number of scholars who study the earth." Dmitri's wife was a scholar of growing renown in her own field of ancient cultures and languages. "All agree there should be no lava at that location and depth. It is not a thing of nature."

Pouring coffee into a mug, Elena knit her brow. "It sounds suspiciously like how Naasir and Andromeda described finding Alexander."

"Alexander has a gift for metals. He deliberately created a barrier that would protect his Sleeping body."

After passing him the coffee, Elena began to pluck the browned leaves off one of her plants. "Is there a chance we've got a Sleeping archangel or Ancient below your territory?"

"If an Ancient chose to Sleep in this place before it became mine, I would have no way of knowing." Even the most powerful immortals gave off no energy while they Slept, the reason why they could rest without being interrupted.

Putting the potted plant back in its hanging basket, Elena moved on to the next one on her bench. "It'd be bad, wouldn't it?" She met him with those eyes of penetrating gray that had become more and more true silver as her immortality advanced. "If another archangel woke up."

"It would fracture the fragile balance of the world." Lijuan's disappearance had alleviated the rising pressure that had resulted from eleven archangels being awake at once. The Cadre of Ten had run at a lower number at times during angelic history, but *never* at a higher one. The world was not big enough to separate out that many devastating powers.

"If another archangel does wake," he said, "we cannot guarantee that their demands will be like my mother's." Caliane hadn't insisted on a large territory upon waking, content with a small part of Japan. Alexander, by contrast, had wanted *all* his former territory.

"Just having that many archangels awake . . ."

"Yes." Too many archangels too close together led inevitably to war and death and destruction. Even Raphael's parents had not been able to stay together always. Love, deep and perhaps a touch mad, had softened the edges of Caliane's and Nadiel's power against each other, but it hadn't erased it.

"Catch." Elena threw him a flower that had gone a spotted brown, its petals crumpled inward.

Plucking it out of the air, he closed his hand around it. When he opened it again, on his palm lay a blush-pink rose with edges of gold.

Elena's smile made him feel a proud youth who had pleased his equally young lover. "I can't get over how you do that." Taking the bloom from his hand, she brought it to her nose and breathed deep, her eyelashes lowering, luxuriant fans far darker than her hair. Then, the scent in her lungs, she tucked the rose behind her ear.

"It is a parlor trick." Raphael flexed his hand. "I'd be more pleased if my ability to heal had not stagnated since the previous Cascade surge. At times it seems as if it is becoming less potent."

"What about the other archangels?" Elena bit off part of a homemade energy bar, and he thought her wrist looked too thin. "Do you know if any of them have developed stronger powers over the course of this pause?"

"As far as Jason has been able to confirm, the entire Cadre is stuck in time when it comes to our Cascade-born abilities." His spymaster had a way of discovering secrets even about the apex predators of the world. "However, Favashi continues to concern."

Elena carefully showered a newly planted seedling with water, her movements as strong as ever even if she'd lost weight under the force of an incredible and ongoing biological change. "She being difficult again?"

Raphael considered his recent interactions with the Archangel of China—and it felt novel yet to refer to Favashi as that, China a place that was so utterly Lijuan's. "It's gone beyond difficult at this point."

"Delusions of grandeur because she got to take over such a massive territory?" Elena suggested. "Might be enough to go to a 'new' archangel's head—she's the newest member of the Cadre, right?"

"Yes." Favashi had only been an archangel for a hundred years in comparison to Raphael's five hundred, though their ages were not so distant in immortal terms. But his history was unlike that of any other member of the Cadre—the beloved and treasured child of two archangels, one of them an Ancient, his ascension had been written before he was born, his progress tracked by angels all across the world. Still, they had been startled and shocked when the sky shattered to rain gemstone blue when he was a bare thousand years of age.

"I worry your Bluebell will beat my record."

Elena's eyes were solemn when they met his. "He's too young, isn't he?"

"I barely survived my ascension and I was double his age."

Swallowing hard, Elena said, "Has an ascension ever failed, an angel unable to handle the storm of archangelic power?"

"Yes." A hard truth angelkind preferred to forget. "It isn't simply a case of raw strength, either. Illium doesn't have the life experience to handle the politics and power plays that come with being one of the Cadre—his heart is . . . vulnerable to bruising in a way it cannot be if he is to survive."

Of all Raphael's Seven, it was Illium who was the most human at heart. Raphael would do everything in his power to assist him should the blue-winged angel indeed ascend, but he couldn't stuff hundreds of years of experience into Illium's head . . . and he couldn't protect Illium the archangel as he had once protected Illium the wild little boy who liked to follow him around.

Raphael, can I fly with you? I brought an apple to share.

Raphael! Look, I can do air tumbles now!

Raphael, Raphael, Raphael, my wings are growing as big as yours!

"Do you think it's certain?" Elena's voice merging with the remembered tones of a little boy who had not yet suffered the three great tragedies that would shape him. "That Illium will become Cadre one day?"

"Nothing is certain. But Illium, too, has an Ancient for a parent." His father had been not much younger than Caliane. "And the Hummingbird . . . she is an old and rare being."

After putting down the empty coffee mug, Raphael began to walk around Elena's greenhouse; he hadn't gone far when he reached up to touch a trailing vine that had leaves covered in what felt like fur. "As for Favashi, Elijah agrees with your theory about her being drunk on her newfound power." The Archangel of South America was Raphael's closest ally in the Cadre—if you didn't count his mother.

Caliane had left him bloody and broken on a forgotten field far from civilization when he'd yet been a youth and she'd been a creature of madness. She'd come back from her long Sleep changed. Sane. And willing to take on any enemy for Raphael.

He remained uncertain how he felt about that—his mother had a way of seeing in him the child she'd left behind. She could not see that the cold loneliness of that grassy field bejeweled with blood rubies had forever ended the final tattered remnants of his childhood. Despite that, he accepted that her loyalty was limitless.

"Favashi's always been one of the more human members of the Cadre." Elena dug her fingers into soil to plant another seedling. "I mean, she's still very much an archangel and distant with it. You're the only one of the Cadre who's been foolish enough to fall in love with a mortal and become a little bit human."

Her words stirred a memory, of Lijuan telling him he must murder Elena, for she would make him a little bit mortal. At the time, he'd thought it well-meaning but misguided advice. For even then, he could've never hurt his hunter. Only later had he come to realize that the millennia-old archangel had understood that Elena could foster in him a power unlike any he'd ever before known.

Their wildfire was a weapon of searing life. Anathema to an archangel like Lijuan, who reveled in death, her power feeding on the life force of others to leave them dried-out husks.

"I am quite content with my choice," he said, walking to stand behind his consort. She tucked her wings neatly against her back so he could put his hands on the bench on either side of her as he kissed her neck, the silken weight of her wings trapped in between their bodies.

Last night, she'd fallen asleep on his left wing, his right her blanket and his palm on her naked hip. Such intimacies were theirs alone. No one else had the right to touch Elena in such a way. Now, she shivered and turned her head. "Raphael."

Their kiss was an erotic dance, a languid brush, and a possessive brand. The latter came from both of them, each as bad as the other when it came to claiming their own. Their tongues stroked, played, their bodies both hungry for more and deeply sated at the proximity.

Breaking the kiss on a rough sigh, Elena pressed her lips to his jaw before turning back to her bench. "My hands are filthy," she said, "or they'd be all over you right now." She wiggled dirt-covered fingers in his direction.

"I see you've been using your gloves again." Frowning as she laughed, he ran his finger over a cut on her forearm, visible because she'd pushed up the sleeves of her top. "How did you do this?"

"Probably from the edge of a pot. It'll heal quick enough." Shrugging off the minor wound, she carried on with her potting. "Thanks to you, I'm no longer in danger of dying because of some weird bacteria that I picked up from the soil."

Raphael went to heal the cut, but his healing energy had flatlined. Teeth gritted together, he tightened his grip on her bench. Elena was a blooded hunter who'd helped bring a mad and murderous archangel to justice. Wounds were a part of her life—but he didn't like the look of that cut. It was too raw and deep, as if it had been newly taken; however, she hadn't done it since his arrival.

Which meant it should've begun to heal at the very edges at least. Because while Elena was an infant in immortal terms, she'd already developed better healing abilities than a mortal.

Yet as he watched, she accidentally stretched the wound while reaching for a seedling on the far side of the bench . . . and a fine droplet of blood welled out over the edge.

7

"Elena, we must clean this cut." Raphael didn't wait for her to respond, instead tugging her to the tap she'd had installed in one corner of the greenhouse, on the far edge of the as yet unplanted garden she'd filled with rich black soil.

"Do you remember when you might've cut it?" he asked as the water washed off the blood, the light pinkness of it soon disappearing into the soil of her garden.

"No." Elena stared at the small wound. "It looks too fresh." Scowling on the heels of her words, she shook her head. "We're probably just being paranoid because of the Cascade restart." She pulled her sleeve down over it. "Let's check it again when we go inside."

Raphael wanted to order a healer to fly here at once, but Elena was correct. It was only a cut. A thing shrugged off by even the smallest mortals day after day.

Elena had returned to her bench, Raphael standing a short distance away, when the door to the greenhouse opened.

Illium's golden eyes took in the tableau, and he hesitated on the doorstep. Conscious of the turbulence that held the younger angel in thrall, Raphael said, *Come, Illium,* at the same time that Elena glared. "In, and shut the door, or you'll let out all the warmth. Then I'd have to murderize you for killing my plants."

"You break my heart, Ellie." The silver that edged the blue of Illium's wings glinted in the light as he walked over to the tray and poured himself half a mug of coffee. There were extra drinking vessels, of course. Montgomery knew far too well that Elena's greenhouse was a beacon that called to many far and wide.

"I've just returned from the sinkhole," the angel said after throwing back the coffee and putting the mug aside with a sigh of satisfaction. "No change."

While the report was appropriate and welcome, Raphael knew the real reason Illium had flown here rather than to his home in the Tower. Elena's Bluebell adored her, and it was to her that he would speak things he wouldn't speak even to Raphael. And tonight was the one-year anniversary of Aodhan's return to the Refuge.

The angel who was Illium's closest friend had asked to be resettled at the Refuge for a short period in the aftermath of his sister's giving birth. The pregnancy had been a shock to the entire angelic community—angelic births were rare in the extreme, and Aodhan's sister was young, comparatively speaking. The shock had been magnified when two other angels fell pregnant three months and six months later, respectively.

But after the shock had come a great celebration, the children to come even more cherished in the face of the battle losses resulting from Raphael's fight against Lijuan, as well as the piercing loss of five angels in the prime of their lives due to Charisemnon's plague. Angels had fallen from the skies that day, to smash into buildings and onto streets, the horror of the Falling one no immortal would ever forget.

Aodhan's sister had given birth to a healthy baby boy.

Though Aodhan wasn't close to his sibling—she'd been seven hundred years of age when he was born—he'd wanted to be there for her as she and her lover settled into their new lives as parents. "I think I would like to be an uncle," he'd confessed. "My sister feels the same. She does not wish me to be a stranger to her child as she and I are to one another."

In turning his wings toward the Refuge and the infant angel of his familial bloodline, Aodhan had left behind a city he loved, and a blue-winged angel with whom his relationship had undergone a seismic shift in the years since he first came to New York.

"I spoke to Aodhan before the earth tremor," Illium said at that instant. "He was babysitting his nephew while his sister and her mate had time alone."

"That baby is criminally adorable." Elena's attempt at a scowl turned into a fascinated smile. "I can't get over those tiny transparent wings stuck to his skin. It's almost as if they're a tattoo on his back, an imprint of where his true wings will grow." A pause before she added, "Though, yeah, I can see how giving birth would be a freaking horror show if babies were born with *actual* wings."

Illium laughed at her shudder.

Raphael's own lips twitched. "The bones will harden over time," he told her, having witnessed the transition in the periods he'd spent standing watch in angelic nurseries as a young angel. "Feathers won't begin to grow for two or more years, and even then, they will be baby feathers so fine as to appear to be fluff." Angelic children took a long time to become capable of flight, their wings growing apace with the development of their minds.

"My mother often thanked the heavens I didn't gain the ability to fly as a toddler," Illium offered. "Apparently I was a walking, babbling emissary of impending disaster. Wings would've been the final straw."

Grinning, Elena picked up the mug of coffee Illium had just refreshed for her. "Did Aodhan send you any new pictures?"

Illium nodded and began to reach for his phone. That was when Elena's mug smashed to the floor in a pungent

stain, Raphael's consort doubling over with her hand pressed
against her chest.

The pain was a spiky ball of razor-sharp knives inside
Elena's chest, the hand she pressed over the spot doing
nothing to ease the agony. She couldn't even cry out, her
voice stolen and red spots dancing in front of her eyes.
Shivers wracked her body.

She clung to Raphael when he swung her up into his arms
and laid her down on her back on the floor of the greenhouse.
Her wings would be filthy, she found herself thinking
through the haze of red, as Raphael tugged away her hand
from the top left of her chest and placed his own on it.

His expression went rigid, his wings limned with light,
and she knew his healing energy hadn't regenerated. Before
she could attempt to reach out with her mind and tell
him . . . something, the pain drained away as hard and as
fast as it had hit.

The vacuum it left behind howled with emptiness.

Sucking in a breath, and conscious of Illium crouching
beside her, his face stark, she wrapped her hand around
Raphael's wrist. The strength of his bones, the warmth of
him, the beat of his pulse, it anchored her. "It's gone," she
murmured in a voice roughened by screams she hadn't vo-
calized.

"You're certain?" A harsh archangelic demand. "No re-
sidual pain?"

"I feel bruised, but that's it." As if she'd imagined the
terrible, overwhelming agony. "Did I just have the angelic
version of a heart attack?"

"Angels don't have heart attacks." Raphael helped her up
into a seated position, and when Illium wove his fingers
through her free hand, he didn't object.

"Ellie." Illium's hand clenched on hers, his left wing
slightly overlapping her own. "What was that?"

"No idea, Bluebell." When she described the sensations,
neither her archangel nor Illium had any answers for her.

"Come." Raphael's voice held no room for argument. "We will go inside and contact Keir."

Elena's face was flushed. Her heart pounded like a hammer. She wanted to say that it had been nothing, but burying her head in the sand wouldn't make the bewildering assault on her body disappear. The dark existed whether you looked at it or not. She'd known that since she was ten years old, since she'd shut her eyes and pressed her hands over her ears and hoped the monster would go away.

He hadn't. He'd slaughtered her older sisters and forever broken her mother.

Night after night, long after the monster was vanquished, she'd heard Belle's dying breath.

Night after night, she'd slipped and fallen in Ari's blood.

And night after night, she'd seen her mother's broken arms and legs dragging on the floor as she tried to crawl to her dying children.

"Pretty hunter. Pretty, pretty hunter. I've come to play with you."

Slater Patalis's singsong voice was a horror Elena carried in her soul and would to her last days, but it hadn't surfaced for the past two years, her sleep free of that nightmare at least. It seemed tonight was her lucky night, complete with ghost owls and being stabbed by knives inside her own body.

"Sire." Illium's cheekbones cut white against the golden hue of his skin. "I'm meant to relieve Dmitri at the Tower within the half hour."

"Go—and send Nisia here," Raphael said. "Elena will tell you the outcome."

She loved Raphael impossibly more for that, for understanding that, right then, Illium needed to know the people he loved were safe. He was having a hard time with Aodhan so far out of reach, the two yet struggling to come to a balance in their relationship—Illium had become used to being the stronger one in the partnership, the one who looked after a badly traumatized Aodhan. But Aodhan was coming out of his shell, and the man he'd become wasn't the boy Illium remembered.

The blue-winged angel walked out of the greenhouse with them, taking off in a wash of wind that flicked up snow into the air in firefly sparks. Normally, Elena would've stood on the cliff edge and watched him fly across to Manhattan. She didn't think she'd ever become jaded enough to not appreciate the sight of an angel in flight.

Tonight, however, she kept her hand linked to Raphael's, and the two of them walked directly to the study entrance into the house. "Take off your boots," she said at the doorway.

Raphael gave her *that* look, the one she called his Archangel look. But Elena wasn't swayed. She needed this instant of domestic normality to fight the roar of fear at the back of her mind. "Montgomery will banish us if we destroy that gorgeous handwoven rug with our wet boots."

Raphael didn't point out that he owned everything in the vicinity, rug included. He took off his boots. And she knew. He was fighting fear, too. She felt an ache deep inside her heart; she was the reason he understood fear, and she wished that weren't true.

Together, the two of them walked to the large screen on one wall, and Raphael initiated the connection to Keir's office in the Medica, deep in the mountainous landscape of the Refuge—a place hidden from human eyes, where angelic young were born, learned to fly, and grew to adulthood.

Nisia arrived midway through their conversation with the healer who'd watched over Elena's transition from mortal to angel. Today, Keir—pretty face, slender body, unparalleled medical knowledge—watched from the screen while Nisia examined her.

Elena might've felt vulnerable sitting there dressed only in her pants and a thin camisole except that she may as well have been a horse when it came to the two healers' interest in her body. *What language are they speaking?* she asked Raphael after trying and failing to pinpoint anything familiar in the words Nisia and Keir were exchanging.

Her archangel was a wall at her back, his hand a welcome weight on her shoulder. *I believe it is a form of Old Ossetian intermingled with snatches of Laurentian and the angelic tongue. Also, now they're throwing in Vietnamese.*

You're making that up, Elena said, though she *had* caught the odd word that made her think of the Southeast Asian country.

There is no humor in me today, hbeebti.

"Take a deep breath and hold it," Nisia told her, switching to English with the fluidity of an immortal who'd seen empires rise and fall.

Elena did as instructed, reaching up her hand at the same time.

Raphael's bigger hand closed around hers, the susurration of his wings as he opened then closed them, the sound of home, of family. Never would she associate it with anyone but him.

"Sire." Nisia frowned, her brown eyes dark. "The shadows . . ."

Only a healer would dare tell the Archangel of New York to step out of her light. Elena's lips quirked; she tipped back her head to whisper, "I think she's saying you're hovering, Archangel."

Raphael moved at once out of Nisia's light, for he would do nothing to diminish her ability to help Elena. He did, however, keep his hand linked with Elena's. She was so brutally fragile. A truth he managed to forget most of the time else it would drive him mad. His consort was fierce, a warrior . . . and still so easy to harm.

Seeing her brought down by pain was a sight he wished never to relive. He had nearly lost her in battle, and in that first fall, when she'd lain broken in his arms, but those things could be foreseen in the context of their lives as hunter and archangel. But to be ambushed by an attack from within her own body?

No. Raphael would not lose Elena to such an insidious foe.

"I can find nothing." Nisia rose to her full diminutive height, her simple gown a dark blue-gray and her pointed features shouting dissatisfaction. "The cut is clean, uninfected, and there are no marks on the surface of her skin to indicate an insect bite or other contagion. I see no signs that denote sickness in her blood or bones, but tests will be done for certainty."

"We should use the human medical device." Keir pushed back the black hair that framed his dusky face, his uptilted eyes intent. "Elena is unique. We cannot predict how her body will change as she matures."

Raphael stirred. "You have no news on previous angels-Made?"

"Just so." Keir's delicate face was calm, but his hand fisted on the wood of his desk. "I have searched the oldest records in the Medica, spoken to healers far more aged than myself, all to naught. Our medical knowledge of ancient angels-Made appears forever lost."

8

"What of Jessamy?" Beloved of Raphael's weapons-master, the angelic historian was Keir's partner in the search for information on Elena's predecessors.

"She has managed to speak with an Ancient one who eschews the world but does not Sleep." Keir pushed back his hair again. "He is rumored to be five hundred thousand years of age. We may find an answer among his memories—but it will take much time for him to search the crevices and fissures where such memories might reside."

Raphael's free hand curled into a fist, but he knew there was no way to rush an immortal of that age. When a being got to be so old, his memories were stacked layer upon layer. Not forgotten but lost in a warehouse that held millions upon millions of recollections.

"The scan"—Nisia's voice was crisp—"I will fly ahead and organize it. Sire, Elena, please follow."

"I will call through there." Keir logged off on those words.

"I feel up to the flight," Elena said after Nisia had left and she'd pulled on clothing suitable for the cold.

"Guild Hunter, do you wish to make me watch you spiral down into the frigid Hudson because of another assault of pain or because your wing has failed?" The words came out cold, clipped.

Rather than responding with anger, Elena pressed her palm to the side of his face. "Hey. It's Cascade weirdness. It'll pass."

"No one can predict the Cascade." It followed its own rules, reshaping immortals and the world as it saw fit. "I will fly you across."

A taut moment before his warrior consort's lips tugged up. "One free pass," she said firmly. "To be redeemed tonight." She pressed a finger to his mouth before he could respond. "After that, you trust me to take precautions."

Raphael couldn't get the image of her plummeting from the sky as a result of a vicious slap of pain out of his mind. That very horror had happened to Illium, though the reason for the blue-winged angel's crumpled wings was apt to be very different from the hurt that had taken Elena to the ground.

Yet his living nightmare could not hold sway here, for he knew one thing about his consort: to clip her wings would be to kill her. "Tonight only," he agreed, even as fear tore at his soul with clawed hands, leaving it shredded.

Scooping her up into his arms, her wings neatly pressed to her back and one of her arms around his neck, he carried her out into the snow then lifted off. Three barges made their laborious way along the Hudson, but the rest of the water was dark on this moonless night dotted with stars hard and cold.

Below them, snow haloed the world in a strange twilight seen only in winter, the effect muted the closer he winged to the brilliant heart of Manhattan. Only four days earlier, he'd flown with Elena through just such a twilight—for no reason but that he loved her and she'd wanted to wing through the winter landscape.

Tonight, the wind whistled past his skin with biting

teeth, but he shrugged it off while curling Elena closer to the heat of his body, well aware she keenly felt the cold. She pressed her free hand over the archangelic heart on which she'd written her name and stayed silent as they flew to the soaring column of light that was his Tower.

•

Allowing a barely dressed Elena to be swallowed by the maw of the machine took teeth-gritting control on Raphael's part.

But nothing went wrong and now his hunter—fully dressed once more—stood in front of him, leaning her back lightly against his chest. The contact soothed the serrated edges of his mood, but the change was temporary and would remain temporary until they had pinpointed the cause of Elena's pain.

"So?" Elena said to Nisia and Keir. "Anything to see?"

"Nothing." Lines marred Keir's ageless face, his frown deep enough to create shadowed grooves on his forehead and at the corners of his eyes. "Other than a minor tear in your wing that's well on the way to healing, there is nothing physically wrong with you."

"Having eliminated all other possibilities"—Nisia folded her arms—"Keir and I believe it to be a Cascade effect. The timing is too coincidental."

It wasn't the answer Raphael wanted to hear. "Elena, has the cut on your forearm begun to heal?"

"It must have." She pushed back her sleeve. "Drat, a piece of fluff caught on it." Tugging off the lint, she stared thoughtfully at the wound. "It's not as angry as it was before. No bleeding, either."

Nisia was already reexamining the break in her skin. "I'm not happy with this progression. It should be close to sealed by now."

Elena's wings moved restlessly against Raphael. "Is it possible my body's just funneling energy into something else and ignoring minor wounds? Because I'm starving again."

"I understand your concern, Raphael," Keir said, having followed along with Nisia's examination. "But in this case, Elena may be correct."

"I'll continue to watch over it, regardless," Nisia added. "Elena's immune system *is* working—it's simply slower than it should be."

No, it was working at *exactly* the right speed for a mortal. The problem was that Elena wasn't mortal any longer.

Elena could feel Raphael vibrating with protective fury at her back. He was an archangel, unused—as he'd pointed out himself—to a lack of control. It was a big part of the reason she'd had to fight so hard at the start of their relationship to get him to treat her not as a cherished lover, cossetted and protected, but as a hunter, a warrior, his *partner.*

Not that she blamed him for backsliding tonight. She'd been fucking terrified, too. But the moment was past, and their relationship would crumble and die if she stopped being herself. Which was why she insisted on flying home under her own power.

Once airborne after gliding off a high Tower balcony, she didn't only fly, she dipped and dived without breaching Nisia's order of "no tricks," and in so doing, succeeded in driving her archangel to insanity until he finally played with her. Spiraling up into the starlit sky together under Raphael's breathtaking physical strength, they fell as one to the earth before separating and sweeping out toward the Enclave.

She was laughing when she landed on the snow, her wings dusted with flakes that had begun to fall from the sky as the clouds moved in. "Come on." She grabbed his hand. "I'm so hungry I could eat my own arm."

Eyes as blue as a high mountain lake held hers, Raphael's hair flecked with snowflakes and his wings wrapping around her in an immortal embrace. *"Elena."*

"I know, Archangel." She and Raphael, they had been

intimate friends with loneliness before their worlds col-
lided. After that fateful collision, they'd made a promise to
one another, to never fall one without the other.

To never leave the other alone.

"I *know*," she whispered again, wrapping her arms
around his body and holding on with desperate tightness.

He held her as fiercely in turn, but the cut on her forearm
stayed unhealed, and one of her wings threatened to drop
into the snow, an injured limb being dragged behind a
healthy body.

9

Montgomery had set up dinner in their suite rather than on the library table that was their usual spot. "It's as if he reads our minds." Elena popped four small savory tarts into her mouth one after the other as she stripped. The flight and the snow had shaken off most of the dust and dirt on her wings, but she didn't feel fully clean.

"I'll be quick." Much as she wanted to wallow in the huge bath—attached to this suite—that Montgomery had already run, her stomach was threatening to gnaw on itself if she didn't give it more substantial fuel.

Raphael's expression as he ran his gaze over her nude form spoke of another, darker form of hunger. The Legion mark on his temple blazed. A glow limned his wings. And in his eyes, she saw a tumultuous wave of emotion that threatened to haul her under.

Her archangel was in a mood.

"Do *not* follow me into the bathroom," she ordered as her skin pebbled, her nipples tight.

Hauling her against his fully clothed form in response,

he sat down in a large armchair built to accommodate wings. Then he reached one hand to the table and grabbed a plate overflowing with delicious hot treats. But it was his scent that had her mouth watering, the heat and rigidly muscled strength of him inviting her to forget her plans for a shower and get even dirtier instead.

He lifted a bite of food to her mouth.

"I should feel very naked right now," Elena said after making short work of it.

Raphael ran his free hand proprietarily over the curves of her body and up to boldly cup one breast, rubbing his thumb across her nipple. "You do not?"

"Not inside." She pushed her own fingers through his hair, fisted gently. "Not where it matters. Because it's you."

It was that simple.

"Eat, *hbeebti*." He fed her bite after bite, each mouthful accompanied by a firm and erotic stroke of her body, breast to thigh. His eyes were hooded, his sensual lips unsmiling—and his wings continued to glow.

Skin hot, Elena drowned in his scent while her body melted, her pulse a roar. Her musk perfumed the air, her thighs pressed tightly together, and her lips felt swollen. "You're a demon in a mood, Raphael." She kissed him, bit his lower lip, soothed the sensual punishment with her tongue.

"Do you need more food?" Rain fell in her mind again, a turbulent hurricane. *We must fuel the changes in you.*

"I need *you*." Was desperate for the wildfire of what they became together to banish the echoes of an unknown future that whispered of death and separation. "I want to hold you so close that nothing will ever come between us."

Elena. Setting the empty plate aside without watching to see if it hit the table or not, Raphael maneuvered her so she straddled his body, her hands on his shoulders. His kiss was a ferocious demand, the hand he thrust into her hair unraveling the near-white strands.

Elena kissed him back with just as much passion, just as much love, just as much need. Fear and worry and love and horror, it all entwined inside her to create a small, intimate madness.

Raphael's hand was rough on her skin, his body unleashed power and desire. Thighs quivering and breasts plump with sensation, she pulled at his clothing until he helped her strip his top half bare. She dug her fingers into the magnificent width of his chest, rubbed herself against the hard, rippled strength of him.

Rising from the armchair on a surge of strength that had her going even wetter, his wings glittering under the light, he took her not to the bed but to the bath. The water was a kiss of heat against her skin when he sat her down into it. Sweeping her arms through the liquid silk of it, she watched him get rid of the rest of his clothing.

A shiver whispered through her.

God, but he was beautiful, all hard lines and lean muscle and hands that knew her every weakness. She returned to his lap the instant he joined her in the bath, once more straddling him as they kissed and stroked and comforted one another.

He lifted her up out of the water to suck her nipple into his mouth. Crying out, she arched her back, and he took advantage of her position to lick along the sensitive undersides of her breasts.

Sliding down until they were face-to-face, she took a breathless kiss, reaching down one of her hands to close her fingers over the iron rigidity of him. He jerked and tore away her hand, his eyes pools of unearthly blue flame. As on edge, she rubbed her passion-swollen folds against him. His response was an open-mouthed kiss without boundaries before he tightened his hands on her hips.

When he thrust into her, it was a hard claiming that made her shudder and clench convulsively around him, her arms locked around his neck and her cheek pressed to his. *Raphael.* A whisper from deep inside her, a shiver of pleasure and a sense of homecoming.

Nothing will take you from me. His fingers dug into her

flesh. *Not even the Cascade.* The wind and the rain in her mind, a relentless storm she never wanted to escape. He was hers and she was his, and together they were a unit that could not be torn apart by forces either mortal or immortal.

Wrapped up in a fluffy white dressing gown while her archangel lay beside her on the bed lazily stroking his fingers up and down her thigh, Elena was inhaling another plate of food when she felt an itching over the exact spot that had been the center of the punch of debilitating pain. She was scratching at it before she realized the connection.

Raphael's eyes zeroed in on her hand.

She shrugged. "It itches."

Neither one of them could divine any reason for the itch when they examined the patch of skin. It was a little red from her scratching but otherwise the same as the skin around it. Raphael pressed a kiss to it, the sweet tenderness laying waste to her tough hunter armor.

Running her fingers over the blue-and-white fire of the Legion mark on his right temple when he drew back, she said, "Maybe I'll get a stylish mark like yours."

Raphael didn't smile, and she wasn't sure he slept that night. Safe in his arms, his wing a silken weight over her, she did fall into sleep . . . and into dreams.

"Mama?" Elena walked across the kitchen to brace her hands on the counter . . . and was startled to discover that she was tall enough to do that. She'd always been a child in this kitchen, never quite able to reach the very top of the counter; so many memories she had, of sitting on a breakfast stool kicking her legs back and forth while Ari and Belle and Marguerite and Jeffrey moved around the kitchen.

Beth would usually be in a high chair at the table, either their mama or papa scooping food into her mouth while making silly noises that had Beth giggling and clapping her pudgy baby hands.

Her mother looked up with a laughing smile, all hair of captured sunlight and eyes of delicate silver. "There you are, azeeztee." Gardenias scented the air, the fragrance warmed and made deeply familiar from its contact with Marguerite's dark gold skin. "I knew you would smell the cookies and come."

Elena took the cookie her mother held out. It was deliciously warm from the oven, the chocolate chips not yet solid. Lifting the treat to her mouth she took a bite . . . and tasted blood.

Spitting out the bite of cookie to the floor, she wiped the back of her hand across her mouth, and it came back smeared with darkest red. The scent of iron filled her nostrils.

"Elena." No raising of her voice, never that with Marguerite, but her disappointment was deep grooves on either side of her mouth. "That, chérie, is not how I brought you up to treat food."

"But, mama, look"—Elena held out the cookie—"it's bleeding." Dark and viscous droplets splattered onto the counter, tiny Rorschach paintings in which were written the stories of their family.

Marguerite's eyes dulled. "I was so hoping they'd turn out nice this time. You know how much your papa loves my cookies." She took the uneaten remainder of the cookie from Elena and put it carefully on the baking tray.

Blood seeped out from the edge of every single cookie.

Her mother was crying.

Elena ran around the counter to take Marguerite into her arms. "It's all right, mama," she said, her heart twisted up inside her chest and her throat thick. "It's only one batch. The next one will be better."

But her mother kept on sobbing, and her slender arms, they held on to Elena so tight. "I love you, my bébé, my strong Elena with my mama's heart," she said between sobs. "I'm so sorry for the blood."

That was when Elena realized the entire room was drenched in red. It dripped down from the ceiling, was smeared on the walls, and was a flood under their feet. Instead of screaming, she closed her eyes and held her mother closer. "It's all right, mama," she whispered again. "I'm not afraid anymore."

10

The strange, haunting dream was still on Elena's mind when she ran into Ashwini in the Tower lobby midmorning the next day. Tall, with long dark hair pulled back into a loose braid, and skin of dark honey, the hunter turned vampire wore a form-fitting chocolate-colored jacket zipped up to her throat, faded blue jeans, and scuffed hunting boots.

Gloves stuck out from her back pocket, and she had knives in one thigh sheath, a gun in the other. Her throwing stars weren't visible, but that meant nothing. Ashwini always had several of the lethal spinning stars on her person. "Where you heading?" Elena asked.

"Quarter. Got two dead vamps." Large gold hoops swung in Ash's ears, multihued jewels dangling from the gold.

Marguerite had often worn long dangles in her ears, their tinkling music the background score to Elena's childhood. "Fight?" she managed to say through the ache in her heart for a woman who'd never again slip on pretty earrings or wear her favorite white dress with the yellow flowers on it.

"Nah," Ashwini said. "Not an ordinary fight, anyway—someone really lost their shit." The other hunter turned the screen of her phone toward Elena. "Swipe through for the full effect."

Elena whistled as she did so. The two vampires in the crime scene photos had been butchered. That their heads had been hacked off was fairly standard—most vampires could be killed by whacking off the head, and so that was the default when someone went after one of the Made. It was the rest of what had been done to the victims that was unusual.

The two looked to have been stabbed hundreds of times, until their flesh resembled ground meat. Not just that but other parts of their bodies had also been hacked off. A hand in one case and the genitals in the other. Nothing surgical about the amputations, either; it looked as if the perpetrator had done the genitals with a serrated hunting knife. As for the hand, the wrist bones were badly shattered. Broadsword, maybe.

"Slight case of overkill."

"You'd be surprised." Ashwini slid the phone into a zippered pocket of her jacket. "Janvier and I see a ton of weird-ass shit working the Quarter. But this one might be more standard—I'm hearing rumors the two vics might've been either angling to horn in on another vampire's cattle, or poking their noses in a vampire gang's drug turf."

"Vics post-Contract?"

"Yep."

Elena shook her head. "You'd think after over a hundred years of existence, people would get to be a bit smarter." Poaching from another vampire's harem of permanent blood donors was considered a mortal crime; and as for the drug gangs, their tendency to eviscerate anyone who encroached on their turf wasn't exactly a state secret.

"Why do you live in hope, Ellie?"

"It's a flaw."

Laughter that faded quickly into a frown. "Don't be afraid of the owls."

Elena froze in place, her breath shards in her lungs. "No?"

"No, they're only messengers of a messenger." A motor-cycle purred to a stop in front of the lobby doors, snagging Ashwini's attention. "That's my ride. Off we go to look at blood and gore—Janvier takes me on the best dates."

Skin yet chilled, Elena watched Ashwini stride out to get onto the bike behind her husband. Janvier passed back her motorcycle helmet. A couple of seconds later the two were gone, racing off toward the sin, sex, and darkness of the Quarter.

Leaving Elena with that unsettling piece of advice about the owls. The last time Ashwini had given Elena something, it had been a blade star, and it had turned out to be the perfect weapon to take down the monstrous angel who'd brutalized Elena's grandparents. Ignoring Ash when she came out with one of her random statements was an intensely stupid thing to do.

"So," Elena muttered to herself, "don't get freaked out by the owls." That in itself wasn't an issue; the owls had been lovely and graceful and unthreatening. No, the problem was that Ash's words implied Elena would be seeing more of the ghost birds with the enormous golden eyes and white feathers.

Fuck.

It was the last thing she wanted to hear when she already felt out of sorts, odd. She'd woken in Raphael's arms, a lump of sadness sitting on her chest. He'd known. He always knew.

"Did you dream?" A masculine face piercingly familiar yet beautiful enough to stun, looking down at her, strands of hair purer than midnight falling over his forehead.

"I told my mother I wasn't afraid." A ragged whisper. "I wasn't, not even when the entire room filled with blood. I was just so, *so* sad."

Enclosing her in his arms, her archangel had shut out the world in which her mother and two eldest sisters no longer existed, and, after a while, she'd permitted herself to cry.

For Marguerite, who would never grow any older than she'd been when she hanged herself.

For talented, mercurial, loving Belle, who'd taught Elena to play baseball and whose legs had been savagely broken.

For smart, kind, bossy Ari, who'd tried to protect Elena with her last breath.

For their small, happy family that had disintegrated into splinters.

Even for her fundamentally damaged father, who'd married a strong, intelligent woman who loved him, and yet who'd once kept a mistress who was a pale facsimile of Marguerite.

Haunted by the memories, the scent of gardenias a sensory echo that clung, Elena had spent the early-morning hours on the snowy lawn above the Hudson, pushing her body through a training routine Galen had designed to teach her to fight with wings. Raphael's barbarian of a weapons-master could be a pitiless bastard, but he was also brilliant.

She'd taken care not to jolt her hurt wing, but she hadn't held back otherwise.

Raphael had watched her until it was time for him to leave to join Illium's elite squadron; they were training over the ocean again today. After all that had happened and the certainty that Lijuan would be a nightmare brimming with power when she rose again, Raphael was taking no chances with his people's readiness.

Despite being based in the Refuge, Galen was in charge of the training schedule. He kept an eye on the reports sent in by squadron and ground-force leaders, and mixed things up so every fighter had periods of rest and recuperation—an exhausted force was a useless one—but no one on the Tower team was ever rusty in their skills. Today, Raphael would act the aggressor so Illium's squadron could practice combat maneuvers.

Elena had intended to go up to Dmitri's office and ask him to put her to use. She'd spoken to Sara again this morning, their conversation focused on another name Sara had added to the Slayer shortlist. "No outstanding hunts," her friend had said at the end, when Elena asked about work. "Keiko, Hilda, and Tyrese just came back from injury leave. Have the day off, Ellie. It's not like your life isn't busy."

But Elena didn't want free time; it gave her too much room to think and worry.

At that instant, however, she decided against speaking to Raphael's second. Dmitri would aggravate her, and in her current mood, she might attempt to kill him dead. Since Dmitri was more than a thousand years old and as deadly as a rabid cougar, he'd probably avoid her attempts and laugh. At which point, her eyeballs would explode and she'd give in to the compulsion to pincushion him with her throwing knives.

No, better she kept her distance from the strongest vampire in the city.

Turning on her heel, she left the Tower to walk over to the Legion building. It rose up toward the heavy gray of the winter sky, its greenery dormant under the frost, but that wasn't what cut through her grim mood to make her chuckle.

Holly was scrambling up the side of the building, one of the ice-encrusted dormant vines her rope ladder. Elena figured the palms of her gloves must have a rough surface to provide an effective grip. As she watched, the lithe young woman vaulted onto the entrance platform and glanced at her watch. Then she did a victory dance, the bright pink of her sweater a blaze against the grayness overhanging the world, and her actions aimed at someone out of view of Elena.

It wasn't Holly's lover, Venom, who stepped forward to bow at Holly in graceful defeat. No, it was Trace. Elegant and assured and with a fondness for exquisite poetry. Also a vampire several hundred years older than Holly. But up on the platform, the two of them grinned at each other like children before scrambling back down to the ground.

Holly's daisy-patterned boots hit the snowy earth at the same time as Trace's more prosaic black.

"Were you two having a race?" Elena was *highly* amused that Holly had managed to talk suave Trace into it, especially today. He needed to prep for his upcoming journey to the Refuge.

"Our Hollyberry is faster than a cheetah," Trace said in his evocative voice, the angular lines of his face put together in a way that created a sharp handsomeness rather than refined vampiric prettiness. "I should know better than to accept her challenges."

Eyes of rich brown intermingled with an unusual acidic green sparkling, Holly reached back to tighten her ponytail. Her hair was currently a vivid purple accented with a streak of gold that began at her right temple and carried all the way down. Dmitri had termed the look "grape jelly with a radioactive rash." But it had been said with an affectionate smile and a shake of the head.

Dmitri's treatment of Holly was like that of a father with a cherished daughter—a daughter who occasionally drove him crazy. A week earlier, Elena had walked into his office to find Holly curled up in a chair in the corner, her nose buried in a college textbook while Dmitri did his work as Raphael's second.

"Venom didn't want to join the race?" she asked.

"He's out at the sinkhole." Holly put her hands on her hips, her nails painted a vivid orange with pink accents. "I'm heading there later this afternoon—after I help Trace pack his fancy duds." A grin at her friend. "You come to visit the Legion?"

Elena nodded. "They inside?" Every so often, the entire seven hundred and seventy-seven strong cohort would rise up and fly off somewhere. Once in a while, it would be to Central Park. The first time they'd pulled that trick, the media had been besieged by calls reporting the abrupt appearance of hundreds of gargoyles in the park.

Agog residents had wondered if it was all an avant-garde art show.

It wasn't only the Legion's way of sitting inhumanly motionless that had people mistaking them for stone. Though they'd gained color since their arrival in New York, their eyes and skin and features no longer palest gray, that color wasn't yet solid. As if it hadn't sunk into their skin and was washed off by the elements.

"I think they're hibernating," Holly said. "I can't blame them—it's so cold. I'm pretty sure my eyelashes are going to freeze and fall off at any moment." Her breath fogged the air, her cheeks pink.

On the surface, nothing remained of the naked and mute mortal coated in dried blood whom Elena had found hiding in an abandoned guard station. Elena knew the truth wasn't so simple. Holly would carry her scars forever, but she'd fought back with feral determination to ensure those scars didn't steal her future, and in so doing, she'd raised her middle finger to the being who'd brutalized her.

Elena approved.

"In case I don't see you tomorrow," she said to Trace, "have a good journey, and say hi to Aodhan."

The vampire who had eyes of the deepest green she'd ever seen, a forest under the veil of night, crossed one arm across his chest with old-world grace and bowed. "I will look forward to my return to the city."

The two headed off to the Tower, while Elena strode to the vines.

The Legion had been alive for eons. Maybe they had an answer for her.

About the heart attack that wasn't.

About the voice in her head.

About the cut on her forearm that she'd covered with a flesh-colored Band-Aid when it began bleeding again at the end of her morning session.

11

Pulling on her gloves, she realized she hadn't brought the ones with grips. But when she checked the vine Trace had used, she saw the vampire's claws—*never* visible in company—and boots had scratched the coating of ice just enough that Elena should be able to get to the top without slipping.

It remained a bitch of an ascent. It didn't help that her wings caused heavy drag on her entire body. "Ellie, you obviously left your brain on pause this morning," she puffed out a quarter of the way up, and spread her wings.

The drag became more manageable.

Reaching the top with a grunt of satisfaction—though her muscles felt disconcertingly quivery for such a short exertion—she stripped off the gloves, stuffing them into a side pocket of her slimline cargo pants. She gave her heart and her breath time to even out before she made her way to the thick strips of plastic that hung at the entrance to the Legion's home. She'd used to call out before she entered, but the Primary had made it clear this place was as much hers as it was theirs, and they didn't understand why she asked for entrance.

Elena walked in.

To be immediately assailed by hundreds of whispering voices in her skull.

Elena. Aeclari. Elena. Aeclari. You come. We are glad.

Having been braced for the avalanche, she managed to push the voices away without being harsh. "Use your mouths!" she called out into the cavernous space with a massive internal core. "Remember what we talked about."

Every one of the gargoyles in her vision—clinging to the walls or crouching on the parts of the building that jutted out to the center—tilted their heads to the side, looking at her with eyes pale and strange.

"One at a time," she said, in case the entire Legion decided to speak at once.

What is one?

Elena rubbed her forehead with two fingers. Every time she thought the Legion had begun to understand the concept of individuality, they'd regress and she'd be explaining it to them all over again. It had gotten to the point where she wondered if they were meant to be a unit always, no matter if they slept in the deep or lived in the world. Yet a few of them *had* indicated a desire to explore the idea of "oneness," so she kept on trying.

Today, however, she decided to let it go. Taking a deep breath of the humid green air, she jumped into the hollow heart of the building. The distance down was just enough that she got air under her wings and could beat her way up to perch on one of the midpoint outcroppings—the remnant of what had once been the forty-fifth floor, if she had her bearings right.

The outcropping had been planted with exotic blooms since her last visit. "Where did you get this?" She pointed at a bright blue flower she'd been trying to source forever. "Can I have a cutting?"

One of the Legion landed near her. Not the Primary, who most often spoke for them. This one was nearly fully gray, except for an unexpected brush of color on the backs of his hands. A deep mahogany shade quite unlike the rest of his skin or clothing. That clothing formed with the members of the Legion when they fell in battle to rise again, and it was an identical gray to their bodies.

Reaching out to touch the discrete patches of the darker shade with gentle fingers, Elena said, "What's this?"

"We are becoming," the member of the Legion said before pausing and adding, "I am becoming. I like this color."

Startled at the individualistic statement, Elena looked at him with more care. "Do you have a name?" None of the Legion had chosen names that she was aware.

"I am Legion," he said, the pinprick points of his pupils black against irises so pale they all but merged into the whites. "We made you a plant." Getting up from his crouch, he moved to one side of the garden and returned with a pot in which grew a smaller version of the plant she'd wanted. "We were waiting for you to come."

A small sun in her heart, Elena ran her fingers over the frond-like leaves. "I'll put it by the entrance so I don't forget to take it with me when I go."

"I will carry it down for you." His bat-like wings flared out in readiness. "We have much to show you."

Elena. Aeclari. Elena. Aeclari. See.

They used that word with such ease, but they still hadn't explained its meaning.

You are aeclari, and the Legion may only serve aeclari. Aeclari is you.

That was all she ever got.

At this point, she'd stopped asking for an explanation. The Legion, millennia of information in their collective brain, believed they were being straightforward in their answers. It was simply that they skipped, oh, about six hundred and ninety-seven steps between one statement and the next.

The whispers rose again in the back of Elena's mind.

Dream. Dream. Blood. Sad.

Shifting to sit with her legs hanging off the edge of this

outcropping, Elena looked down at the plants that thrived in this massive and multilevel internal garden. The member of the Legion who'd given her the plant flew back from his errand to crouch next to her while several of his brethren came to crouch on the outcropping facing her. Others flew to cling to the vines that crawled down the walls.

"How do you know my dreams?" she said, somehow not creeped out by the idea.

We are Legion. We are yours.

Actually, technically, they were Raphael's, the power capable of calling the Legion from the deep archangelic in nature—but the strange and *truly* immortal beings tended to treat her and Raphael as one.

As *aeclari.*

"My mama," she said, her hands curling over the edge on which she sat. "I dream of her. She's gone." It hurt to say that, to admit she'd never again feel Marguerite's soft arms around her except in her dreams. "Dead."

Dead.

An echo, not a question.

"Do you understand the concept of death?" Cut down in battle, the Legion had arisen over and over again, an army that could not be vanquished.

We know. We die. Eons we die. Then we wake.

How could Elena argue with that? Surely, an endless sleep at the bottom of the ocean would feel like death. "But you hear the world passing by?"

"Not all," several voices said aloud. "Only the ones who listen. Then we know."

Working that through, she realized that during their times in the deep, only groups of the Legion were "awake" at a time, but as they shared all knowledge gained, it made no difference long-term. "Why seven hundred and seventy-seven?" Another question she often asked.

It is the number.

And that was the answer she always received.

Laughter bubbling inside her, she said, "Have you grown any new fruit?"

Come. Come. Come. See. See. See.

Following the sweep of a pair of silent gray wings, she rose higher after dropping down to gain momentum and found herself on an outcropping situated near the apex of the skyscraper, underneath a glass cover, which was closed against winter's frigid kiss. In the summer months and in spring, the Legion often left it open. Sunshine drenched the building then, and the rain fell in, helped quench the thirst of their gardens.

Today, beneath the anemic winter sunlight and the yellow glow of heat lamps attached to the walls, she saw a perfect patch of strawberries. When one of the Legion plucked out a strawberry the size of a small plum and handed it to her, she bit into it with relish. The juices flowed onto her tongue and down her palm to her wrist, the trail as thick and darkly crimson as blood. She jerked but didn't drop the strawberry . . . And when she looked again, the trail was a pale, watery pink as it should be.

"Did you do that?" she demanded of the Legion, a hot ball of lead in her stomach.

You did. You did. You did.

"Stop." The voices had been rising in volume, mirroring one another and threatening to drive her to madness.

Quiet, broken only by the sound of her own breathing. The Legion could be quieter than death, quieter than stone. "I did it?" She stared at the thin stream of juice. "A bad dream brought to life?"

The Primary's voice reached her from inside the silence. "Yes."

She wasn't the least surprised to turn and discover him crouched beside her—with his gray eyes that had a ring as blue as Raphael's irises, and his hair of black, the Primary was the most individual of all the Legion. But she saw now that the gray had begun to creep through his hair once again.

Backward, he was going backward.

Like Elena.

"What's happening?" She indicated his hair. "Have you stopped becoming?"

He tilted his head to the side, his bat-like wings folded tight to his back and his body otherwise static. "No, this is the second becoming."

Her heart was a bass drum. "What will be the end result?"

"We do not know. But we feel the spiral of energies, the cataclysm of change."

The tiny hairs on her arms rising, Elena held out the strawberry. "Why do I see blood? Why won't my cut heal?"

"Because you are becoming, too."

The Legion lifted off together without warning, a flock of silence. They'd scattered across the skyscraper in a matter of minutes, and she knew that if she asked more questions on the topic, their answers would be exactly the same.

She finished eating the strawberry with slow, deliberate focus on its ripe sweetness then flew down to look at the other new plantings. By the time she reached the exit again, it held a collection of ten potted plants.

Affection bloomed inside her, a strange thing to feel for these ageless creatures who were so clearly not human. "Thank you," she said aloud. "I'd appreciate it if you could fly these gifts to my greenhouse."

We will. We will. We will.

Elena was about to walk out when she remembered another question she'd meant to ask. But agony burst inside her chest before she could speak, red-hot iron pokers searing her organs and perforating her lungs.

She screamed without a voice, would've fallen to her knees except that two of the Legion caught her, one on either side. They lowered her gently to a seated position on the ground, her wings spread out behind her on the lush green grass they'd somehow coaxed to grow inside their haven.

The Legion crouched all around her, watching, waiting, eerie but unthreatening.

Hand still clutched to her chest, she clenched her jaw and rode the pain. Scarlet waves, black nothingness, crushing stone in every breath, this attack went on and on.

It was instinct to reach for Raphael, but she held off with grim will. There was no reason to remind him again of the mortality that lingered in her bones. Even now, the pain was fading, the edges softening until she could breathe again without the air slicing her lungs.

Sorry. Sorry. Sorry.

She shook her head at the rising swell of echoes. "It's all right. It wasn't you."

The becoming, the Legion said. *The becoming.*

Elena rubbed at her chest again. Finding the Primary in the sea of faces, she said, "Have you been through a second becoming before?"

"The Cascade does not always surge."

Instead of tearing out her hair at the cryptic answer that intimated the "second becoming" only came into play when the Cascade cycled from active to dormant, she asked another question. "Am I in danger of dying from this pain?"

A long pause during which she could hear a million whispers at the back of her head but couldn't make out the words. The Legion consulting among themselves.

"The pain will not kill you," the Primary said at last. "We have not seen this in our past wakings, but we have felt the energies. The pain energy will not kill you."

It was, she realized, a highly specific answer. "What about the *reason* behind the pain? The root cause? Is that energy dangerous?"

Another wave of background whispers, cresting and falling.

It is not known to us, was the ominous final response.

Gut tight, Elena hooked her arms around her raised knees and stared. The Legion had been around since before vampires; for them to so bluntly say they had no knowledge of what was happening to her, it hit a solid ten on the terror meter. "I guess this Cascade will be one for the books."

They tilted their heads to the side all at once, a comical row of fairground clowns whose paint had washed off. *We do not keep books.*

Finding a laugh inside her, Elena said, "If you remember

anything about this"—she tapped the internal bruise left behind by the attack—"let me know, okay?"

Yes. Yes. Yes.

Hidden in the echo of their final yes was another voice, old and heavy with sleep: *Child of mortals. Vessel unawakened. You step closer to your destiny. For one must die for one to live.*

Who are you? Elena said inside her mind.

No answer. No sense of a presence. Just a promise of death.

Fuck it, she thought. If death was coming for her, she'd face it with teeth bared and weapons unsheathed.

The pain down to a dull throb, she said her good-byes then left the Legion to transfer the potted plants across the river. At least she didn't have to climb down the slippery ropes of vine. Flaring out her wings, she floated easily to the ground, but she'd only taken five steps when her phone began to buzz with an incoming call.

Retrieving it, she stared at the name that flashed on the screen. Great, this was exactly what she *didn't* need. "Father."

"Elieanora, I need you at Beth and Harrison's home," Jeffrey Deveraux said in a curt tone. "Harrison is badly injured. Do I give him blood?"

Elena was already running toward the Tower. "No, it's too dangerous." If Harrison was so badly hurt that Jeffrey was calling Elena, he could fall into a blood fog and drink Jeffrey dry. Elena's father was strong and in good shape, but Harrison was both younger and a vampire—in a physical fight, he was the one who'd reign supreme. "I'll bring a healer." Her bruised lungs fought to keep up with her pace. "Beth and Maggie—"

"Eve has messaged Beth," Jeffrey interrupted. "Both are safe."

"Stanch the blood loss as well as you can. I'm on my way."

Shoving the phone into a pocket, Elena ran full tilt. Every second that passed felt like an eternity.

After reaching the infirmary floor, she found only Laric

in attendance. No one had expected the badly scarred and emotionally wounded young healer to accept Raphael's invitation to visit his Tower, but eight months after they'd first met, Laric had surprised everyone by coming to New York to visit Aodhan.

And somehow, he'd stayed.

He never ventured to the ground and kept his scarred face hooded even among friends. However, he seemed to find fascination in sitting on the Tower balconies and watching the colorful life of the city, and he flew in the skies above New York. The violent archangelic energy that had burned him down to the bone had done catastrophic damage to his wings—but a long-overdue examination had found that enough of the crucial substructure remained to offer hope.

It turned out that Keir had, in his records, designs for pair upon pair of prosthetic wings that he'd worked on as a young man in an effort to find something to help his friend Jessamy take flight. None had proved suitable for the historian's congenital malformation . . . but one pair, when modified, extended and supported Laric's devastated wings enough to give him back the sky.

He couldn't fly for long, but he *could* fly.

And from afar, his wings looked like any other angel's.

"Can you make it to my sister's home?" Elena asked, telling him the distance. "You'll be dealing with a severely wounded vampire." Laric was in training under Keir, with Nisia his tutor while he was in New York.

His hands flowed rapidly in the silent tongue he used nearly all the time and that Elena had learned after he came to the Tower. Most of the other senior staff already knew it, and the ones who didn't had learned alongside Elena; Laric would not be isolated here as he'd been in the place where he'd spent more than a thousand years.

I have this knowledge, he was saying. *Flight possible.* A short pause before his hands formed another word. *Witnesses?*

"Only my father and sister will see you, and they know never to speak immortal secrets." As with Jessamy, Laric was careful never to be really seen by mortals; humanity needed to believe angelkind too powerful to be hurt. It kept the balance of the world and stopped mortals from trying to pick fights with immortals they could *never* hope to win.

Nodding, Laric took a moment to grab his kit, then the two of them stepped off the closest balcony. Today, Elena didn't see the glittering winter-draped beauty of her city, and she barely felt the ache in her left wing.

All she heard was that tone in her father's voice.

Cold, controlled, clipped.

Harrison had to be critical.

12

Elena would never like her brother-in-law—he was a weak man, weak enough that he'd gotten himself Made into a vampire while Beth was still waiting to hear back if she'd been accepted. It turned out Elena's younger sister was incompatible with the toxin that turned a mortal into a near-immortal. She couldn't be Made. Harrison would have to watch his wife grow old and die. He might well have to bury his daughter, too.

But Beth loved him and that was what mattered.

"There!" She pointed out the house to Laric.

Landing on the pathway swept clear of snow, Elena dropped a knife into her palm before running into the house, Laric following . . . to be greeted by a scene of horror. A choking, gurgling sound filled the air, and on the sofa, Jeffrey had both hands clamped around Harrison's neck. The wound was spurting blood, the dark red liquid flowing over her father's hands, macabre ink that smelled of iron.

Red splattered Jeffrey's wire-framed glasses.

More blood smeared the space on either side of Harrison's mouth, and at first glance Elena thought his mouth was twisted into a rictus of a smile. But no—*Christ*—his assailant had slit open the sides of his mouth.

She took in the rest of the room in that same initial glance.

A gaily wrapped box lay on the fog-gray carpet, while Elena's half sister, Eve, a petite Valkyrie, stood in an offensive posture, her eyes huge and her newly issued long blade held out with guild hunter precision.

Muddy boot prints led from the back of the sofa to the kitchen.

The strides were long. Running. Whoever had left those prints had been running.

"Ellie." Eve lowered her arm, her breath a touch uneven but her stance solid. "I think we interrupted the robber. I was afraid they'd come back."

Elena wasn't sure this had anything to do with robbery, not when she could see Harrison's wallet sitting right there where even a fleeing robber could've grabbed it. "You did good, Eve." Striding to the kitchen door while Eve continued to stand guard in the living area and Laric worked on Harrison, she nudged it open with care—if the assailant was a vampire in the throes of bloodlust, she couldn't expect him to act rationally.

But the kitchen proved empty.

She swept the entire space inch by inch regardless, to make sure no one was hiding in a cupboard or under the island at the center.

The back door lock was broken.

After jury-rigging it with a piece of twine from Beth's junk drawer then reinforcing that with a fork bent to block the mechanism, Elena returned to the living room and told Eve she was going to clear the rest of the house. "I'll lock the front door on my way. Keep an eye on the entrance from the kitchen."

Eve nodded jerkily as Elena left. She moved quickly and was able to confirm the house was free of intruders within minutes.

She returned to find Laric motioning for Jeffrey to remove his hands. Blood began to gush out the instant Jeffrey obeyed . . . only it was slow.

Too slow.

Harrison had lost most of the blood in his body. Replacing Jeffrey's hands with his own, Laric began to do whatever it was that healers did to encourage healing in immortal and semi-immortal bodies. Keir had once told her it felt like coaxing a flame in the wind, or waking a sluggish sleeper.

Their job was to lead the body to heal itself.

It was wholly unlike Raphael's ability to heal without any involvement from the injured's own body.

Laric's hands were a stark and icy-white ridged with fine pink lines that quickly became streaked with viscous red. The lines had been much thicker when Elena first met him, and Laric had said they were impossible to cut through.

Of course, buried as he'd been in the isolated stronghold of Lumia, he hadn't ever tried lasers.

His body remained badly damaged within, but he was getting regular treatments to shave away the worst ridges so that he had better movement and flexibility.

"You must stop panicking and start trying to conserve your energy," he said aloud; his voice was crushed gravel, so rough and broken and painful to the ear that it was rare for him to use it.

Aodhan had told Elena it actually hurt Laric to talk.

Shifting into Harrison's line of sight, Elena took one of his hands so that Laric could get on with his work without having to deal with her brother-in-law's desperate attempts to cover his wound with his own hands. Bloody and sticky, Harrison's fingers gripped weakly at hers.

She squeezed back. Whatever Harrison's faults, he didn't deserve this. Beth and Maggie didn't deserve this.

"If you're going to survive," she told him, "you need to stay calm and let Laric help you." Beth's husband was fewer than ten years old in vampiric terms. He couldn't have survived even a partial decapitation. Thankfully, Eve and Jeffrey's interruption had stopped the blade from transecting his spine. Add in the rapid arrival of a healer and he *might* have a fighting chance.

She damn well hoped so. Beth loved him, and, to Harrison's credit, he treated both Beth and their daughter, Maggie, like princesses.

"Think of Beth." It was the one topic guaranteed to get his attention. "You know what she's like. If I tell her you're bleeding out, she'll have a panic attack. But if I tell her the healer has things under control and you're handling it without worry, she'll do fine."

That wasn't quite true—the youngest of Marguerite's four daughters had far more depth to her than most people realized. Even Elena hadn't understood that for a long time. Beth might prefer to live in a bubble of joy, but she understood the harsh realities of life. And when it counted, she'd always been there for Elena.

It was Beth who'd gathered up Elena's things after Jeffrey threw them out in the rain and the snow.

I have no desire to house an abomination under my roof.

Her oh-so-loving father's words to his eldest surviving child. Elena might've spent her life hating him for them if she hadn't figured out that her father was as fucked up as she'd once been. Jeffrey Parker Deveraux had watched his hunter mother be beaten and decapitated by vampires, then lost two cherished daughters and the woman he loved beyond life to another killer, only to discover that one of his surviving children was the reason the monster had come to their door. Elena's hunter-born scent had been the irresistible lure; Ari, Belle, and Marguerite the casualties.

Yes, Elena had a certain amount of sympathy for her father.

Forgiveness for his rejection, however, that would take a lifetime.

All the years when Elena had walked alone but for her friendship with Sara, it was Beth who'd held out a hand and kept her connected to their shattered and ruined family. Her younger sister had become lost in trying to please Jeffrey for far too many years, but no matter how bad their sibling relationship had become at times, Beth had refused to cut the bond or just ignore it. She had a quiet stubbornness most people never realized.

But the mention of Beth didn't calm Harrison. Eyelids blinking rapidly, he pulled even more desperately at her hand.

Elena froze. "Is Beth in danger? Maggie?"

Jagged nods.

Fuck. She considered the time of day, where her sister might've gone. "Has Beth taken Maggie to visit our grandparents?"

Another nod.

Relief rocked her. Jean-Baptiste was a far older vampire than Harrison, and ruthless with it. Elena didn't know who he'd been before surviving decades of torture, but the Jean-Baptiste she knew wouldn't hesitate to summarily execute anyone who threatened to harm his own.

She dug out her phone and sent through a warning regardless: *Beth and Maggie at risk. Stay alert.*

Jean-Baptiste acknowledged her message with a single word: *Understood.*

"They're safe," Elena told Harrison. "Now focus on staying calm so Laric can help you."

Harrison gave as much of a nod as was now possible for him to give. His breathing seemed to have improved, but his olive-toned skin was deathly pale. He'd lost an exponential amount of blood before Laric arrived.

"Will my blood make any difference?" she asked the healer—consort to an archangel or not, she was a baby immortal who had a flicker of wildfire in her blood. That wildfire was a weapon capable of wounding Lijuan. Who knew what it'd do to Harrison? But if there was no choice . . .

"I don't want to use your blood when I cannot judge the impact it might have," the healer said in his broken voice.

"I can donate," Jeffrey said, stiff but resolute, while frowning at Eve.

Elena's youngest sister closed her mouth.

A headshake from Laric.

Understanding, Elena translated: "Harrison's injury is beyond the rejuvenating capacity of human blood."

She knew Laric himself couldn't donate without losing the energy he needed to help Harrison—and Laric was young, too. Not in years, but in development. He'd been in a kind of stasis for the hundreds of years he'd spent hidden from the world, his growth stunted.

Thinking quickly, she pulled out her phone again and called Dmitri. "We need strong blood to save a vampire's life," she said the instant he answered. "My brother-in-law." She rattled off the address, though she was sure Dmitri already knew it. It was his job to know anything and everything that could impact Raphael.

"I've got someone nearby," was the response before he hung up.

Only three minutes later, Harrison's eyelids trapping birds as he fought to lift them and failed, another angel walked into the room. He was the night, his wings an inky black and his clothing obsidian. The intricate tribal tattoo that covered one half of his face only added to the impression of danger and darkness and a man who walked his own path.

Elena hadn't even known that Raphael's spymaster was in the city. Not an unusual circumstance with Jason. He came and went like the wind. Which was why it caused her no surprise whatsoever that he'd made his way through a locked door without a whisper of warning noise.

Walking up to Harrison, he used a small blade to slit his own wrist. The scent of blood—*powerful* blood—had Harrison's eyelids flickering again, but he was too weak to even angle his head toward the source of the life-giving fluid. Jason pressed his bleeding wrist against Harrison's lips after tugging back Harrison's head just enough that he could drip the blood directly into Harrison's mutilated mouth.

Elena couldn't tell if her brother-in-law had enough of

his throat left to swallow, and she could see no sign he was trying to suck in the blood. Jason had to remove his wrist and cut it again multiple times before Laric signed, *He has had enough.*

Harrison's fingers went limp on Elena's hand at the same time, dropping heavily to the sofa. No blood dripped from his throat, though the gash was wet and red. As if he'd run dry. "Is he still alive?" She did not want to have to tell Beth that Harrison was dead.

Yes. I've put him in a deep sleep. Blood as powerful as Jason's may have otherwise caused a seizure.

"Here." It was Eve, holding out a slightly damp dish towel toward Jason and doing an excellent job of hiding her awe at being in his presence. "I went into the kitchen and got these." A glance at Elena as she gave her a towel, too, before putting one on the coffee table for Laric. "I was careful even though you'd cleared it."

"Good girl," Elena said, as Jason inclined his head in a silent thank-you. He wiped the cloth over his wrist to remove the smears of blood. His warm brown skin, she saw, had already sealed up again. Jason was at least seven hundred years old; more important, he was seven hundred years old and powerful with it.

Prior to her fall into the immortal world, Elena hadn't understood that power and age didn't always correlate. Some of the difference had to do with inborn strength—immortal genetics, if you would. But some of it had to do with dedication and persistence. The two elements—inborn strength and a resolute will—combined in angels like Jason and the other members of Raphael's Seven.

"Thank you," she said to an angel she might never truly know, he was so contained and private.

"There is no need," was the quiet response. "He is your family." Putting the dirty dish towel in a pocket instead of giving it back, likely an automatic reaction from a man used to being a spy and leaving behind no traces, Jason held Elena's gaze with the bitter chocolate of his own. "I will continue on my way. I must speak to the sire, then I will head homeward. Mahiya was not able to come with me on this last journey."

And he missed her, Elena thought, happy for this dark angel that he'd found a lover to whom he *did* show all of himself. "I'll see you both when you're next in the city."

The door closed behind Jason seconds later.

When she looked to her father again, she saw Jeffrey had already finished cleaning his hands and was now polishing the glass of his spectacles using a handkerchief he must've pulled from his pocket.

She put her used dish towel onto the coffee table, then caught Jeffrey's eyes, angling her head. He, Elena, and Eve moved closer to the front door, leaving Laric to work in peace. There probably wasn't much more he could do at this stage. Vampires were creatures of blood, and Jason's blood was the biggest piece of first aid that could've been offered.

"Tell me how this happened," she said to the man who'd once blown bubbles with her in a sunny backyard. The same man who had thrown her out of the family home when she'd been only eighteen.

For a long time, she'd believed he hated her because she was the reason the monster had come to their door. It had taken her more than ten years to understand that in her sophisticated, intelligent father lived both a forever-broken-hearted man who loved his children too much . . . and a scared four-year-old boy.

Do you know what it's like to watch a woman get her head torn off? The blood spurts hot and dark and it gets in your mouth, in your eyes, in your nose, until it's the only thing you can see, all you can smell!

Jeffrey Parker Deveraux had lost too many loves. He was never going to be whole again, never going to be her playful papa again.

13

It was Eve who spoke first.

"I wanted to drop off my gift for Beth's birthday," she said, her hand clenched to bone-white tightness around the hilt of the long blade. "I'm going away tomorrow for two weeks for that out-of-town Guild training session. I won't be here for her actual birthday."

Elena broke contact with the gray of Jeffrey's eyes, eyes he'd bequeathed her and Eve both. "Yes, I remember." The two-week camp would teach her sister tactics she couldn't learn in the city.

It would also be a time of friendship and freedom.

She half expected Jeffrey to comment on Eve's plans—their father could barely deal with having one hunter for a daughter, and in a few short years he'd have two. But all he said was, "I have a key to this home." He pulled the key out of the right pocket of his suit pants then slid it back in. "When Evelyn received no response to her knock, I decided we should leave the gift inside. That way, even if we were unable to track Beth down, she'd have the gift and card."

That sounded like her father: decisive and coolly rational. He'd always been that way, except when it came to the butterfly of a woman who'd been his first wife—and the four daughters she'd given him.

Only Elena truly remembered Marguerite's Jeffrey. Beth had been so young when they buried Belle and Ari. What they hadn't known until it was too late was that they were also burying Marguerite. Jeffrey's butterfly and Elena's beloved mama, the lovely, soft-spoken woman who'd kissed Beth's chubby cheeks until she giggled and giggled, had never come back from the hell of so horrifically losing two of her babies.

"I heard the back door slam as we came in, like someone had left in a rush," Eve added, her voice mingling with that of a sunlit childhood that had lasted only a few short years. "I pulled my blade out before we walked into the living room."

"Clearly," Jeffrey said, his voice as calm as if they were talking about a business deal, "we interrupted an intruder in the act of violently assaulting Harrison."

Elena looked over at Laric, who was swathing her brother-in-law's throat with bandages. "I'm pretty sure he'd be dead if you hadn't arrived when you did." A little deeper on the cut and Jason's blood would've come too late.

"Beth can't walk into this." Jeffrey held her eyes.

"No." Beth hadn't been there the day Slater Patalis turned their family home into an abattoir. Neither had she seen their mother's body swinging from the ceiling, a painful shadow that lived forever on the wall of Elena's mind. Elena had been able to grab Beth and get her out of the house before her baby sister came far enough inside to see the end of their fractured family.

Beth had the terrible sorrow of having lost her mother and two of her sisters, but no horror stained her memories of them. Elena wanted to keep it that way. It was enough that Elena carried the blood and the death and the nightmares. It was enough that Jeffrey carried the same. That was their dark bond, the viciousness and the pain that connected the two of them and that would probably always hold them apart.

"It's okay, Ellie." Jeffrey's big hand stroked her hair as they stood in the morgue beside Ariel and Mirabelle's bodies, tears thick in his voice. "There's no more pain where they are now."

The memory broke her with its glimpse of who Jeffrey had once been. A father who'd fought to give her the closure she needed—to show her that Slater Patalis hadn't turned her sisters into monsters like him. Jeffrey had held her hand and kept her safe, a tall, strong bulwark against the darkness.

"We should go to Maggie's great-grandparents'," he said now. "Break the news before Beth hears it in some other way."

Maggie's great-grandparents.

Never my parents-in-law.

Never, *ever* Marguerite's parents.

Elena wondered if he'd even spoken to Majda and Jean-Baptiste Etienne. They'd been in the city two and a half years, but Jeffrey was very good at drawing a line in the sand and holding to it.

Tap. Tap.

Eve jerked at the quiet knock on the front door.

Putting one hand on her sister's shoulder, and aware of their father's eyes going hyperalert, Elena opened the door after a glance through the peephole. "Tower vampires," she told Eve and Jeffrey.

The more senior of the two, his black hair tightly curled to his skull and his night-dark skin a stark contrast to the snowy background against which he stood, said, "Dmitri sent us," in a voice that held the formal intonation of many of the old vampires.

Relieved she could go to Beth without leaving Laric unprotected, Elena pointed to the living room. "Help Laric transfer Harrison wherever he needs to go."

"We brought a van." The other member of the team, shorter and freckled, with floppy hair of pale brown paired with a broad Midwestern accent, jerked his thumb over his shoulder. "Big enough for wings. Dmitri figured the healer would want to accompany his patient to the infirmary."

It would also, Elena realized, excuse Laric from having to fly again.

Every so often, Dmitri acted human and she almost liked him. Then he'd play his scent games with her, trapping her in a seduction of fur and champagne and decadent chocolate, and she'd remember why the two of them would never braid each other's hair while singing camp songs around a bonfire.

After speaking to Laric to ensure he was happy supervising the transfer, Elena nodded at Jeffrey and Eve. "Let's go see Beth."

Jeffrey put his spectacles back on. "Shouldn't we call the authorities?"

"The Tower will deal with that. It has forensic teams that'll come in and sweep for clues. Given that Harrison is my brother-in-law, we have to treat this as an immortal crime until we have evidence otherwise."

No barbed response from Jeffrey about how she'd put Harrison in danger.

The three of them walked out of the house in silence. It was only then that she noticed the gleaming black sedan that sat at the curb in front of the equally dark van with opaque windows belonging to the Tower team. "You want to drive?" she asked her father.

"No, it's close enough to walk. Let me get my coat." A glance at Eve, his gaze penetrating behind the lenses of his spectacles. "I'll get yours, too, Evelyn."

Elena put a gentle hand on her sister's upper back once Jeffrey was out of earshot—Eve was much shorter than her. "Sheathe the long blade, Evie." She couldn't walk around the city flashing the weapon.

Cheeks coloring, Eve whispered, "You won't tell my team leader, will you?"

"Your secret's safe with me." She watched to make sure her sister's hand was steady as she slid the blade home in the sheath she wore down the side of her leather pants.

Those pants weren't an affectation but a necessity for new hunters. Sewn with a protective inner layer, they were harder to cut through.

Elena had once almost stabbed herself in the arm while putting away her own blade. Ransom had laughed at her—then promptly speared a hole through his pants. There was a reason baby hunters were issued weapons with only fifty percent sharpness.

Her blade safely stored, Eve took the jacket that Jeffrey had retrieved for her. It was a puffy thing, dark green in color and with fake brown fur around the hood that suited Eve's face with its soft layer of baby fat that was already being honed to adult sharpness by age and the strenuous training regime at Guild Academy.

Jeffrey's coat couldn't have been more different; tailored black, it reached halfway down his calves.

He held out something to Elena.

Startled, she took it, unraveling the soft gray fabric to realize he'd handed her a scarf. She knew it was his the instant she put it around her neck. The scent of his aftershave lingered in the woven strands, bringing with it a thousand childhood memories.

Of being held against his chest when she got too tired to walk.

Of laughing wildly with him as they played a game of tag.

Of watching him dance with Belle and Marguerite in the living room while Ari took photographs with her new camera and Beth played with her dolls.

Of walking in on a kiss in the kitchen between Jeffrey and Marguerite and feeling her heart *squeeze* so hard in happiness.

Shattered pieces of a mirror with jagged edges, memories of a life forever destroyed.

Part of her wanted to tear off the scarf, tear off this resonance of yesterday, but she didn't reject the offer. With her and Jeffrey, it was a tightrope, a fragile balance that could be upended with a single word.

They began to walk the five blocks to Majda and Jean-Baptiste's home.

It was three minutes later that Eve said, "Ellie, *psst*."

Following her sister's gaze, Elena saw that Eve was pointing to where Elena's left wing dragged through the snow. A chill filled Elena's blood, and it had nothing to do with the winter white that blanketed the world and made her breath create small, icy clouds as it left her mouth.

She hadn't felt the slack in her wing muscles.

Neither had she felt the wet cold of the snow.

"Thanks." Winking conspiratorially, she lifted both wings to the correct position . . . while keeping a surreptitious eye on the one that had dropped.

The muscles responded to her commands, but she couldn't feel them. And though her right wing appeared fine, it wasn't. It might not have weakened far enough to drag, but there was too much slack in it.

Rocks in her abdomen, hard black weights that crushed and scraped.

But Beth came first; she'd deal with this later.

It took tight and conscious control to keep her wings from dragging as they walked the rest of the short distance. Her grandparents had chosen their house because it was close to Beth and Maggie.

They loved Elena and Beth for being "children of their child," but it was Marguerite "Maggie" Aribelle Deveraux-Ling who'd so totally stolen their hearts. Beth's chubby, pretty baby had turned into an energetic and sweet little girl who laughed as often as not.

Cherished and protected and loved, Maggie would have a far different life than either Elena or Beth. She'd probably end up a little spoiled, but far better that than the bone-deep sorrow that had led an adult Beth to sob in Elena's arms.

Beth, the baby of their original family, had wanted Marguerite when she fell pregnant herself, wanted to learn how to be a mother from her own. But Marguerite had left them long ago, so broken inside that she'd forgotten it was one of her surviving daughters who might find her body.

"Mama?"
A single high-heeled shoe lying on the tile.
A burst of hope that Marguerite was getting better.
The gently swinging shadow.

Eve's gloved hand wove through Elena's right then, tugging her from a past too full of pain to bear. Another baby of the family. The youngest of the six daughters Jeffrey had fathered. Holding on to her big sister even though she was fifteen now and far too sophisticated to act like a child.

Elena curled her fingers tight around Eve's.

"Will Harrison be all right?" her sister asked solemnly.

As solidly practical as Maggie was carefree, Eve reminded Elena fiercely of Ari at times. Jeffrey's second-eldest daughter had been pragmatic and solid, too, a point of calm in the madness—and the most like their father. Elena remembered how the two of them would escape the chaos together at times, fishing rod and camera, respectively, in hand.

Today, Jeffrey walked silently on Eve's other side, but Elena could tell he was listening.

"Harrison has Jason's blood in his system now," she said after a cough to clear her throat—the memories were haunting her today. "It gives him a far higher chance of survival."

Eve shivered. "I've met lots of angels because of you, but he made all the hairs on my arms stand up—like he carries a storm with him."

Pragmatic and perceptive, that was Eve. "Jason's one of Raphael's Seven." And an angel who could create black lightning that broke the sky, his power a dark storm.

Her wing dropped again.

14

Having caught the motion out of the corner of her eye, she managed to pull it up before her sister or father noticed.

"What do we tell Beth?" Jeffrey's tone held no wrenching emotion, but that was the thing with her father—he hadn't cried when they'd discovered Marguerite, and he'd stood stone-faced at her funeral. Two days later, Elena had woken from a nightmare and walked down the hall to see Jeffrey crumpled on the floor of his study, sobs wracking his frame. An empty whiskey bottle had lain on its side beside him.

Elena had gone in even though the two of them were already broken by then, and she'd hugged him and they'd cried together.

That was their terrible history. Pain and love entwined in equal measures.

"We tell her the truth," she said as a prickling sensation ran over the back of her hand, "but we lead with Harrison being alive and in excellent hands. She needs to know what's happening to take precautions to protect herself and Maggie."

"I don't think we should tell her about all the blood in her lounge, though," Eve suggested. "Father—"

"I'll organize a cleaner," Jeffrey said. "In the interim, and for her and Maggie's safety, she needs to stay with either myself and Gwendolyn or Maggie's great-grandparents."

"Jean-Baptiste is a trained fighter," Elena said. "It's probably better if they stay with him and Majda until we figure out what's going on. Majda can also look after Maggie when Beth visits Harrison at the Tower."

Jeffrey didn't point out that he had the capacity to hire round-the-clock bodyguards, and that Gwendolyn didn't work outside the home and could also babysit Maggie. He knew as well as she did that Beth had bonded far deeper with her mother's parents than she had to Jeffrey's second wife.

There was no enmity between Gwendolyn and Beth, but Beth saw her mother in Majda's face. She saw the same fine bones and small stature, the same darkly golden skin, the hair that could've been Marguerite's under a waterfall of sunshine. And in Majda and Jean-Baptiste's piercing love for one another, a love that had survived decades of torture and isolation, she saw an echo of Marguerite and Jeffrey.

Those were the very reasons Jeffrey couldn't stand to look at Majda and Jean-Baptiste. Majda most of all. Elena knew that her grandmother and grandfather had reached out to Jeffrey many times. As far as she was aware, he'd rebuffed each and every approach, politely but firmly.

She wondered what he'd do today, but that he was coming with her was a good sign. Beth might've bonded to her grandparents, but she was still a daddy's girl. Jeffrey's presence would help her weather the shock.

Two little boys playing in the snow up ahead stared at Elena with huge eyes, their impressive snowballs forgotten in their hands. "Whoa," one of them said as she passed. "Those real?"

Taking the chance to confirm everything was functional, Elena flared out her wings—and heard excited chatter behind them as the boys ran off to tell their parents they'd spotted an angel walking around the neighborhood.

Poor kids probably wouldn't be believed unless someone else snapped a pic and uploaded it online.

She closed her wings, using the excuse of avoiding a broken piece of fencing to glance back and check everything was where it should be. No drag. No obvious sign of weakness. She remained unable to feel her wing muscles.

Her stomach gnawed at her spine.

Shit.

Elena couldn't have felt less like eating, but she took out two energy bars and methodically finished them one by one. Eve didn't pay much attention, her face set in a determined frown and her eyes looking straight ahead, but Jeffrey said, "You're still transitioning?"

No one would ever call her father anything but sharply intelligent.

"Long process." Which appeared to be going backward.

Bars eaten, she tucked the wrappers into a pocket then rubbed her fingertips gently over the worry lines on Eve's brow. "She won't believe us if you look so gloomy."

Sniffing out a breath, Eve leaned a little into Elena.

And Jeffrey ran his hand over the raven black of his youngest daughter's hair.

Then there it was, the pretty town house Elena's grandparents had made their own, complete with a low-slung black sports car in the drive. Jean-Baptiste had taken to technology like the proverbial duck to water—not only had he quickly learned how to use phones, he loved driving. He *especially* loved driving the fast car he'd been assigned by the Tower after Dmitri caught him admiring the red Ferrari that was Dmitri's pride and joy.

At first, Jean-Baptiste had been given the courtesy because he was Elena's grandfather. Not that Elena couldn't have bought him the car herself, as she could've bought her grandparents this home—the hunt that had ended her mortal existence had also left her a wealthy woman, and then she'd fallen into the blood-café business.

Money wasn't a problem.

But the Tower had insisted on providing for the couple—

and she'd realized Majda and Jean-Baptiste would be more likely to accept the help from their archangel than their child's child. Especially as Jean-Baptiste, experienced and valued for his skill, was now a commander in charge of an infantry unit.

Even had Jean-Baptiste decided against such service, he and Majda would've been treated with the same courtesy.

"They are your grandparents," Raphael had said as he and Elena lay tangled in bed one night, "and so they are mine, too." A pause before he'd added, "I also do not feel the desire to murder them as I so often do your father."

The door Jean-Baptiste had painted a bright pink at Majda's request opened before she reached it. As with Beth's home, this door was wide enough to allow Elena entry. And it was Beth whose smiling face filled the doorway. Jean-Baptiste must've spotted them coming and not stopped Beth. From the joy of her, he also hadn't alarmed her with a warning about nebulous danger. *Good.*

Before Beth could say anything, a smaller body wriggled out from around her side and pelted down the walk. "Auntie Ellie! Grampa! Auntie Eve!"

Bending, Elena scooped Maggie's body into her arms and snuggled her close. Her niece was dressed in pink jeans with pink snow boots and a white furry jacket that was open over a white top that had a sparkly design on it. Her head was bare, the shoulder-length strands of her silky black hair awry, but she'd no doubt be wearing her pink sparkly hat when she ventured out into the snow again.

Her eyes were a sweet brown, tilted up at the edges, and her light olive-toned skin held a brush of gold. In the cheekbones hidden beneath the little-girl softness, Elena saw the promise of dramatic beauty. Most of all, in Maggie's tiny body, she saw myriad threads of their family—strands of Morocco, of France, of New York, of her other great-grandparents' history in Hong Kong and India.

But Maggie's smile was a reflection of the pretty woman with strawberry-blonde hair who stood in the doorway, clad in skinny blue jeans and a fuzzy green sweater with threads of silver.

Beth's face had lit up at seeing the three of them, but her smile began to fade at the edges almost before Maggie finished digging in Elena's top jacket pocket for a treat. As Maggie knew her aunt often had a small sweet for her, Beth knew that Elena and Jeffrey didn't go out for companionable walks in the snow. Her eyes zigzagged between them to finally land on Elena. "Ellie?" A shaky question.

Maggie kissed Elena on the cheek, even though all she'd found today were a couple of crumpled energy bar wrappers. The foil backing of the wrappers caught the snow-amplified sunlight when Elena passed her niece to Jeffrey. Then she gave Beth a hug and tugged her sister with her as she walked into their grandparents' home.

Majda and Jean-Baptiste sat in front of the fire, cakes made from the colorful clay children used to form their dreams spread out in front of them. A plastic tea set sat nearby. Heartbreakingly young in appearance, Majda and Jean-Baptiste could've been two twentysomethings who might have a three- or four-year-old of their own, but Majda was more than eighty years old and had been trapped in hell for much of that time. Jean-Baptiste, muscular and golden blond with a square jaw and eyes of silvery blue, was older than his wife by a hundred and forty-five years.

Majda's face was solemn when she looked at Elena. Her eyes, a hauntingly clear turquoise identical to Beth's, spoke to Elena without saying a word. Jean-Baptiste had told his wife of the threat alert.

Elena gave a small, barely perceptible nod.

Rising in a graceful move, Majda held out a hand. "Maggie, *azeeztee*. Would you like to help me ice the cookies we made?"

Over the years since she'd found her grandparents, Elena had become used to hearing the affectionate word from Majda's lips, the same word Marguerite had once used with Elena and Beth, Ari and Belle. But she sensed more than saw Jeffrey go rigid, as, across from them, Jean-Baptiste got to his feet.

None of them spoke until Maggie was in the kitchen, safely behind the closed door. Then, aware Beth had to be imagining all sorts of horrible things, Elena cupped her sister's face in her hands. "Harrison is alive."

Beth's pupils flared.

Elena didn't give her a chance to panic. "He was hurt, but Father and Eve found him in time," she said in a voice as calm as Jeffrey's had been at Beth's house. "By now, he's at the Tower under the care of a team of experienced healers."

Beth lifted her hands to clamp them over Elena's wrists. "How badly is he hurt?"

Elena didn't lie to her sister. She had once, softening the edges of reality because she'd thought Beth couldn't accept the harsh truth, but she knew better now. Though Beth lived in a world of sparkles and pink coats and a little girl who was her starlight, there remained inside her a Beth who understood death and loss and having to stand at gravesides while the people you loved were put in the cold ground.

Elena wished she didn't, but life had stolen that choice from them.

"Bad," Elena said. "But one of Raphael's Seven donated blood to help him heal. You know that blood is powerful, Bethie."

Her sister's trembling lips firmed. "Oh. That's good." She took a shuddering breath. "Raphael's angels and vampires are scary and tough." She turned toward Jeffrey, and, to Elena's surprise, their father held out an arm.

Beth fell against his chest, let him wrap his arms around her. "Harrison got the best possible help at the right time. Barring any unforeseen complications, he'll be fine," he told Beth with curt practicality. "Your house, however, is a mess—you should stay with your grandparents for the time being. We'll make sure you and Maggie have what you need from the house."

"I need to see him."

Elena had expected as much. "I'll organize it." As her sister, Beth was always welcome at the Tower, but Beth was intimidated by the vampires and angels who called it home.

"We'll take care of Maggie while you're with your husband." Jean-Baptiste touched his hand to Beth's shoulder after she stepped out of Jeffrey's embrace.

Another deep breath. "How was he hurt?"

"Someone attacked him," Elena said, because Beth couldn't protect herself in ignorance. "Harrison was afraid you and Maggie might be targets, too—you'll have guards until we figure out what's going on." She'd talk to Dmitri, get Jean-Baptiste some help.

Beth didn't dispute the order, her pupils hugely dilated. But even after the shock passed, Elena had no doubts that Beth would acquiesce to the protection—her sister was agreeable and gentle, and she'd do anything to keep Maggie safe.

Now, she took Elena's hand again, holding on as she had as a bewildered little girl. "I'll be able to think properly after I see him."

"Do you wish to say good-bye to little Marguerite so she doesn't worry?" Jean-Baptiste asked, and Elena felt her father go impossibly stiffer. They all knew Maggie's full name, but neither Jeffrey nor Elena ever used it. It was too hard.

Beth straightened her shoulders. "Yes." A determined smile on her face. "No stressing out in front of my baby."

Jean-Baptiste's eyes narrowed after Beth was gone, his hands on his hips. "You have the details of the assault on Harrison?"

"The assailant attempted to decapitate him." Elena took care to keep her voice low. "Harrison couldn't speak, but he was desperate to warn me that Beth and Maggie were in danger."

"No one will take another child from us," Jean-Baptiste said grimly. "I promise you this." Then he turned to look at Eve and, though she was no blood relation of his, leaned in to press a kiss to her forehead. "And how are you, Evelyn? Such a fierce look you have on your face."

"It was horrible." Eve gave him a hug, was warmly hugged in turn. "But I stood watch with my long blade while Father tried to help Harrison."

Meeting Jeffrey's gaze once Eve broke the embrace, Jean-Baptiste held out a hand. "It is good to meet the man who loved my child and was loved by her."

Perhaps because this was Jean-Baptiste, who didn't remind Jeffrey so terribly of Marguerite, he shook the proffered hand. "If you'll excuse me," he said afterward. "I need to organize a cleaning crew for Beth's home."

"I'm going to steal a cookie," Eve said after Jeffrey stepped outside to make the call.

Alone with Elena, Jean-Baptiste sighed. "Majda wants so much to know the man who was our child's husband and who spent so many years with her, but your father is . . . difficult."

A very diplomatic word. "She reminds him too much of Mama." Her grandparents could have no idea of the staggering resonance of the resemblance—photographs didn't capture her mother's spirit or her innate gentleness. Majda had the same gentleness, though her spirit was wilder than Marguerite's. "Father loved Mama more than he's loved anyone else his entire life. He broke inside after he lost her."

"I understand, child of my child." Her grandfather's tone was bleak. "But we will keep trying. You and Beth are living pieces of our Marguerite, but Jeffrey has memories you cannot know."

Eyes threatening to burn, Elena nodded.

Beth returned from the kitchen a couple of seconds later. She had her coat with her, was already shrugging into the deep purple of it. "Maggie's more than happy to stay here while I go out for a little bit." She pulled out a set of keys. "My car's parked on the street."

Jeffrey confiscated Beth's keys the instant they got outside. "I'll drive you."

Beth, being Beth, agreed.

Elena didn't veto the arrangement either; Jeffrey's car was bulletproof and the distance to the Tower short. To be safe, however, she made a call to Dmitri so he could alert angels in the air to keep track of the vehicle. That done, she waved Jeffrey, Beth, and Eve off . . . and tried not to flinch when two huge white owls appeared out of the snow to fly past within inches of her on either side. Her hair lifted in the wind created by their wings, a soft brush against her cheek from the very edge of a feather.

But when she swiveled to follow their flight, the owls were gone.

Ghosts.

Her own wings dropped to drag along the cold stone of the path.

15

Heart chilled, Elena pulled them back up and tried to decide what to do. A vertical takeoff wasn't a realistic possibility, but she didn't want to ground herself without reason. She had to test the status of her wings, see if they could hold her aloft.

At the same time, it'd be foolish to run the test alone.

Raphael was out on the water, and so was Illium. There was no point asking either one of them to come in when she was simply running a controlled test. She still needed a spotter—someone loyal enough not to say a word about the problems with her wings but strong enough to ease her fall if her wing *did* collapse.

"Izzy," she murmured with a smile.

She made the call, then went in to ice cookies with Maggie and Majda while she waited.

"Elena"—Jean-Baptiste poked his head into the kitchen, a frown on his features—"your very young friend has just landed in the drive. You're sure the boy is over a hundred? He looks ten."

Elena laughed and kissed Maggie's cheek in good-bye then hugged a worried Majda before going to join her grandfather. "Izzy's one of Galen's protégés. Trust me, he knows what he's doing."

Jean-Baptiste walked her to the front door. "Your wing," he said quietly. "There is a problem? Young Izak is here to act as your escort?"

No surprise that he'd figured it out; he was a senior vampire who'd worked with two archangels and was trusted enough to be on a first-name basis with both those archangels. "Yes. I'll tell you more when I know."

Eyes solemn, he touched his hand to the side of her face. "Take care of yourself, Elena. My Majda's heart cannot bear another loss." He pressed a kiss to her forehead as he'd done with Eve. "If Majda reminds Jeffrey of his wife, you are the living embodiment of our daughter."

Elena made no promises as she walked out.

"Izzy," she said when she reached the baby-faced angel with a tumble of blond curls and a painfully earnest heart. "Thanks for coming."

"I'm part of your Guard, Ellie." His brow wrinkled. "Of course I would come."

She smiled—it was difficult to do otherwise when with Izak. "Let's walk around to the back of the property." Majda and Jean-Baptiste had a private fenced-in garden there, and thanks to the tall trees that edged the garden, none of the neighboring houses looked down on it.

Once there, she double-checked to confirm no neighbors would see what was about to happen. It didn't matter if they saw her and Izzy linked—a lift from one angel to another wasn't uncommon, especially among friends who might be playing games in the sky. But strangers couldn't be permitted to see the initial lift in case the problem with her wings was obvious.

Only when she was satisfied of their privacy did she turn to Izak and tell him what she needed and why. His face turning solemn, he nodded. Izzy, she knew, would do anything for her—even if what she asked would get him in trouble with Dmitri or Raphael himself. She just hoped she'd always be worthy of his devotion.

Putting his hands on her waist, because he wasn't yet strong enough to pull her off the ground using her hands, he waited for her to tighten her wings to her back then rose into the air. A small face pressed to the kitchen window waved excitedly at her as they left the ground.

Elena waved back at Maggie . . . while the owls perched on the branches of a dormant tree watched on with eyes of luminous gold.

Seconds later, they hit the gunmetal gray sky and Izzy said, "Shall I let go?"

"Yes." Elena spread out her wings the instant he released her, not snapping them out as she normally would, but unfurling with more care.

She didn't fall.

Breath shuddering from her lungs, she was conscious of Izzy dropping slightly below her. The position would make it easier for him to halt her descent should she suffer a midair wing failure. But they made it across the snow-dusted landscape and over the jagged height of the skyscrapers to land on the balcony outside the infirmary.

She waved Izzy off to his other duties, then escorted Beth—who'd just arrived—to Harrison's side. Her next stop was Nisia's office. The healer's expression darkened when Elena described her inability to hold her wings off the ground without conscious effort. "How did your wings feel once you were in the air?" the healer asked, going around to Elena's back to examine her wings.

Elena stood still for the slow and thorough inspection. "I had all the normal controls, but I felt . . . weaker." She frowned, trying to narrow down the reason for the feeling. "As if each wingbeat took more effort than usual."

"We will go into an empty training room," Nisia announced. "I need to take you through some tests."

Urgency pounded at her, the need to eliminate the threat

to Beth and Maggie overwhelming, but she'd be no use to her sister and niece if she fell out of the sky to splatter onto the streets of Manhattan.

The tests took two hours.

Somewhere in the midst of it, Elena took off her jacket and shoved up the sleeves of her long-sleeved thermal T-shirt. Nisia's eyes went immediately to the Band-Aid on her forearm. "Elena?"

"Shit. I forgot about that." Hard to keep a scratch in mind when Beth's lounge looked like the site of a massacre. "The cut broke open again." Holding her breath, she peeled off the Band-Aid. "Hey, it's looking much better."

"No, this is not good." Nisia's cheekbones jutted sharply against her skin as she stared at the small wound. "Such a cut should've been nothing for your body to repair. Your current level of healing is close to a mortal's."

Okay, yeah, put that way, they had a problem—but her wings were the bigger one, so she and Nisia returned to the tests.

Elena, I'm almost home. Dmitri informed me about Harrison—have there been further developments?

Archangel. A hot rush of blood through her veins. *I haven't had much of a chance to follow up—I'm with Nisia in the internal sparring ring.* It had been free when Nisia enquired, and was the better space for testing the range of her wings. *More issues with my wings.*

I am on my way.

He walked into the ring only a few minutes later, an archangel dressed once again in the worn softness of warrior's leathers, with his hair tumbled by the wind and his expression dangerously calm. And his wings . . . they were rippling white fire. Wings of pure silence that he could summon at will but that appeared most often when his emotions were running high.

"What has happened?" Liquid blue flame danced in his irises.

A stab of fear deep in Elena's heart; she couldn't help it when he got like this. So very *other* that she feared he'd evolve into a level of existence where she wasn't welcome, where she couldn't follow.

"Elena's wings show evidence of further degeneration," Nisia said without stopping her most recent examination of Elena's flexed left wing. "You can continue to fly," she said directly to Elena, "but I'll need to keep a close eye on things." The healer came around to face her. "We'll begin with an examination each morning and night."

Stomach dropping, Elena didn't even try to stop herself from shifting so that Raphael's wing overlapped her own. Though the white fire *felt* like him, she was glad when his wings solidified, the warm weight of bone and tendon and feathers pressing against her wounded wing.

"Is this damage a result of the original strain?"

"It doesn't matter if it is." Nisia unfurled then folded in her own wings. "You should be healing." A thoughtful pause. "Have you been eating enough? We know from previous growth spurts that you require a prodigious amount of energy at such times."

"You saw me inhale the food we had sent down here." Elena shoved a hand through her hair, remembering too late that it was in a braid. Pale strands of near-white fell around her face when she pulled her fingers out. "Do I need even *more* fuel? I might as well just get a stomach tube and pour things in."

Ignoring her muttered aside with the ease of an angel who dealt with warriors all day, many of them snarly, Nisia said, "It's highly possible if this growth spurt is a larger one than the others. I'll speak with your household staff about increasing your energy intake." The healer considered things for a moment. "I'll also personally prepare a liquid supplement for you that you need to drink every hour. One full glass."

Elena thought of the owls and the voice in her head that predicted death—and told both otherworldly manifestations to stuff it. "Full glass every hour," she promised.

After Nisia bustled off to prepare her supplement, Raphael turned and lifted up the arm with the cut.

"I had another heart attack, I'm healing at the rate of a mortal, and I keep seeing the owls," Elena said, because keeping secrets from her archangel was a no-go zone.

Raphael's jaw worked. "We've beaten far more dangerous foes than this."

"Yeah—but this enemy isn't playing fair. How can we fight what we can't see?" Frowning, she said, "Ashwini told me not to be afraid of the owls, that they're just messengers of a messenger."

A chill whisper across her skin, an old, *old* voice on the far edge of her hearing.

"What do you hear, *hbeebti*?" Raphael's voice was cold with power, his eyes liquid flame again. "Lijuan could be unseen, and we brought her down. An invisible enemy cannot conquer us."

Elena scowled. "You're right." But no matter how hard she tried, she couldn't capture the words spoken . . . then they faded altogether. "It's gone. Like . . . someone moving in a dream."

Elena and Raphael met with Dmitri, Ashwini, and Janvier later that afternoon, when the winter sky was already giving up its fight against the dark. Added to which, a thick fog-colored blanket made the world smaller and more claustrophobic, and dampened even New York's vibrant spirit. People were picking grocery store shelves bare in anticipation of deadly blizzards.

"Or maybe a volcano," Ash said with a shrug when Elena voiced her thoughts. "It'd make as much sense as a lava sinkhole."

Everyone stared at the hunter turned vampire.

She threw up her hands. "That was just me mouthing off, not a prediction."

Elena exhaled quietly, while Dmitri scowled at Ash, and Raphael's expression remained unreadable to anyone but Elena. He wasn't brushing off Ash's mad forecast, despite the other woman's disclaimer. He was probably already thinking of an evacuation plan—just in case.

The ongoing monsoon rains that had hit Africa's deserts less than an hour earlier had everyone jumpy. According to early media reports, the Sahara was already so wet it had begun to turn into a river of orange sludge while the Kalahari's drenching had people fearing catastrophic "flooding" from the sand. Desert residents all over the continent had begun to evacuate their homes, taking only what they could carry.

The situation was bad enough that Charisemnon and Titus, neighboring archangels and mortal enemies, had laid down their arms and were cooperating to move large numbers of people out of danger. Charisemnon was a sick bastard who preyed on impressionable young mortals in his territory and had everyone convinced he was all but a god—Elena figured he was helping so he didn't end up with too few acolytes.

Titus, in contrast, was one of her favorite archangels, a hugely powerful being with a warm heart who was beloved by his people. And by the women he favored with his smile. He loved and he left and no one was angry with him. Women sighed and bit their lower lips and melted when reminiscing about their time with the Archangel of Southern Africa.

Raphael had spoken to both Titus and Charisemnon when news of the rains hit the world. The latter was no ally of his—not after the horror of the Falling—but he'd offered help if needed regardless. Because in some matters, the Cadre laid down all enmities and got on with saving the world. The two archangels had acknowledged the offer but held off from accepting it.

Titus had said, "We do not know what disasters may yet come, my friend. We must all husband our strength."

Charisemnon had been even blunter. "I may need you when the plagues of locusts and snakes descend. I'm no longer so sure all of Mad Cassandra's prophecies were so mad."

So now, the five of them focused on a problem that had hit much closer to home.

Playing a blade restlessly through her fingers, Elena laid out the facts of Harrison's attempted murder. "He wasn't stabbed," she said to Ashwini, "but the forensic team that took images of his throat wound say it looks like it was made by the same weapon as that used to decapitate your Quarter victims."

To say the connection had come as a shock would be a gross understatement.

16

"Well, shit." Arms folded, Ashwini braced her back against the wall nearest the door. "We just cleared our only suspect."

Raphael's wings whispered as he resettled them, white fire dancing along the edges of his primaries and his presence holding a razored edge. Her archangel was not taking the changes in her well. Neither was Elena. She wanted answers, but all she had were questions and—strapped to one thigh—a bottle of Nisia's energy drink that tasted like chocolate and fruit at the same time.

Might as well embrace the silver linings where she could find them.

"Tell us what you discovered at your scene," Dmitri said to Janvier and Ashwini. Raphael's deadly second was wearing a black T-shirt and black jeans, as he so often did, the bronze color of his skin unchanged even in the heart of winter and the weapons on his body so cleverly hidden that Elena could spot only one.

"Two dead vampires in the same apartment," Janvier said in his deceptively lazy Cajun accent, his body holding up the wall beside Ashwini. "Simon Blakely and Eric Acosta. Acosta looks to have been lying on the sofa. My brilliant Ashblade"—a slow smile at Ashwini—"tracked down the addict from whom he took a honey feed about six hours before the bodies were discovered."

Honey feeds were the vampiric equivalent of shooting up. A mortal junkie would take a drug of the vampire's choice and then, while that junkie was high, the vampire would sink his or her fangs into one of the junkie's remaining uncollapsed veins. Actual inhalation, injection, drinking, or eating of drugs stood no chance against the vampiric metabolism, but a honey feed high lasted long enough to make it worthwhile.

Rich vampire junkies often "kept" human junkies as pets. The vamps supplied the drugs, and in return, the junkie was the resident source of a honey feed high. Sex was often but not always part of the bargain—the ones who wanted sex during a feed made sure to keep their pet junkies healthy and pretty. Less well-off vampires did deals with junkies on the street.

"Our honey feed connoisseur made good money as a bouncer for one of the high-end clubs," Ashwini continued. "But, from what I got on the streets, he blew most of that on feeding his addiction. Preferred junkies on crystal meth. Said it made their blood taste like acid."

"Appetizing." Dmitri's voice said he'd seen it all before.

"He used so much that he'd have been a meth zombie if he didn't have the vampiric metabolism," Ashwini added. "According to our users, he tended to zone out on the crash, hallucinate, nobody much home upstairs for a while."

"So he may have been in a drug haze when he was murdered?"

"*Non.* We believe Acosta was in a drug dream when he was *bound*," Janvier replied. "The killing came later."

"Pathologist found evidence of rope burns around his wrists and a nasty gag around his mouth." Ashwini reached over to tuck in the tag sticking out from the back of Janvier's dark green T-shirt. "Nothing obvious on his ankles, but we figure he must've been bound there as well."

Arms folded, Dmitri leaned back against his desk. "It would seem your killer wanted the victim to know what was being done to him."

"Yep," Ashwini said. "Amputations came first, the throat-slitting the coup de grâce."

Janvier said a string of words in his native tongue that sounded like a tease. Ashwini showed him a blade star in return. Janvier's grin was wickedly playful.

Catching the byplay out of the corner of her eye, Elena chewed on the information the couple had shared. "How could a single person have gotten the drop on two vampires? Could we be talking more than one assailant?" She was thinking about Ash's earlier mention of vampire gangs.

"We considered that, but everything points to one scarily organized murderer." Ashwini pressed a boot up against the wall. "Indications are that Blakely was secured first, while Acosta was spaced out and pretty much useless. A yeti could've walked past him and he'd have said 'groovy suit, dude.'"

True enough. Honey feed highs didn't last long, but crystal meth, cocaine, heroin, or ketamine, the short period was intensely euphoric for users. A habitual user like Acosta had probably been used to hallucinations, even craved them as the sign of a good hit.

"Also, Blakely was . . ." Janvier's moss-green gaze went to Ash. "What is the quaint saying, *cher*?"

"Caught with his pants down," she supplied. "In flagrante frickin' delicto."

That certainly explained how one perpetrator had gotten the better of two vampires. "Blakely's sexual partner?"

"In the wind." Ashwini's earrings moved gently as she spoke. "All we found of her were her panties. Could've been a small man who likes frilly panties—I'm not one to judge—but word on the street is Blakely was strictly into women, so I'll go with female."

Elena thought of Harrison's panic about Beth and Maggie. "Escaped or was let go?"

"She would've been as naked as the victim, and, as the pros I talked to were happy to share, Blakely liked to be on top. No way she could've put up a fight."

"That tells us something, does it not?" White fire continued to dance on Raphael's wings as he walked to the plate glass window behind Dmitri's desk. "Our killer isn't indiscriminate."

Elena bit down hard on the inside of her cheek, unable to forget Harrison's sheer fear. "Yet from Harrison's reaction, this unknown threatened Beth and Maggie."

"Your sister is married to Harrison, and Maggie is his daughter," Raphael pointed out. "The woman in the Quarter was apt to be no one important to the dead vampire. She wasn't on the killer's target list."

Jesus, that made too much sense.

"Which amputation goes with which victim?" Dmitri asked into the grim silence.

"Our friend in the bed had the family jewels hacked off—while he was very much alive and gushing blood. Assailant then stuffed said jewels into his mouth." Ashwini glanced quickly at an incoming message on her phone before putting it back into her pocket. "And, yeah, I'm not finding that a coincidence, either. Same informants who told me about his sexual habits say the vic was a bit of a Don Juan."

"A different jeune fille every night." Janvier's shoulders brushed Ash's, the two of them having shifted subtly during the course of the conversation. "Such men leave a trail of anger in their wake—and often tread where they shouldn't."

"Any chance the killer is a woman?" Elena asked, slipping her knife back into an arm sheath.

Ashwini shook her head. "Can't say either way right now. One other thing—second mutilation was also done while the victim was alive."

"He slit Harrison's mouth," Elena murmured. "A different kind of mutilation, but mutilation all the same. Also done while he was alive and trying to hold his throat together."

"Agreed." Dmitri was nothing but business right then, all hard angles and violent vampiric power under total control. Not a man who would ever be led by blood hunger, ever be made a slave to the need to feed; no, Dmitri had fought that battle and won it long ago.

"All else aside," he said, "it's the intelligence involved that makes this killer dangerous. They might enjoy torturing their victims, enjoy watching the victims' panic and pain, but they haven't been careless."

"He also had the willpower to cut his losses when necessary." Janvier's eyes, the rich green color reminiscent of the bayou, held Elena's. "He ran rather than attack your father and 'tite Eve, likely because he had no idea of the threat he'd be facing. He's a planner and he's patient."

Elena felt cold seep into her bones at the thought that Eve and Jeffrey could've easily ended up sprawled bloody and lifeless on the carpet.

Two more lives lost.

Two more graves dug.

Two more ghosts to haunt the living.

One more sister gone forever.

Shifting from the window, Raphael held her gaze with the crushed sapphire of his. *You did not lose another sister, Guild Hunter,* he said in a voice chill with the ever-growing power that scared her so for what it might mean for them. *And that sister was armed and ready. Eve will not be caught unawares like your elder siblings.*

Elena remembered Eve's fierce concentration, the gleam of her long blade, thought of the way Jeffrey had given Eve her coat and Elena a scarf. He would've fought bitterly for his daughter's life. She let herself believe the two would've won against a murderous assailant, because the alternative was a crushing blackness that suffocated.

I needed that, Archangel. More than his words, she'd needed to know he remained her Raphael even while power burned hot and blue in his eyes.

"Harrison might have answers for us," she said aloud, "but he's been put into a coma." Beth's husband had lost so much blood prior to Jason's donation that his young vampiric body was in a state of violent shock.

"We'll have to work with what we have until he wakes." Ashwini straightened. "Janvier and I'll continue to dig into the Quarter killings while you come in from the Harrison angle. We'll pool information."

Elena nodded; Ash and Janvier now had far deeper connections in the gray underground of the city, of which the Quarter was ground zero. "You said you cleared a suspect?"

"A junkie who got into an altercation with Acosta earlier in the week," Ashwini clarified.

"He was naked in the glass display mezzanine at Club Masque during the time of death and for hours on either side." Janvier's liquid voice held a shrug. "The man, he has endurance."

Ashwini parted her lips, paused, finally said, "Do you think Beth knows anything?"

Elena had already considered that particular question. "I'll ask her." But she wasn't hopeful of a positive outcome. Beth and Harrison had a different relationship to Ashwini and Janvier—and Elena and her archangel. Beth was the homemaker and Harrison the man of the house, the one who handled finances and everything else outside of Beth's domain of family and children.

Elena didn't know if Harrison spoke to Beth about the more dangerous aspects of being a vampire, or if Beth would even *want* to know those facts. Everyone dealt with tragedy and loss in a different way; Beth had done so by insulating herself in a happy routine with defined lines. Elena just hoped her questions wouldn't bring her sister's fragile construction tumbling down.

It will begin in liquid fire
In sand that flows
In ice sharp as knives
In the death of one

—ARCHANGEL CASSANDRA, ANCIENT AMONG ANCIENTS,
LOST TO AN EONS-LONG SLEEP

17

Ashwini and Janvier left first, off to prowl the Vampire Quarter for new leads.

Desperate inside in a way she couldn't explain, Elena was about to drag her archangel out for a kiss before she went to Beth, when Dmitri got a call from Naasir.

"Ice?" Dmitri wasn't a vampire who often betrayed surprise, but that one word was spiky with it. "How bad?"

The answer had his skin going tight over the bones of his face. "I will inform the sire." A short pause. "If he requests it. Otherwise, head back to the Refuge." Hanging up, Dmitri looked to Raphael. "Naasir and Andromeda decided to make a short trip to Alexander's territory."

That territory was Persia. Elena had no details of how Naasir, a wild and unique member of Raphael's Seven, was tied to Alexander, but she was aware that Naasir had an open welcome to the Ancient's territory—and, technically, Naasir's mate, Andromeda, belonged to Alexander's court.

"Ice in Alexander's sun-filled lands?" The Legion mark burned almost too bright on Raphael's temple.

"Not only ice. An ice storm in Qatar."

Elena sucked in a breath. "Those poor people won't have the clothes, the heating . . ." She knew parts of Alexander's territory could get frigid, but Qatar was warm even in the winter months. "Are Naasir and Andi safe?"

"Yes. I've told Naasir to assist if asked but to return to the Refuge otherwise." Dmitri's features were grim. "There is little we can do quickly."

"I will speak to Alexander." Eyes of deep Prussian blue held Elena's. *Go to your sister,* hbeebti, *I will tell you the outcome.*

Filled with a raw need for him at this moment when life drew them in different directions, she blew him a mental kiss, but his eyes didn't lighten, his features set in lines so perfect they were brutal.

Drink, Elena. A hard order. *You must not get any weaker.*

Elena stopped in the corridor to rub her fingers over the spot under her heart, her wings slumping for a moment. *I'm a fighter, Raphael.* A reminder to herself as much as him. *Even if the weapon involved is some weird healer mixture that tastes like chocolate blueberries and ripe apples.*

Raphael's response was a sea storm inside her mind, the lightning flashes within it incandescent. Letting the searing power of him sweep through her, she finished the drink she had in the bottle then detoured to refill it. That done, she ate three energy bars . . . while considering the new cut on her left arm.

She'd absently shoved up her sleeve while mixing up more of the drink and there it was. Higher up than the first, the cut was a fine line she could've gotten anywhere.

The problem was that it was paper-cut thin but an angry red. She checked both arms then pushed down her sleeves. She'd examine it again in a couple of hours. Right now, her priority was Beth. Elena had sat with her after Nisia finished the tests on Elena's wings, only leaving her to attend the meeting. Holly had arrived at the same time to return a book she'd borrowed from Laric and somehow ended up chatting with Beth.

Elena's sister had immediately warmed up to her. Maybe because Holly looked so very young and human, with her playful hair and bright clothes. Beth could have no idea of the murderous alien power that had once run through Holly's veins.

Holly would never be an ordinary vampire. Her reaction times were dangerously fast, as fast as Venom's—and he was hundreds of years older. She also had the ability to turn liquid in a way that was difficult to describe, but that meant she could avoid broken bones even if thrown against a wall at great force.

Elena could've never predicted that the two women would hit it off so well. Holly was as tough as Beth was soft . . . but Holly did love fashion as much as Beth, and Holly, too, had once been a far softer creature.

However, when Elena walked into the infirmary, it was to find Beth alone. She sat beside Harrison's bed with a steaming mug in her hands and a fashion magazine on her lap. A small plate of cakes lay on the side table, the plate itself decorated with gold foil and hand-painted feathers.

"I see we're looking after you." Elena leaned down to press a kiss to her sister's hair, her chest squeezing; some part of her would always see in Beth the lost little girl who'd clung to Elena's hand beside far too many fresh graves.

"The magazine's Holly's," Beth confided. "And she just raided a kitchen somewhere and brought me the tea and cake. She had to leave to do her shift at the sinkhole, but I knew you were in the Tower."

"You two spent a lot of time talking."

"I like her. We're going to go shopping at that new mall after Harrison is better." Smile fading, Beth put down the tea. Her fingers trembled as she brushed her husband's hair off his forehead.

Harrison's face remained too pale, his throat swathed in bandages. Elena knew Laric had stitched up the wound to hold it together. It wasn't the standard procedure with vampires, but with Harrison being so young and his throat so badly cut, Nisia had made the unusual call and supervised

Laric in its implementation. There was zero risk of Harrison healing around the stitches.

He was recovering too slowly for that.

"The senior healer was here a few minutes ago." Beth tugged the finely woven blanket higher up Harrison's body. "She said it's going to take time, but that Harrison will wake up. I just have to be patient." She leaned her head against Elena's thigh. "I can be patient, Ellie. I waited all that time while Harrison was being Made. I trusted that he'd come back to me."

Elena ran her fingers through the rough silk of her sister's hair. "I know you can be patient, Beth. I see how you are with Maggie." Beth never yelled at her daughter, always spoke with a sweet gentleness. It was at those moments that Elena most saw pieces of their mother in Beth. Marguerite had never yelled at her children, either, and yet even rebellious Belle had listened when she'd spoken.

Maggie minded Beth the same way, a piercing echo of memory and family.

Beth looked up with a smile before putting her head back against Elena. "I'll have to work out certain times when I can come see Harrison. I can't sit with him twenty-four hours a day, no matter how much it hurts to leave him here. I have to look after Maggie's heart."

"Harrison would agree with you. You're the two most important people in his life." That, too, was true; regret was an emotion with which Harrison Ling had plenty of familiarity.

As if she'd read Elena's thoughts, Beth said, "I know you think he was selfish in being Made, Ellie. So did I for a while, but then . . . it gives me such comfort to know that he'll be around to look after Maggie after I'm gone." A quiet pause filled only with the subtle sounds of the machines that monitored Harrison. "I never considered that he might go first one day."

Elena squeezed her eyes shut for a moment, her jaw clenched.

She'd had nearly the same conversation with Sara. And

she'd thought more than once that she'd have to watch her baby sister grow older and older while she stayed ageless. But her body was running backward, and she had wounds she couldn't explain that wouldn't heal. Beth might outlive both her and Harrison.

If that happened, Elena knew her sister would deal. She might be heartbroken beyond repair, but she'd *deal*. Because no matter her pain, she would not abandon her child as Marguerite had abandoned them.

"We have to live in today," she said, speaking to herself as much as to Beth. "Worrying about the future just steals the now from us."

"So does living in the past, doesn't it, Ellie?"

Swallowing hard, Elena put her hand on Beth's shoulder. "Yes. I'm glad you never did that."

"Father's still back there, with Mama and Ari and Belle." Such terrible sadness in Beth's voice, so much compassion for a man who'd died when Marguerite chose to leave him behind rather than trust him to help her navigate the darkness. That old Jeffrey was buried with his wife in a cold grave she'd never wanted to inhabit.

Elena would always be angry with her father for that, for burying Marguerite in the unforgiving earth when her mother had wanted to be cremated and scattered to the winds, so she could be part of the wind itself.

That had been her mother, brilliant and light and always in motion.

Yet even in her anger, she remembered the empty bottle of whiskey and a man who'd cried heartbroken sobs in the dark of the night. "I don't think we can pull him back to the present," she said, her voice rough. "He has to make that choice himself."

"I feel sad for Gwendolyn, too." Sitting up properly, Beth took a sip of her tea, then held up the mug in a silent offer.

Elena wasn't much of a tea drinker, but she took the mug from her sister and had a drink before handing it back. The heat ran through her in a sweet rush. "Yes, Gwendolyn's got

no fault here." If she'd made a mistake, it was to fall in love
with a man who'd left the best part of himself in the past,
but as Elena knew, love wasn't a thing to plan or control. It
just was.

"I'm trying to figure out who'd want to hurt Harrison,"
she said a while later.

"Do you want to ask me questions?"

"If you think you're ready to answer them."

"If it'll help protect our baby, I can manage," Beth said
softly.

"Has anything been worrying him, or has he been afraid
of someone?"

Picking up a cake, Beth handed it to Elena. "You should
eat this. Holly said the chef would be insulted if we didn't
eat his cakes."

"The chef" happened to be Venom, a little secret to
which not many people in the Tower were privy. They just
knew that, over the past couple of years, extraordinary cre-
ations occasionally appeared in the communal areas utilized by those who called the Tower home.

Elena knew the truth only because Illium had let it
slip—then sworn her to blood-oath secrecy. "Usually," she
told Beth, "I'd be lucky to get a crumb. The cakes and pas-
tries disappear at the speed of light—then everyone sulks
when the chef goes quiet for weeks or months at a time."

Smile a faded copy of its luminous reality, Beth took a
bite of her own cake and chewed, swallowed, before saying,
"Harrison hasn't really said anything, but I know my husband. Something's been on his mind the past couple of
days." She paused and took a drink before continuing. "I
used to never ask him things, but that changed after Maggie.

"I want to know how to look after her if anything happens to Harrison. I want to know how to access our
money—and I want to know if there's a danger that could
hurt her." Anger in those last words, though the look she
sent her wounded husband's way still held more love and
worry than anything else.

Elena looked down at the top of Beth's head; she'd been

foolish to think Beth would be in the dark about Harrison's secrets. She should've remembered her own thoughts about how motherhood had changed her sister. "What did he say when you asked him what was bothering him?"

"I never got the chance with his work shifts and my volunteer work with the suicide hotline." White grooves bracketed her mouth. "I planned to do it today, after I got back with Maggie and she was snuggled up for naptime." Putting down her half-eaten cake, she said, "But this morning, before Maggie ran in for breakfast, he said, 'Baby, what if I did an innocent thing once and it ended up hurting someone? Would it be my fault?'"

Elena's gaze lingered on the brutal slashes on either side of Harrison's mouth, the mutilation that further linked this assault to the murders in the Quarter. "What did you say?"

"Maggie 'attacked' him before I could answer. She was pretending to be a lion, and he growled back and started playing with her." She sighed, sorrow in her touch as she smoothed back Harrison's hair once more. "He had to leave for his angel's home ten minutes later, but he was only on for half a shift today. Just a few hours, I thought. We could talk after." Her voice broke.

It was six by the time Beth left the infirmary. Jeffrey picked her up. Gwendolyn was in the passenger seat of the dark sedan and got out to hug Beth. Raven haired, with eyes of dark blue and rich cream skin over bone structure that shouted her high-society lineage, she was an elegant beauty two decades Jeffrey's junior.

"Let's get you home," she murmured to Beth, and settled her in the car, then smiled at Elena. "Thank you for being so good with Eve. She felt so much better because you told her she did the right thing."

"I have tough little sisters."

Another smile before Gwendolyn got into the car. Shutting her door, Jeffrey nodded at Elena and went to get into the driver's seat . . . only to turn without warning and come wrap her in a furiously tight embrace. Elena's arms went around him almost by instinct, buried childhood memories rising to the fore as the smell of his aftershave mingled with the wool of his coat.

Neither one of them spoke.

It was over seconds later, and he was gone.

Elena.

She glanced up at the sound of Raphael's voice to see him looking down at her from a high Tower balcony. Heart in a vise, she said, *He's afraid.* It came out a whisper, the rapid beat of her father's heart yet imprinted on her skin. *He only has two of Marguerite's daughters left now, and he can't bear losing us, too.* It was the very force of her father's need to keep her safe that made Jeffrey so angry with her . . . with the daughter whose profession and life put her in danger on a regular basis.

Wings glinting white-gold against the night, Raphael soared down to land beside her. His eyes were flames of a blue so pure, it pierced her to the core. "Raphael." She brushed her fingers over his cheek. "You can't put me in a steel box as Jeffrey can't wrap me up in cotton wool."

Her archangel, his face harsh and beautiful, ran his fingers firmly over the arch of her wing. "How is your strength?"

"Good." She'd had a full pre-dinner meal with Beth, astonishing her sister with how much she could put away. "Nisia's cleared me for flight. No further degeneration since the first round of tests, so her magic drink must be helping."

Putting his hands on her waist, Raphael said, "I have to return to the sinkhole." No smile, no hint of softness. "Then I must fly deep into the territory."

The fear of losing him to his power, it bit at her. Focusing on how he held her, how he felt like her Raphael no matter what, she said, "Has something happened?"

"The sentries have reported changes in the movement of the lava, and I'm receiving reports of geothermal activity in a slightly distant region not known for it."

"Ashwini's volcano?"

"Let us hope not."

"Be careful." She watched the wind riffle through the midnight strands of his hair. "Did Alexander want help?"

"This storm has passed for the time being, but we will be shipping over winter supplies to be used should another one hit." He gripped her jaw. "You will not come with me?"

Haunted by memories of three cold graves and a small hand clutching tightly at her own, she fought her gnawing need to cling to him. As he couldn't box her up and put her in a safe place, she couldn't stop his development. All she could do was love him and hope he'd remember her no matter how the Cascade changed him. "I need to get to the bottom of the attack on Harrison, neutralize the threat to Beth and Maggie."

Tightening his grip on her waist, Raphael lifted off. *You will land the instant you sense trouble with your wings.*

"I will," she promised.

A hard kiss that burned with archangelic strength and had her wrapping her arms around his neck as she fought to assuage both her desperate need and his. They spun against the starlit sky, and when they parted, it was with heaving chests and dilated eyes. "I love you, Raphael."

"*Knhebek, hbeebti,*" he said in return . . . and then he let her go, this being of excruciating power who understood that her mortal heart would wither and die in a cage.

She turned to watch him fly away from her and saw wings of white fire. Of an archangel who was becoming . . . more.

18

Elena touched her gloved fingers to her lips, remembering his kiss. Her Raphael's kiss. Then she turned in the direction of Beth's home. When her head throbbed, she took stock, but it was nothing, just a passing pulse. Probably a stress headache. It wasn't like she didn't have cause.

Once in Beth's neighborhood, she did slow and wide glides in the air as she considered how things currently stood. The Tower forensic team had processed the entire scene and locked up the house using the key Jeffrey had provided. Both the front door and the—repaired—back door had been discreetly rigged to show evidence of any unauthorized entry.

Elena didn't think the assailant would return—not unless he had firm evidence Harrison, Beth, and Maggie were back in residence. It wasn't coincidence that he'd attacked Harrison first. No—her face stiffened—the unknown intruder had wanted to terrorize Harrison by promising to murder Beth and Maggie.

That didn't mean the threat was a toothless one, especially since Harrison had survived the attempt on his life. Anyone angry or motivated enough to break into a vampire's home to slit his throat wouldn't hesitate to get at the target by harming his family.

The fruit of Harrison's innocent act that had harmed someone? Possible. Also possible was a drug connection, or another illegal business enterprise. Harrison had always thought himself smarter than others—the reason why he'd once tried to escape his Contract.

Elena was the hunter who'd hauled him back.

That had been just great for family relations.

Deciding on a course of action, she landed. It felt far too good. Her muscles had begun to strain and quiver. As if she were a fledgling barely used to flight. And fuck she was hungry again. After gulping down Nisia's mixture, she grabbed a chocolate bar from a pocket where she'd stashed it.

She was halfway through it when her phone rang. "Sara," she said through a mouthful of pure dark chocolate. "Sorry I didn't reply to your message." It had come in while she'd been with Nisia.

"Forget that—Ransom said he saw pretty senior Tower vampires at Beth's house. Is she all right? Maggie?"

Elena gave Sara the details. "I'm about to start knocking on neighbors' doors, see if anyone heard anything." As a mortal-born angel, she'd get a better reaction than the people she might've asked for help—Izzy was adorable and sweet but not practiced at this type of task, and the more experienced Tower vampires and angels tended to scare people. As for her mortal hunter friends, Elena tried not to pull them into immortal problems if at all possible.

Humans had a way of ending up hurt or dead once in the immortal world.

"Shit, I should've asked Honor." Dmitri's wife wasn't only highly capable at gathering intel, she was handy in a fight, and had only been a vampire a short time. Most people didn't even realize she wasn't human.

"She's out with the advance team prepping the training site for Eve's group, remember?" Sara said.

Elena rubbed her forehead with her fingers. "I did know that." It had simply become lost in the mess of memories and worries in her head. "Did you approach anyone on your Slayer shortlist?" Good thing Sara had rejected her as a choice—the way things were going, Elena wouldn't be able to chase a ninety-year-old escapee from a rest home, much less a hunter gone bad.

"No," Sara answered. "I realized we both forgot about one person who'd be perfect—probably because we hate the thought of him walking alone." A sigh. "Archer was unusual in being a family man. Most Slayers are single. And I have a highly intelligent hunter who's both single and not easy to anger. Like Archer, he wouldn't act without thought, wouldn't be vulnerable to psychological games."

"Hell, Sara." Elena blew a white cloud visible against the night. "You're talking about Demarco." Cheerfully good-natured Demarco, who liked to tease her by wearing a *Hunter Angel* T-shirt, but who fought like a demon.

"It'll ruin him." Sara's tone was weighted with the dark responsibility of her task. "I need more time to make sure I'm not making the wrong call."

Because if Sara asked, Demarco wouldn't say no. He'd step into the breach, the courageous idiot. The possibility of losing a friend to the darkness was too much on top of her failing wings, Raphael evolving further and further from her, the ghost owls, all the crazy shit. "Why do we have to have a sole Slayer anyway? Who made that stupid rule? Why not a team?" Friends and comrades could get you through a hell of a lot.

Sara was quiet for a long moment. Elena took that time to tear off the last hunks of her chocolate bar. Imani had it right: change sucked. Even her beloved Guild was in turmoil.

"You know," her best friend murmured at last, "I don't know the reasoning behind having a single designated Slayer." Intrigue in Sara's tone now, pushing aside the heaviness. "I'm going to do some research. Good luck with the door-to-door."

"I'll need it." She allowed herself a small, fierce smile. She might not be able to feel her wing muscles, but maybe she'd saved Demarco and future Slayers from a lonely life in the shadows.

A small win, but she'd take it.

The next hour was full of failure.

Beth's neighbors were all home now. However, most hadn't been around during the incident, and the ones who had been had seen nothing suspicious. Wings tugging heavily at her back and frustration mounting, she was about to write off the entire thing as a colossal waste of time when she walked around the block to knock on the door of the property situated directly behind Beth and Harrison's home.

It proved to have a full security system, cameras included. Better yet, that system had been on at the time of the assault on Harrison. Her skin prickled, her heart kicking. The camera, contingent on its angle, could've caught the assailant's rushed exit.

"Would you be willing to give me the footage?" Elena asked the middle-aged man who'd answered the door; his hair stuck up in black tufts, the eyes behind his round lenses a rich shade of brown, and his unlined skin two or three shades darker.

"Oh, of course." The neighbor shivered. "Terrible what's happened. They're such a lovely young family. We talk over the fence sometimes."

"Imagine, that could've been you, Al!" interjected the neighbor's wife.

A short Hispanic woman wearing a T-shirt bearing the logo of a local boutique bakery, she'd introduced herself as Anita, then asked Elena if she wanted a slice of fresh pie. Elena and her bottomless pit of a stomach—she probably had ringworms, *immortal* ringworms—had been tempted, but demurred. "Where's the recorded footage stored?"

"It's on my computer." Al gestured for her to come inside, quickly realized her wings would make that awkward. "Hold on, I'll bring the laptop out here."

He returned just as the snow began to fall, the flakes soft and delicate.

"Pretty," he said. "But I'm glad I'm not outside in it."

"Al!" Anita glared at her husband.

Shoulders going up and head lowering, he said, "Sorry," to Elena. "Just came out."

"I'm not as vulnerable to cold as I used to be." True enough, except that her teeth were threatening to chatter and her skin felt encased in ice where the snow kissed it.

Putting the laptop on a small hallway table his wife quickly cleared, a reassured Al angled the table so that Elena could see the screen. "I haven't actually looked at the footage myself," he said. "You never do, do you? Not unless something goes wrong."

"We only got the entire setup to help out a friend who was selling them," Anita confided. "Otherwise, who thinks of cameras? But Al's good with computers, so we use all the features. Can even see through the cameras when we're on vacation!"

Al pointed to a file icon on the screen. "That's the recording from the past forty-eight hours." He scratched his head. "We leave the cameras running on a loop, but I delete the files every few days, and this is the only one we've got right now."

"It's more than enough." Elena clamped down on her excitement. "Can you pull up a specific time?" She gave him a time five minutes before Jeffrey and Eve's arrival.

"Yes, I just type the time in here . . . and . . ."

Anita hovered beside him as he worked.

"There we are." He hit play.

As expected, the relevant security camera was focused on their own backyard, but the angle meant the camera *did* also catch a relatively large section of Harrison and Beth's property as well.

"Stop." Elena leaned forward, breath hitching, as the image of a fleeing individual disappeared off the side of the screen.

"Oh, my goodness." Anita pressed her fingers to her

mouth; Al was already backing up the footage then setting it to run more slowly. "Well, gosh darn it." Lines furrowed his brow. "You can hardly see him. He must've run down that left-hand part, where the camera can't see."

Nonetheless, Elena had seen enough to confirm their theory about intelligence and planning. The assailant had been dressed in a long coat, boots, and a brimmed hat, with a scarf wrapped around their face. From this distance, she could see no details of their features, but even their run was measured and purposeful rather than panicked. A person who moved as if they had a right to be there. A visitor in a rush.

Nothing to cause alarm.

"Can you copy the footage to me?" Elena caught Al's gaze. "I'd also recommend you not try to do anything yourself. This individual is dangerous."

"Oh no, don't worry, dear," he said while his wife gasped, "I leave the heroics to young people like you." He took down her details. "I'll put the files in the cloud and send you the access link."

"Thank you."

"You take care in the snow, honey!" Anita called after her. "And if you decide you want pie after all, come on back!"

Smile curving her lips, Elena continued to do the rounds, but no one else had anything to offer. Her back and shoulder muscles ached badly by the time she called things to a halt—all from just making sure her wings didn't drag on the ground. The task hadn't been this wearing since the weeks after she woke up with wings and was learning how to fly, her body unused to the exertion. Good wing posture had become second nature in the years since.

Her left wing threatened to drop again.

She was standing by Beth's house fighting the urge to lie down flat to ease the strain on her back when the throaty purr of a motorcycle engine sounded down the street. She glanced over . . . and grinned.

"Why are you prowling these streets?" she said to the

black-leather-garbed rider who stopped in front of her.
"Sara said you were around earlier, too."

Ransom pushed up the visor of his helmet to reveal gorgeous green eyes that had seduced more than one woman.
"Coupla kids tagged a pic of you walking around the
neighborhood. Showed up on my feed."

When she raised an eyebrow, he sighed. "Nyree wants
to move around here in preparation for when we start trying
for a mini-me. I'm doing reconnaissance."

Elena knew him well enough not to fall for his put-upon
scowl. The hunter who'd avoided entanglements like the
plague was delightfully entangled with a woman who took
no bullshit and who loved Ransom with ferocious honesty.

Elena grinned. "How about a ride?"

"Any time." He patted the back of the motorcycle he'd
only recently bought, after his previous one fell down a cliff during
a fight with a young vampire in bloodlust. He'd loved that
bike, but he hadn't sulked at the loss—he'd said it was worth it to
stop a vampire who'd already murdered three innocents.

The vampire's angel had paid for the new bike—and
requested Ransom for all future hunts. Elena wondered
how her friend would handle things when he did have children. Most people transitioned to teaching at the Academy
or low-risk hunts for stupid vamps, but Ransom wasn't the
kind. Hunter-born rarely were.

"Hold still." She straddled the bike behind him but didn't
sit—no way to do that safely with wings. Instead, she got her
feet settled on the foot stands and put her hands on his shoulders. "Ready." She lifted her face to the wind as they roared
off and, yes, it was just as much fun as she remembered.
Especially when they stopped at traffic lights and a bored
driver glanced over . . . to do a serious double take.

Elena waved at him. He waved back, his eyes like small
moons in his face.

"You should take a photo or no one will believe you!"
she yelled over.

Scrambling for his phone, he managed a shot before the
light changed and they roared off. She could feel Ransom's

shoulders shaking as he laughed. Whooping, she enjoyed the ride with a friend she'd known since she was sixteen. It was only as Ransom brought the bike to a stop by the Tower that she remembered the cuts on her arm.

Yeah, she probably shouldn't be acting the hooligan on a motorcycle without a helmet. "Thanks." Getting off, she exchanged high fives with Ransom before he roared off to pick up Nyree from a book club meeting.

Elena went directly to her and Raphael's Tower suite to eat two loaded sandwiches and drink more of Nisia's mix. After which she found the healer to ask her about immortal ringworms.

Though Nisia was seated while Elena was standing, she managed to look down her nose at Elena. "You don't have worms."

"Did you check?" Immortals had a way of assuming certain things, and what if she did have a very normal mortal problem? "I'm not fully immortal. They could survive in my gut."

"Ringworm isn't caused by worms. It's a fungus. Which you also don't have. Your skin didn't fluoresce under black light when I ran it over you as part of my tests."

Elena stared at her. "You keep up with modern medicine?"

"No, I prefer to treat my patients with bucketloads of leeches." A stern pursing of the lips. "Now go away so I can continue to study the results of your various tests. Though . . ."

That sounded ominous. "Though what?"

"I didn't check for a parasite of another kind."

19

Elena's heart raced as Nisia walked over and put her hands on Elena's abdomen. "Not a flicker of power," she announced, "and considering the other genetic donor, it'd be a conflagration."

"What?" Elena demanded again.

Raising an eyebrow, Nisia said, "If you were pregnant."

"Christ, Nisia, you can't just say things like that!"

Back at her chair now, Nisia waved off Elena's shock. "You're not with child, so stop panicking."

"I'm not panicking," she squeaked out; she was *so* not ready for a baby.

"Yes, of course not." Dry words. "You're far too young anyway. But with the Cascade"—Nisia shrugged—"I thought better to check."

"Right." Elena's head spun madly at even the idea of it. "Wait a minute. Did you call the possible baby a parasite?"

"The basic definition of a parasite is an organism that lives on or inside a host and feeds off that host. Therefore, all fetuses are technically parasites. A fetus with DNA from an archangel will be a super-parasite," she added cheerfully. "It'll suck you dry of energy, so you'd better be *really* old and strong before you start thinking about the flitter-flutter of tiny wings."

Elena slitted her eyes and pointed. "You're having fun making my future offspring"—and jeez, she was never going to be ready for those—"sound like energy-draining horrors."

Nisia smiled beatifically. "Strange how that happens when you question a four-thousand-year-old healer about immortal worms."

"It was just a question!" Elena protested but decided to haul ass before Nisia got in the mood to put more nightmare images in her head. "Parasites," she muttered under her breath. "No wonder she's not in angelic obstetrics." Keir was the expert in that, and she bet he didn't take pleasure in terrifying poor hunters who had perfectly legitimate questions about ringworms.

And why was it called ring*worm* when there were no worms involved? That wasn't playing fair.

Also, maybe she should talk to Keir about contraception. He'd said it was unnecessary because she *could not* fall pregnant. She wasn't immortal enough yet, quite literally a different and biologically incompatible species from Raphael. But with the Cascade going on . . .

Then again, she appeared to be becoming even more mortal these days.

Chastened and ringworm-less, Elena made her way to Vivek's domain. "Where's V?" she asked a passing vamp when she couldn't spot the other hunter.

"Being tortured by a physiotherapist. Sadists even check to make sure he's not wearing an earpiece. Man's totally cut off from comms." A shudder at the idea.

"I guess he finally got on their last nerve." Vivek had a way of interrupting sessions to follow up on incoming pieces of information.

"Whatever." The vampire wasn't buying it. "Anyway, he's out for an hour. You need help?"

"No, I think I can handle it." With that, she made her way to the area at the back that was set aside for Tower residents who needed computers but didn't have an office. Elena could've had an office, but she preferred working here or in Raphael's office. Today, bones heavy with missing her archangel, she wanted to be around the buzz of life in the tech center.

She'd just sat down when she sensed a current of power in the air. Turning, she scowled at Illium. "Are you following me?" She wouldn't put it past Bluebell—he was very protective of his people.

"You wound me, Ellie." A hand pressed to his chest, golden eyes wide in innocence. "I was visiting my friends." He indicated a couple of angels hunched over the computers, their wings flowing gracefully to the carpet.

That sight always took her a moment or two to process even though she knew full well that part of the reason Raphael's Tower ran so well was that he'd changed with the times—and he had Illium. The blue-winged angel handled a phone with the same ease he did the sword he wore in a spine sheath.

"What are you doing?" He leaned over the back of her chair, his scent familiar and as welcome as the heat coming off his body.

Elena was so cold deep inside.

Shrugging off the odd sensation and telling herself she'd be fine once she could wrap her arms around Raphael for a long embrace, she logged onto the computer. "Looking at security footage from near Beth's place."

Illium stayed where he was, watching along with her. "I heard about Harrison."

First, she replayed the section she'd watched at Al and Anita's house. But no matter how many times she ran the footage, the camera just hadn't caught enough of the assailant.

"Now comes the boring part," she murmured. "We have no idea how long Harrison's attacker was lying in wait, so I'm going to cue it up to the time of the incident and go backward at speed from there. Even then, it'll take time." She dug out an energy bar to eat while they watched.

Illium's stomach rumbled.

Elena blinked and paused the footage to look up at him. "Seriously? You haven't eaten for so long that your stomach is actually *rumbling*?" Angels didn't need to eat as often as mortals, which meant Illium had skipped a serious number of meals.

"I've been busy." He rubbed his stomach, the blue-tipped black of his eyelashes lowered.

Rising from the chair, Elena thrust half the energy bar at him. "Proper food for both of us, I think." Her body had already digested the sandwiches, and that wasn't scary at all. "We can eat as we watch."

Illium went with her to the suite, where the two of them got busy preparing more sandwiches, as well as rolls. "You're missing Aodhan, aren't you?"

"I have to set him free." Illium's answer was quiet. "I finally figured that out. He's doing what he didn't do for two hundred years." Eyes of aged gold held Elena's. "Those years when he buried himself in the Refuge, I had a chance to grow and become who I am today. Now it's his time."

Elena ran her hand over his wing with the intimacy of long friendship; though the silver filaments glittered, the texture of his feathers was incredibly soft and silken. "That doesn't mean you can't miss him—especially after you waited two hundred years for him to emerge from the shadows."

"I'm scared all the time," he admitted, bracing his hands on the counter. "I know he's powerful, I've seen him in battle, and yet the fear crushes me."

"Of course it does." Elena let her wing overlap his. "That's what it means to love someone." She gave him a lopsided smile. "I worry about Raphael and he's an archangel. I've been known to warn him that if he gets hurt, I'll kill him dead."

Illium's laugh pierced the darkness around him to reveal her Bluebell who had so much light in his soul. "Let's go watch your boring footage. I know how to program it to stop on movement, so we don't have to keep it to a speed the eye can track."

As it was, Illium had gone through half his sandwiches and she'd finished off her filled rolls and all they had was a big fat nothing. The only movement so far had come from a couple of prowling cats, two snowfalls, and a flying plastic bag. No indication of an intruder in Beth and Harrison's yard.

"Assailant could've been hiding in a section the camera doesn't cover." Elena threw back more of Nisia's mixture as the footage continued to run backward.

"He'd still have to enter the house," Illium pointed out. "Only two options left if he didn't use the back door. Either he was in the house for hours—and that doesn't seem reasonable with how you've described the layout of your sister's home—or he went in another way."

Tapping her fingers on the table, Elena said, "They do have a large window on the other side of the house." She rang the forensic team and asked if they'd picked up anything unusual near that window.

She groaned inwardly at the answer. "We could've saved ourselves the mind-numbing boredom," she told Illium after she'd hung up. "The techs found shoe prints on the windowsill. Nothing in the snow outside, but depending on when it snowed, any footprints could've been buried."

Illium dropped his wings in a dramatic slump. "Does this mean we can stop the visual torture?"

Elena went to nod then thought better of it. "No, let's watch it through." She scratched absently at the older cut on her forearm through the fabric of her long thermal tee; she'd long ago stripped off the jacket. "Harrison's attacker must've scoped out the property at some point, and we've got two days of data."

"I must really like you to subject myself to such punishment," Illium said as they settled in to watch more of the same endless scene. Even at the speed they had it going, it seemed a static image.

The only break came when a giggling Maggie ran outside dressed up like a little polar bear—complete with bear ears on the hood of her snow jacket. Harrison stepped out after her, the two of them playing in the snow until Beth came to the doorway to call them back in. It was odd watching the entire scene in reverse, but one thing was clear.

"He's a good dad." For the first time, she saw a glimmer of what Beth must see in her husband. Saw the gentleness with which he swung Maggie up in his arms, the tenderness with which he stole a kiss from Beth while she tried to shoo husband and daughter out of the snow.

"Andreas likes him better these days," Illium told her.

Had Elena not hauled Harrison back to his angel when she had, Andreas would've signed an execution order with Harrison's name on it—a fact that Harrison hadn't understood when he attempted to escape, or even in the aftermath of his punishment.

Angels didn't play when it came to rogue young vampires.

After taking a drink of cola to swallow down another bite of sandwich, Illium said, "Last time I spoke to Andreas, he said your brother-in-law's knuckled under and put his nose to the grindstone."

"I think some of that has to do with Maggie." She rubbed the back of her neck to ease the stiffness without taking her eyes off the endless snow-draped white of the footage. "I know motherhood's changed Beth."

"Your niece might be the making of her father," Illium agreed. "Andreas can be harsh, but he doesn't ruin the vampires who work under him."

Elena thought of the punishments she knew the angel in question had meted out over the years: the precisely flayed skin and vicious whippings, the enclosure in coffin-sized boxes, the removal of a fucking eye with a rusty blade. "Are you sure about that?"

"Vampires can be blood-hungry monsters, Ellie. Normal punishments mean nothing to them."

In Elena's mind ran the images from one particular hunt: she'd found her target with his face burrowed in the torn open body of a young woman, her viscera—slick and gleaming—clutched in his greedy fingers. He'd been so glutted on his victim's blood that Elena'd had no trouble removing his head from his body.

His angel had sighed when she reported the circumstances and her decision to execute the vampire rather than bring him in. "I suppose I should be angry," Nazarach had said, his piercing amber eyes lit from within and his power bruising her skin. "But Richard was eighty years old. If he could not maintain a hold on his blood hunger at such an age . . ."

Wings of burnished amber in her vision and the ebony of his skin taut over fluid muscle as he turned to walk to a large arched window that offered a view of his gracious and lush estate full of magnolia and cypress trees. "It is a shame to lose one of mine, but Richard chose to run rather than come to me with his unacceptable urges. He dug his own grave." Age and death lived in Nazarach's voice, ancient and cold as the darkness of a crypt.

To this day, Elena found Nazarach as disturbing as fuck. But Andreas wasn't far behind Nazarach in the disturbing stakes. "What else have you heard about Harrison?" she asked Illium.

His shoulder brushing hers, he said, "Turns out he has a gift for administration. Andreas is training him to run a household."

"Like Montgomery does ours?" The Enclave home would be a shambles without him; Elena certainly would have no idea what to do.

"No one will ever be a Montgomery," Illium said, "but Harrison could deal with a more standard household. Trained that way and with Andreas as a reference once he finishes his Contract, he'll never have to fear being out of work and unable to support his own household."

But Beth would be gone by then, perhaps Maggie, too. Her heart twisted.

"So if he hasn't pissed off Andreas," she said through the screaming wrench of it, "and he's walking the straight and narrow, what could he have done that got him targeted for murder?"

"Andreas mentioned Harrison broke away from his previous friend group a while ago."

Pausing the recording, Elena turned to face Illium. "Since when are you and Andreas such good buddies?" she asked suspiciously. "He's not taking advantage of you while Aodhan is gone, is he?"

Illium's shoulders shook before he threw back his head and laughed. If Nazarach's voice was death and age and pain, Illium's was golden light and a playful joie de vivre that had the others in the room looking up with smiles. No one liked it when he wasn't himself. Once he finally calmed down—and after wiping tears from his eyes—he picked up one of her hands and brought it to his mouth for a kiss.

"I love you, Ellie." Solemn words, but his eyes were dancing.

"I have a crossbow, Bluebell, and I won't hesitate to use it."

An unrepentant grin. "Andreas and I have known each other for centuries. In battle, he leads one of the other elite squadrons." He pointed to the recording and she started it up again, both their eyes on the unmoving scene as they spoke. "We've had more contact recently because the squadrons are in the process of evaluating our total fighting capacity and ability to work with one another."

She'd known Andreas led a squadron but hadn't realized it was one of the elite ones that held their deadliest angelic fighters. "Tell me what your buddy Andreas had to say about Harrison's old friends." In spite of Illium's perfectly rational explanation, she remained leery of this relationship she'd never known had existed. "Why were you talking about Harry in the first place?"

Illium reached over to tug at her braid. "Because he's your sister's husband, of course. I knew you'd want to know if there was a problem." Still playing with her braid, he told her the rest of what he'd discovered. "In short, Harrison is on an upward trajectory, but the others—all post-Contract—were heading in the opposite direction last Andreas heard. Drugs, lack of ambition, the usual."

Elena's instincts prickled. Eric Acosta had been a junkie. So were hundreds of other vamps in Manhattan. But dead-beat former friends were a better lead than anything else she had right now. "You know the names of the post-Contract vamps?"

A shake of his head she caught out of the corner of her eye. "Andreas will, but he's out of the city tonight. He should be back tomorrow." A pause. "We show each other our diaries—then make playdates."

"Ha-ha." She poked him in the side while continuing to watch the footage.

She'd been looking at the whiteness of Beth's snow-draped home and yard for so long that when the movement came and the video slowed to normal speed, she stared dis-believing at it.

20

The same long coat Elena had seen in the footage when the intruder fled through the back door, the same hat, the same scarf wrapped around the face. Her heart pounded. "Can you skip through until you find the initial entry?" she said to Illium. "I want to watch this in the right order, from arrival to exit."

It only took Illium a minute to cue up the recording to the intruder's first appearance in the yard.

The unknown individual walked with quiet purpose, scoping out the house with intense attention to detail.

It was nighttime in the video, the resolution grainy, but . . .

"He moves like a man." She didn't know how else to explain it, but the gait, the way he held his body, the breadth of his shoulders, it all said male to her mind.

"Agreed."

Though they watched with unblinking focus, they could discern nothing of the man's face.

He walked out of camera view as stealthily as he'd arrived.

Elena had already seen that there would be snow later on that night, which would have hidden all signs of his passage. No way was that a stroke of luck. The assailant was too well-organized to have left such a thing to chance. He'd checked the weather, known that more snow would fall after his visit.

"Go backward again?"

Elena nodded at Illium's question. "Let's run this recording down to the final second. Our intruder might've been by earlier."

But that proved a false hope. Not about to give up, Elena cut ahead to the first glimpse of him, trying to glean even a minor detail. But it was Illium, leaning forward with his forearms braced on his thighs, who said, "A man—*and* one who moves like us. Like you. Trained."

"You're right." It was there in the fluidity of his walk, in his watchfulness, in the ease with which he pulled himself up to look through a window. "Could be military, ex or present. A mercenary. Even a guild hunter." Bill James had taught her that hunters weren't immune from going bad.

"Could also be off-grid," Illium pointed out. "A lot of old vampires who were once soldiers have kept up their skills, and not all work for the Tower." A shrug. "We can't eliminate every single Tower vampire, either."

Elena nodded; the suspect pool was huge. "About the only thing we can be sure of is that he isn't an angel."

Noting down the times of the relevant sections of footage, Elena sent off an e-mail to Vivek asking him to have a look. "Maybe he can spot something or zoom in further."

Stiff after such a long vigil, she and Illium both rose to stretch out their bodies. Tiredness lingered in her shoulders, but it didn't feel as if she had any new damage there. As for the cuts on her arm, she made a conscious decision to ignore them.

She *would* look, but only when her archangel was home.

Because she was fucking terrified the second barely-there scratch was actually starting to *hurt*.

"What are you doing the rest of the night?" she asked Illium after surreptitiously scratching that itchy spot on the left side of her chest. It was only a half hour till midnight, but Illium needed far less sleep than she did.

"I was thinking of flying down to the clubs, watching the entertainment."

Ordinary enough words, but Elena knew Illium. As he spoke, the last echoes of their shared laughter drained away from his face, his wings stiffer against his back. Nudging her shoulder against his, she said, "What is it?"

He linked one hand with hers, the warmth of his skin imbued with a power she felt as a prickle against her palm, a tiny lightning bolt that would've disconcerted if she didn't sleep skin-to-skin with an archangel.

"Today is the anniversary of the day she forgot me." A lopsided smile. "It seems all my loves leave me in the winter snow."

She. Illium's mortal lover to whom he'd spoken angelic secrets. Secrets she'd then spoken to others—it'd be easy to judge them, but there had been no malice on her part or his. They'd both just been young and a little foolish. Unfortunately, in their case it had equaled a far bigger consequence than waking up hungover with a bad tattoo, or with your wallet gone.

Caught by angelic law that left him no other recourse, Raphael had been forced to wipe the mortal woman's mind. Illium, in turn, had been stripped of his feathers and forbidden from contacting her again. He'd watched her live out her life without ever remembering that she'd once been the cherished love of a young angel with wings of astonishing blue.

Illium hadn't had the silver filaments then.

Those had come when his feathers regenerated.

At times, Elena thought Illium was over that long-ago heartbreak, and then there were days like today, when he'd say something and she'd be reminded all over again of how much he'd loved that unknown young woman. It would've been different had she died after spending her life with him. He'd still have mourned her, but he'd have also had a lifetime of memories to balance the sorrow.

Raphael had said something interesting once when they'd spoken about Illium's past. "He mourns a dream. He was so young, and in his mind, their love was perfection. Life is rarely perfect, however." But Illium only had the dream, the bittersweet poignancy of a first love lost in a way that had scored a permanent mark on his psyche.

"I'll come with you." She grabbed her jacket from where she'd hung it on the back of her chair. "There isn't much I can do on Harrison's case at the moment."

"You don't have to babysit me, Ellie."

"In that case, you can babysit me." Shrugging into the jacket, she met his eyes. "I've got a few ghosts whispering to me today, too." Only Raphael knew the whole of her blood-soaked history, but Illium knew enough to know that she was haunted as he was haunted. "I don't want to go home without Raphael."

He helped her find the right strap to snap her jacket closed over the wing slits. "Let's go paint the town red."

First, however, she drank two glasses of Nisia's energy supplement then stopped by to see the healer. Nisia cleared her to continue flying—with conditions. "If you experience the heavy tiredness you've described, you land." No give in her voice. "Even if you're over water. Your wings will keep you afloat after a controlled landing, but a crash into the water from a high enough height could tear you to pieces. Much like when the flying machines hit the water at speed. It may as well be concrete."

Elena winced. "Understood." Neither a panicked fall into suddenly unforgiving water nor a horrifying tumble into New York City traffic held any appeal.

Having waited on the balcony for her, his profile a clean line against the night sky, Illium looked over when she came out to join him. "Prognosis?"

"No new damage, but I'm going to stay at lower altitudes." It'd make for a quicker landing if her wing began to crumple.

Frowning, Illium shook his head. "You'll have a longer window and fewer obstacles in your path if you go high. I'm fast enough to catch you—you won't crash."

Raphael was the only person Elena trusted that much, but she couldn't bruise Illium's heart any further. Not tonight. And he *was* fast, the fastest angel in the city. Not only that, he was strong.

Pulse a drumbeat in her throat, she spread out her wings. "Since I have irrefutable proof that you can catch a helicopter and turn it upside down in mid-air, I suppose I'm willing to trust you with my scrawny body."

Illium's responding grin made the risk worth it.

Turning his back to the city, he fell back off the balcony with a "Yee-haw!"

"You've been watching Westerns again!" Elena called out as she glided more sedately off the edge.

The cold dug in its teeth and shook, but it was painfully beautiful to fly through the glittering color and lights of the city. Illium seemed to feel the same way, because he was in no rush to angle his wings toward the club district and Erotique, the club he frequented most often. At one point, Elena'd been sure he had something going with Dulce, one of the hostesses there, but Dulce wore a wedding ring these days and managed her own smaller club.

Illium continued to spend more time at Erotique than he probably should, especially with Aodhan gone. Elena didn't think that environment—sophisticated and full of vampires jaded and often no longer capable of simple happiness—was the greatest for him, but she couldn't exactly ground him. She'd done plenty of self-destructive things herself before she met Raphael. Mostly involving hunts with major hazard payouts.

Illium turned in a direction that would take them to the Catskills if they kept on going.

Sweeping closer to him, she said, "You just want to fly?"

Hair rippling in the quiet but cutting wind, he twisted

down in a complicated fall before flying back up to her side. She laughed at his showing off. *That* was Illium. An angel of violent power who had a heart that might almost be mortal. And, these days, she could appreciate his tricks again. Not a single angel in the city had been ready to witness his acrobatics in the immediate aftermath of the day he'd crashed out of the sky.

Elena would never forget her screaming fear.

To his credit, Illium had flown with absolute discretion for months, letting the memory dull and fade.

When he returned to her side today, his face was flushed, the gold of his eyes rich. "Sky's too beautiful to shut ourselves away in a club."

"Just don't forget I'm not as fast as you. Also, I'm currently lame."

Illium lifted one cupped hand close to his shoulder, the other moving back and forth . . . and she realized he was playing a tiny violin in response to her morose tone.

"Crossbow, Bluebell." Narrowed eyes. "Remember the crossbow."

He dived, his wicked laughter floating up on the night air. Lips twitching, Elena continued to glide, letting the air currents sweep her along with cold but gentle hands. Illium, meanwhile, flew circles around her—but he never went far, always close enough to halt her descent should she tumble.

She landed a number of times to rest her wings, once in an isolated park, whispering and dark. A luminescent insect appeared then disappeared from sight before she could truly see it, an earthbound star. The ghostly owl sitting on a tree branch watched her with eyes even more luminous.

A sigh deep in her mind, an old, *old* presence restless in Sleep.

The hairs rose on her arms.

Then Illium shot them both up into the sky again, and together, they flew far beyond the diamond-bright skyline of the city and over the sleeping homes of ordinary people who lived in a world of vampires and angels, blood and immortality.

Another rest stop for Elena.

Another throb of pain from the cut on her forearm.

Another watchful owl, this one landing on Illium's shoulder without his knowledge. Ashwini had told her not to be afraid of the owls, so Elena ignored the goose bumps and said, *Hello*, with her mind. *A good night to fly.*

A vein began to throb at her temple.

The answer came a long time later, after they were in the air again, the glow of the sinkhole visible from the distance.

It has been an eon since I flew.

Gritting her teeth against the devastating weight of age in that voice, Elena said, *Do you plan to wake?* The throbbing vein kept on pulsing.

A sense of stirring, two owls flying in languid patterns in front of her. *I am tired, child of mortals. My Sleep is not yet done.*

A bead of sweat running down her temple from the pain, Elena fought to hold on to the conversation, find out more about what was happening to her. *Then why are you talking to me? Why are you partially awake?*

I saw you once long ago, the old voice said. *I felt the approach of the markers even in my Sleep, and I thought to see you again before the becoming.*

Elena's pulse spiked. The Legion had spoken about becoming, too. *Who are you? Where did you see me?*

But the owls were gone, the Sleeper once more at rest. Nausea churned in her stomach from the pain at her left temple, and she thought she'd have to land—but a long drink of Nisia's concoction and the pain began to fuzz at the edges.

I love you, Nisia.

"It is a carnival," Illium said to her with a grin.

He wasn't far wrong.

The air around the sinkhole buzzed with activity—while unsmiling angelic guards kept the impatient and arrogant immortal audience from flying across to the heart of the cauldron of lava. No one seemed to be aware it was after two in the morning. "Forget a carnival," she muttered, "looks like we found the hottest club in town after all."

"Dance over the lava?"

"Hot, hot, hot."

Despite the byplay, she and Illium stayed outside the border. Seeing Raphael's consort and one of his Seven following the rules had the encroaching angels remembering their manners. The guards sent the two of them looks of exhausted gratitude.

Jurgen, who'd always put Elena in mind of a Viking, flew close enough to mutter, "I feel like I'm in the Refuge, corralling Jessamy's fledgling students." His neatly trimmed beard of dark blond shimmered with fine droplets of frost, his eyes an icy blue. "You'd think a particular seven-hundred-year-old angel had never once seen lava in his long and idiotic life. I'm of the opinion he has an amoeba for a brain."

Elena snorted out a laugh before she could stop herself. Amoeba-angel was dressed in flowing robes of purple velvet with inserts of white lace that looked like a rash crawling up his neck and over his shoulders. He also had diamonds woven into his hip-length hair. Not so surprisingly, he wasn't part of Raphael's Tower.

It wasn't, however, his flamboyance that made him unsuitable: Tower angels could clean up crazy-good when they felt like it. Elena had seen pearls braided into hair, gauzy dresses of handmade lace, shirts with more ruffles than a pageant gown paired with circulation-obliterating pants, all of it carried off with aplomb.

The difference was that the amoeba was a professional dilettante with no appreciable talent or expertise, the angelic equivalent of a socialite who lived large on an inherited fortune. Vampires had a term for it among their own kind: "gilded lilies."

"You didn't see me do that," she said to Jurgen. "I am a highly professional consort who does not laugh at jokes about amoeba-brained angels."

Stroking his beard, he said, "Do what?" and winked before sweeping back to his patrol.

"Amoebas," Illium mused with a deadly light in his eyes. "It's an even better description than gilded lilies. Jurgen is hiding genius."

And Elena knew the description would catch on among the non-amoebas. "I see and hear nothing. I am impartial."

Illium didn't call her out on her blatant lie. "Let's do the rounds, your Impartial Consortness."

The vast majority of the sightseeing angels wanted to talk about the lava, but a couple mentioned the vampiric killings in the Quarter. It seemed word of the attempt to slit Harrison's throat hadn't yet spread.

Then Elena ran into an angel who'd known one of the dead vampires.

21

"I always knew he'd do something foolish," Miuxu said to Elena after the two of them decided to land and take a leisurely walk around the sinkhole fence.

"Eric Acosta or Simon Blakely?" she asked the tall angel who wore intricate and heavily embroidered gowns as a matter of course—and kept her black hair in a short, spiky cut dusted with gold dye.

"Simon."

The victim on the bed. The Don Juan.

"I'm hearing he had a weakness for women."

Miuxu threw up hands gifted at the piano, the tawny eyes she'd lined with black kohl flashing. "He was a handsome man and he knew it." A shake of her head. "But handsome men are plentiful among immortals. You flew here with one of the prettiest of them all."

"Simon Blakely thought himself beautiful enough to surpass others?"

"It wasn't so much that." Miuxu tightened pale brown wings threaded with delicate filaments of shimmering bronze. "I'm not one of those angels who believes in breaking down a vampire in order to shape him. I prefer to treat them as adults and give them choices."

The angel sighed. "I've had brilliant successes, but I've also had more than one spectacular failure. Including with Simon." She spread out her wings before folding them back in, her coloring unusual in that her left wing had a band of black primary feathers while her right didn't. "He was intelligent, and he was vain, and he was a gifted enough lover that he was never short of bedmates."

Eyebrows rising to her hairline, Elena glanced at the strong angel as handy with a war hammer as she was at the piano. "You?"

Miuxu angled her head closer to Elena's, her contralto voice low as she said, "I was tempted, it's true, but I knew the instant I entered into bedsport with him, he'd think he could breach his Contract with impunity. That was the thing with dear, imprudent Simon; he thought he could manipulate everyone with his body."

Elena listened . . . and kept a furtive eye on her wings to make sure they weren't dragging. In the good news department, her temple was no longer throbbing and, having eaten three energy bars on the flight over, she had her hunger under control.

"Simon's sensuality could've held him in good stead in the immortal world." Miuxu's voice was contemplative. "I made sure he could support himself in a legitimate profession at the end of his Contract, but I thought it far more likely he'd find himself a wealthy mortal or immortal. You know how such things are."

"Yes." Plenty of the genetically blessed made their living as arm candy. Elena saw nothing wrong with that when it was an honest exchange and when both parties were adults in full control of their faculties. "How did he end up in a bad part of the Quarter? My friends working the case tell me he was sharing an apartment that was one step above a dump."

"Simon didn't seem to understand that once you make

an agreement with an immortal, you stay loyal." Miuxu's gaze looked out beyond the blackness of the night. "He quickly gained a reputation for being untrustworthy and liable to cheat." Another shake of her head. "Angels and vampires old enough to support lovers to the lifestyle to which Simon aspired are not forgiving. He was lucky that he escaped with his life."

The hairs on Elena's nape prickled. "Is it possible one of the people he cheated on decided to punish him with death?"

"It has been some years since he was active in the immortal world in that way." Clasping her hands behind her back, Miuxu took a moment to consider her next words. "I would say he was punished with the most painful cut of all—he has been forgotten," she said at last. "But I wouldn't be at all surprised if there was a woman involved somewhere."

A glance at Elena, Miuxu's eyes a light brown with an unusual yellowish cast that reminded her of a tiger's penetrating gaze. "He was firm in his tastes. Always women. Young, yes—but adults, you understand? He had no liking for children when it came to pleasures of the flesh, and I would not have him accused of that perversion."

"I understand."

"Nubile and lovely were also prerequisites—and many vampires as well as mortals fall into that group."

"Do you know anything about the other vampire who was murdered? Eric Acosta."

"No." Miuxu nodded politely to an old vampire strolling in the opposite direction, before picking up the thread of their conversation. "I believe in giving my vampires true freedom when they've finished their Contract. I don't keep them on any kind of a leash—but I am proud to say many of mine stay in touch. Even black sheep like Simon swing back into my orbit now and then."

A sad smile. "He never told me of his cheating ways—I got that from the wronged angels who knew he had been one of mine. From Simon, I got grand plans and even grander promises of what he would one day become."

"You've given me a far clearer picture of him." Elena'd work with Ashwini and Janvier to see if they could dig up more about Simon's love life, any jealousies or spurned lovers capable of ruthless, brutal payback.

The problem was that motive left too many gaping holes unfilled. Acosta she could explain away as collateral damage for having been there at the time, but Harrison had been stalked. Also, Simon had only liked women, but the possible killer Elena had seen was male. Jealous husband, boyfriend, maybe?

A wash of wind, tendrils of her hair flying back in it, before Illium landed in front of her and Miuxu. Bowing with old-world grace, his wings flaring out in a showy display, he said, "My lovely Miuxu, it has been too long since I've heard you weave fever dreams with your fingers."

Husky laughter from Miuxu. "You are as playful and as wicked as ever, I see."

Elena caught the glances shared between the two and wondered . . . If so, Illium had excellent taste. Yet when Illium joined her and Miuxu, the two spoke only as intimate friends who had a cherished history between them, but no present entanglement.

Stopping at one of the large glass windows that allowed the curious to peer in, Elena watched the lava bubble and spike, forming and reforming into strange unearthly patterns. In front of her eyes formed the molten image of an owl. "It's alive," she murmured, scratching at that spot on her chest again.

Child of mortals.

Elena froze at the ethereal feminine voice in her head. *You're awake again.*

A whispering sigh that held such exquisite tiredness. *Child of mortals,* the voice repeated. *I will not awaken in time to see you. You are destined to fall.*

Screw that. Elena glared at the lava. *I'll write my own destiny.*

This is not destiny. This is a birth. You must end for the other to live.

Cold in her blood now. *Raphael?* A stiff whisper. *Do I need to die to save Raphael?* She'd do that without thought, without hesitation.

No answer, no sense of a presence, the sounds of Miuxu and Illium's conversation filtering in past senses that had been locked in silence while she spoke to the being who wasn't there. Except it *was*. Feminine. *Old*. So achingly old. Barely awake.

That was the imprint in Elena's head.

An imprint that forespoke her death.

You must end for the other to live.

What the hell was she supposed to do with that? How the hell was she supposed to process it?

Illium gave her a discreet boost into the air when it was time for them to head homeward. He made it seem that they were just playing a game, that Elena was being tugged along for fun. She wondered that he wasn't anchored down by the weight of the stone in her abdomen, her blood like lead.

They'd barely reached Manhattan when she felt the crash of the wind in her mind, the whisper of the sea. *Hbeebti, I see you have been playing with your Bluebell in my absence.*

Elena's clenched heart slammed into thudding joy as she searched for her archangel. *Where are you?*

A sweep of air, Raphael soaring down from the night sky far above. Spotting Raphael, Illium lifted a hand in a wave before zooming off in another direction. *Now look,* Elena said with a mock scowl, *you've scared him off.*

Your Bluebell is made of sterner stuff. I've asked him to check a border line. Winging down then up, Raphael grabbed her by the waist.

Elena folded her wings instinctively to her back and locked her arms around his neck. *You remember.*

Old memories on his face, of a love between a young angel and a mortal woman, of an archangel forced to make a cruel decision. *It is a hard thing to hurt a boy you've watched grow to manhood.*

Elena couldn't imagine the horror of that day, Raphael and Illium both caught by angelic law and left with no way out. If Illium's lover hadn't spoken . . . But she had, and in so doing, sealed both her and Illium's fate. *Did you keep him busy most of the day on purpose?* Illium had run down his packed schedule for her as they tried to stave off boredom while watching the security footage.

It is the one gift I can give him on this day. Holding her with one arm around her waist, he cupped her jaw and cheek with the other. *Dmitri intended to set him another task when he saw the two of you together in Vivek's domain.*

"I'm glad he didn't interrupt. We ended up having fun." Perhaps enough to take the edge off the painful anniversary. "Do we have to brace for a volcano?"

"Not just now. I have left a team behind to monitor the geothermal activity—it should not exist, but it is mild in the scheme of things." The pad of his thumb brushing over her cheekbone. "Your face speaks of exhaustion and yet you fly in the darkest hours before dawn. Why are you not in bed asleep?"

Unable to hold her need back any longer, Elena turned to kiss his palm. "You've been gone so many hours."

Raphael bent his head toward her own. "Did you miss me, Elena-mine?"

Like the air from my lungs, like the blood in my veins. No shields between her and her archangel, no secrets. "Will you dance with me?" she whispered with her lips against his, the second cut on her forearm a dull pulsation in the background that she ignored with ferocious focus. "I missed you so much today."

"*Hbeebti.*" Flame-blue eyes burning with archangelic power, each obsidian eyelash defined against the crystalline clarity. "What darkness holds you in thrall? Are your wings causing you pain?"

"Later." The rest could wait—inside her was a hunger to feel real, feel strong, feel *Elena*. "I need you."

In answer, he rocketed them up into the sky with violent power. She screamed out her delight, knowing that no one could hear them, no one could see them. Raphael had wrapped her in glamour, that skin of invisibility that only the archangels could produce—and not even all of them.

"To the river or the sea?" Raphael murmured the question in her ear, his breath hot, his arms strong, and his body a powerful haven.

Elena knew he'd never let her fall.

From the moment he'd become hers, Raphael had been there for her in a way no one else had been her entire life. Not even her mother.

Marguerite's betrayal had been the most hurtful of them all.

"The sea," she said. "I'm too angry for the city today."

"You are thinking of your mother again," Raphael said as he took them high across Manhattan.

"I love her till it hurts, and I'm *so* angry with her." In that strange, sad dream, she'd told Marguerite she wasn't afraid, but what she hadn't spoken of was the other emotion that was a scalding heat in her psyche. "Sometimes I think I've forgiven her, then I remember the loneliness and the fear and *how I found her*. I saw my mother's body hanging from the ceiling! How could she do that to me, Raphael?"

His answer held a knowledge that not many people would ever possess. "Caliane asks herself the same question and she cannot divine an answer. It is a thing of madness that causes a mother to forget her child."

"That's exactly what makes me want to find her and shake her and shake her." Elena's voice was crushed stones and coarse sand. "Mama was so lost in her grief over Belle and Ari that she forgot me and Beth. She forgot Jeffrey." Marguerite had been no trophy wife. She hadn't even been the "right kind" of wife for a man of Jeffrey's wealth and standing.

No, she'd been a beloved wife.

"I can almost understand what he's become," Elena said. "The way he is now." She ran her fingers through Raphael's hair as the two of them flew on into the night. "It'd be as if you chose to leave me. I'd spend the rest of my life wondering *why* you couldn't come to me, why you couldn't trust me with your hurt and sorrow."

I would never leave you, Elena. A lethal edge in every word. *Such a thing is an impossibility.*

"I know you'd never leave me, not by choice." The Cascade shoving him full of power, other forces in the immortal world, sought to steal him from her, but Raphael would never make the choice Marguerite had made. "I was just using it as an example."

Find another example.

Laughter burst through the anger, shattering it into icy shards that melted in the heat between them. Sinking into the force of his love and commitment, she used her most penitent voice to say, "I apologize for even using it as a hypothetical example."

He gave her a stern look, before nodding downward. "See there."

Following his gaze, she spotted a jetboat scything through the water. It was a sleek black thing with what might've been flames licking up the sides. It was hard to see in the darkness, the only light coming from the boat itself. "Fancy."

"Look closer."

She squinted as he dropped lower, but it was a wisp of scent that floated into the air—chocolate and fur and champagne—that gave her the identity of the man at the helm. "Dmitri? I didn't know he had a boat."

"That's the *Honor*, Dmitri's new personal launch." A pause before he said, "Shall I name something after you?"

Elena pretended to think about it. "Maybe the next time you buy a jet," she said solemnly.

"I will call it the Hunter Angel."

Elena threatened to punch him. He laughed until his eyes were pure light and white fire danced over his primaries and it felt like intoxication. His kiss was food to her parched soul, the angel dust that coated her lips without warning luscious and erotic, delicious and addictive.

The special blend he created only for her.

"Raphael." She licked her tongue against his, a molten quickening at her core.

22

Body hard, her archangel speared up into the sky again and this time when he fell it was like a bullet, his wings arrowed to his back. They smashed into the water but felt no impact. A bubble of energy that arced with Raphael's power protected them as they fell, going deeper and deeper, two bodies locked in a primal dance.

Kiss after kiss. Touch after touch.

His mouth at her throat, her fingers finding the most sensitive spot on his wings.

Elena's need a wild thing, Raphael's touch earthy and physical.

Skin, I need skin. She pulled at the zipper of her jacket, de—

A stab of heat in her arm, cruel enough to have her breaking their kiss. Her hair tumbled around them, her clothing askew. But her eyes were on the arm she cradled to her body. "It burns." The shocked words slipped out past her guard . . . because this was Raphael.

Face set in brutal lines, he gently pushed up her jacket

and T-shirt sleeve at once, the glow of his power lighting up the dark below the surface of the ocean. In that glow, she saw that her flesh was translucent, her bones morphing shape. A scream built inside her . . . and the illusion faded. "Did you see?" she asked through a throat gone raw. "My flesh was see-through."

"No, I see only inflamed skin." Raphael brushed away the piece of lint that stuck to the cut that continued to throb. "Describe what you saw." Healing power sank into her, power that tasted of her archangel.

Exhaling shakily in the aftermath, perspiration chilling on her face and the back of her neck, she stared at the spot where the cut had been and told him all of it. "I'm changing somehow. Becoming, the Legion said. Maybe my brain's trying to make sense of it and short-circuiting."

"Perhaps, and perhaps the ancient being who speaks to you has encroached into your life while asleep." His voice was frigid, emotionless. "Does the injury feel better?"

"Yes. No more pain." Only echoes of it, serrated pieces of metal twisting under her skin.

Raphael's face went impossibly more emotionless, the Legion mark on his temple ablaze and his wings pure white fire. "Home, *hbeebti*."

"Home." Elena closed her arms around him, a crushing suffocation in her lungs.

The house was lit up in welcome. Someone had even strung fairy lights amidst the trees and along the rooftop. "Those weren't there before," Elena whispered, a pressure behind her eyelids, a pounding at her temples, and a sense of *wrongness* in her limbs. As if her bones had truly changed shape.

Raphael didn't speak.

Instead of turning toward the house after they landed, Elena stood toe to toe with her archangel. His fury was a living thing between them, his power crackling the air and dancing along her skin.

Spreading out his fiery wings, he closed his hands over the top arch of her own wings and stroked down firmly.

She shivered and nuzzled his throat. "Activate the glamour."

"You need to speak to a healer, then go to sleep."

"What I need is you." The wrongness faded, her skin settling back on her bones. "I won't let anything, even the Cascade, steal us from one another." Thrusting her hand into his hair, she kissed him until he was no longer stone, until he was her Raphael again, her archangel who feared for her as he'd never feared in his life.

Red flushed his cheekbones, his pupils dilated when they came up for air. White fire and feathers, his wings shifted from one to the other in a pulse timed to his heartbeat. "We are wrapped in glamour." He pulled off his tunic to reveal a sculpted chest that made her want to bite.

So she did.

He laughed and bit her back oh so lightly on the curve of her neck, his hand possessive on her breast. "Clothes, Elena," he ordered with another bite, another squeeze of her swollen flesh.

Barely able to wait, she stripped off her jacket and dropped it to the snow, then placed her various knife sheaths, assorted other weapons, and the crossbow onto the protective leather. The rest of her clothes disappeared in a flash. "I must love you a great deal, Archangel," she pointed out as an icy wind brushed her bare skin. "It's freaking freezing."

"I'll take care of that," Raphael said before leaping with her into the sky.

Limbs interlocked and minds entwined, flesh against flesh, warrior to warrior, they danced that most intimate, erotic dance.

He kissed her mouth, her neck, her breasts.

Nipples hard against the beauty of his chest, she petted him everywhere she could reach, her lips determined to cover every golden inch of his body.

His hands were rough with need, with fear.

Her fingernails were claws as she fought to cling to their future.

Thighs quivering and body liquid, she pressed wet kisses along his jawline high above the Hudson River. "Inside me, Raphael. I need you inside me."

His hand squeezing the curve of her flank where she had her leg wrapped around his waist, the Legion mark on his right temple glittering diamond-bright . . . and his stone-hard cock thrusting into her with an earthy passion that had nothing of distance or otherness in it.

Her body clamped around his as a cry left her throat. *Mine, you are mine.*

Eternity, Elena, that is what you promised me. His mental voice was ragged, his body possessive and primal in her, around her. *I will never release you from that promise.*

They clung, two lovers in freefall.

The waters of the river closed over their heads, a dark blanket.

Wrapped around him in every way, Elena whispered, *Knhebek, Archangel,* and the words of love held her every fear, her every hope, her very soul . . . even as her forearm began to burn and the vein at her left temple felt as if it would burst.

Raphael sensed his consort's excruciating pain even as their bodies rocked with pleasure. It was instinct to drench her in his healing energy. Paltry though it was after his earlier usage, more a false promise than a truth, Elena trembled around him on a shudder of relief before she surrendered to the incandescent energy between them.

Her eyes glowed at the end, the rim of silver dazzling . . . only for it to flicker and fade out like a candle extinguished by a sudden wind.

Back bowing as his own pleasure broke on a cresting wave, Raphael couldn't hold on to the image, and when he looked at his hunter again, she was smiling softly, her body languid and her eyes boasting the rim of silver that spoke of her growing immortality. He ran his hand over her back, kissed her temple, used his free arm to hold her close to his warmth.

Hair wild silk against his skin, she made a near purring sound, so strong and alive and vibrant in his arms.

And being hunted by forces Raphael wanted to annihilate out of existence. "Home?"

"Mmm." A nod, followed by the grumble of her stomach.

No annoyed huff this time, his consort too lazy-limbed in the aftermath of their loving. Bringing them out of the river, he carried her to the clifftop on which stood their home.

"Hey, wait!" Jolting out of her heavy-lidded laziness when he strode past the pile of their clothing, she said, "My crossbow! My knives!"

Taut as he was with a worry that went down to the immortal cells of his body, Raphael felt his lips kick up. "Ah, now I see your priorities."

"No funning, Raphael." A heavy scowl as she twisted to look over his shoulder at the pile retreating into the distance. *"Archangel."*

Placing her on her feet inside the doorway of the study entrance, he said, "Stay out of the snow. I'll retrieve your precious jewels."

She was dancing on her feet and rubbing at her arms and legs by the time he returned. "Glamour, quick," she ordered. "I don't want to flash Montgomery." A shudder of horror.

Raphael was an archangel, feared no man, far less his own butler. But there was an innocence in sneaking out of the study like misbehaving youths, the laughing glance Elena threw him over her shoulder stirring a part of him that awakened only for her.

The house was warmly lit at this pitch-dark time before dawn, but of Montgomery, there was no sign.

"He has a wife now," Raphael murmured with a stroke of his hand up Elena's bare flank. "I'm sure he's engaged in

far more pleasurable matters than in rising predawn to wait
for us."

"Hush." Elena threw him a quelling look. "I can't think
about Montgomery *that* way. As far as I'm concerned, he
sleeps in his suit."

"Sivya may have some disagreement with a husband
who is never naked."

Elena put her fingers in her ears. "La-la-la, I can't hear you."

Holding on to the simple joy of this instant when they'd
set aside the problem of the dangerous changes in Elena,
Raphael teased her with heavy strokes of his palm across
her wings as they went up the stairs. His warrior threatened
to kick him. He pressed a kiss to the dimple at the base of
her spine.

She pounced on him the instant they were behind the
closed doors to their suite.

Weapons and clothes dropping to the floor, they tumbled
onto the bed in a warm tangle of limbs, their wings wrapped
around each other.

"I love you too much," she said without warning, her
smile wiped away. "What if one day something happens to
you like what almost happened to Harrison yesterday?"

He brushed back the strands of her hair that stuck to her
cheeks, living pieces of gossamer crackling with life. The
strands clung to him. "I am difficult to hurt." He didn't have
to say the rest, didn't have to point out that she was the one
who threatened to break him.

Swallowing hard, she caressed her fingers down his
cheek then gave him a concise summary of what had happened to her while they'd been apart. The watching owls,
the horrific pain in her left temple, the continued problems
with her wings . . . and the voice in her head. "Describe it
to me again," he ordered.

She twisted up her face. "Old, old, *old*. Older than Caliane. Than Alexander." Biting down on her lower lip, she
considered it. "A female energy. No sense of overt threat,
but the words she says, Raphael. '*You must end for the*

other to live.' That's not exactly a warm and fluffy bedtime story."

Shifting so that he was braced over her, his wings blocking out the night and offering her a canvas for fingers that painted affection over him, Raphael forced his brain to think. Raw archangelic power was no use against a foe unknown and unseen. He must be intelligent, fight with will and knowledge. "We will speak to Jessamy. The words are in the pattern of a prophecy. It could be that such a prophecy was recorded in our histories."

"But if the speaker is an Ancient among Ancients . . . Age and time eat away at even great civilizations. Libraries are lost, entire histories erased."

"Yes, but angelkind has living histories, whose memories simply need to be mined." Even then, the task might be impossible—he knew of no angel older than five hundred thousand years who was awake. Their forebearers Slept an endless night, immortals who wished no more to walk the earth. "We must ask."

Elena nodded. "Never know what someone's great-uncle Bert might remember."

The joke fell flat, both their hearts beating too fast. Raphael almost wished Lijuan would rise again. She, even in her deadly and dreadful "evolution," was a foe he understood and could battle.

Having his hands tied while Elena hurt . . .

"*Enough* of this." His consort placed her palms against his glowing wings. "You don't have to save me, Archangel. We are *us*. *That's* how we fight this. Together." One hand against his heart. "You're a little bit mortal and I'm a tiny bit immortal. *We* did that to each other. *We* created the wildfire. *We* beat Lijuan. *We'll* beat this together. The one thing we won't do is surrender who we are to this menace."

Yes, she was magnificent, his warrior consort. She was also right. All their greatest successes had come when they acted as one. He would do well to remember that. "As you say."

"I do so say." She poked a finger to his chest. "Also, we're both covered in angel dust."

Bending his head, he licked the tip of one breast. She shivered.

The result was inevitable.

Afterward, her skin gleaming with a layer of perspiration mingled with angel dust and sleep not yet on her mind even now so close to dawn, she rose from the bed to raid the table on which Montgomery and Sivya had laid out a feast of covered dishes before they retired the previous day.

One of the two had also placed a heating device on the table. A microwave, he recalled, that was what it was termed. On the microwave was a note in Sivya's hand that she'd be happy to rise to prepare fresh foods whenever Raphael and Elena returned home, but Raphael knew his hunter would never think of intruding on the couple's sleep for such a small matter.

"Those two would keel over stone-dead if they knew what I used to eat as a mortal at the end of a long day in the field," she said as she put a full plate in the microwave. "This kind of a spread would've been beyond my wildest dreams."

After the food was ready, she filled a second plate with cold items then came back to sit on the bed facing him, her right wing lying heavily on his thigh as he remained on his back in bed.

"Tell me about your day and I'll tell you about Nisia's warped sense of humor," she traded.

"You are too late, *hbeebti*. I learned of Nisia's leanings when she solemnly told my three-hundred-year-old self that I had a growth on my back that was for life but should cause me no harm. I spent days twisting around to try to find it."

Elena paused with a slice of pie halfway to her mouth. "What was it?" Wide eyes.

23

"You have the same growth."

Elena twisted instinctively before groaning. "Wings? She was messing with your head the whole time? God, she's diabolical. What did you do to piss her off?"

"Broke my bones once too often trying to gorge-dive." He'd been much younger, with weaker bones, the gorge that bisected the Refuge a massive crack in the mantle of the earth. "But I will tell you about my day and then you can tell me how you discovered Nisia's sadistic streak."

He plucked a grape off her cold plate, bit into the tart sweetness of it. "Jason found me before he left to return to his princess. We had a long discussion."

"About Favashi, I'm guessing." Finishing off her pie, Elena fed him another grape.

Raphael accepted the gift. "She appears to be gathering a much bigger standing army than she's ever before had."

"China's bigger than her previous territory." Getting up off the bed with hunter fluidity, Elena refilled her hot plate. "Maybe she thinks she needs more people?"

Her left wing was dragging on one side.

A primary feather, shimmering dawn and white-gold, floated to lie on the carpet as he watched.

His gut tensed. Losing a feather so significant for flight was not a common thing.

Elena's gaze followed his when he didn't respond, the bones in her face standing out against her skin. But when she looked to him, it was with challenge and a furious will to fight.

We are us . . . The one thing we won't do is surrender who we are to this menace.

Wrenching his eyes off the feather on the memory of her words, he spoke to her as his consort and the most integral piece of his existence.

"The problem," he said, "is that Favashi's army is not spread out across the country as it would be if she intended to use it to maintain order. It is gathered in one place, and though Jason has no specifics as yet, he's heard whispers that she is thinking of conquest."

Elena resettled on the bed. "Conquest?" Her voice rose. "She barely has China under control."

Stroking his fingers over her thigh, he attempted to send more healing energy into her body, but the well had run dry. "I'm not saying any of this makes sense," he said past the ball of cold rage in his chest. "Regardless, Dmitri spent much of the day ensuring there are no holes in our defenses. We will be ready, should she cast covetous eyes toward this territory."

"Wouldn't it be more logical for her to target the territory closest to her?" Biting into a small pastry that crumbled buttery flakes onto her plate, she made a humming sound in the back of her throat.

Even in the depths of the rage that surged past his resolution to search for a solution together with his consort, Raphael's body stirred. "If Favashi dares look to India, she will have a war on her hands—you said it yourself, Neha can be a warrior goddess when necessary." He brushed off a piece of soft white lint on her thigh.

"I can't figure out where that's coming from," Elena muttered. "My clothes maybe got laundered with a tissue. Stuff's everywhere."

Keeping one hand on her thigh, Raphael folded his other arm behind his head. "Favashi will alienate the rest of the Cadre if she tries anything against another territory, no matter whose. She already has one of the biggest landmasses on the planet despite being the newest member of the Cadre."

"You know," Elena mused, "it's like an ancient Egyptian curse"—wiggling her fingers as if casting a spell—"anyone who becomes Archangel of China will go batshit crazy."

"The angels who ruled Egypt were often melodramatic, but yes, it appears so." He hoped for Favashi's sake that hers was a small madness brought on by the sudden ascension to such a huge territory—because there was no way she could win against the rest of the Cadre. She was no Lijuan, who had evolved into a truly immortal terror who appeared impossible to kill.

The war when Lijuan rose again would forever scar the world. She wouldn't wake sane, as Caliane had done. No, Lijuan had gone to ground to bloat herself with power.

Her rising would augur a new Dark Age.

Perhaps the darkest since angelkind's first death and the birth of vampires.

Favashi, however . . . she risked annihilation by her fellow archangels should she truly be planning to encroach on the territories held by the rest of the Cadre.

"Enough of Favashi's descent into megalomania," he said. "Tell me what you discovered today." He understood the history that drove her to try to protect her sister by solving the mystery of Harrison Ling's attempted murder, but still had to bite his tongue from telling her she needed to be concentrating on her health and the changes going on in her body.

Falling in love with Elena had taught him many things—not the least of which was the dubious art of patience. He would battle a thousand Lijuans to keep on learning such lessons.

Making a face, she said, "I caught a glimpse of the assailant, but there's precious little to go on."

As he listened, she took him through her day, focusing on the investigation. She didn't linger on her ride with Ransom, nor the lift from Izak, but neither did she hide her concern about why those decisions had been necessary. His consort had always been strong; as a hunter-born, she'd been stronger than most ordinary men. And the instant she settled into her wings, she'd begun to learn how to utilize her new body.

She'd fought him for her freedom when he would've cocooned her in safety.

Weakness, helplessness, was her enemy, returning her to a childhood in which she hadn't been able to stop a monster.

Later, once the food was gone and she lay in his arms, she said, "I'm afraid, Archangel. What's happening to me?"

Rage tore through him all over again, and he knew that if he lost her this way, to an unseen assailant, he would become a monster himself. "I have no answers yet, Elena, but I will tear the world apart until I find one."

Her fingers spread over his heart. "We," she reminded him.

Closing his fingers over hers, he said, "We."

Her body went soft and unguarded against him not long afterward. She slept . . . and dreamed. Her breath caught, her pulse increased, and a thin sheen of perspiration glimmered on her skin.

Speaking into her mind, he said, *I am here, hunter-mine. Nothing can harm you.*

A slow exhale, her breathing beginning to even out as she turned into his body and fell into a deep, restful sleep. Raphael didn't sleep. He watched over her. The attack on Harrison entwined with the voice that spoke ominous things to her, and the changes in her, they were clearly stirring up the darkest memories of her childhood.

Raphael could open her brother-in-law's mind without effort, discover what it was Harrison Ling had done that had made him a target. Except that would cut Elena to the quick. She would feel complicit in his violation of Harrison's mind—because that was how she'd see it: as a violation.

If Raphael acted now, he did so knowing it would bruise her and cause a fissure in their relationship. Such a fissure might heal over time, but enough fissures and the whole thing would break apart.

"Love," he said to his warrior, "is a most inconvenient thing." She stirred, a soft smile curving her lips . . . and he saw a small feather of darkest blue detach from her wing to lie orphaned against the white of the sheets.

24

Raphael watched his consort dress after breakfast; she'd slept a bare three hours before waking. He hadn't pushed her to attempt more rest—he knew Elena. She wouldn't truly rest until she'd nullified the threat to her sister and niece. As it was, she'd eaten and drunk five times what she normally would, but her facial bones were starting to become more obvious nevertheless, her clothes a fraction looser on her frame.

Her body was burning fuel at a phenomenal rate.

"Where do you go this morning, Elena?"

She strapped on her crossbow. "To talk to Andreas—I'm going to see if I can track down some sketchy friends of Harrison's."

He settled slightly; the senior angel was loyal to the core. "Pass on my greetings to him."

"You know I don't like him." Scowling, she slid her long blade home in its spine sheath. "He's got a streak of cruelty in him that's disturbing."

"So did I." Raphael had once broken every bone in a

vampire's body to the size of small pebbles, turned the vamp into nothing but a fleshy sack incapable of conscious movement—and he'd made sure the male stayed awake through all of it. "Perhaps Andreas needs to fall madly in love with a hunter."

Elena shuddered. "I wouldn't wish that on any hunter—and no, he's way worse than you." A pause, then grudgingly, "Though I guess my perspective is skewed since I'm passionately in love with you." She watched him put on leathers of gunmetal gray with an appreciative gleam in her eye. "I mean, Honor's a sane woman with advanced degrees, and she married Dmitri, of all people, so maybe being part whackadoodle is a prerequisite to falling in love."

He clasped on wrist gauntlets of beaten steel not because he needed them today but because Elena had given them to him. "Such romance you give me, *hbeebti.*"

Laughing, she zipped up her jacket, a lethal black-clad woman who took no prisoners. "What are you doing today dressed up like the sexiest warrior I've ever seen?"

"Archangel business."

Her eyes danced at his deliberately arrogant tone. Closing the distance between them, she rose on tiptoe, her hands gripping his bare biceps to demand a kiss that held naked need. Raphael gave and he took and they broke apart on a rasp of breaths.

"Will you be in the city?" his consort asked, her fingertips tracing the lines of the Legion mark.

"No." Much as he wished to keep Elena in his sights so he could catch her if she fell, such suffocating protectiveness would be a small death for her, and he did in fact have archangel business to which to attend. "I go to meet Elijah. I want to ensure he's heard about Favashi's recent actions and that he's willing for us to work together to protect our territories—and such discussions between archangels are a thing better done in person."

The Archangel of South America had once been a general in Caliane's army, and even after he ascended to become an archangel, he hadn't forgotten that old loyalty. He treated Raphael's mother with a deference unusual among archangels, and he treated Caliane's son with the warmth of an older brother who wished to see his sibling succeed.

Raphael didn't always know what to make of that, but he trusted Eli. While friendship was a complicated thing between archangels, they had the beginnings of it, a foundation on which their relationship over the centuries to come could be built.

"Tell him to say hi to Hannah for me." Elena's phone buzzed with an incoming message on the edge of her words. "It's been a while since we've had dinner together." Digging out her phone, she quickly checked the message before securing the phone back in a pocket. "Maybe we should organize something before the Cascade causes even more chaos."

"I leave that in my consort's hands."

"Don't think that I don't see you laughing." She pointed a finger at him. "But Andreas's secretary just confirmed he's home and willing to meet me, so I'll deal with you later."

He walked her to the balcony, running his hand down her spine one more time as they stepped out into the frosty morning air. His healing energy was limited, merely what had regenerated while she slept, but she gave him a grateful look. His jaw hardened. "Your wings are worse?"

"I'm pretty sure it's just morning stiffness." She scratched at her chest.

Catching her hand, he stared at the spot. "Elena."

"Damn, was I scratching again?" A grimace. "You saw me naked in the shower—did you spot anything? I didn't."

"No, I saw nothing."

"Then we keep on living." A fierce vow. "We do not let the Cascade manipulate us into limbo."

"Fear will not ruin us," he vowed in turn.

Elena's smile was of a warrior, full of teeth.

He took both himself and his consort into the air before dropping her so she could glide into flight. She swept out in a wide curve then back in to head deeper into the Enclave,

while he flew toward the Tower to speak to Dmitri before
he left for his meeting with Elijah. When he glanced back,
he saw that a number of the Legion must've been crouching
in the trees around their home. They rose into the air to join
Elena, providing a silent escort as she flew toward Andreas's property.

Raphael smiled grimly and flew on.

In his hand was a piece of lint he'd brushed off Elena's
shoulder when he took off her robe after breakfast. Gossamer soft, it was the color of her hair.

Elena looked to the Primary, who flew next to her on silent wings. "Why are you shadowing me?"

"We want to."

Elena narrowed her eyes; sometimes she thought the Primary was deliberately using inscrutable language to perplex
and confound, but then she'd remember the Legion weren't
human in any way, shape, or form. They weren't angels or
vampires, either. They were *other,* and their minds didn't
walk known paths.

"You're here because Raphael wants you to be here."
Her archangel's protective urges were riding a dangerous
edge, but he hadn't tried to chain her. No, he'd taken her to
the sky and set her free. But the Legion were so much his
that they acted on his emotions.

The Primary cocked his head to one side. "You also
want us here."

Elena went to say no she didn't—then realized she didn't
actually mind her Legion followers. She liked them whereas
she didn't like Andreas all that much. "Did you spend the
night in the trees? Why didn't you go inside the greenhouse?" She often walked in there to find one of the Legion
among her plants, exotic garden statues who woke at the
sight of her.

"We like the winter. Many trees sleep, but they exist.
And in the spring, new leaves are born fed by the energy of
the leaves that sighed to the earth in fall."

"Very philosophical." Goose bumps broke out over Elena's skin, an eerie sense of déjà vu thick in her mind. "Have we had this conversation before?"

"No. Perhaps we will have it in the future."

Shaking off the chill, Elena flew on with the Legion silent and old yet paradoxically young.

"Elena?"

She looked over. "What is it?"

The Primary's pale eyes held hers. "We remembered a memory. It is old."

Skin too hot, her internal thermostat malfunctioning today, Elena had to force herself to break the eye contact so she wouldn't fly off-course. "Tell me."

"A memory of white owls who sit with a woman with hair of lilac. She smiled before the Cascade of Terror changed her. Then she bled tears of dark red."

Shivering at the reference to the last time the Legion had woken, during a war that had "unmade" angelic civilization and sent the battered survivors into an eons-long Sleep, Elena said, "Do you know her name?"

A shake of his head. "We remember only that the owls cried for her after she was gone."

Elena found her phone and sent a message to Vivek with the description. *Please make sure it gets to Jessamy*, she wrote.

Sure, Ellie, was the response. *Any more creepy things you'd like me to forward?*

Tell Aodhan I'm waiting to rewatch Psycho *until he gets back.*

I'm so glad I'm not in your film club. Messages will be sent.

Putting away her phone, Elena flew on, the Legion keeping pace with her slow flight. When she landed in Andreas's front yard, it was to find the angel out in the snow. He was dancing through a martial arts routine using dual swords, and he was good. Better than good. Intellectually, Elena had always known that Andreas was powerful, but despite his position as a squadron leader, she didn't tend to think of him as a warrior.

Seeing him stripped to the waist, however, his muscles moving fluidly and his wings—a rich amber leavened with gray—held with warrior precision as he manipulated the swords at brutal speed, she remembered something Jessamy had once said to her: *"An immortal has many facets, Ellie. Millennia of existence create myriad strands of personality."*

Andreas wasn't only shirtless, he was also barefoot.

Elena looked down at her boots, told herself she didn't need to show off. She'd rather keep her feet warm and frostbite free in the nice thermal socks Sara had given her as a gift. They had vampire smiley faces on them.

Finishing up the kata on a suicidal whirl of blades, Andreas came to a halt on one knee, his dark hair falling around the aristocratic lines of his face.

He looked up with a glint in his eye, and for the first time since she'd met Andreas, she saw the man Raphael knew. A warrior who fit seamlessly into an archangel's forces, a leader who'd have a squadron's respect, and a fighter who'd throw back a beer while sweaty and dirty.

"Consort," he said. "Thank you for waiting."

"You're a master with the blades." Elena wanted to scowl as she spoke that grudging compliment.

Rising to his full height, Andreas flipped the blades and held them out hilt first toward her.

She accepted the offer but took only one blade. As she'd expected, it was heavy. "The workmanship is exquisite." While the hilt bore the soft patina of hundreds of years of handling, the blade itself gleamed razor-sharp in the weak sunlight amplified by the snow into a stinging brightness.

"It was made by a famed angelic weapons-master who now Sleeps." Andreas handed his other sword to one of his vampires who'd just walked out. Taking a bottle of water in return, he pointed up. "Does your escort require anything?"

"No, they're happy crouching on your roof." She handed

the weapon back to Andreas using both hands to display it as a work that beautiful should be displayed. "Deacon would love to see this sword."

He took the sword the same way she'd presented it, warrior to warrior, and passed it back to his vampiric assistant. "Deacon has already held it." A sharp smile. "I have commissioned him to make me another pair for the dark future when his mortal existence is no more."

It could've been an ugly statement dismissing the value of a human life, but startlingly, she heard a strong thread of regret in his voice. And she knew Andreas foresaw a future centuries ahead where he would one day show someone Deacon's work and tell them of the gifted human whose life had run far too short.

"I'll look forward to seeing what he creates," she said, consciously stepping back from that pathway into a future unseen.

"Would you give me a moment to shower quickly and dress?"

"Of course." Impatience sank its teeth into her, shook like a dog with a bone, but Andreas was an old-world angel. A gracious response would gain her far more than pushing at him to rush.

She walked to the house with him. Acres of glass and right angles dominated, the building designed by a living contemporary architect. It had always struck her as odd that such an old angel would have so modern a home until Illium pointed out that the Tower wasn't exactly of a "colonnades and arches vintage."

Point well made, Bluebell.

The vampire who waited in the doorway wore a simple gown that reached her ankles. "Sire. Consort." She bowed and moved aside as they neared.

Once inside, Andreas gave a short nod and headed upstairs, while Elena followed the woman—who proved to be his housekeeper—to a contemporary living area decorated in tones of gray and black, with unexpected splashes of aquamarine. She was resigned to having to wait a half hour at the very least, but Andreas was true to his word and took fewer than five minutes to shower and return.

His slightly overlong hair—a deep brown-black—was still damp, and roughly combed, as if he'd run his fingers through it and considered it done. The amber gray of his feathers glimmered with the odd droplet of water. He was also dressed more casually than she'd ever seen him, wearing khaki pants and a simple white shirt with no buttons and an open tunic-style collar.

"I realize you've just returned home," she said. "Thank you for fitting me in."

His cheeks creased in a smile that reached his eyes, a pale greenish-hazel she'd always before found disturbing in their acute directness. "It is an honor to have the consort in my home." Waving a hand at the sofas, he said, "Would you sit?"

"Actually, do you mind if we walk?" Despite her continuous low-level hunger and lack of sleep, she felt jumpy with energy, her skin burning from the inside out.

"If you do not mind the snow, there is a path through the back gardens."

When they went out there, it was to find the path had already been swept clean. The gardens slept under a thick blanket of white, haunting in their simulacrum of death and burial. "This must be lovely when it's in full bloom." Ever since she'd discovered Andreas's punishments included hanging vampires naked from the trees that surrounded his home, she tended to avoid overflying his property.

At least she knew no one was buried alive out there.

A small mercy.

But she still listened for distant screams.

"My father is enamored of growing things." Andreas's voice broke into her gloomy thoughts. "He often laments at having a warrior for a son."

"I didn't know your father visited New York." A sudden sinking feeling in her stomach. "Oh God, was I supposed to know that as Raphael's consort?"

Andreas threw back his head, his laughter deep and resonant and clashing with what she knew of his pitiless methods to break the insubordinate. "You are safe," he said afterward. "My mother and father both visit but have said they wish to give you time to settle in before expecting an invitation."

Elena winced. "Were they being sarcastic?"

"No. In their mind, you have but met Raphael." He used his boot to nudge aside a small branch that had fallen on the path. "My parents are both over a hundred thousand years old. Their sense of time is not ours."

Andreas, Elena recalled, was older than Raphael, but by a matter of hundreds of years rather than millennia. "Your parents had you late in life."

"Not in immortal terms."

"Wow. No wonder everyone's lost their minds over Aodhan's sister having a baby." Imalia was only twelve hundred years old, give or take.

"An infant having an infant," Andreas agreed, and she didn't think he was joking.

Shuddering within as she recalled Nisia's talk of superparasites and pregnancy, she said, "I promise to invite your folks to dinner the next time they're in town—but help me out and give me warning of their next visit."

An incline of his head. "Mother and Father will be most astonished that you are already so well organized." That glint in his eye returned. "I should warn you, my parents are . . . dedicated, and they remain uncertain Raphael isn't a bad influence."

Elena didn't know which thread to follow first, went for the most fascinating. "I didn't realize Raphael had a reputation."

"He went wild in the two centuries after Caliane's madness. It was to be expected, but my parents worried I would be led astray."

At nineteen, Elena had once gone after a vampire with only a single throwing blade and no other weapons. Yes, she understood the wildness engendered by grief and anger. "You can reassure your parents I'm being a good influence on him," she lied.

Andreas's lips curved. "I admit I am but teasing you. Their worries have long been laid to rest, and they will be honored to be welcomed into your home."

Elena had the strange feeling she'd successfully navigated the social necessities that came with being an archangel's consort. "As I said when I contacted your secretary about speaking to you," she began, returning to the reason for her visit, "I need to ask you about one of your vampires."

Her left wing threatened to drop. Catching the movement out of the corner of her eye, she pulled it back into the correct position . . . just as her left forearm began to burn.

25

It took every ounce of strength she had not to scream.

Elena. Aeclari. Elena. Aeclari. Seven hundred and seventy-seven echoes in her head, a wall of noise drowning out the pain.

Then. Silence.

Snow that absorbed all sound.

The pain a low and bearable thread, she realized she'd stopped on the path and Andreas was looking at her with a puzzled expression on his face. "All is well?"

"Sorry," she said through the roar of blood in her ears. "Legion were talking to me." The spot on her chest itched unbearably.

"Ah." A glance up at the roof but he asked no more questions before they resumed their walk. "You wish to ask about Harrison, I presume?"

Elena forcibly shoved aside what had just occurred to focus on why she'd come to Andreas's home. "You've heard?"

"Dmitri briefed me as Harrison is one of mine." He frowned. "I was surprised to hear of such violence visited on him, given his recent conduct. He has learned the wisdom of holding to contracts made." A hardness to his tone as he spoke the latter words; they held nothing of the charm he'd displayed only minutes earlier. "Harsh methods were necessary, but they have borne fruit."

Elena told herself to keep her mouth shut, failed. "There's harsh and then there's cruel."

"True." No insult in his expression. "I often cross that line, but I would rather cross it than go too far in the other direction. Vampires who do not fear and respect their masters create carnage far more vile than the worst of my cruelties." A whisper of wings as he settled his. "You are a hunter. You've seen how the blood-maddened feed, how they defile the bodies of their victims. Better I whip them into line prior to that."

Now she was beginning to agree with the man. *Shit.* "I'm looking at Harrison's past," she said rather than continuing down that rabbit hole. "Illium said he used to have deadbeat friends."

"Yes." Andreas narrowed his eyes, his arms held loosely behind his back. "I cannot recall their names, but there are records." Reaching into his pocket, he retrieved a phone. "I now appreciate such devices, but I recall my consternation when I was first given one—a gift from Illium."

"I am shocked." Bluebell appeared to be on a one-man crusade to get holdout angels into the twenty-first century.

"It is a trial having young friends," Andreas said with a hint of a smile on his lips. "Perhaps I will order similar devices for my parents. They will think I have run mad."

As she watched, he made the call. Putting away the phone after a short conversation, he said, "My record keeper will come meet us in the gardens."

The two of them continued to walk through the peaceful snow-draped landscape, while the Legion gargoyles looked on from the rooftop. *Thank you*, she said to them. *Whatever you did, it worked.*

We are . . . A pause, whispers at the back of her head. *Energy. We are energy. The Cascade is energy.*

So they'd fought primal energy with primal energy. But she knew they could help her only in limited ways. This Cascade was a world-devouring beast, too big for even seven hundred and seventy-seven Legion hearts.

"Should I be worried the sire no longer trusts me?" Andreas had his eyes on the Legion as he spoke.

"Every so often, they like to follow me around." Elena had learned enough about immortal politics to have picked up the subtle but real tension in the question; her words were one truth and the only one Andreas needed to know. "They tell me I'm different, and they like to be with those who are different." She scowled. "I'm not sure if that's a compliment or not."

"It is," Andreas said solemnly. "When you live hundreds upon hundreds of years, anything different and unique is a treasure to be cherished." His disturbingly penetrating eyes lingered on her. "Had I met you before Raphael, I would've seen only a mortal and dismissed you as that—and that would've been my loss."

"You did see me," Elena said, and had the pleasure of watching him start. "Back when I was a wet-behind-the-ears hunter-trainee, my mentor and I retrieved a vampire for you."

"And so," Andreas murmured, "I could've been the one who won a woman so unique that she charms beings old beyond time."

"Nope. You aren't Raphael."

He stared at her for a long second before smiling again, wide and deep and intensely real. "I feel my loss more keenly now, for you are a woman who loves true. Such is . . . rare across time."

Unsettled by how human the cruel angel was acting today, Elena nearly sighed in relief when a stunning woman appeared around the corner of the pathway. Dressed in a charcoal-gray pantsuit that looked bespoke and with her bronze-threaded black hair intricately braided then wrapped into a bun at her nape, she didn't seem a woman who would fit in with Andreas's old-world viewpoint.

The impression of cutting-edge modernity was further solidified by the miniature tablet she held in her hand.

"Nara. You have the file?"

"Yes, sire." She held the tablet out to Elena, her skin a tawny brown that bore a slight winter pallor. That or Nara hadn't yet fed. Andreas's keeper of records was an old vampire who smelled of thick honey and ice crunched under the teeth.

"I've pulled up the information for you, Consort," she said.

"Thank you." Accepting the tablet, Elena was aware of Andreas dismissing Nara.

"Terence Lee and Nishant Kumar," she read out. "Nara's highlighted their names on this note about Harrison's lack of delivery on a project."

"Yes, the memories come back to me." Andreas spread then folded his wings back in, being careful not to brush them against hers. "The trio of fools." Returning his arms to behind his back, he said, "I made it clear to Harrison at the time that he was on his final chance—and I used the cruelty of which you accuse me. He has not failed me since."

Elena didn't ask him what he'd done to Harrison; she had to be able to look her brother-in-law in the eye and not see him screaming as chunks of flesh were dug out of him, or as his skin was marked with red-hot brands that would take years to fade. She read the report through a second time, but there wasn't much else, just the one note that Harrison's friends were likely responsible for his lack of attention to the task.

"These two," Elena said. "They're post-Contract?"

"Almost certainly if Nara has not noted the name of their supervising angel."

Realizing they'd reached the front of the house, Elena handed him the tablet with a word of thanks. He looked down at the device and said, "I am not like Imani, who eschews change, but I wonder at this age we live in where information must always be at the fingertips. Why does no one value patience?"

"Human lives are shorter," she reminded him quietly. "A mortal life must be lived in fast-forward."

Andreas held her gaze before inclining his head with warrior grace. "I think, Consort, you will teach me more than I care to know."

Not sure quite how to take that, Elena asked if it would be possible for her to speak to his staff. "They might know more about Harrison's friends." Plenty went on in an angel's household that was never brought to the attention of said angel; a good housekeeper or butler took pride in running a smooth household that caused only a modicum of disruption in their angel's life.

"My home is open to you," Andreas said.

Nara was waiting for them by the front door. After giving her the tablet, Andreas told his record keeper to cooperate with Elena and to inform the other staff to do so as well. "I will take my leave," he said to Elena. "Illium and I are to meet for a drill."

"Thanks for the help."

"It was a most agreeable walk," he replied before heading into the house, his wings held with automatic warrior control.

Elena did an unobtrusive check on the status of her own wings.

So far, so good.

Stomach tight and that vein on her temple throbbing in odd bursts, she forced her attention back to her task—and to Andreas's seriously old record keeper. Nara's power was a slow-motion punch against Elena's skin. If all she did for Andreas was keep records, then Elena would eat her own foot. With hot sauce.

"I'm looking for information on Harrison Ling," she said. "Any friends he might have, interests that could've brought him the wrong kind of attention, that type of thing."

"I'm afraid I will be of no help, Consort." A furrow in Nara's otherwise smooth brow, tiny lines flaring out at the corners of her feline eyes. "I deal near-exclusively with senior members of staff."

Elena had figured as much; half the household was probably as terrified of Nara as they were of Andreas. "Point me in the direction of the younger staff—no need for an escort." Elena might be Raphael's consort, but she was also a former mortal; she'd be more likely to get the truth without Nara around.

Andreas's scary record keeper gave her what she needed without hesitation.

When she walked into the kitchen a couple of minutes later—a large and gracious space that boasted shining metal ovens and a huge obsidian slab of a central island—everyone froze, the room abruptly a painting devoid of breath.

Elena fought the urge to pull out her crossbow. Vampires could be *seriously* creepy when they did that no-movement thing.

"Consort." The greeting came from a petite vampire who wore a white apron and had flour on her hands. "What may we do for you?"

"I was hoping to talk to members of staff who know Harrison Ling."

A sigh seemed to ripple through the room, the others within it spinning back into motion now that they knew she brought no dangerous tidings.

The vampire who'd spoken—she had to be the head cook—said, "Most of the young ones have gone out into the gardens to clear the snow." She waved over the taller woman who'd been working beside her when Elena first came in. "Iris supervised Harrison for a time."

"Only the two months he was in the kitchen," Iris said, a flush high on her cheekbones as she twisted a tea towel in her hands. "Not to speak ill of the wounded, but oh, that man was terrible in the kitchen." A flash of fangs as she grimaced. "I spent half my time overseeing him so he wouldn't burn whatever it was he was meant to be watching."

"Did you ever speak about anything that might've caused someone to hold a grudge against him? Even in passing?"

Iris shook her head. "He was too young and foolish for conversation. I simply tried to teach him some skills before Cook here finally abandoned the idea that he might be useful in the kitchen."

"It was right when he first came to us," the chief cook added. "I do always have hope, but so many of the young have no comprehension of good food and the skill of preparing a nutritious meal."

"Yes." Iris pursed her lips. "Fast food and store-bought rubbish." A snort. "Then they become vampires and suddenly don't see the *point* in cooking."

The cook nodded darkly. "As if an art form has no value."

Elena decided not to confess to her less-than-amazing skills in that area. "Thank you for the help. I'll head out to the gardens to speak to the younger staff."

Once outside, she asked the Legion if they'd seen anyone in the garden, and they pointed her toward the far west of the sprawling area. It took her ten minutes of brisk walking to find the three vampires, all in good spirits. Digging their shovels in, they were throwing the snow to the side in neat piles. Elena figured this couldn't be a major part of their day. Andreas was too smart to lose people out of boredom.

As it was, the three seemed to be enjoying their task, their conversation peppered with laughter. The first one to see her spluttered to a stop in the middle of a sentence. "Elena!"

She halted, looked at him more carefully even as his coworkers paled. Sharply pointed face with bright brown eyes and pink-flushed white skin, a height just over five feet, a small dark brown goatee . . . and an ability with cards that had made a pauper out of her one long-ago January.

Smile cracking her face, she held out a hand. "Phineas. It's good to see you."

Phineas took off his glove, shook her hand with open

enthusiasm. "I heard you became an angel. Thought me mates were having a good laugh at old Phineas's expense at first." Breaking their handclasp, he peered around at her wings. "Blimey."

"You still fleecing innocent hunters out of their earnings?"

"I'm an honest man now," he said with a grin that was as infectious now as it had been when they first met. "I even cheat honestly."

Elena remembered why she'd liked Phineas, despite his cardsharp ways. "Introduce me to your friends."

"These miscreants aren't friends," he said with a scowl. "They're silly boys I'm breaking in to the real world." The younger vampires grinned despite the dark words. "Andreas would go mad if he had to deal with their idiocy."

That explained what Phineas was doing here. He'd completed his hundred years of service decades ago.

"The one with the ridiculous fluff on his upper lip is Vernon, and the one who thinks purple is some kind of color for a shirt is Tepe. The youth of today." A shake of his head. "What brings you to us, then?"

Phineas's face fell at her explanation. "Sad business, that. Harrison's a good man."

One of the "silly boys" choked back something before bending to industriously shovel away at the snow again. "Too late, Tepe." Elena kind of liked the purple shirt he'd paired with a thick black coat that boasted a gold zipper. "You may as well tell me."

The younger vampire looked at Phineas and waited for his "Go on" before saying, "Look, Harry's all right—I actually like him now, but back when I was newly Made, he'd been a vampire for . . . what? About a year?" A glance at Vernon, who nodded. "And honestly, he was a total asswipe."

Vernon found his voice, his words coming out in a puff of white as his breath froze in the cold air, his bushy mustache—nothing flufflike about it—coated with shimmering flecks of frost. "Before he tried that dumb escape attempt, he thought he could get into Andreas's good books by snitching on other vampires."

Elena stilled. "Did he snitch on anyone who might hold a grudge?"

26

The two vampires looked at each other, then nodded in concert. A gold stud glinted in Tepe's ear, catching the light and hitting Elena's eyes for a flashing second.

"Jade's not at the house anymore," he said, his skin as dark as Vernon's was pale. "Man was on a post-Contract job deal, but Andreas didn't renew his employment after it expired, and I think it had to do with what Harrison told."

"Well, spit it out, then." Phineas lightly slapped the back of Tepe's head. "What did Harrison have on this Jade man?"

"Had to do with money." Tepe leaned his hands on his shovel, dropping his voice as if afraid of being overheard. "Jade was *stealing* from Andreas."

"Feckin' idiot. I'm surprised boyo's still alive."

"He's alive *now*." Vernon shuddered. "I don't think he was that alive the months he spent hanging in the woods with his flesh scraped from his bones on a regular basis with a fucking kitchen carving knife." The vampire crossed himself with every evidence of true faith. "You couldn't pay me enough to make Andreas that angry."

That kind of torture, Elena thought, could very well make an enemy of a man. But, in her eyes, Harrison hadn't snitched in telling his angel of fraud in his home; no, he'd been loyal despite the fear he must've had of the older and more powerful Jade. "What's Jade's full name?"

"You won't say it was us that told you about him, will you?" Tepe whispered, his shoulders hunching in. "Jade's *mean*."

"Raphael has the best spymaster in the world. I'll let Jade assume I got the information that way." No one would dare threaten Jason.

Both vampires blew out relieved breaths before Vernon said, "He just uses the name Jade. Never had a last name the whole time I knew him."

Tepe tugged at the lobe of his bejeweled ear. "I heard he hangs out in the Quarter a lot, but I think he might live outside it." A glance at Vernon. "Remember that time Claire said she ran into him and he talked about moving out of the Quarter?"

"Oh yeah." Vernon pulled off his knit cap to scratch at his bald head. "She was too scared to ask for details, though—and she's in Prague for training now. You could call her. Her last name's Vargas."

Elena made a mental note of the detail. "Does he have money?" Wealth or lack of it would influence which areas the vampire could afford.

"Yes, I think so—I mean, he had to pay back what he stole, but I always figured he must've had more money stashed away. Jade's pretty old."

"Older than Phineas, for sure."

Phineas pointed his shovel at the two. "I'm a young whippersnapper as far as you're concerned."

"Yes, Phineas." The two grinned before Tepe returned his attention to Elena. "That's all I can think of that could've gotten Harrison into serious trouble. Everyone else he snitched on only got a slap on the wrist. Andreas isn't so bad if you're just goofing off. He only cares about *actual* betrayal, like with Jade—or if you run."

"I don't think the money thing was snitching, to be honest," Vernon added. "I mean I'd tell Andreas, too, if I thought someone was stealing from him. Not right to come into your angel's home and be a thief."

"Yeah, yeah, you're right. I'd tell, too," Tepe said after a thoughtful pause. "But Harry didn't stop at the big stuff. Like, he told when I took off for a couple of hours to see a friend without getting official permission. I don't think Andreas was too impressed with him for that."

"Andreas is a warrior under all the elegant manners." Phineas leaned on the top of his shovel. "He'd have seen that kind of telling as disloyalty between comrades."

"Yeah, that's a good way of putting it." Tepe bit down on his lower lip, frowned. "Can't think of anything else useful except that Harrison ran soon after the Jade thing, and you know the rest."

"Do you think he ran because he was scared of Jade?" That would put a whole different slant on Harrison's escape attempt.

"No way." Tepe shook his head hard. "I mean, Jade's a psycho, but Andreas is stone-cold terrifying. Harrison could've gone to Andreas if he was scared of Jade, and Andreas would've handled it. Harry just thought he could have the near-immortal life without paying the price."

"We even felt sorry for him after he was brought back," Vernon admitted. "Andreas was *pissed*."

Tepe said a little prayer while his friend spoke.

"I kept my head down, never knew anyone could be that angry and that icily calm. But"—Vernon's voice dropped—"it was hard to ignore the screaming."

"Well, the lad shouldn't have signed on the dotted line if he didn't want to play by the rules. Near-immortality's no feckin' free lunch."

Elena moved to steer the conversation away from any specifics on Harrison's punishment. "Anyone—other than Claire—on Andreas's staff who might know more?"

After a short discussion, the two offered her a couple of other names.

However, when she found those members of staff, they were cooperative but didn't have much to give her.

"He does his work and he goes home," the male said. "Doesn't hang around to chat."

"Harry knows his wife and baby are going to die before him," the female added, her lips downturned. "Can't blame the man for wanting to spend every minute he can with them."

Her partner nodded. "He's the only one of us who has a kid, so we all get why he doesn't party with us when we have time off. Must be sad as fuck to think of outliving your little girl."

Yes, "sad as fuck" described it perfectly.

The end result of Harrison's devotion to Beth and Maggie was that he didn't have any close friends among the staff. No one to whom he'd tell his secrets. But she had the Jade angle to follow.

Considering her next move, she walked to the front of the house without going inside then headed to the cliffs that edged Andreas's property. Her takeoff was a smooth glide over the Hudson . . . and it took teeth-gritted concentration on her part to make that happen. Her wings felt heavier, less responsive to her control on takeoff. But once up, she felt no undue stress and decided to continue on rather than detouring to the infirmary.

She had to use her time wisely. She knew others would pick this up if she was grounded but, as long as she was mobile and could think, she couldn't stop in the hunt. She needed to keep this monster from reaching the door, keep a little girl's life untainted by torture and death.

The Legion flew with her on silent wings. When the Primary came close, she said, "Can you share your energy with me in other ways?" If they could, she might be able to extend her safe operating hours.

"We did not share energy," the Primary said. "We pushed the other energy out."

Elena considered that. "Could you do it again?"

"The other energy is of the Cascade. It is . . . deep." In

the pause that followed came hundreds of whispers at the back of Elena's mind. "We can try again, but we may fail, should the power surge."

"Better than nothing," Elena said, then reached into a pocket to grab her phone. Calling Vivek, she asked for the addresses of the other two members of Andreas's "trio of fools."

"Sorry, Ellie," Vivek said after running the search. "Terence Lee and Nishant Kumar used to live in the Quarter, but as of two months ago, they're permanently unavailable."

Elena's hand tightened on the phone. "Why didn't this come up when Blakely and Acosta were found?"

"Because no one knows if these two were stabbed, decapitated, or mutilated. Lee and Kumar were turned into crispy critters so fried their bones cracked from the heat. Their shared apartment went up in flames."

27

Raphael landed on the border between his and Elijah's territory after a long flight from New York. Elijah had flown approximately the same distance from his home. A number of birds of prey sat on the branches of the tree under which he waited for Raphael.

"I see you have an escort," Raphael said.

"They can be possessive creatures." Elijah, dressed in worn leathers of dark brown, drew him into a backslapping hug.

Raphael returned the gesture because he knew it was meant in good faith. "You are well?" he asked afterward. "How is Hannah? I am instructed to tell you to say hi to Hannah from Elena."

"I have been given much the same task." Elijah's hair glinted gold even under the dappled sunlight, his smile open. "Hannah and I are content. It is good to have peace, and to be able to remain at my home with my consort—and the vast array of creatures who consider my court their personal playground."

The Cascade had brought with it new powers for all of them. Where Raphael had inherited the Legion, Elijah had gained the ability to control cats both large and small as well as birds of prey. The wild beings were drawn to him, like metal to a magnet. "No one will ever again be able to sneak up on you at least."

"There is that." Elijah held up an arm clad in a heavy leather gauntlet, and a large eagle flew to land on his forearm, its claws closing tight. Rubbing the fingers of his free hand over the creature's head, the bond between the two apparent, Elijah said, "I think you bring me no good tidings, Raphael."

"No, though I would be glad for any you have to share."

"I'm afraid I will disappoint you." Elijah lifted his arm so the magnificent bird could fly aloft into the sky once more.

After watching the eagle soar against the gray-blue of the sky, the two of them fell into step beside the tree-shadowed stream that was their meeting point.

"Jason has come back with disturbing reports of Favashi gathering an army," Raphael told his fellow archangel. "It's concentrated near her stronghold." A stronghold that had been built for Lijuan by an architect gifted and tragic.

"My spymaster has not returned home yet," Elijah murmured. "I thank you for the warning, and I have something I can share with you in turn." He folded back his wings even tighter, his feathers a pure white. "The reason my spymaster isn't home is that he's investigating reports of ghost villages on the edges of Favashi's territory."

"People missing or killed?"

"The very question he seeks to answer." The sunlight spearing through the canopy highlighted the strong angles of Elijah's face. "The villages are rumored to just be sitting there empty, as if the residents had simply stepped out for a moment and been sucked into the ether."

A long silence filled only with the sound of water tumbling over rocks.

"We are both thinking the same thing," Raphael said as they came to a halt at the curve of the stream.

"Lijuan Sleeps," Elijah pointed out. "An archangel in Sleep cannot affect the external world. Else chaos would reign."

"Lijuan was no ordinary archangel when she went into Sleep. She is the only one of us who has ever been able to turn noncorporeal." Raphael thought of the old voice in Elena's head, her sense of a being that was stirring awake. "It's also possible she's begun to come out of Sleep and to interact with the world once more."

"I see your point." Eli didn't flinch when a gyrfalcon, most likely a resident in Raphael's territory, winged over to land on his right shoulder, its claws curling into the leather that now reinforced the shoulders of all Elijah's shirts and tunics. "Do you think she is feeding on the disappeared?"

The suggestion wasn't an outlandish one, not when it came to this one archangel. During the course of their battle above New York, Raphael had seen the dried-out husks of the ill-fated from whom Lijuan had sucked their life force. "It's possible—I have a theory that she has found a way to create a reservoir of power for her eventual return. That is why she went into Sleep. To glut herself."

"I hope you are wrong, my friend." Ice threaded Elijah's voice now. "She is already almost beyond our ability to defeat. She does not need access to more power."

"It's also possible her people are joining her at an unknown location." Despite her depravities and how many of her own she'd massacred in her lust for power, Lijuan was considered a goddess by many.

But Elijah shook his head. "The lost are simple villagers— not the kind to be welcome in Lijuan's court as anything other than menial servants." Eyes of golden brown held Raphael's. "We cannot neglect the probability that Lijuan truly Sleeps and the disappearances have nothing to do with her. Favashi's current behavior is not what anyone would expect from her."

The two of them began to walk again.

"Perhaps," Elijah continued, "she has ordered her generals to take ruthless action to instill fear in the populace and the ghost villages are only the tip of the iceberg. China is a large territory for a young archangel to control—and she is fighting an uphill battle, given her predecessor."

"Yes." Lijuan's people were used to being under the hand of the most powerful archangel in the world—there was little doubt that the older vampires and angels in the territory were only giving lip service when it came to their loyalty to Favashi.

Such was the unavoidable side effect of taking over a territory where another archangel had either died or gone into Sleep. The new archangel had to earn the fidelity of those left behind—or rule by creating a primal fear that overwhelmed history and loyalty in favor of pure, animal survival.

In some cases, the balance was never struck, and those loyal to the previous archangel scattered on the winds, to find new homes and positions. The vast majority were capable of loyal and devoted service to another archangel—just not to the one who'd usurped *their* archangel.

Many of Alexander's people had served others with utmost fidelity but had tendered their resignations the instant he rose again—then they'd flown home. It would be the same with Raphael's people, should he ever go into Sleep. As for his Seven, that was a certainty. No one would be surprised when Dmitri, Jason, Naasir, Illium, Aodhan, Galen, and Venom returned to him. Even were Illium to ascend, he would be as Eli was to Caliane—forever loyal.

Some bonds did not break.

"Lijuan might've been mad to our eyes," Elijah said quietly, "but to many of her people, she is a living goddess. It does not matter if she is in this world or if she Sleeps, she remains the one to whom they direct their prayers."

Raphael watched the gyrfalcon preen Elijah's hair. "Her most loyal people could be erasing villages in order to make it seem as if she is present in the world, so her grip on her territory never fades. Their belief in her is fanatical." Even the horror of the shambling "reborn," that mockery of life everlasting, hadn't altered their faith.

Elijah reached up and the gyrfalcon hopped from his shoulder to his forearm. Stroking the wild creature, he said, "I know it is not the way of the Cadre to interfere in the affairs of another archangel, but I feel we cannot leave Favashi to stumble into war." Elijah's voice was of a man who had seen too much battle in his long lifetime. "Before I left to meet you, I received a call from Neha. She has withdrawn her ambassadors from Favashi's court, and she tells me Michaela's ambassadors are also not happy."

Raphael considered the water, the clarity of the liquid over the stones. That Neha hadn't spoken to him was no surprise. Their relationship had broken on the blade of her daughter's lust for power. But that she'd taken the step of recalling her ambassadors . . .

It was a prelude to war.

"Your thoughts are sound, Eli, but we will invite war ourselves if we step into Favashi's territory without invitation."

"Then, my friend," Elijah murmured, "we will have to inveigle an invitation."

28

Elena had decided to see Nisia after all. Just in case. The healer made no attempt to hide her concern about the new tears in Elena's wings, but she didn't ground her. To a being born to flight, Elena realized, such a step was an absolute final recourse. "Can you sense anything about my left forearm?"

Nisia spent several minutes checking it, even taking a scan. "Your bones have tunnels through them," she said afterward, her expression grim. "As if your immortal ringworms have eaten their way through."

Too bad it wasn't actually anything as prosaic as worms. It was fire and an energy that sought to reshape the world. "Can you fix it so my arm won't fracture?"

A curt nod. "I am still able to stir your body to heal enough for that, but Elena, we are merely putting plasters on the wound. I cannot define a cause." Hot flags of color rode her cheeks, but her hands were calm and competent as she worked.

"I know," Elena said, though her throat was dry and her

head stuffy with all the emotions she couldn't afford to feel right now. "But before I ground myself so you can run as many tests as you want, I have to make sure my sister is safe. That her daughter is safe."

Nisia pursed her lips. "Work quickly. You're not just regressing—this bone is now weaker than a mortal's."

Fifteen minutes later—after a huge meal she bolted down—Elena began to go over the file on the fire that had claimed the lives of Nishant Kumar and Terence Lee, while Vivek tried to track down Jade. There wasn't much there. The entire thing had so obviously been arson that it was as if the arsonist were advertising his work—or didn't care about being subtle.

The investigator believed said arsonist had also rung the fire alarm to empty the building of other residents; he'd based his conclusion on the fact that multiple residents had reported a man knocking on their door to warn of a fire before they'd so much as caught a hint of smoke. All had described the man as white or Hispanic, wearing a long coat, a hat, and a scarf wrapped around his mouth.

Nishant Kumar and Terence Lee had been the sole casualties.

It held to the pattern: leave unconnected innocents alone, even save their lives where possible. But as Raphael had pointed out, Beth and Maggie were intimately connected to one of the killer's targets.

Muscles bunching, Elena read on.

Thanks to a liberal dousing with accelerants, paired with the materials used to construct the old building, the two vampires had burned down to—as Vivek had put it—crispy critters. The problem with using fire to murder vamps was that the older ones could survive it—Elena had once rescued an eight-hundred-year-old vampire from a malicious fire. He'd been charred bone barely held together by warped tendons. Lighter than a small child in her arms.

But when his eyes opened, they'd been moist and bright with pain.

She'd nearly dropped him, unable to believe the impossibility of it.

Later, another vampire had told her that the one she'd rescued couldn't bear to be without sight and so had used the rest of his body to protect his eyes. That had been over a decade earlier and the old but not very strong vampire was yet recovering. His face had regenerated, as had most of his body, but he needed a cane to walk and his endurance was limited.

Nishant Kumar and Terence Lee had been barely out of their Contracts. Nowhere near an age to survive the fire had they been alive when it was set, but there was a good chance both men had been dead at ignition. "He amputated Blakely's genitals and Acosta's hand while they were alive," she reminded herself. "And he threatened Beth and Maggie to Harrison." The man liked to torture his victims.

She revised her conclusion: Kumar and Lee must've been alive but immobilized when the fire was set. The two had been burned alive.

Flexing her left arm to ease a muscle ache deep within, she turned the page with her right hand. With no viable DNA samples recovered and the fire so hot it had damaged the men's teeth—though the pathologist had made a note the teeth damage could've been perimortem—Kumar and Lee had been identified by the process of elimination.

No one else in the building was missing; further, neither man had accessed any of their accounts in the aftermath. A neighbor had seen the two come home that evening, but no one had seen them leave—and neither had been spotted since.

Nevertheless, was it possible either Kumar or Lee had pulled off a hoax and was the murderer?

Possible, Elena decided, but unlikely. Especially since both victims had been of a slender and short build, while the man who'd knocked on doors the night of the fire was uniformly described as tall and well built. Muscular. That coincided with what Elena had seen on Al and Anita's security footage.

Flexing her arm again, she turned another page.

As the victims had been vampires, the police had copied the Tower into their investigation, but the Tower hadn't interfered, leaving the seasoned human detective in charge to do his job. That detective had uncovered Nishant Kumar's qualifications as a chemist, been able to link him to new designer drugs that catered to the vampiric market.

Elena sat up straight at the drug connection.

Bored old near-immortals were constantly hunting for a new rush. Ninety-nine percent of the designer drugs just didn't work, the vampiric metabolism simply too efficient— it was why honey feeds were so popular. However, every so often, one of the designer drugs *would* work just enough to make it viable . . . and deadly.

Umber, the last big vampiric drug to hit the market, had turned ordinary, law-abiding vampires into murderous machines. One of the saddest cases Elena had heard of involved a vampire who'd torn the woman he loved to shreds.

Picking up the phone on Raphael's desk, where she'd set up shop, she called the detective in charge.

"Santiago," was the gruff response on the other end.

"Hello, detective." Detective Hector Santiago and Elena had worked more than one case side by side over the years, where the Guild's job intersected with the police force's. Their relationship had hit a wobble when she first became an angel, became consort to Raphael, her loyalties different, but the two of them had figured out a way through it.

"So *now* you call me." A mechanical groan on the other end, probably Santiago's chair straining as he leaned his big body back. "After blowing off my cookout."

"Gimme a break, Santiago," she said, settling into the familiar banter as if it was a favorite old coat. "I was on the other side of the freaking world at the time." She and Raphael had flown to visit Caliane.

"Excuses, excuses." Rasping sounds this time, Santiago

likely rubbing the salt-and-pepper stubble on his jaw. "You got a case?"

"No, I wanted to ask you about a recent one of yours. Nishant Kumar and Terence Lee."

"The deep-fried vamps," Santiago said at once. "We figured the vics to be humans at first—my whole career, I've never seen vampires burned down that bad."

Elena squeezed her forearm to ease the increasing ache even Nisia's healing abilities couldn't keep at bay. "The drug connection, you ever track down specifics?"

"Nothing but rumor—and I dug deep." A rumble of frustration down the line. "Ash and that slow-talking smart-ass husband of hers hooked me up with folks who'd normally rabbit if they smelled a cop, and my own informants were happy to talk, too."

"Unusual." Quarter residents usually clammed up to outsiders; they couldn't afford to shit in their own pond.

"Kumar and Lee had a history of running scams," Santiago told her. "Penny-ante stuff like mixing up an innocuous substance and telling low-level buyers it was a powerful designer drug—you know, poisonous shit the junkies would never be able to afford."

Elena nodded. "You have a note in the file that it's possible they did stumble on a dangerous drug at some point."

"Yeah. I got approached by a couple of vamp street hookers—Red Cutie and Monique Darling—who swore up and down that Lee and Kumar had given each of them a taste of a 'high' that caused psychotic hallucinations then a blackout. When the women came to—in a back alley in Red's case, and dumped in the stairwell of her building in Monique's—their clothes weren't quite right, and both were sure the bastards had raped them."

And these men had been Harrison's friends? *Fuck*.

"No memories, though—couldn't even get dates from them because their sense of time is fucked up after years on drugs," Santiago added. "But both women remembered that they woke up wet, their clothes sticking to their skin. Their take was that the two rapists hosed them off inside and out to get rid of DNA. Not that they would've reported it." Tiredness in his voice now. "You know what it's like in the Quarter."

"Yeah. Quarter takes care of its own—except it's vamp-eat-vamp." Elena's stomach churned at the idea of Harrison being involved in such repugnant crimes. If it proved true, it'd destroy Beth. "If a woman did remember what had been done to her . . ."

"Hell of a motive," Santiago agreed. "But then I had the guy who warned people too early. No smoke, none of the early evacuees saw any sign of a fire. I had him as the doer."

"You had no luck tracking him down?"

"People were so happy the bastards were dead, they weren't particularly interested in finding out who'd done it. If anyone knew the identity of the firebug, they weren't telling. I got handed plenty of dirt on the dead guys, but other than the two street girls, no one came forward as a victim of rape."

Laric walked in during the last part of Santiago's statement and placed a fresh glass of Nisia's energy drink in front of her. Smiling her thanks up at him, she said to Santiago, "The pros weren't suspects?"

"Had airtight alibis for the time the fire was set—one locked up for disorderly behavior, the other admitted to a local clinic after a john broke her collarbone. I checked to see if they had pimps who'd maybe taken exception to the lack of payment for use, but these two are individual operators." More mechanical groans, followed by tapping, a pen hitting a desk over and over. "Don't vamps get a payout after their Contract?"

Putting down the glass after drinking most of the mixture, she said, "Yes, some more generous than others."

"Add in a hundred extra years to figure life out and they end up selling their bodies to losers on the street. I don't fucking get it." Not waiting for a response, he said, "Why're you so interested in the deep-fried rapists?"

Elena told him the truth. There were many things she could never tell him, secrets that would endanger his life, but three connected attacks against vampires didn't fall under that umbrella. "Asshole threatened my sister and niece."

"Fucker." No give in his voice; Hector had a prettily plump wife he doted on and four energetic boys who were his pride and joy. "Blakely and/or Acosta might've been dealers, but there's a strong case for saying Blakely at least used the rape drug on women—would explain the amputation of his genitals."

Elena had been thinking the same. "Eric Acosta was a honey feed addict who sourced his own drugs. Could be he bought the rape drug for Simon Blakley, had his hand hacked off for his trouble."

"Works," Santiago said. "But I'll tell you one other thing— there are flat-out insane vampire gangs in the Quarter. Crazy bastards don't blink at disemboweling a man to make a point. Lee and Kumar could've been whacked for encroaching, same with Blakely and Acosta."

"It feels too personal." Elena went to drink the last of Nisia's concoction but almost dropped the glass when her forearm spasmed.

Clenching her jaw to withhold her grunt of pain, she put the glass back down. "There's also the timeline," she managed to say. "Lee and Kumar were murdered two months ago, Blakely and Acosta only the night before the attempt on Harrison."

"Serious escalation," Santiago agreed. "Boy's on a rampage. More bodies are gonna start turning up."

They wouldn't, Elena vowed, be of Beth or Maggie.

After hanging up the call with Santiago, the detective having promised to talk to a few informants, Elena swallowed hard and pushed up the sleeve of her top. Her forearm was rigid, the muscles bunched tight, but nothing was translucent or lava-like. The good news ended there.

Because what she could see was a new crack in her skin. She brushed off the lint clinging to it. Where the hell was that stuff coming from? It must've been the tissue to end all tissues that had gotten in with her laundry.

With her skin clear, the discoloration around the break

in her flesh was impossible to miss. Bruise-colored, it spread out from the cut in a strangely delicate bloom. That wasn't the worst part. When she turned her arm to look at the underside, she found more breaks. Not only that, but her wrist protruded noticeably, and the ring she wore on her right pinky finger fell off in front of her eyes.

She'd lost more weight.

Curling her fingers into her palm, she decided against going to the infirmary. No one knew what was happening to her, Nisia couldn't help her any more than she'd already done, and the threat to Beth and Maggie remained. She'd be smart, take several of the Legion with her in case of a sudden decline, but she had to keep moving on this. Time was falling away from her like water from a gushing tap.

Child of mortals. Vessel unawakened.

She jerked to her feet, her head swiveling to the balcony doors out of instinct. But no ghostly woman with lilac hair stood outside, her hand pressed to the window. No, it was a golden-eyed owl that sat on the edge of the balcony, its feathers whiter than the snow.

Don't be afraid of the owls.

Mouth dry and heart thudding like a live creature trapped inside her ribcage, she walked to the doors and slid them open with quiet stealth. The owl just watched her, unperturbed. When she stepped out into the icy air, it turned its head and lifted a talon to preen its feathers.

Elena held her breath until her chest ached . . . and hunkered down to touch the bird.

29

Its feathers were luxuriantly soft under her palm, its body warm.

And it looked at her with its golden eyes suddenly fathomless, the gold holding the glow of an old, *old* power.

It is a sadness, child, to die. But it must be so. One must die for one to live.

You must die.

"Who the hell says so?" Elena growled, her hand tensing on the owl's back.

The silence was . . . odd. As odd as the way the owl watched her. When it tipped its head to the side, she was reminded forcefully of the Legion.

It is written in time.

The earth will boil.

The marker will fall.

And the one to die will falter.

Elena's wing threatened to drag as if in silent agreement. "Fuck destiny and fate," she said without care. "I will fight to my last fucking breath."

The owl looked at her again, its eyes endless and beautiful and strange. Under her hands, its warmth was a soft glow, and in her mind spoke the voice that wasn't there. *Child of love. Child of grief. Child of courage. Watch for the broken blade. Watch for the mourner. He is your death.* A long sigh . . . and the owl spread its wings.

Unwilling to even attempt to cage the wonder and wildness of it, Elena removed her hand and watched the owl take flight. It went up into the sky . . . and was no longer there. She made herself look at the part of the balcony where it had sat.

No clawprints in the snow, no signs of disturbance at all.

"Elena."

She jumped up, her knives in her hands even as she turned. "Oh, it's you."

The Primary stared at her from his silent crouch on the far side of the balcony, his eyes a deeper blue today and his skin carrying a touch of gold. "Who did you speak to?"

Breath rough, Elena put away her knives. "Did you see the owl sitting there?"

"No." Wind blowing back his hair. "We felt you reach for us. Will we fly again?"

Her phone rang before she could answer. "I'll take this inside." She was cold deep within her bones. "You want to come in?"

"I will watch the snow and remember it."

Leaving the Primary to his unfathomable vigil, she stepped in, phone to her ear. "V, what is it?"

"You still in Raphael's office? I'm patching in a call on his screen."

"Thanks."

The screen cleared to reveal a woman with curls of golden brown against skin the shade of rich honey. Her eyes were a clear brown with a burst of gold in the center, the wings that rose up behind her shoulders the evocative shade of bitter chocolate. "Andi." Elena's blood grew hot. "Did Jess put you on my research question?" Mated to Naasir, the young angel was Jessamy's student and a nascent historian in her own right.

"The white owls." Andromeda's voice trembled. "Legend says they are Cassandra's—she's often described as having lilac hair and it's said she clawed out her eyes to stop her visions."

. . . tears of dark red.

"I think Jessamy mentioned her once." Elena frowned, fighting to remember what her friend had told her. "She was an archangel long ago?"

"Cassandra is more myth than memory now. Many people think she never existed, the few of her prophecies that survived, nothing but the fantasies of a Sleeping poet." Andromeda's curls vibrated with her energy. "Ellie, the legends say she was kin to the Ancestors—the first ones of our kind, the angels said to Sleep under the Refuge."

Elena staggered inside at the idea of an archangel of such enormous age. Cassandra had Slept a *long* time. "Is she waking now?" she asked, a rasp in her throat. "Is that why I see her owls?" Elena had spoken to Jessamy right after leaving Nisia, given the historian the necessary background to her request.

"Jessamy and I don't know." Andi hugged an old book with a battered leather cover. "We spoke to Caliane, and she says she dreamed in her Sleep. You may be part of Cassandra's dream—she might not be conscious she's woken enough to impact the world."

Rubbing at her forehead, Elena tried to quiet the incipient headache. "Do you know anything else about her?"

"Not yet," Andromeda said. "But I won't stop hunting."

After saying good-bye to the other woman, Elena got dressed for the weather then went outside and asked the Primary the same question she'd asked Andi.

The gargoyle that was the Primary didn't so much as blink as snow began to fall on him. Within seconds, he was coated in a fine layer of white, a stone creature who had always been on the balcony in that position. When he spoke, his voice was inside Elena's head, his lips unmoving. *We remember the snow. She loved the snow. She loved our first aeclari.*

And Elena knew. *Cassandra ascended during the Cascade of Terror, didn't she?* A time of such violent energies that it had changed the fabric of the world—and given an archangel the terrible gift of endless foresight.

The Primary didn't answer, only said, *She saw what was to be. She dug out her own eyes to stop. But she could not stop seeing. She saw you, Elena.*

Elena stared at the Primary. "What?"

We did not understand then. We did not know. The Primary's voice held an echo now, the others of the Legion coming through. *Mortal born. Mortal fall. Mortal heart. Ambrosia's sweet kiss. Wings of dawn. Wings of night. This will be.*

Elena's heart still felt like ice ten minutes later, though she'd come inside again to give herself time to calm down before she went looking for Jade on the ground while Vivek continued to try to find an electronic trail. He'd even contacted both Claire Vargas and Andreas's Nara, but so far had nothing. In this case, talking to certain connected people might get her the answer faster.

Mortal born. Mortal fall. Mortal heart. Ambrosia's sweet kiss. Wings of dawn. Wings of night. This will be.

"Fuck, fuck, fuck!" She screamed it out and felt immediately better. "Right, Ellie, pack it away until your archangel gets home. Your focus is fixing this mess of Harrison's."

She couldn't think about how if Cassandra had foretold her ascension to angelhood so long ago that she'd been forgotten by immortals, then it was unlikely the Sleeping archangel was wrong about her upcoming death. So she'd push that cheery thought aside till she had Raphael beside her. She knew her limits, and she knew this was archangel-level insanity.

She'd just taken a step to the balcony door when her pants sagged.

Giving in to another scream because, *goddamn it*, she could not get a break, she wrenched her belt tighter around her waist and carried on—after grabbing three chocolate bars and ripping into one as she decided to talk to Ash and Janvier before she headed out. The two might have contacts inaccessible to her.

Also, she needed to brief them on what she'd discovered this morning. She was pretty sure she'd heard them in the hallway earlier, but if they'd left the Tower, she'd call. No point letting her research go to waste if her brain turned to paste when her wings sent her on a swan dive into a sky-scraper.

She ran into Dmitri during her search. Dressed in a slick black-on-black suit, his hair brushed perfectly, he just raised an eyebrow when he saw her.

Elena pointed the half-eaten chocolate bar at him. "Mess with me and I will shoot you through the heart, I swear to God. I am so far past hangry, I'm homicidal."

A twitch of his lips. "Have you tried drinking blood?"

Elena nearly pulled out her crossbow and carried through on her threat—the asshole was *powerful*, would survive it—then she realized he was serious. "Blood?"

"Archangelic blood in particular. Violent amount of energy in it."

Finishing off the chocolate bar, Elena considered it. "I'm not a vampire. Would it even work?" Forget about the actual drinking blood part of it; if it would stop the hunger gnawing at her from the inside out, she'd pinch her nose closed and throw it back like medicine.

Dmitri shrugged. "What have you got to lose?"

"I'll talk to Raphael." Walking past, she said, "Sometimes, I can *almost* believe you might once have been human."

"Clearly, I need to up my game." A hint of fur and champagne wrapped around her, sensual and caressing and mocking.

"Argh!" Swiveling, she had the crossbow in her hand and was shooting the bolt before she could think about it.

Dmitri *moved* . . . and the crossbow bolt thudded home in the wall behind him. "Destroying Tower property again." A headshake followed those censorious words. "'Don't get involved with the white-haired accident-on-legs,' I said to Raphael, but did he listen?"

"Give me back my bolt you scent-infested-excuse-for-a-vampire."

Grabbing it out of the air when he obliged, she strode off without another word . . . and heard Dmitri laughing behind her, the sound deep and unrestrained. Her own lips were twitching hard, but she managed to keep it together until she was in the elevator and he couldn't see her. Her laughter was near-hysterical and it was a release.

God, she wanted her archangel home.

She was sane again by the time she tracked Ashwini and Janvier to the sparring ring in a lower level of the Tower. As members of her Guard—which she would never need if Cassandra's prophecy held true—the couple had to spend a certain amount of time honing their skills with the blade and any other weapons in which they were or could become proficient.

Since the two were in the middle of something, Elena sat down on the bleachers and reviewed all she knew. With Santiago digging up more on Lee and Kumar, Jade remained her best lead. She had to eliminate him from the suspect list, if nothing else. That was, unless he had a connection to Lee, Kumar, Blakely, and Acosta—*or* had decided to use their deaths to cloak his attempt against Harrison.

She was getting ready to interrupt Ash and Janvier when Dmitri—now dressed in an olive-green T-shirt and camouflage pants suitable for sparring—appeared from a ringside entrance and assumed the role of adversary. Janvier was older than Ashwini, but she was better at taking on Dmitri.

Because Ash saw the future, too.

A cold wind infiltrated Elena's blood, a wind that tasted of incomprehensible age.

She did interrupt then—she had no time to waste. When she updated them on Nishant Kumar and Terence Lee, Janvier's bayou-green eyes widened. "There is our connection, *cher*," he said to Ashwini.

It turned out the couple had heard the same rumors—of a drug that caused psychotic hallucinations and blackouts in vampires and could be used for sexual assault. Street name: Vamhypnol. "We had no reason to connect it to Blakely or Acosta—or Harrison," Ashwini said, hands braced on her hips. "But we've been gathering intel on it as fast as we can around investigating the murders, because this stuff is bad news."

Dmitri spoke. "Why is this the first I'm hearing about it?"

"Not enough for a report," Janvier replied. "We're waiting to hear back from a woman who might give us more."

As the couple laid out all they knew, Elena heard two familiar names.

"Wait," she broke in. "Unless Red Cutie and Monique Darling are common working names among pros, those are the two who spoke to Santiago about how Kumar and his buddy, Lee, raped them under the drug's influence."

"Shit, Ellie." Ashwini played restlessly with a blade star. "Both women are dead."

Elena's gut clenched. "Murder?"

"*Non.*" Janvier's languid tone had turned grim. "What was the word our doctor friend used, *cher*?"

"Brain aneurysm," Ashwini supplied. "Each had a massive one."

"As effective as decapitation in causing vampiric death." Dmitri folded his arms. "Cause severe damage to the brain and there's not enough left for the body to know how to regenerate it."

Elena's own brain snagged on something. As if she had a crucial bit of the puzzle and didn't know it. But when she tried to follow up on the thought, it vanished without a trace. Frustrated, she said, "When did they die?" Santiago had spoken to them a bare two months ago.

"Been five weeks for Red, four weeks for Monique," Ashwini said.

The timeline didn't work to answer the questions of this confusion of a case. "Any hint of other victims?"

Ash nodded. "One other—her friend that told us about her said she'd ask the victim to call." A frown. "It'd be good if she did that now."

They all stared at her when her phone rang from where it sat at the side of the sparring circle.

"You are *not* sending telepathic messages now." Elena scowled.

A grin. "Just playing with you." Ashwini grabbed her phone. "She messaged before to say she'd call when she was on break from her shift at the strip club. I got lucky with my timing."

"Lucky as only your wife gets," Dmitri murmured to Janvier under the cover of her conversation.

The vampire grinned. "My Ashblade is always lucky— she has me for a husband."

"You, on the other hand, won't be getting lucky anytime soon, if you keep that up," Ashwini threatened after hanging up. "Our third victim didn't black out, but she did get hazy after drinking a glass of blood offered to her by her date. Her memories of the hour that followed are patchy, but she's sure she was sexually assaulted." Voice a blade, she continued. "Date was Simon Blakely."

Silence as they absorbed that information.

"Accidental lower dose . . . or a purposeful one because Blakely fancied himself a ladies' man?" Elena thought aloud. "A comatose 'lover' wouldn't feed his ego." She was starting to feel more and more in harmony with the man who'd amputated Blakely's genitals. "Maybe Blakely figured a lower dose would mean a compliant, semiconscious woman."

"We must get this woman medical assistance." No humor in Janvier's voice or expression now. "We don't know when the two dead victims were raped, which means there's no way to work out the time it takes for the aneurysm to strike."

"Lower dose, she might survive." Dmitri's face was dangerous. "Tell her the Tower will cover her costs."

Yes, Dmitri could act human at times.

"A rape drug that kills down the road is one hell of a motive." The only problem was Harrison—either Elena didn't know him at all and he was hiding an ugly secret, or they were missing a critical piece.

And what was it that she couldn't *remember*?

"Is the drug widespread?" Dmitri asked, all deadly power and taut control.

Ashwini shook her head. "Low-level vamps have heard of it, but the only people we know to have had personal contact with it are the three rape victims—and the men who gave it to them."

Running his hand through the dark chestnut strands of his hair, Janvier picked up the thread. "Our Holly and Venom know a fixer who works in the higher levels of the city, with the richer vampires and angels, and he says none of them are using it. No one wants to risk it after you came down so hard with the umber situation."

"Blakely, Kumar, and Lee didn't care about the risk to their victims." Elena wanted to stab the rapists herself. "It's possible Acosta didn't, either." Though the amputated hand made her think he hadn't been involved in the sexual abuse. "It was about control, about power." Same as rapists everywhere. "This drug, it only works on vampires?"

"Yes," Ashwini confirmed. "But two human pros who work the Quarter"—a tap on her neck to indicate they offered honey feeds—"said Kumar picked them up a time or two, and they came out of it without memories. Symptoms fit in with a human rape drug." Her eyes flashed. "Only reason they kept going back was because he paid them in cocaine."

"He chose his targets well." Dmitri's voice was like ice, so cold it burned. "Your brother-in-law," he said to Elena, dark eyes flat. "You think he's capable of this crime?"

"As far as I know, Harrison isn't into rape or drugs." She clenched her jaw. "If I find out different, I'll execute him myself." It'd break Beth to discover that kind of evil in the man she loved. "He has a wife, a child, both of them innocent of any wrongdoing—we give him the benefit of the doubt until we have proof either way."

Dmitri gave a curt nod.

"As for suspects—a well-trained human could've taken out Nishant Kumar and Terence Lee." Elena could've done it as a young hunter. "Per the police report, they were small, not particularly strong, and had no real combat training. Did admin work during their Contracts."

"I examined Blakely and Acosta," Ashwini said, "and they were flabby for vampires. Strong because of the vampirism, but not old enough for that to be a serious advantage against a skilled opponent."

Elena went to reply when her forearm cramped again, giant screws twisting her muscles tight enough to snap. *Raphael!* An instinctive call as the pain threatened to bring her to tears, the agony in her arm joined by the throbbing vein on her temple. *Archangel, I really need you.* It was a desperate mental whisper even though she knew he was too far away to hear her.

30

Elena.

She nearly staggered at the faint echo of water crashing against rock, the sea winds in her mind. Excusing herself from the group with a mumbled statement that probably didn't make sense, she made her way to the elevator. *Raphael? Where are you?*

Two hours from home. His voice was stronger now . . . and it held strange echoes.

Swallowing hard, Elena clamped her hand down on her cramping forearm and tried to breathe. *You sound like the Legion.* Sweat broke out along her forehead, the vein in her temple a hammer ringing down beat by beat. *I'm not doing so good.*

I am sending Nisia to you. Where are you?

Why hadn't she gone to the infirmary herself or told the others to call a healer? She didn't know. Her thoughts weren't running in straight lines. It was difficult to think past the wall of pain.

ELENA. Where are you?

Corridor outside our suite. Stumbling out of the elevator, she just barely made it inside their suite before collapsing on the plush white carpet. It felt so soft against the side of her cheek, almost like a cocoon.

She curled up on it, a sleeping cat, her eyes fluttering.

Elena!

I'm so tired, Raphael. It took too much effort to speak.

The doors from the balcony shoved open to admit a whip of icy air; the power that swept in with it was violent and familiar. *I'm hallucinating you now.*

"Guild Hunter." Raphael's arms scooping her up, his wings burning white fire, the glow coming off him so blinding that she had to squint her eyes to see through it.

When she put her hand on his chest, his heart pounded in a beat that was far too fast for an archangel of his power. "Your skin burns." Her brain struggled to comprehend what was happening. "Two hours . . ."

Elena went limp in Raphael's arms on those confused words. But he felt the pulse of life in her veins, the rise and fall of the air in her chest. Taking her through to their bedroom, he put her down on the bed just as Nisia ran inside. The healer was flushed from her headlong flight . . . and came to a jagged halt at spotting Raphael.

Healer instincts kicking in a second later, she went straight to Elena. "Tell me what happened." Already her hands were on his consort as Raphael explained Elena's call to him, and the confusion and enervating sense of tiredness that had come with it.

"My apologies for the glow, Nisia," he said at the end. "I cannot currently restrain it." His body *burned*, as if his cells had boiled to an impossible intensity.

"It won't affect my work, sire."

Raphael tried to have patience as Nisia worked on the hunter who was his heart, but a kind of quiet fury ravaged his veins.

Raphael? Izak just reported that you dropped out of the

sky onto a Tower balcony. I'd think the boy had been in the
wine, but he sounded both earnest and astonished.

Glad for the distraction of Dmitri's voice reaching for
his mind, Raphael answered, *I am in our suite. Elena is
down.*

*Wounded? She left us with unexpected quickness but
appeared fine.*

Because his hunter hated showing weakness. *I wait to
hear from Nisia.*

"She is out of energy," the healer said a minute later, her
tone dumbfounded. "There's barely enough in her cells to
keep her breathing."

Raphael stared at the healer. "Has she not been eating?"

Frown dark, Nisia tugged at something sticking slightly
out of one of Elena's pants pockets. She had to unzip the
pocket to get it out. "A chocolate bar wrapper . . . No, there
are three."

Nisia dropped the wrappers on the nightstand. "She's
eating and drinking but even with the potent and double-
strength mix I made for her, she isn't intaking enough energy to fuel the changes in her body."

Raphael could literally see Elena's bones becoming
more prominent against the dark gold of her skin as her
body consumed itself from the inside out. "Will my blood
make any difference?" Elena wasn't a vampire, formed to
metabolize blood into energy.

"We have to try." Taut desperation on Nisia's face.

It thrust a cold dagger into his gut. The practiced healer
never panicked.

Lifting his wrist to his mouth, Raphael went to tear open
his vein when the taste of a haunting golden richness licked
across his tongue, a richness he'd tasted only once before in
his immortal existence.

His canines elongated.

Life filled him to overflowing.

He bent, scooped Elena into his arms, and lowered his
mouth to her lips. *You must live,* he said into her mind, as
he had once before, when they fell broken and bloodied to

a New York that was jagged splinters and shattered buildings below them. She had been a dying mortal then, her body so badly damaged that her soul was barely clinging on. *You must live, Elena-mine. I would rather die with you than walk into eternity without you by my side.*

A sigh into his mouth before her body began to warm, and she raised a hand to wrap it around his neck, her fingers locking in his hair. Her eyes remained closed, but he saw a glow through her eyelids and it was silver. Like moonlight on water, a gift of light and shadow.

Their kiss went on for always . . . and it wasn't long enough.

When they parted, his canines were the size they should be and Elena's cheekbones were no longer threatening to cut through her skin, but when her lashes lifted, he saw the eyes he'd seen the day she first stood her ground against him, on the Tower roof. The ring of silver she'd developed since they'd become one was gone. All he saw was a clear, pristine gray.

Fear was an anvil falling on his heart.

"I know that taste." She released his hair to brush her fingers over his lips. "We fell on that taste."

"And we rose together." He crushed her close. *Go, Nisia. I must be with my consort.*

The healer slipped away without a word.

Elena kissed him again, warm and languid and deeply alive. "Raphael," she said against his lips when she broke the kiss this time. "I'm not hungry for the first time in days." A nuzzle of his throat. "Put me down. My wings feel different."

He did so with care. "More damage?"

"No." She flared them out, a wonder of midnight and dawn. "No." A smile brighter than the dawn. "No damage at all."

He saw the strength of her, and when she snapped her wings to her back and turned so he could check her wing posture, that posture was precise. "No drag," he told her. "No weakness."

Laughing in a relief that gave her voice a sharp edge, she said, "I guess all I needed was the kiss of ambrosia."

Raphael went to agree when a feather floated to the carpet. Indigo blue.

Then another. Midnight.

And a third. Violet.

Elena followed his gaze. Face stilling, she bent and picked up the three feathers. Neither one of them spoke for long minutes as they waited.

The rest of her feathers remained on her wings.

"Fuck." Shuddering, Elena dropped the feathers she'd picked up and walked into his arms.

He held her tight to the blaze of his body. When she lifted her face to his, he kissed her with a passion that devoured. Elena's response held no gentleness, either, only a primal need. He would've torn off her knife sheaths if he didn't know how much she treasured the soft leather.

So he broke the kiss and forced himself to undo the straps that held the sheaths to her forearms.

Elena kissed the side of his jaw, her fingers settling on his face. "I love how you love me," she whispered, raw need altering into a poignancy that was a knife thrust to the heart.

Kissing her fingertips when they brushed his face, he continued with his task. Both knife sheaths, then the crossbow and quiver, and the hunting blade she wore at one ankle. Her hair was down so he didn't have to check for blade sticks hidden in her braid. "Any other sharp objects on your person today, *hbeebti*?"

A grin that seared his heart. "Down my back."

Raphael couldn't smile yet, the memory of her collapsed body too fresh, but he reached to her back. Sweeping the tangled near-white of her hair over one shoulder, she bent her head, and he pulled out the long blade she wore in a spine sheath. He placed it on the pile of discarded weapons . . . then slammed his mouth down on hers.

He had no memory of stripping her bare, but she was naked in his arms, all skin of dark gold and a determined

strength. Her hands were on his own skin, his clothing
abandoned. Covering her in angel dust, the intimate erotic
flavor in every kiss, he captured her moan with his mouth
and wrapped her up in wings of white fire that would never
burn her.

Rubbing up against him, her nipples hard points, she
whispered his name.

He spoke into her mind. *Yours*, he said, *always yours.*

They fell on the bed together, wings and limbs entangled. Her eyes reflected back the glow pulsing off him, luminous in their inhuman beauty, but the ring of silver that
was a promise of her growing immortality, it hadn't returned.

Her fingers in his hair, her mouth on his throat, she
wrapped her legs around his waist. "Love me, Archangel."

Raphael surrendered to his consort and to this coupling
as rawly physical as it was imbued with a painful love he
hadn't understood until he met Elena. Hope, fear, need, the
hunger to cherish, the twist of the heart when she laughed.
His eternity was encapsulated in Elena's not-yet-fully-
immortal body. She was so easy to break, his consort, so
easy to damage.

And she kissed him like the warrior that she was.

Raphael stroked her with rough hands, molding and
shaping her breasts until her spine arched, a needy sound
emanating from her throat. He kissed his way down her
throat, lower, lower, and he made her scream his name
while her fingers clenched in his hair.

She was quivering in the aftermath, her skin shiny with
a light layer of perspiration and her breathing ragged, when
he shifted position to brace himself over her. She stroked
his chest with lazy fingertips that moved down to grasp his
rigid cock.

Muscles stone, he gritted out, "I have no patience today,
Elena."

Slowly spreading her thighs, she guided him to the dark
heat of her. "Me, either, Archangel."

Her hands came around to his back on that husky

admission—and he pushed into her. The musk of her was a deeply private caress against his senses, her nails sharp bites that anchored him to the physical even as dangerous archangelic energies seethed inside him. Their eyes locked as he sank home, and in the luminous gray, he saw forever.

Legs around his hips once more, she held him possessively tight as he began to move. All at once, it wasn't enough to be braced over her. He lowered his body to hers but wrapped both arms around her upper back so he wouldn't crush her. As close as two people could get, not a breath between them, they loved until there was no fear, no pain, no prophesied death, only Raphael and Elena. An archangel and his consort.

"You're not glowing anymore," his consort pointed out when she'd caught her breath.

The two of them lay together in bed, Elena on her front on one of his solid-once-again wings, Raphael on his back. She'd spread one of her wings over him, and he ran his fingers over her feathers, checking for any sign of weakness. "Good. I'm not used to having no control over my physical reactions."

"Oh?" An arch sound. "I could've sworn you were swept up in uncontrollable passion not so long ago."

"This is not a time to tease, Elena."

Of course she just leaned over and kissed him on the jaw. "It's exactly the time." But her gaze was solemn. "You shouldn't have produced ambrosia, should you? It's only ever meant to be produced once, to turn a mortal into an angel."

"That is the legend, but we have precious few facts." No one, not even the oldest angels who walked the world, could remember the last angel-Made, it had been so long ago. The only thing that had survived was the legend of ambrosia. "It might be that the transition requires multiple doses." Raphael traced the perfect beauty of a feather that graduated from deepest blue to violet.

Elena frowned. "Stage one, stage two, and so on." Propping herself up on one elbow, she considered it. "I could see that. All my weird issues could've just been a signal that we were nearing the deadline for the next dose." A dazzling smile. "At least we know your body will produce it when the time comes. No panic before dose three."

Raphael couldn't stop searching for the silver in her eyes. "What happened today?"

She told him all of it . . . then blinked. "Raphael"—her fingers spread on his heart—"you were *two hours* away. How are you here?"

31

"I have no answers for you, *hbeebti*. As I had no answers the day I caught Illium out of the sky."

"Yeah, you were too far away then, too, but you got to him in time." Elena bit down on her lower lip. "But that was across the city and this . . ."

Raphael continued his careful investigation of her wing. "If I have gained a new Cascade-born ability tied to speed, it is a valuable one. Unfortunately, I have no knowledge of how to access it." When he attempted to focus on what had occurred so he could re-create it, all he got was a turmoil of emotion and blinding power.

"I knew only that you needed me and I was too far away." He'd reacted with anger and determination. "I pushed myself faster and faster, and then I was lightning stretched across two universes."

Elena listened with silent attention, her hair a glorious tumble over her shoulders.

"It felt for a single endless instant as if I was in two places at the same time. My position when you contacted me, and here, at the Tower. Then the two ends crashed into one and I dropped out of the sky to land on our balcony."

"Like a rubber band stretched too tight snapping back together."

"An apt description." Bracing one arm under his head, his other one on her wing, he tried to think through the entire happening again but his brain saw only chaotic flashes, as if the speed of it had been too much for his mind to process. "My skin was afire when I landed—no pain, but a searing heat."

"Kinda makes sense, if you went supersonic."

Raphael began to reply when his attention was caught by a glimmer on her shoulder. He'd almost missed it because it was the same shade as her hair, but when he reached out and picked it up, it came away with ease. Long, silken white strands that floated against his palm.

"Am I shedding?" Elena said, tugging at her hair as if to check on its health.

"Elena, this isn't hair."

Frowning, she leaned in to pick up the delicate strands from his hand. "It looks like the lint that's infested my clothes." Her face went motionless, her breathing too quiet. "It was never lint, was it?"

"I don't know what it is, but this morning I dropped off a sample at our labs for testing."

Lines formed on her forehead. "So?"

"No answer yet." And no return of silver to her irises. "Let's go speak to them now—but first, *hbeebti*, you must look in a mirror."

She noticed the change at once. "Shit." Her fingers rose as if to touch her eye, dropped before she made contact. "I guess we wait and see. Maybe the ambrosia takes time to reboot me for stage two."

Raphael glanced out the balcony doors as they went to leave their suite. A number of the Legion sat outside, watchful gargoyles whose huge mind had amplified Raphael's senses when Elena called out to him. *Stay with her when she leaves*, he ordered, because he knew his hunter and the demons that haunted her.

"I need to look in on Harrison, too," she said right then. "And I've been trying to track down that Jade guy I told you about."

Raphael cared nothing for her brother-in-law when the unpredictable changes in her had him by the throat, but some battles had to be fought. Elena had to keep this monster from her sister's door, had to save Beth as she hadn't been able to save Ariel and Mirabelle. *You should speak to Dmitri. If Jade is any kind of power, Dmitri will know his whereabouts.*

No response from Elena, though she did raise her fingers to her temple and rub it absently.

Raphael stopped. Hbeebti, *do you hear me?*

Halting, Elena turned to face him, and he cursed himself for a worry that had no cause . . . then she said, "Raphael? What's up?"

"Elena, I want you to send me a mental thought." She'd developed the ability to speak to him on the mental level far faster than anyone had expected, and now the steel and wildfire of her was a familiar presence in his mind.

She'd braided her hair after showering quickly, and the single plait swung a little as she tilted her head, her expression acute. "I just did."

"I heard nothing."

Elena's throat moved as she swallowed. "No silver in my eyes, and now I've lost mental speech." Pressing her fisted hand against the center of her chest, she took a deep breath, exhaled slowly. "But my wings work and feel fine. This could be a normal part of my development."

"I don't care about the silver or the mental speech." Raphael cupped her face. "I care about what they say about your immortality." No matter how they worked it, how they justified it as a part of her development, she was steadily going *backward.*

"No signs of forward momentum, huh?" she said, as if they'd spoken mind to mind after all.

Elena had always understood him, even as a mortal with too much courage and not enough self-protective instincts.

At times, he thought he'd fallen for her that first day on the roof, when she'd closed her hand defiantly over a blade, her blood dripping to the floor.

"I have asked Keir to journey to New York. You will cooperate with him and Nisia." It came out an order.

Rather that bristling, his fiercely independent warrior shook her head. "I don't think they'll be able to do much. Right now, with all records of previous angels-Made lost, I may as well be one of a kind."

Unique beyond compare.

Words spoken by a fascinated Alexander. The Ancient still had trouble with the concept of a mortal turned angel, though he, too, had heard the legend of ambrosia.

"Come on, let's go find out about the lint before I run down Jade." Firm resolve in Elena's voice.

No, his warrior would not sit and wait for events to overtake her. "We'll speak to Lucius on the way, get him to run tests on your blood."

"Yes, good plan. Maybe he can figure out what the ambrosia's doing to my insides." She held up another strand of the gossamer "lint." "Just saw this on my wrist. No idea when it appeared or if it was caught in my clothes already and got shaken loose when I put them back on."

Raphael said nothing, but three minutes later, he watched Lucius draw Elena's blood, and he told the angel with wings of softest yellow exactly what he wanted him to check. "Focus on any changes. You have the results from Elena's blood over the years." Taken by the healers as part of routine checkups to monitor the progress of her immortality. "Find out if anything has altered."

Lucius bowed his head. "Sire."

"Compare my blood against mortal, vampire, and angel exemplars, too," Elena said, her jaw set. "No point avoiding the truth if I'm regressing."

Their next stop was Nisia's office.

"I've just received the results," the senior Tower physician said when Elena held out the gossamer strands in a wordless question. "It is a natural byproduct of some process in your body."

"Like hair or nails?" Elena dropped the strands into a sample receptacle Nisia held out.

"Yes. Its structure comes closest to hair, though its tensile strength is far weaker."

"Am I going to turn into Elena Haireaux?"

"At this stage, there are no indications the material is adhering to your skin. My working theory is that it is a waste product—your body discarding that which it does not need. But it's a theory only, with no proof."

"That is not a satisfactory answer, Nisia." Crackling with ice, Raphael's voice created frost in the air.

Elena shot him a scowl, her thoughts written on her face. *Stop bullying Nisia for what she can't control.*

Clenching his jaw, Raphael wrenched himself back from the edge. Elena was right; Nisia had done nothing to earn his anger. "You have the apology of your archangel, Nisia."

A wideness to the healer's eyes he'd rarely seen, she was so competent and self-assured. "There is no need, sire. I am as frustrated as you." Picking up a medical device, she pressed it to Elena's heart.

It was merely the first test.

Heart, lungs, muscles, bones, Nisia ran Elena through the gamut.

"Can I fly safely?" Elena asked that question in a calm tone, but Raphael could feel her need to fly as a second heartbeat.

"Your wings are in perfect condition and your bones no longer have the tunnels," Nisia said. "I see no reason to ground you."

Leaving Nisia to continue her work, Raphael's hunter walked with him to the privacy of the balcony outside the infirmary. "Do you have more archangel business today?"

He couldn't smile at her reference to their earlier play. "Partway through your tests, Dmitri informed me of a kiss of vampires in an area some distance from here who appear

to believe they are out of the Tower's sights." He could send
Illium or Dmitri to remind the vampires of the fallacy of
their thinking, but an archangelic reminder would rever-
berate through the entire territory, nipping any other such
erroneous thoughts in the bud.

"Go," Elena whispered.

"Elena."

"I know. I'll land if I feel the merest twinge." Elena
placed her hands on his chest, her expression strong and her
words a promise. "I would never make you watch me fall
out of the sky."

Closing his hand over her wrist, Raphael bent his head
so their foreheads touched. There they stood for long minutes even as the snow began to fall and the Legion landed
all around them.

32

Elena watched Raphael soar into the sky, the snow melting against her skin. She knew exactly how hard it had been for him to leave her; she fought the urge to fly to him, stick close. Never, as an adult, had she been so deeply afraid. Not even when she fell the first time.

Then, she hadn't understood what she and Raphael could be together, hadn't tasted the full glory of a love that was her breath and the reason for her being. Hadn't lived with an archangel who loved her more than eternity.

Her eyes burned.

A flutter of snow and silence, vast numbers of the Legion rising from this balcony and from rooftops across the city to fly in the same direction as Raphael, an eerie gray wave whose voices no longer whispered in her head. The Primary, however, still waited for her—and she wasn't so arrogant as to shrug off the escort. "I have to check on my brother-in-law, then I'll be out and we'll fly."

No movement, the living gargoyle waiting patiently.

She checked her phone as she made her way quickly to

Harrison's bed in the infirmary and saw a message from
Ashwini. The hunter and Janvier were in the Quarter, running down the exact depth of the relationship between Lee
and Kumar, Blakely and Acosta. *We're also taking another
stab at the drug angle, talking to people in the gangs to see
if there are rumors of a hit.*

The pragmatic nature of it all, the banal predictability of
evil, was an antidote to the mystery of her transition. *I'm
going to chase down Jade*, she wrote back, then made herself add, *Dig about Harrison, too, in connection with the
others.* It made her sick to her stomach to consider that
Beth's husband might've been a party to rape, drugs, death,
but the questions couldn't be left unasked.

Her brother-in-law himself could tell her nothing; he remained unconscious.

Your sister was here earlier today, Laric shared in the
silent tongue, his hands flowing with subtle grace. *She said
she told their little girl that her father had gone away for a
while for business.*

"Good on Beth. No point in Maggie seeing him like
this." Elena placed her hands on her hips. "She'll be mad at
him for leaving without saying good-bye, but she won't be
afraid." And Maggie was secure enough in her father's love
that she wouldn't consider it an abandonment.

I think so, too, Laric said. *I know little of children, but I
believe, once he wakes, it will not be a hard thing for him
to mend the small anger. To root out fear is sometimes impossible.*

"You're certain he's going to recover?" Harrison's skin
was bloodless.

Laric touched her gently on the arm to get her attention
on his hands. *Jason's blood has had enough time to bond
with Harrison's own, and it has restarted that which
stopped in Harrison. He will heal.*

Switching to the silent tongue herself, because she
needed the practice, she said, *How long before I can talk
to him?*

She thought Laric might've smiled at her awkward

movements. It was one thing to be fluent at "listening" to the language, another to speak it. The gestures were subtle, small, the curve of a little finger able to alter the entire meaning of a sentence.

He is no longer in an imposed coma but in a more natural unconscious state. The healer made sure the blanket over Harrison's body was neat and tidy. *Nisia says we cannot predict when he might wake—it will depend on his own body's healing capacity.*

Nodding thanks at Laric for the information, Elena stepped out to check in with Vivek. "Any news on Jade?"

"I was just about to call you." Vivek's voice hummed with the thrill of the hunt, his hunter-born instincts riding him hard. "Your man Jade's shed his old skin and set himself up under his two-hundred-and-fifty-year-old real name, Jadchenko Simnek, and yes, that was a bitch to track down."

Elena's own instincts hummed. "Damn, you're good, V."

"Never forget it," Vivek said in smug pleasure. "Anyway, he's got an apartment on the Upper West Side. I'm messaging you the address. Looks like he's living large off the income generated from a gaming website. Got himself a view of Central Park."

"A gaming website?" It didn't seem like the kind of thing that'd interest a vampire from the tail end of the eighteenth century.

"He has a track record in the share market under both his old and new names. Nothing big, but the man's invested in tech companies before—he's smart enough to keep up with the world. Be careful." A pause. "And hey, Ellie? Thanks for pulling me into the hunt."

"You're the best partner I could imagine." He'd be a lethal danger once he could hunt on the ground as well as via his byzantine network of computers. "I'll let you know what I find at Jade's."

The sun had gone behind the clouds when she flew off with the Primary her silent shadow, and the city looked metallic and gray. Snow was falling, but it wasn't heavy, nothing she couldn't handle. Once airborne and despite the healthy condition of her wings, she flew with a sedateness that wasn't her natural state, trying to glide as much as possible.

Below her, New Yorkers moved in a chaotic dance of pedestrians and cars and trucks that somehow wasn't a total mess. More than one pedestrian looked up and waved before carrying on their way. A taxi driver stopped at a red light hung out his window to grin and wave at her.

Her city was proud of having produced the only mortal turned angel in the world.

Elena waved back before the winds carried her away.

Hundreds of the Legion had left with Raphael, but she saw scattered groupings of them throughout the city as she flew. A couple of new gargoyles appeared on the tony building that housed Jade's apartment just before she landed in the entrance courtyard. The Primary joined his brethren. She looked up at them without smiling, never forgetting why the escort was essential.

"Consort." The vampiric doorman bowed and held open the door for her.

Irritated at the deference but gripping it in a steely fist because her inability to handle this consequence of being Raphael's consort wasn't the poor doorvamp's fault, she entered the building. One of these days, she'd have Raphael issue a proclamation that everyone was to treat her as just Elena.

Inside, she took in the thick carpet, the glossily painted walls, and the equally glossy people behind the counter. Both humans rose to their feet at Elena's approach. "How may we assist you?" the female of the pair asked, her voice smooth but her hands clasped so tightly in front of her that she had to be cutting off circulation to her fingers.

"I'm here to visit one of your residents," Elena said through her discomfort. "Jadchenko Simnek. Apartment 7C."

The male receptionist gulped. "Do you have an appointment?"

Elena smiled, suddenly feeling a lot more centered. This was reality and normality, not the silver disappearing from her eyes and not the loss of Raphael's voice in her head. God, she *missed* it. "No appointment," she said, "but I'll wait while you call him."

Eyes huge, the woman picked up the phone and spoke to Jade. It took only a moment for her to hang up and say, "Mr. Simnek will be most delighted to welcome you." Her smile no longer a plastic caricature, she added, "You can take the elevator directly up to the seventh floor. I've cleared it."

Elena was striding to the elevator when she heard, "Consort! Elena!"

Shifting on her heel, ready to drop a knife into her palm, she found the male receptionist jogging toward her. He held something in his hands. "They fell," he whispered after coming to a breathless halt. "I wasn't sure . . ."

One feather gleamed darkest midnight shading to deepest blue. The other was nearly pink, one of the odd feathers hidden in among the gradient that flowed across her wings. Throat dry, she dug up a smile. "Must be shedding season. If you have a use for them, go ahead."

"Oh!" His fingers curled covetously over the edges. "I collect angel feathers," he blurted out, a soft madness in his eyes that told her he walked a line very close to the angel-struck. "I've never found one on the ground this beautiful and undamaged." A glance over at his partner at reception. "I'll give Rose one, too. Her little girl will go wild."

Elena thought of Zoe, with her collection of feathers that she treated like jewels. Even her adored daddy had to ask permission to touch them. Elena wondered if she'd soon have far too many feathers to give her goddaughter. The feathers rescued by the receptionist hadn't been loose or damaged. Raphael had checked her wings with intense care while they lay in bed, then Nisia had done a secondary inspection.

She'd just lost two healthy feathers.

Leaving the delighted receptionist, Elena resumed her short journey to the elevators. The doors opened as she arrived, gleaming mirrored walls reflecting back her face. Stepping in, she quieted the manic voices in her head with a single command: *Get this done before it all turns to shit—make sure Beth and Maggie are safe.*

When she stepped out onto the seventh floor, it was to find a tall man dressed in a designer suit of pinstriped navy waiting for her. His eyes were a brilliant green, his skin a black so deep that it held a blue-black gleam, and his hair shaved off to reveal a perfectly shaped skull.

His scent was marigolds in the sunlight splashed with butterscotch.

"Jade, I presume."

The vampire bent into a deep bow. "I am honored to welcome the consort of my liege." A graceful wave toward the left, his hands bare of ornaments except for a chunky signet ring on his pinky finger. "My apartment occupies this quadrant of the floor."

Elena followed him inside through the impressively wide doorway. Conscious that she was more vulnerable in her current physical state than she'd ever been, she never took her eyes off the vampire strong enough to be a deadly threat. When she spotted one of the Legion fly past a window, she knew they must be clinging to the wall outside, ready to respond to a call from her.

Ignoring the sofas in the living area, Elena walked to the large sliding doors that led out onto a small balcony. Jade obligingly opened them for her, and they stepped out to speak in the cold winter air.

She spotted two of the Legion on the walls of the building, one on either side of the balcony. Jade, however, didn't seem to notice their motionless gray presence. "I'm guessing this has to do with good old Harry Ling?"

"You keep track of him?"

"I have better things to do than spend my time on that pissant." Jade sniffed and straightened the cuffs of the pristine white shirt he wore under the tailored lines of his suit jacket. "But I keep my ear to the ground—I heard someone finally got tired of his brand of ass and tried to slit his useless throat."

Jade clearly didn't know her link to Harrison. Elena had

been careful not to broadcast her family connections; newspapers and magazines that tried to run articles on Beth or Jeffrey or their tragic family history invariably received a visit from a cold-eyed senior angel or vampire—and had learned to leave that hot potato alone.

It was the one point on which Elena had no scruple in using Tower might. She wasn't about to put her family and friends in an enemy's sights when she could keep them out. Not that the information wasn't out there. People just had to dig to find it.

It was obvious Jade hadn't bothered. A stroke of luck for her. "No fan of Harrison's, then?" she prodded.

Jade brushed off the snow that had settled on the balcony railing. "Why else would you be here? You know Harrison tattle-taled on me to Andreas." Leaning one arm on the clean railing, he looked at her with eyes gone hard as gemstones. "Andreas is not a forgiving angel."

33

"Where were you when Harrison was attacked?" Elena asked point-blank, then gave him the date and time of the assault.

Jade frowned . . . before flashing a smile wide enough to show fang. "I have an alibi. Fucker picked a perfect day to nearly get dead—otherwise, I might've been working alone in my apartment." Retrieving his phone, he brought up a photograph of a pretty black woman wearing pink lipstick that matched her pink dress, her gaze coy and her lashes long. "I was on a date with this sweet thing."

"You have her contact information?"

"Sure—we met on Fang Love."

"The vampire dating site?" Elena looked him up and down. "Why do you need a dating site?" Jade might have sticky fingers, but he also had the sexy-danger thing going on *and* he had money to burn.

He ran his hand down his lapel, his smile pleased at the implied compliment. "I work and work. No time to meet women in the clubs—and I want to meet a nice girl, not one of the barflies. Senataye and I went to that little blood café in Soho."

That "little blood café" was part of Elena's accidental business investment that had struck a vein of gold. What had started off as a source of cheap blood in the Vampire Quarter had expanded into multiple outlets across the country—including a high-end boutique in Soho that offered premium blood and was open twenty-four hours a day.

Marcia Blue, the publicity-shy brains behind the entire thing, was already planning blood café world domination.

Elena knew their properties had surveillance cameras, so Jade's alibi would be easy enough to check. She also knew that a vampire as wealthy as Jade could've hired an assassin to do the dirty work for him—however, that didn't dovetail with the personal nature of the threat against Beth and Maggie. "Why didn't you ever go after Harrison?"

"Well, first," Jade said, "I was too busy begging and screaming at Andreas that I was sorry." His face hardened again, eyes flat. "Then, after I'd healed enough to get even, the imbecile ran off on his half-witted escape attempt."

No one, Elena thought, should be able to switch moods that quickly. "Talking of imbeciles—stealing from Andreas? What were you on?"

He groaned. "High on my own bullshit. I want to go back in time and slap myself stupid."

"I like you better for owning your idiocy." In reality, she was fairly sure Jade was a sociopath with very little actual empathy for anyone beyond himself.

"It was either that or stay an idiot like Harry." Snorting, he looked out over the snow-blanketed shadows of Central Park. "By the time a hunter dragged him back home, and Andreas got through with punishing him, time was dragging on. Because *then*, I had to wait for *him* to heal, because what use was it beating him to a pulp if he started off as pulp anyway?"

"Understandable."

Laughter that melted the green and made her understand

why nice-girl Senataye had accepted a date with a man who probably saw her as a trophy. "And then, when he finally wasn't a sack of broken bones anymore, I had my fingers in other pies." An avaricious gleam in his eyes. "That was when I realized the smug shit had done me a favor. After Andreas terminated my contract, I couldn't even get a job cleaning toilets. Angels blacklisted me."

"Big, fat motive right there. Lots of prestige working for a senior angel."

"Sure, but a lot *more* prestige being a big man on my own." Jade flashed his fangs. "I was fucked after clearing my debt to Andreas, lived on cheap blood, and used what funds I had left to set up an online gaming enterprise designed for long plays, bets that last years. It. Took. Off."

Taking out his phone again, the vampire showed her his figures. "No other site caters to immortal gamblers like this, and the best thing is, I collect my money from every angle. Registration fee, per-bet fee, yearly renewal fees for long bets, cut of final winnings. And the membership keeps growing."

Elena folded her arms. "You're telling me you got too busy to worry about vengeance? Like Andreas, you don't seem the forgiving type."

"I know, I know, it sounds like pure bull." Jade held up his hands. "But I like money and the power that comes with it—that's what got me in trouble in the first place. Not that I wouldn't enjoy pounding on Harry if he appeared in front of me, but I'm not going to waste my valuable time hunting him down."

"Say I believe you," Elena said, because the money angle did make sense in light of his personality. "If you didn't have any reason to harm Harrison, do you know anyone else who did?"

"No one with enough balls to creep into his house and slit his throat," he said after several seconds' thought. "And when his kid could've walked in on it? Ice fucking cold." Elena didn't think she was imagining the hint of admiration in his tone. "I was the only big fish he tried to sink. Others were all small fry, admin, maids, trainees. No one dangerous or physically inclined."

Elena felt like kicking the balcony railing. She found Jade disturbing, but her instincts said he was telling her the truth.

Another dead end.

"I have been a bad host." Jade straightened. "May I offer you a glass of wine, or a cup of coffee, if you prefer?"

"No. I'll be on my way." She'd tell Vivek to keep an eye on Jade electronically, see if he made any questionable moves financial or otherwise, but she didn't expect Vivek to turn up anything relevant to the murders. "Thank you for your time."

Even as Jade turned to walk her back to the front door, Elena pulled herself over the side of the railing, spreading out her wings as she fell. Five gargoyles detached from the building to join her. She caught Jade's startled face looking down at her as she angled up, and she raised one hand in good-bye.

Smile bright and as happy as she figured someone that cold-blooded ever got, he waved back with something in his hand. It glimmered white-gold with a hint of another color.

That was one of her primaries.

Stomach falling and face going scalding hot before chilling to a shiver, she told herself losing another primary feather wasn't a problem. Molting then growing new feathers could be part of the process. Birds did that, didn't they?

She felt Jade's eyes of stone track her in the air. And she thought that if she was ever powerless, he'd have no compunction in ripping off her feathers to sell to the highest bidder. As for his success, it didn't eliminate the black mark against his name. No invites to big angelic events for Jade, she bet. A self-confessed "big man" would be enraged by the insult.

If he proved innocent of the murders, she'd have to make

it clear to him that Harrison and his family were off-limits forever. Jade would never forget what Harrison had done, but he was also too clever to set himself up against an archangel. Beth, Maggie, and Harrison would be safe.

Calling the Soho blood boutique, she asked the manager to check the security files to confirm Jade's alibi. "No need," the manager said. "I remember him because he ordered our most expensive bottle. The five thousand dollar Blood Noir."

"Christ, what the hell are we selling, liquid gold?"

"Almost. Marcia talked an older angel into donating a cup of his blood—each bottle has a droplet. Most vamps will never get near angelic blood, so . . ."

"Do I want to know how Marcia convinced this angel?"

"She traded looking over his business plan."

"Then the angel got a good deal." Marcia was still more diffident than she should be, but that woman's *brain*. "No mistake on Jade's attendance at that time?"

"None. We also had a proposal in the café that day. Made my cynical heart go pitter-patter."

Ending the conversation, Elena was about to put away her phone when a message from Vivek pinged onto the screen: *Order from Nisia on threat of her wrath—you need to eat regardless of the earlier situation. Montgomery's been alerted.*

Elena didn't feel hungry, but with her feathers falling off, she wasn't about to chance fate. She landed at the Enclave home minutes later. While the Legion went to poke around in her greenhouse, she scratched at the spot on her chest that continued to itch. "It's probably a mosquito bite," she muttered to the white owl that had landed with her. "The original vampires."

The owl yawned, looking very real and not a ghost of Cassandra's cherished birds.

After eating the meal Sivya had prepared, she checked to ensure she hadn't lost any more primaries. Only when she'd confirmed that did she take off in a glide across the Hudson. Before she did anything else, she had to see Beth;

she knew regardless of who else was around Beth, her sister would be waiting for her. Always, in the end, she would look to her big sister.

A quick exchange of messages told her the entire family was at a small neighborhood park.

Reaching the park, she spotted Maggie running around in the churned-up snow with two other children. Sparks glinted off her favorite pink woolen hat with woven silver threads, and her little body was clad in the pink coat with big glittery buttons that she loved almost as much as the hat. She was also wearing her matching snow boots, the perfect little pink princess.

Elena wondered if she'd grow up that way, or if she'd rebel in her teenage years, and drive Beth to distraction. Her lips quirked at imagining a goth Maggie, complete with a pierced lip and a tattoo designed to infuriate Mom and Dad. Elena looked forward to watching her niece's journey, and seeing who she became. One thing was certain—no matter where Maggie chose to go or the path she decided to follow, Beth's love would remain a fierce force of nature. She would *never* abandon her baby.

Elena's landing caused squeals of glee, with Maggie running up to hug her legs. "Tag!" she cried out. "You're it, Auntie Ellie!"

Making a growling face, Elena said, "Run!" The children took off while she pretended to chase them as fast as she could. She saw one of the other parents take photos, and after the game was over and the children went back to playing on the available equipment, she asked the woman if she could see the images.

As she looked through them, she quietly deleted the ones that featured Maggie, leaving the woman with only those that showed her own child with Elena. It was unlikely the beaming woman would even notice, she'd taken so many shots.

That done, she went over to where Beth sat in a child-sized swing, her feet dragging heavily on the ground.

"Afraid I can't push you on that one, Bethie."

Her sister rose to lean into her. Elena wrapped her up in her arms . . . and she hoped to hell that she'd be there for Beth as time continued its inexorable march. As Maggie grew. As Harrison healed.

Because she'd just seen another feather float to the ground.

34

Night was a black cloak around him as Raphael flew home, the city winter-dark though it was only early evening. It had taken teeth-gritted control on his part not to check in on Elena every ten minutes after he left her—and then she'd messaged him, his hunter who knew him well enough to understand his need.

The contact had held him through his time dealing with the vampire kiss that had been flexing their muscles. It had been the wrong time for them to act out—and for the area's angel to fail in his duties to keep the vampires in check. Raphael had been in no mood to go easy on anyone.

When he spotted lights on the Tower roof, he headed that way in case Elena had chosen to wait for him up there as she did at times—most often in the company of one or more of the Legion, or Illium. Once in a blue moon, it would be Dmitri or Venom—and they'd usually be throwing verbal knives at one another.

He often thought the three had come to enjoy their barbed interactions too much to ever be any friendlier.

Closer now, he saw colored lights strung all along the sides of the roof; the snow had also been brushed to the edges of the large space to leave a clean area in the center. Chairs surrounded a brazier that burned hot . . . lighting up a face he hadn't seen for far too long.

His wings sending up a flurry of snow as he landed on one edge, he closed them back then stalked across to meet his weapons-master halfway. "Galen." He clasped the other man's opposite forearm in the way of warriors, their other arms coming around each other's shoulders, the embrace warmed by centuries of loyalty and of battle beside one another. "This is a surprise." His weapons-master was based in the angelic stronghold of the Refuge and ran all of Raphael's interests there.

"We thought we'd take advantage of Aodhan being in the Refuge." Galen's pale green eyes were bright even in the night, though his hair appeared brown rather than the true red it was under sunlight. "He's happy to handle my duties while I make this visit."

"I am glad to see you." He looked past Galen's shoulder to spot Illium, Venom, and even Jason on the roof. The others must've called his spymaster when Galen landed in New York.

"Where is Jessamy?" He wanted to speak to her about Cassandra, see if she knew more than what Andromeda had imparted to Elena.

"Your consort has kidnapped her to parts unknown." Galen ran his fingers through his hair, the amber amulet that hung from the metal band he wore around his upper-left arm aglow in the firelight that reached them. "I was told not to wait up."

"They're going to Sara's!" Illium called out after catching their conversation. "A girls' night, Ellie said, while we have a gathering here."

Raphael's hand curled into his palm, but this—having so many of his Seven together—was a rare gift. Elena was giving him a silent message: *Enjoy this night, Archangel. With the Cascade unleashed once more, we can't know when it'll come again. The rest can wait a few more hours.*

Putting a stranglehold on the fury of his worry, Raphael joined his men just as the rooftop door opened to admit Dmitri and Janvier. Also with them was Deacon, the weapons-maker husband of Elena's best friend—and a mortal who reminded Raphael of the man Dmitri had been when they'd first met. The same quiet confidence, the same dedication to his family, the same way of interacting with Raphael—as a friend.

Raphael would mourn Deacon when he was gone.

So, he thought, would Galen. His weapons-master's face had lit up more brilliant than the winter moon. "Deacon! Don't say you have it already?"

Dark-haired, with eyes of dark green, Deacon reached into the scabbard he wore across his back and, giving a slow smile, pulled out a heavy broadsword that gleamed with the colors of the lights ringing the roof.

Galen, hard as granite and not known for emotional displays, looked near to tears. Taking the broadsword with reverent hands, he moved away from the main group and began to put the blade through its paces. It sang like music in the air, the balance so tuned to Galen's hand that it would never sing as well for another.

"Well," Janvier drawled, "I guess that puts me in my place." Hands on his hips. "I'm never entering a room with you again, *mon ami*," he said to Deacon.

The weapons-maker removed the scabbard from his body. "Give Galen the scabbard when he's done, and he might realize he's not imagining a Cajun accent near me."

Laughter filled the air, along with insults and rejoinders.

"We're only missing Naasir and Aodhan," Dmitri murmured to him.

Raphael nodded. It was difficult to gather all his Seven in one place at one time. The last time had been just under a year prior to Aodhan's departure, when Raphael had taken advantage of the peace to send Andreas to the Refuge, alongside Trace, Janvier and Ashwini, and Nimra and Noel.

Galen and Naasir had helped Andreas and his caretaker team settle in then left to spend time in New York with the others of the Seven. It had been a necessary and important month—an archangel could rule with his power alone, but an archangel bonded to such strong vampires and angels as Raphael's Seven had a critical advantage. More, Raphael valued his bonds with his men, and if he'd learned one thing from watching his mother, it was that such loyalty was a treasure not to be squandered and taken for granted.

There was a reason Eli looked to her with respect to this day.

It was also good for Andreas, Janvier, and the other strong vampires and angels in his territory to have a taste of what it meant to run his Refuge stronghold. Andreas, in particular, was old and powerful enough—and now had enough experience at the task—that he'd need less of a team the next time Raphael asked him to step in.

The trust Raphael had shown in assigning him the critical duty had further solidified the strong angel's loyalty. As for Nimra, she was both powerful and one of his calmest angels, and Andreas valued her counsel. Even Nazarach had been known to speak to her when he needed advice. Janvier, Trace, and Noel had skills to back up Andreas and Nimra, and all were blood-loyal to his territory.

Technically, Ashwini was much too young to have been shown the secret of the Refuge that protected angelic young and held the histories of angelkind. But Janvier's wife was a most unique vampire. She had the third eye, could glimpse the future—though, thankfully, her gift was not a thing of madness as Cassandra's had been.

While in the Refuge, she'd been a popular guest invited to many homes. All of whom were hoping to be bestowed a glimpse of what was to come. And every so often, Ashwini would let something drop. It was never on purpose, Raphael knew. That was what made her so very likable— she was swayed neither by power nor by wealth, and when the words came, you knew they were honest.

She'd visited the home of Aodhan's sister, Imalia, at some point—and halfway through the cake she'd been served, had said, "Your lover should really start building that crib. It takes time, you know, even for people gifted with their hands. And he's such a perfectionist."

That prophecy had been politely ignored—especially after Ashwini told another angelic couple to fit out a nursery, and a third angel to learn to play music because his daughter wouldn't go to sleep without it. Everyone had thought she'd made an embarrassing mistake.

Angelic births were rare. Three in close proximity? Ludicrous.

Yet today, Aodhan cradled his nephew's fragile body in his arms, while two other babes slept in the Refuge. Needless to say, Ashwini had an open invitation to any territory she wished to visit.

Galen finally came to a stop. His hair windblown and his face flushed, he moved to shake Deacon's hand. "It's even better than I imagined. Are you sure you don't want to become a vampire? I have connections."

"I am quite sure," Deacon said with the smile of a man deeply content with his life. "I'll create to the end of my days, then I will sleep in peace."

Illium hefted a bottle of champagne over his head. "We have this stuff for those of you whose taste buds can stand it," he said with a shudder. "There's also fancy blood from Elena's café, beer, and a bottle of truly excellent Scotch." He held up the latter with a grin. "What's your poison?"

The drinks were poured, conversation began, and Raphael sat down to spend the evening with a group of men he'd trust at his back no matter what the battle. However, not thinking about Elena and the changes wracking her body? An impossibility.

On the Tower floor directly below the roof, Elena called her grandfather while Jessamy went to get her cloak. The historian had long come to accept her wing malformation, but as with Laric, she took care never to reveal it to ordinary mortals.

Angels could not be seen as fallible.

For angels were not like mortals and never would be.

"Better that I wear a cloak than be the cause of a reign of blood," Jessamy had once said when discussing her reasoning. "Let the world believe me so haughty an angel that I do not think mortals deserve a glimpse of my wings."

Those wings were startlingly lovely, a luxuriant magenta that flowed into blush then purest cream. Jessamy wore her wings openly in the Refuge, and when the sunlight fell on the fine filaments, they lit up from within exactly like the glow of Jessamy's soul. The historian and teacher of angelic young was the kindest, gentlest angel Elena had ever met.

"Beth is fine," Jean-Baptiste told her after picking up the call. "She's reading stories to Maggie."

"Jessamy and Galen have flown in for a visit. I'm taking Jess to Sara's for drinks and conversation."

"Good. Don't feel guilty for living your life, child." Rough words, so much unspoken. "Enjoy your friends, enjoy the world."

Elena thought of the tiny feather she'd picked up an hour ago. A deep black, it had come from where her wings grew out of her back. Wings that had begun to feel heavy again, her back aching under the pressure. "I will," she said to her grandfather, her heart a knot.

Ten minutes later, she and Jessamy rode through the gaudy and bright and laughing color of Manhattan in back of a converted truck that had no sides to block the view. "How's Sam?" Elena asked. "I haven't had a chance to call him this week." The young angelic boy was one of Elena's favorite people in the Refuge.

"I had to stand him in the corner last week for throwing pieces of rotten fruit at another boy." Laughter in Jessamy's voice. "He planned the whole thing in retaliation for a mudpushing incident. And of course they are the best of friends who find it all hilarious."

As Elena grinned, Jessamy looked around, her eyes brilliant with reflected light. "Even when Raphael was a young archangel building his Tower," the historian said, "there was a life to this place that was both joyful and frenetic." She watched two angels sweep low through the skyscrapers before swinging back up again. "Now, it burns with energy."

"I like that it never sleeps," Elena murmured, her mind on other thoughts of energy. "There's a discovery on every corner. No restraint, pure heart."

Jessamy met her gaze across the space between them, her soft brown eyes incisive. "What is wrong, Elena? Will you not tell me?"

Hand clenching on the metal bar above her head, Elena tried to figure out where to begin. In the end, she spoke the dark truth at the heart of it all. "I'm regressing in my immortality." She told the other woman about no longer being able to speak to Raphael with her mind, about the changes in her eyes, about the feathers she kept losing. "I'm terrified I'll wake up one day mortal again, my wings lost."

Distress on Jessamy's features. "If I had known, I wouldn't have left the Refuge. When we spoke about the owls and the woman with the lilac hair, I thought it simply a Cascade dream—I was in Amanat then and looking forward to surprising you." Her wings moved agitatedly under her cloak. "Galen and I must return at once, so I can continue to scour the archives for—"

"*Jess.*" Elena shook her head. "Andromeda answered the question about the owls and the woman, and from what she said, not much else is known about Cassandra. As for the rest . . . you've been digging for years at this point, and all you've discovered are mentions of the same legend about ambrosia and an archangel loving true."

"I've never before failed so badly at a research task."

"You can't find what's not there." Elena knew how hard Jessamy had searched, the countless hours she and Andromeda had spent among the dustiest records. "The last angel-Made was so many eons ago that the Legion can't recall it. Any records have long since turned to dust."

A rare frustration in the fine lines of Jessamy's face. "I am keeping exact records of your transition. No other angel-Made will ever go blind into the future." Her wings moved again under the cloak. "You're certain you don't want me to return to the Refuge?"

"Yes. This is a journey into the unknown. Raphael and I will walk it together."

Child. The Sleep-heavy whisper fell into her mind.

So, at least one person could still talk to her on the mental plane. Maybe because Cassandra was entering through another part of her mind. The part that dreamed while she slept, only this dream happened while she was awake and conscious.

Yes? She'd made the choice not to antagonize Cassandra—after all, the Ancient only saw as Ash saw; she wasn't the reason for what was happening to Elena. As for the golden-eyed white owl seated next to Jessamy, it was a hauntingly beautiful creature that lived in an archangel's dreams.

The second marker in time nears.

Elena straightened. *Will someone else die? Can I save them?*

Not death. Rebirth. The owl flared its wings. *The gift is not yours, child of mortals, and will not give itself to you.* The voice was sad and adamant both. *Your death is written in the stars. For you must die for the other to live.*

Goose bumps broke out over Elena's skin. *How many markers in time are there?*

Three.

The drinker of blood lost.

The agony of rebirth.

The last feather to fall.

Three markers. The second was about to happen. And she'd just seen one of her feathers float to the truck bed.

This was not looking good for Elena.

35

Raphael stood with Galen near the edge of the roof, an archangel renewing ties with a member of his Seven. But Galen had things to tell him that had nothing to do with the bond that had tied them together for centuries.

"Sire," the weapons-master said, "we came through Amanat."

Raphael had expected as much. His mother's home was a place out of time. She'd taken an entire town with her into Sleep. When she had arisen, she'd brought it all back, a living city from another land now extant in the depths of Kagoshima, Japan. As a historian, Jessamy couldn't resist its lure.

"Lady Caliane sends her love."

"You will go back that way?" At Galen's nod, Raphael said, "I would ask that you carry a gift for my mother." It was Raphael's hunter who had chosen that gift: a finely balanced blade two centuries old.

"There is plenty of room in the metal death trap Jessamy insists on flying." Galen scowled at the thought of the plane that Jessamy piloted with calm expertise. He flew on the wing beside her, while she controlled the small but sturdy craft that gave her wings of her own.

Amanat itself had no landing strip, but Caliane had ordered her people to create one not far from the city—a place where Jessamy could land out of sight of other human eyes. In his mother's home, she could walk in freedom. The people of Amanat were loyal to Caliane beyond anything Raphael had ever seen, would never reveal the secret of Jessamy's twisted wing.

No, he corrected himself, he'd seen such loyalty with Lijuan, too. Both archangels whose people looked to them as goddesses. The difference was that Caliane did not consume the life force of her people . . . but his mother had sung thousands of souls into slavery, and she'd once executed every adult in two neighboring cities. It had led to hundreds upon hundreds of child-sized graves, the children of the dead struck by a heart-sorrow unknown to immortals.

So perhaps Lijuan and Caliane were more alike than they knew.

Elena, her heart forever bruised from the loss of her own mother, saw Caliane's rise as a gift. Raphael's feelings were more complicated. He was glad his mother was sane again, but part of him watched always for the madness.

"It is held together by bolts and screws," Galen was muttering. "How can that be safe?"

Wrenching his mind back from thoughts of madness and murder, Raphael clapped Galen on the shoulder. "You will have to get used to it one of these days. The people who service the plane that carries my own consort on long journeys have deemed Jessamy's plane safe."

"My arms would be safer."

Listening to Galen, no one would guess that he was the one who'd placed the order for Jessamy's custom-built plane with extra cockpit space for her wings, as well as an extra-wide door for ingress and egress. Till then, Jessamy had been borrowing the far less comfortable plane of the vampire pilot who'd taught her to fly.

Another time, Raphael might've used the knowledge of

Galen's contradictory actions to nudge his weapons-master into laughter, for they were not simply liege and warrior, but today, tension knotted his tendons and crackled through his veins, his eyes drawn toward Sara and Deacon's home. He hadn't realized how often he and Elena spoke mind-to-mind until he could no longer reach the steel and wildness of her.

Reminding himself of the silent message she'd given him about this night, he took a sip of the twenty-five-year-old Scotch that Galen had brought as a gift. It had no impact on his archangelic system, but the complex and smooth taste was pleasing. "Did you notice anything else while you were in the region?"

"Yes," Galen said, his eyes on a small squadron of angels silhouetted against the glittering nightscape of Manhattan, on their way to relieve the guards at the lava sinkhole. "Lady Caliane says that a number of vampires and angels previously resident in China have resettled in Japan."

"Is Favashi playing power games?" If so, it was an act of true madness. Caliane was an Ancient content with a tiny territory *and* who'd offered Favashi her assistance. A young archangel struggling to enforce her rule over a large territory could ask for no better ally.

But Galen shook his head. "Caliane's people weave like smoke through the landscape, and, per their reports, these new residents are scared, their only aim to move out of Favashi's sphere of influence."

Raphael knew a significant number of strong angels and vampires who'd once served Caliane had quietly resettled in Japan after fulfilling their obligations under any contracts they'd signed in her absence. An archangel's madness could be forgotten with far more ease by her warriors and courtiers than by the son she'd left broken and bleeding on a lonely field far from help.

"Leaving aside the age and strength of those who oversee various parts of Japan for my mother, Caliane is far more terrifying in power than Favashi."

"But Lady Caliane is gentle with the people under her care," Galen said, for he had only ever known *this* Caliane.

Raphael's weapons-master had not yet been born when Caliane's madness painted Raphael's world in pain. "Her punishments can be harsh, yes," Galen continued, "but she only ever metes them out when the crime deserves it. She does not seek to seed fear in the veins of those who call her their liege."

That, too, was true. Prior to her madness, Caliane had run a stable and peaceful territory renowned for its art and its scientific discoveries, her court a place that often hosted other archangelic guests. "Elijah has told me of empty towns and villages, where it appears the residents abandoned their lives and left without warning."

"Such can't be explained by the immigrants." Galen's brow was heavy. "Their numbers are limited—and it's not poor mortal or vampiric villagers who have moved in. These are people with wealth and power enough to get out without being noticed."

Jason, he said to his spymaster. *Will you join us?* He had no interest in Favashi's games right now, not with one of Elena's feathers lying healthy and shedded in his pocket, but those games could not be ignored.

Archangels who destabilized could take down millions with them.

When Galen filled in Jason—Raphael had already told him of Elijah's news—the spymaster said, "I will return to that corner of the world." His face gave nothing away. "I focused on gaining as much information about her army as I could. Clearly there are more shadows I need to penetrate."

"You have just come home after a long sojourn, Jason." His spymaster had walked alone for hundreds of years, even in the midst of the Seven, his aloneness a ghost he couldn't shake. It had taken a princess from Neha's court to pierce the veil.

"Mahiya will understand." Light and shadow played over the curves and dots of the tattoo that marked his face. "Whatever is occurring in China, it could have implications for the entire world."

"Elijah's consort is reaching out to Favashi," Raphael

told Galen, having already shared the same with Jason. "Her goal is to get an invitation to visit Favashi's court. Should Hannah succeed, she and Elijah would be right in the heart of Favashi's territory."

A cascade of whispers at the back of Raphael's mind, hundreds of bat-winged beings settling on the buildings around the Tower, hundreds of gargoyles peering at them in interest.

"Sire." Venom came to stand with Raphael as Galen and Jason stepped away to talk. "I know they are your Legion, but they are also creepy as hell."

"That is very amusing coming from you," Raphael said to this member of his Seven who enjoyed using his slitted viper's gaze to disconcert and, at times, frighten.

"But there's only one of me—imagine over seven hundred vampires with viper eyes staring at you."

"You make an excellent point."

Beside him, his eyes unshielded among friends, Venom raised his glass toward the Primary, who'd landed directly across from them. "Would you like a drink?"

Taking his words as an invitation, the Primary came to crouch on the small wall that edged the roof. When Illium walked over with a tumbler full of amber liquid, he took it.

As they watched, he sniffed it several times then drank the entire thing down in a single movement. Placing the glass on the roof wall beside him afterward, he said, "This is a thing I have tasted before." As if he'd logged the experience against the millions of memories in his mind.

With that, he opened his silent wings and flew off to join his brethren on the buildings around the Tower. All those buildings were considerably shorter, but the attraction for the Legion was clearly the Tower roof.

They were there two hours later, when the night sky began to crack with gold. The lightning was silent and uncanny and beautiful. The white-gold filaments in Raphael's wings vibrated in time with the strange lightning . . . and the sky, it was golden fire.

The thought raised every hair on Raphael's arms. He'd

last seen a sky full of golden fire as a youth, when Caliane
executed Nadiel. The death of Raphael's father—of an
archangel—had released energy so violent that it had scarred
Laric through time.

His mind reached out, searched. *Elena.*

Silence.

A searing star above him. All that golden lightning co-
alescing into a single spot directly above Raphael. Flaring
out his wings, he flew up while ordering the winged members of his Seven to stay down. This, he knew, was not a
thing that could be dealt with by angels.

It was a thing for an archangel.

But as he flew up, he turned in the direction of the
rooftop that belonged to Sara and Deacon, and though his
hunter was too far for him to see, he knew she'd taken off
and was flying toward him. This was not a thing for angels,
only for an archangel . . . but he waited for her to make her
way to him.

Aeclari, sang the Legion. *Aeclari.*

Then she was there, breathless and with her gray eyes
stark against the lightning-lit dark gold of her skin.

Taking her into his arms, he said, "Close your wings,
hbeebti."

She did so without hesitation, her trust a gift.

Holding her close, he lifted them both into the burn of
light.

It cascaded into him in a thousand tiny lightning bolts
that sparked through his skin and wings. Elena, though she
was pressed against him, was touched by none of it. He was
the lightning rod and the energy knew to come only to him.

His hunter traced a jagged crack in the skin of his upper
arm. It was what had happened to Illium when the Cascade
shoved him full of power too huge for his body. Unlike with
the blue-winged angel, Raphael was in no danger of being
overwhelmed or killed. "It causes me no pain." As one
fracture healed, another appeared. But his cells were ab-
sorbing the power as rapidly as it jolted out of the sky and
into him.

He felt full to the very edges of his wings by the time the storm ended.

Elena stared at his face, her eyes a mirror of the incandescent light. "It's beautiful in an eerie way," she murmured. "Your face is covered with fine lightning-bolt cracks that glow with power." She raised a hand to his skin but didn't touch. As if afraid of hurting him.

He moved his face so that her fingers brushed his jaw. "There is no pain," he repeated. "The power simply needs time to be absorbed into my flesh."

When Elena drew away her hand, her fingertips glowed with light. Rather than seeking to sink into her, however, that light flew back to him, golden dandelions against the night. Undaunted, she brushed her fingers over his arm where the light glowed through the cracks in his skin. That light reached out and twined around her hand, crawled up her arm.

Raphael watched ready to intervene, but at no point did it merge into her skin.

Instead, after a moment, it drew back toward Raphael.

"This energy is too strong for you," he told his hunter. "It is archangelic and it stretches my power to places unknown." He could feel himself changing on the most basic level, his cells altering shape. It had happened once before, but this . . . it was bigger, the changes deeper.

A fine tension in Elena's features. "So much power, Raphael." She spread her fingers over his heart. "Promise me you won't stop being a little bit mortal."

Closing a hand alive with golden lightning over hers, he spoke an unalterable truth. "My heart will always be a little bit mortal, this I promise." He could feel the wildfire born of them both concentrating around the organ, as if protecting it from the surge of Cascade-born power, protecting the small vulnerability Elena had introduced into his archangelic body.

"This new power will soon learn that some things are set in stone." Right now, it was a thing without shape, unimprinted by any living being.

It was pure, raw energy.

Elena's pupils flared. "The voice told me of a gift and that it wasn't meant for me," she whispered, her free hand caressing the side of his face. "It must've meant it could only be handled by an archangel."

Cupping her cheek, Raphael lowered his head to claim a kiss that glowed with light. Her lips were rimmed with it when he drew back, but again, the energy returned to him after a moment.

He tried to funnel the energy into her through his healing ability.

"Raphael." A gasp. "Pinpricks all over me. Sharp, hard."

He stopped his attempt, coldly enraged at being given such power but being helpless to protect his warrior. "I was seeking to use the new power to fix the unknown problem with your feathers. This energy is pure; I should be able to reshape it as I wish." Including changing it into a form that healed. "I wasn't attempting to give you the pure power—that's too violent, would kill you. I was filtering it through my ability to heal."

"Oh," Elena whispered. "*This* is the gift . . . and it's not mine." A crooked smile. "Don't you see, Archangel? I'm too mortal now. My body can no longer absorb any immortal energy. Even Nisia failed this afternoon—digesting archangelic energy is far beyond my grasp."

They stared at one another, the truth of her words a slap. "That is impossible," Raphael ground out. "You have wings."

"A slowly failing relic of my brush with immortality." Somber knowledge on her face. "We can check with Lucius, but I know. I'm weaker again, my body is having trouble supporting the weight of wings, and I can't heal even a hangnail."

Raphael realized on a roar of rage that his new power could only hurt her, hurt the one being in all the universe whom he never wanted to hurt. Lightning cracked the sky again, his power threatening to break the universe.

36

Elena gripped his hair and hauled his face to her own, pulling him back from the edge of the abyss. "Don't you dare give in to the darkness," she ordered. "This energy is yours. Shape it to your will. Don't let it shape you."

And he saw at last what she already had—if he wasn't careful, the Cascade surge would alter him to its own design. "No one," he said coldly, "manipulates an archangel."

Elena's smile was fierce, his consort well aware he wasn't speaking to her. "The voice said the second marker is a painful rebirth . . . and isn't it strange, how the power surge occurred when Jessamy is in the city? Do you think this energy could heal her?"

"If it is a marker—"

Elena pressed her fingers to his lips. "We fight destiny other ways. We don't attempt to nullify this marker . . . and it's only a marker. Whether it takes place or not, events continue."

Raphael fought his black rage to say, "I will wait for you and Jessamy to return."

"Laric is in the city, too." She frowned. "He qualifies as well as her, if I'm reading the prophecy right."

"I'll speak to him."

"What about Vivek?" she asked, and he could feel her hope.

"This power is too strong. It would burn out a vampiric body." Raphael tried to think of others, not only of her. "He will recover, Elena. Unlike with Laric and Jessamy, all Vivek needs is time."

"Yes, you're right." She claimed a kiss, as was her right as his lover and consort. "See you soon, Archangel." Grin wild, she brushed her hand over the mark on one side of his temple, the mark of the Legion. "And after, we'll plot how to foil destiny and a prophecy spoken by an archangel who saw me at the dawn of time."

A small cloud of light glowed through her own clothing before he could release her for flight. It came from the spot where she'd felt the pain in her chest, but this time, she didn't collapse.

"Whoa." Unzipping her jacket, she pulled up the top she wore underneath to expose that patch of skin. It was the merest pinprick of smudged light, and it settled into her skin even as they watched, but what it left behind was a small darkness in the shape of the Legion mark on his temple. But where his mark crackled with light, this one absorbed it.

"Huh." Elena stared at it. "Ask the Legion if they know what this is."

When Raphael did, the ancient beings said: *A dark mirror.* Whispers in his head, the Legion in conversation. *Not our mark. Your mark. It is a mirror.* A sense of a huge mind straining. *Aeclari are . . . mirrors. They are more. But they are also mirrors.*

Raphael's heart accelerated. After sharing with Elena their first piece of concrete information about what *aeclari* meant, he asked, *Is this as it should be?*

No, came the storm of voices. *The mirror should not be dark. This mirror is wrong.* Agitation in the Legion mind. *This becoming is wrong.*

Elena's face stilled when he repeated that unequivocal response. "A mirror," she whispered. "To reflect power back to you, maybe magnify it?"

He thought of how the wildfire came from both of them, and said, "Perhaps."

"It explains why all my problems are concentrated on the left." She touched her fingers to his right temple. "Mirror images."

Raphael wasn't thinking with enough clarity to have seen that. His head rang with the Legion's cry that this mirror was wrong, Elena's becoming was *wrong*.

"But this mirror absorbs light," she said, her brain working better than his. "And my body isn't magnifying your power, it's just rejecting it. It makes no sense."

Comprehension cut through the chaos and he understood what the Legion were telling him. "This mark"—he ran his fingers over the lightless black of it—"is a brand. Mine on your flesh."

Scowling, Elena tugged and zipped her clothing back into place. "Fucking Cascade needs to learn I'm not a cow, to be branded. And what's the point anyway, if I'm mortal?"

"This isn't over yet." Raphael kissed her hard. "I will find a way to erase the brand."

A smile full of teeth, followed by a kiss as possessive as his own. "On the other hand, I suppose it's fair, since you wear mine." Her gaze went to the starburst pattern on his left wing, where she'd shot him once. "And look, we screwed up the mirror image thing there."

In her wild smile, he found reality again, the Cascade-born power no longer swamping his senses. He had it held tightly in his fist now, under his control and beyond the Cascade's ability to shape. "I suppose you will say you shot me in preparation for this moment."

She laughed, the rising night winds whipping her hair from its braid to stream around them. And in her face, he saw bones too close to the surface once more, saw too the small break in the skin of her neck that hadn't been there when she first flew to him.

And when Elena fell from his arms with a sound of joy
to flare out her wings, two feathers of indigo blue fluttered
silently to the earth.

"**W**ill you tell me what you saw up in the sky with Raphael?" Jessamy asked Elena as they rode up in the Tower
elevator. "I won't put it down in any official record until you
tell me it's time."

"Yes," Elena said, her throat rough. She'd never forget
the heartbreaking rage in Raphael's eyes when he realized
he couldn't heal her. *Fuck fate!* She refused to sit back
and let the Cascade screw up her archangel into some
twisted bitterness haunted by watching his consort die
mortal and wingless.

It is foretold, child, whispered the old, old voice in her
head. *One must die for the other to live.*

Elena stared into the endless golden eyes of the owl that
hovered in front of her. *Why can you talk to me when Raphael can't? Is it because this is a waking dream?*

He is altered, as you are altered. You must . . . A deep
stirring. *But you do not have time. One must die. You
must die.*

*Yeah, well, I'm not convinced on the whole predesti-
nation thing. Forget one to die for one to live. I and this
unknown other will both live.*

The owl tilted its head to the side. *Child of change. You
alter the fabric of the universe.* A sense of waking in the
voice that was Cassandra's, an old being disturbed in her
Sleep. *You rewrite time.*

The doors opened and the owl flew out, to disappear into
the distance.

Elena smiled deeply within. So, she could rewrite what
was foretold. Good to fucking know—because she had no
plans of being a meek lamb led to the slaughter. She walked
through the open door of her and Raphael's suite on that
vow. Her archangel was overflowing with golden energy—
though it wasn't as obvious as it had been in the cold night

sky. The lightning-bolt cracks were thinner, the energy a shimmer of light against his skin and wings rather than an inferno.

Galen stood with his hands on his hips, talking to Raphael. The weapons-master's expression changed the instant he spotted Jessamy. It didn't go soft—Galen was too rough and tough, but it turned gentle in a way that it only ever did for Jessamy. He held out his hand, and she walked across to take it.

The first thing he did was unhook her cloak and throw it aside.

The pale blue of Jessamy's simple but elegant gown skimmed her slender form to froth at her ankles, soft waves crashing to shore. The historian pressed a tender kiss to Galen's cheek. Her twisted wing overlapped by his, she looked at Raphael with eyes soft in wonder. "May I?" She lifted a hand.

At Raphael's nod, she released Galen's hand to reach over and brush her fingers over part of Raphael's forearm. Curious, Elena watched. But when Jessamy raised her fingers, no light came with her.

"Ellie," she said. "You do it."

Elena stroked the same part of his arm, the warmth and heat and strength of him sinking into her and making her smile even in the midst of the continuing madness. Her fingertips glowed when they lifted off his skin. Pursing her lips, she blew the light back into him. The flickers flew like fireflies to become a part of him once more.

Raphael stroked his hand over the arch of her wing. "It knows who you are to me." Unsaid was the angry coda: it didn't matter if his power accepted her if it couldn't help her.

God, he was *so* angry. This could ruin him if they didn't figure out a way through it. She hoped he was able to help Jessamy—that might take the edge off his rage. "Jess," she said quietly. "Raphael is overflowing with power."

A moment of incomprehension before Jessamy's face went still.

Galen strode forward at the same instant. "Sire." His

hands were fisted, his shoulders rigid. "The decision has been made."

Elena didn't try to get in the middle of that conversation—this was between an archangel and one of his loyal Seven. Raphael had attempted, if not to heal, then at least to ease Jessamy's twisted wing before. However, his healing power hadn't been able to affect the malformation that kept Jessamy bound to the ground except when she flew up in the plane or in Galen's arms.

"I will honor that wish." Raphael closed his hand over Galen's shoulder and squeezed. "But I would not be your archangel if I did not offer you this chance."

Jessamy spoke for the first time since Elena's words. "Laric?"

"He was caught in the energy released by the death of an archangel," Raphael said. "According to Keir's tests, his cells have altered in unusual ways that make those cells unlike ordinary angelic cells. It has also made them unrecognizable to my power—that may change as he grows older and his own healing processes restart, but for now, I can do nothing for him."

Raphael's eyes began to glow. Not only the cerulean blue that was his own but a ring of golden light that hadn't existed prior to the energy surge. "The choice is yours."

Jessamy ran her hand down Galen's arm to his bunched hand. Unfurling it at her touch, he locked his fingers with hers. "What will happen to the power if I say no?"

"I do not know. It doesn't feel too much for me, so it may simply stay until I use it. Or it may dissipate."

Power enough to shatter the night and he wasn't overwhelmed. No wonder Cassandra said he was changed—but he was guiding that change now, shaping it to his will. Yet Elena still felt a jagged rock in her gut . . . because what if the worst happened? Would Raphael fight the Cascade forces then? Or would he allow those forces to shape him into a cold and ruthless immortal untouched by mortal vulnerability?

Jessamy turned to Galen and put her free hand on his

chest. Elena and Raphael both stepped away as the couple spoke in low voices tense with withheld emotion.

"What if we're doing the wrong thing, Archangel?" Elena asked out of earshot of the other couple, suddenly afraid. Not only would a failure hurt Jessamy, it would be another darkness whispering to Raphael.

Eyes inhuman with power held hers, and when he spoke, his voice was different. Heavy with archangelic power. He sounded more like the archangel she'd first met than he had in years. But the words he spoke, they were her Raphael's. "Hunter-mine. To not make the attempt would be a disservice to Jessamy. Especially after I could do nothing the first time we attempted to ease the malformation so it would not ache."

Until then, Elena hadn't known that Jessamy's wing caused her physical discomfort. Not on a daily basis, and the pain was a dull throb rather than a sharp stab that made her cry out, but the muscles did spasm and lock up at times. The historian had described it as a bad cramp—to Elena, that would be an awful pain, but Jessamy had become accustomed to it over the centuries and centuries of her existence.

She didn't seem to understand what that said about her strength, this slender woman who was no warrior and who, to this day, tried to avoid the fighting lessons Galen gave her so she would never be helpless against an opponent.

"Sire." Stiff but resigned, Galen's voice split the heavy silence. "Jessamy wishes to try."

Raphael moved around to Jessamy's back without further discussion—and that, too, was different. The Raphael she loved would've said something to reassure his weapons-master. Or maybe she was just jumpy and Raphael was too concerned with reigning in this wild power to waste his energies on anything that wasn't strictly necessary.

"I need you to spread your wings as far as possible," he ordered Jessamy.

One strong wing whispered out in a glow of delicate magenta and luscious cream against the pale sky-blue of Jessamy's gown. The other stayed close to her back, the bones, muscles, and tendons formed wrong and unable to stretch outward.

Elena and Galen both moved so they could see what Raphael was doing, one on his left, the other on his right.

"Describe it to me," Jessamy said with the frustration of a historian missing out on what might be the making of a piece of angelic history.

"The sire is staring at your back," Galen muttered bad temperedly. "If I didn't know that he was madly in love with Elena, I'd have to thump him for looking at you with such intensity."

Jessamy's laughter was a warm, gentle thing.

"His hands are full of light now," Elena murmured. "It's like the lightning we saw from Sara's roof, not the blue of his usual healing energy." Her heart thundered at seeing the violence of it, quite unlike the delicate dandelions that had floated back to him. "Archangel?"

"Sire, that is archangelic energy meant to level cities and battle others of the Cadre," Galen said harshly at the same time.

"Yes," Raphael said in a distant tone, "but it is also mine to mold."

In front of them, the lightning became shot with streaks of healing blue. Elena shuddered inwardly at the sign that he continued to carry a touch of mortality, a touch of humanity. He'd always said that his ability to heal came from his love for her and how it had changed him on a fundamental level.

"Someone tell me what's happening."

Elena responded to Jessamy's demand. Galen was too focused on Raphael's hands, his big body all but vibrating in readiness. And Elena knew that if he thought Raphael was hurting Jessamy, he'd unsheathe his broadsword and take on an archangel himself.

"The light coming off Raphael is almost too much to look through now." Elena's eyes teared even though she'd narrowed them as much as she could without totally cutting off her sight. "He's moving his hands closer to your wing."

She blinked away the tears. "The energy's touching you. Small lightning bolts arcing against your wing."

"I can't feel the touch," Jessamy said, attempting to look over her shoulder.

"Be still."

Jessamy went motionless at the command, and Raphael— Everything blurred in an incandescence of overwhelming gold, light sparking behind Elena's lids as she instinctively closed her eyes. When she opened them back up a milli-second later, the light was retracting back into Raphael, sucked in until it no longer lay like a second skin on his arms and his hair and his eyes.

The breaks in his skin sealed up in front of her gaze.

Elena jerked her attention to Jessamy's wing. Disap-pointment slammed her in the gut, an ugly two-fisted blow. It was exactly as it had been, and she saw from the angry sadness on Galen's face that he was an inch away from punching Raphael.

About to tug away her archangel so the weapons-master could focus on his beloved Jessamy, she halted at a keen of sound from the angelic historian. "It hurts."

Galen moved in a burst of raw strength, cradling her trembling form against his chest. "Where?" His voice was like stone, murder in the pale green of his eyes.

But Jessamy pushed back from his chest, her hands braced against it and her nails digging into his shirt. An-other animalistic keen of pain, a helpless creature with its limb caught in a trap.

"*Sire*, you must fix this," Galen demanded.

"It is an old and tight muscle," Raphael said with unnat-ural calm, his gaze yet intent on Jessamy's wing. "It has not been stretched in nearly three thousand years."

"Jesus." Elena saw it then, saw what was happening. "Galen, look at her wing."

37

Keeping one arm around Jessamy's waist, his features set in brutal, unforgiving lines, the weapons-master came around Jessamy's other side so that he could look at her back. The twisted part of Jessamy's wing was moving. The motion was slight, but it was *there*.

"Has it ever moved before?" Elena asked both Jessamy and Galen. "Jess, have you ever been able to manipulate that part of your wing?"

Gripping hard at Galen's forearm, Jessamy shook her head. "I can feel it now." Her words were breathless, pain dripping from each one. "Before, it was a knot. It didn't hurt except for the odd cramp, but there was no flexibility in it, either. This . . . it is the most horrifying agony I've ever experienced."

Breaking unwritten angelic law, Elena pressed a hand against Jessamy's wing on that sensitive upper section. "Stop."

"Elena," Raphael warned, even as Galen's hand rose toward her.

Elena broke contact. "Jess, really, *stop*." She fought for the words to explain. "We need to get one of Vivek's physiotherapists in here. Regardless of your final range of movement, we're talking about the rehabilitation of a part of your body that hasn't been used for close to three thousand years."

All three immortals in the room froze.

Jessamy turned to stare at her. Her eyes were dark hollows in her face, pain a purple bruise under them, and her bones striking. "Physiotherapist?" So much disbelief it was gray fog in the air. "Such practitioners are not used by angelkind."

"Um, we're not exactly in a normal situation." Honestly, angels could be aggravating at times. "Vivek goes to physiotherapy every single day, sometimes twice a day. We're talking about *exactly* the same thing here, bringing to life part of your body that hasn't been used your entire lifetime. Being an angel might mean your process moves faster, I don't know, but given your pain and the way your wing looks to the naked eye, no way can it be immediate."

"Elena is right." Gripping the back of Jessamy's neck on those surprising words, Galen pressed a kiss to her temple. "I know you are impatient, my love. But we must take this slowly."

Jessamy nodded at last, pressing her face into Galen's chest. "I can feel it," she whispered again, her voice wet. "As if I could open it if only I tried hard enough."

Galen ran his hand over her hair and tenderly across the painful wing, before looking to Raphael. "Sire . . ."

Raphael shook his head. "If you had caused Elena pain, Galen, I would've taken off your head too."

And that was that.

Elena had taken those moments to call the physiotherapist, a honey-skinned and gently muscled vampire who'd been born in what was now Vietnam four hundred years ago. As a senior member of the Tower team, Nga was fully aware of Jessamy's wing. Elena had also deliberately called her rather than her male counterpart. Galen was already at

the limit of his patience—and she didn't think Jessamy
would be as comfortable with a male, especially since the
treatment would mean hands-on contact.

When the physiotherapist arrived—dressed in sweatpants
and a fitted tank top—she listened to Elena's breakdown of
the situation before speaking. "First, we need scans of your
wing," she said directly to Jessamy. "Are there previous
scans for comparison?"

Jessamy, more in control of herself, said, "Yes."

No one was going to be sleeping tonight, and no one was
going to be waiting another day for the scan. They tracked
down a qualified vampire technician and began. The machine had been modified to accommodate an angel, but
even so, it couldn't do Jessamy's entire wing in one go.

Two hours later, they had a full scan.

Elena was no medical genius, but even she could see the
change.

In the original scan, done prior to Raphael's first attempt, the muscles and tendons and even bone of Jessamy's
wing had been locked together in what Jessamy called a
knot. It must've happened at a very early stage of growth—
everything had merged instead of separating out.

In the current scan, Elena could see the fine bones of
Jessamy's wing as separate pieces. Everything remained
bunched in, and her muscles were undoubtedly too short
after lack of use, but there were tiny particles of light in certain areas, as if those parts of the wing were attempting to
stretch out.

Nga took over at that point, guiding Jessamy through a
range of test exercises to judge her current capacity for
motion. Jessamy gritted her teeth and got through the
gentle set, but she was sweating by the time it ended. Galen managed not to intervene, though Elena could see the
muscle jumping in his jaw as he fought not to break poor
Nga in half.

"I think we can get that wing to open out, but it'll take
considerable time," the physiotherapist said in her practical

way. "You risk tearing things if you rush it—then it'll be a long recovery and we'd be starting from scratch again."

"She's saying you can't pick up a sword before you've learned to handle a knife, Jess," Galen murmured against Jessamy's temple, his body her anchor.

One arm around his waist, Jessamy swallowed. "I can't stay in New York. Vivek—"

"My partner will continue to work with him—Vivek will not begrudge you my shift in allegiance," Nga interrupted. "In fact, he has been known to call me the chief servant of Satan, so he may celebrate my departure." She turned and bowed deeply to Raphael. "If the sire authorizes it, I will return to the Refuge with Jessamy and begin to torture her instead of Vivek."

Raphael resettled his wings, but he didn't smile. "Stay as long as you need."

Galen looked at Jessamy. "Are you happy to fly a passenger?"

She smiled, though pain webbed her eyes. "This passenger, I will fly as many times as she wishes."

After Nga had left the room to put together her bag, Jessamy moved to stand in front of Raphael. "When you were a boy who would not listen to me in school, and who ran off laughing when I attempted to chastise you, I couldn't imagine that you would one day give me this gift beyond price."

Her fingers brushed his hair with the maternal gentleness of a woman who'd taught him as a child, and who saw him not only as the archangel he'd become but as the laughing boy he'd once been. "I was deeply happy with my life when I entered your suite, but this adventure will take me to new places. I wish the same wonder for you, Raphael."

Raphael gathered her into his arms, the moment poignant with a thousand unspoken emotions—and a relief to Elena. He was acting like her archangel, compassion in his heart no matter how huge his power.

She caught the feather about to slide free from her wing,

slipped it into a pocket before anyone could see. This was a moment full of light. She wouldn't mar it with shadows.

Galen and Jessamy left at dawn—as soon as Jessamy was certain the pain in her wing wouldn't hamper her ability to pilot her craft. The couple planned to stop a number of times so Jessamy could stretch out her wing according to Nga's instructions, but their goal remained to get to the Refuge as fast as safely possible.

It might take years for Jessamy's wing to fully straighten out, but as Jessamy herself had remarked, even a decade was but a moment in the span of her thousands of years of life.

"Show me," Raphael said to his consort after Galen, Jessamy, and Nga had left. He and Elena stood on the Tower roof under the painted sky of dawn, the orange-hued light coloring Elena's hair like a watercolor.

Face solemn, his consort reached into a pocket and pulled out a feather of deepest blue with the merest hint of indigo. It lay against her palm, a silent witness to her descent into mortality. Again, she angled her hand downward and let the feather dance away on the air currents.

"Spread your wings so I can assess their status." Rage continued to burn in him, a black cauldron, but it was also oddly distant, leaving his mind crystalline.

"It is not patchy," he said after a close examination, "but there are places where you now only have a single layer of feathers, with no overlap."

"Let's hope I don't lose more there. I don't want to look like a plucked chicken." Shutting her wings, she turned to face him with a ferocious expression on her face. "That power, it's doing something to you. You're *letting* it manipulate you."

"Nothing manipulates me," Raphael reiterated. "I allow it freedom because it gives me clarity." Else, he was nothing but anger under the skin, constantly fighting the urge to demolish the world.

"Bull. Shit." Elena pressed a finger into his chest. "This

reminds me of when you went into the Quiet. Not that bad, but the same scary lack of emotion."

He gripped her wrist. "I *boil* with emotion, Elena. You don't want me to set it free." Mercy would no longer live in him if he was forced to watch her die.

"Archangel." A hard shake of her head. "Don't let the Cascade steal who you are. Protect that little bit of mortality in your heart. Please."

He made her no promises he might not keep should he lose her. Inside, his cells morphed under the fury of a power that was making him stronger, more deadly.

"Argh!" Elena clenched her hand but didn't tug away her wrist. "You infuriate me at times." Her kiss was a ravaging, but she smiled when she drew back. "You're angry enough to make me afraid for you, but you still taste like my archangel." Narrowed eyes when he didn't respond, his anger at the world was so vast and deep. "I had another conversation with the voice in my head. Told it I didn't believe in the predestination crap, and that I was going to change the future."

The words reached him with their sheer impudence— only his Elena would argue with an archangel who was kin to the Ancestors. "What was the response?"

"I messed up the future timeline." A tight, satisfied smile. "I'm going to keep messing it up until we're on the other side." Challenge in her voice. "Do you see?"

"Yes." Resolve roared through him, and he wrenched the reshaping power back under his reign. "The prophecy is not set in stone. We will break it."

"Together."

Storm winds howled around them without warning.

Elena bared her teeth. "Looks like the Cascade doesn't like that."

"Fuck the Cascade." He kissed her laughter into his soul and stole some of her human warmth to heat the icy cold of the power that sought to alter him to a form that would not understand pain . . . or love.

38

When they spoke to Nisia, it was only to check if Elena could still fly.

The resulting scan showed a subtle weakness in the under-structure of Elena's wings.

"They're weak but won't collapse," Nisia reassured Elena. "I will confirm with Keir, but this is likely what your wings looked like when you first took flight."

Elena's eyes locked with Raphael's, and in her gaze lived the knowledge that one more step backward and she'd lose her wings, be earthbound once more. "I have to finish the investigation on Harrison," she said with quiet determination once Nisia left the room, as if they had been in the middle of a conversation. "I need to know my sister and her child are safe."

Even drenched in immortal power so violent that the small touch of human vulnerability in his heart threatened to be subsumed by it, Raphael understood her nightmares, understood why this was so important to her. Beth had lost nearly everyone she loved as a child. Only Elena and Jeffrey remained.

And Elena's body was shedding its immortality.

"Finish it," he said. "You have my wings and my hands. Use them and finish it." Lightning crackled over Raphael's skin as he curled his hands into fists. His skin split and closed in fine fractures.

His hunter walked to him. "Black clouds, darkness, it's all gathering on the horizon." A glance at the turbulence beyond the Tower windows. "If the omens were any more obvious, we'd be beating them off with a sharp stick." She ran her hand firmly over the arch of his wing in a caress he'd permit no one else on this earth. "I know the promise we made, but I'm asking you not to keep it—if the worst happens, if I fall, you can't fall with me."

Raphael set his jaw. "You'd sentence me to eternity alone?" The lightning crackled over him again and again, the Legion mark on his temple brilliant with wildfire, until the space around them was blurred out by his power.

Elena stood unafraid in the midst of the storm. "You're a burning sword, Raphael, a creature of endless light." His energy twined up her arm, sparked in her hair, slid down the curve of her cheek. "If you fall, the world will stand no chance when Lijuan rises."

A sudden, luminous gold in her eyes.

"Archangel of Death," she whispered. "Goddess of Nightmare. Wraith without a shadow. Rise, rise, rise into your Reign of Death."

Raphael's power spiraled around her body.

"For your end will come." Elena's voice, Elena's touch, but not Elena's words. "Your end will come. At the hands of the new and of the old." Tears shimmered in her eyes now. "An Archangel kissed by mortality." Her lips pressing to his. "A silver-winged Sleeper who wakes before his Sleep is done. The broken dream with eyes of fire. Shatter. Shatter. Shatter."

Elena's breath on his skin, her eyes no longer unearthly

gold. "This she saw," she said, her voice a rasp. "The old one in my head. Cassandra. She saw this long, long ago."

Cassandra.

Seer of nightmares and dreams, haunted by visions.

"Do you see, Raphael?" Elena raised her head to meet his gaze. "Come what may, you *must* live until Lijuan is vanquished, or her reign will murder this world and rewrite it in her image. Death and horror, that's what our world will become."

Raphael gripped both her upper arms, nearly lifting her off her feet. "How can I be kissed by mortality if you are not with me? I feel the power fighting to change me already—without you, I'll sink into the cold arms of immortality until the Raphael you know is gone forever." He and his Elena, they had been together for a firefly flicker of time, at the bare edge of their immortality together. Not enough time. *Never* enough time.

"No." A single firm word. "No matter what, you'll stay my Raphael." A war in every word. "You won't let eternity or Lijuan steal the humanity in your heart. You *will* protect that part of me you carry in you. Promise me this, Raphael. *Promise.*"

"We will alter destiny and you will live, Elena," he said flatly. "That is the only option."

A jagged smile. "I'm not about to give up, Archangel, but I'm also not arrogant enough to think it'll be a slam dunk against forces that wrenched Cassandra from her Sleep." A kiss so wild that their wings became entangled, their breaths one, his hand buried in her hair, hers bunched in his tunic. "Promise me."

"No." Raphael would give Elena anything on this earth, but he would not promise to be whole should she fall. "It would be a lie. I will become a monster without you." This new Cascade-born power was too huge to allow for anything else; he could see how Lijuan had fallen to its seduction. It made a man feel good, his mind a vastness untrammeled by the physical.

Elena was the heart of them, the one who reminded him

to never surrender to the seduction. For to surrender would be to lose her, lose the piece of her he carried protected inside his own heart. But when she was gone, no one would love him so fiercely that it was a force larger than the Cascade. No one would anchor him to life with the wildfire of her own. No one would teach him to be human. "Better I break than I become as Lijuan."

A shudder ran through her at his uncompromising words. "Then," she said, spine going stiff and face stubborn, "we figure out how to give the Cascade an ass-kicking." Hauling him down with two hands bunched in his tunic, she said, "I am *not* leaving you to turn into a bad movie villain with a thwarted love in his past."

Raphael didn't smile, couldn't smile, the coldness in him the spaces between stars. "I will undo the universe for you." Tear it to pieces, leave it as broken as his heart would be if he didn't have Elena. "Tell Cassandra I don't believe in the predestination crap, either."

The geothermal field that shouldn't exist erupted into life two minutes later.

"Destiny is fighting back," Elena said when Dmitri briefed them on the showers of lava and heated rocks.

"It's building," Raphael's second said, his tone dark. "The team on duty is attempting to contain it, but the energy is too catastrophic."

Raphael's hand fisted at his side. "It attempts to separate us," he said to Elena, while Dmitri looked from one to the other with a frown.

"Maybe," Elena said, "but neither one of us can just ignore this when our people are fighting for their lives." She pressed her palm over his heart again. "I can't come with you." She was too weak, would be a liability. "And you're too scary to come along with me anyway—my informants would expire on the spot."

She had to ensure he didn't start making the wrong choices, didn't start falling into the chill of immortality devoid of a little human vulnerability. "Go, do what's right. Save those who look to us for safety." Lowering her voice, she added, "The final marker is the last feather to fall. I have a lot of feathers left. I can't lose them all in a day."

Raphael's face was like granite.

"Raphael." She shook her head. "We are who we are. What is the use of surviving if we become monsters?"

It was the echo of his own words that fractured the granite. He left her with a kiss that seared her with its love and admonished her with its fury, flying to contain a disaster that needed archangelic power. Her own task was smaller, more intimate, relating only to a single broken family, but she had to finish it.

After that, she'd worry about lava and ice storms and geothermal fields.

She took three of the Legion with her, her first destination a rooftop not far from the Tower. She landed near a familiar food cart—and when she saw strands of the white not-lint on the back of her hand, she rubbed it off with a single hard brush.

With the rooftop currently clear of customers, the owner of the cart grinned at her. "Cream cheese bagel?"

"I'll never say no." Her hunger had returned overnight, was an even more vicious gnawing than before.

"You lost weight. Getting too skinny."

"You think these wings move themselves?" she said with an inner melancholy.

"Eat more bagels," Piero said. "Imma gonna put extra cream cheese on this for you."

Accepting the treat he held out, Elena bit in then walked with the short, solid man to take a seat on one of the wide benches placed near the right edge of the roof. "How are you?" she asked, because to help her sister, she had to be human.

"Can't complain." His black curls shiny with hair product atop a cleanly shaven face with cold-reddened cheeks, Piero waved off the money she dug out from her pocket. "Least I can do is spot you a bagel now and then when you gave me a loan after no one else would. My old lady can't believe I've gone legit, become a real-deal businessman."

Neither could Elena, but it appeared to be true. "You said you had something for me."

"I put out my feelers, like." After first offering to pour her a lidful, he took a swig from a thermos of hot coffee. "You know about those two vamp hookers whose brains went kapow?"

Same old sensitive Piero. "Uh-huh," she said around the last of the bagel.

"Them two pros worked the Quarter exclusive-like, didn't step out of it." He screwed on the lid of his thermos after a satisfied belch. "I've got friends there. Most of 'em don't see the appeal of going legit." A shrug. "What can you do? I tell them to keep me out of the shit, and we can stay on being friends."

"What did your friends pass on?"

"Word in the low-bucks 'vampire set,'" Piero said, "is that that Nishant Kumar dickweed had a hard-on for 'nice' young women—from good families, like. Once he had 'em, he liked to mess them up in the head until they started walking the streets."

From his sour expression, Piero found that execrable behavior—probably because the reason for his turnaround from crook to cart owner was an orphaned eleven-year-old sister who had only Piero for family now. His "old ladies" tended to come and go. "Pros were to fill in the gaps if he couldn't find a good girl who'd gone off the tracks." A scowl. "Girls, you gotta work so hard to keep 'em safe."

A faint tug at the back of Elena's mind. She frowned, couldn't quite grab hold of it. "You in debt for this intel?" Nothing was free in the gray underground.

A glint in Piero's eye, but he resisted his inner thief. "Nah, fuckers gave me a freebie because they're always coming up here and eating my bagels. Like bagels grow on trees." Another grin. "Assholes are my friends, though, and they're good to my kid sister, too. Bring her presents and shit. So we're square."

"Your friends have any details of the girls he might've targeted?"

Piero shook his head. "No one pays attention to the chicks, you know. Revolving door in the Quarter." His tone wasn't uncaring, just practical. "But my buddies said there was this one father who went after another of your vics. Would've been like a year back."

Elena frowned. "What?"

"Yeah, exactly what I said. Why go after this Blakely character when Kumar was the one aiming to turn good girls bad? Boys say it's because Kumar passed on his girls to Blakely. He didn't like them after they weren't so shiny, but Blakely got off on chicks who were broken."

Elena wanted to murder both men herself. If not for the threat against Beth and Maggie, she'd say good luck to the assailant and leave him be. "So one girl had a father who came after her?"

"Yeah, bashed Blakely up pretty good." Sincere approval in Piero's tone. "Man hauled his daughter out of there, too—parents who care don't hardly show, so yeah, folks *did* notice."

A jolt of adrenaline, the connections all falling into place . . . while something stayed stubbornly out of reach. What was she forgetting? *A year ago*, Piero had said. She knew something important that had happened a year ago.

"Girl's dad was human." Piero rubbed his hands together, his breath fogging the air. "Shocker, right? I mean, this Blakely prick was a vampire. Word is the girl's father turned him into hamburger even though he had that druggie vamp friend of his around."

Elena whistled through her teeth. "Anything else on the father?"

"One badass motherfucker, that's what my friends told me. No one saw his face. He ambushed Blakely at night, while the creep was in bed with the girl." Going a little green, he quickly unscrewed the lid of his thermos and took another gulp.

"Man, that had to be tough," he said after the coffee hit. "I hope to God my sister doesn't grow up to sleep with assholes." He crossed his chest, the words a prayer. "I'd probably end up in prison for life."

Bagel finished and her stomach quiet for the moment, Elena stared into the distance, trying to catch that whisper at the back of her mind, but it remained elusive. "That all?" she asked Piero.

"Nah, I wouldn't call you over unless I had solid stuff." Rich brown eyes gleamed as he dropped his voice. "Word is there was another girl in the apartment the night the father came looking for his daughter. She did a runner when the human went psycho on Blakely Sack O' Shit and his druggie roommate."

Elena sat up straight. "Tell me you have a name for her."

Piero beamed so hard his face would crack if he wasn't careful. "China. On account of her skin being like that fancy stuff they use to make teacups and shit." He twisted up his face. "I can't see it, not in the Quarter. Even vamps show damage, and this girl's human. But my one buddy swore to it on his dear departed ma's life. Says China's got perfect skin and big blue eyes, black hair cut like this." He scissored his fingers across his forehead. "Real doll-like."

"You know where she is now?"

He pulled out a wrinkled piece of notepaper from his pocket and handed it to her. "Never say Piero doesn't pay his debts."

"Consider this month's loan repayment done."

A gleeful rub of his hands. "Pleasure doing business with you."

Not in a mood to smile, Elena memorized the address before shoving the paper into her pocket.

"Hey, wow, can I take those?" Peiro sounded like he was going to explode.

A knot in her gut, Elena didn't want to look down, didn't want to see.

39

Three of her feathers lay on the fine layer of snow that glittered on the roof. Shimmering indigo fading into dawn. Deepest black. A charcoal gray with indigo edges she hadn't even realized she had in her wings. No primaries, but three large feathers at once was bad.

"Yeah," she said, her voice rough. "Sure. Try to sell the three together—collection will get you more than if you separate them out." Especially since she wasn't going to have any soon.

"You want a cut? Forty to me, sixty to you?"

"They're all yours, Piero." Then feeling as if she might as well do something good with her decline, she took the crushed bagel wrapper, grabbed the pen from his pocket, and, smoothing out the wrapper, wrote: *I certify these feathers are mine.—Elena Deveraux.* "That should double the value."

"I'm gonna buy a lottery ticket today," Piero said as he scooped up the feathers, tears in his eyes. "It's my lucky day! And you got free bagels for life!" he called out after her as she swept off the roof.

Her wings were so heavy. Her shoulders ached. Pushing the sensations to the back of her mind, she called Vivek and asked him to run a search on the address Piero had given her. "Place belongs to a senior Tower vampire," he said mere seconds later. "Hiraz Weir."

Elena frowned; she knew Hiraz. There could be nothing whatsoever suspicious in the unexpected Tower connection, or there could be something extremely suspicious. "Thanks, V." Phone safely stored, she and her Legion escort turned in the direction of Weir's residence. It proved to be the dual-level penthouse suite in a hotel that also catered to those who wished to live in serviced apartments.

After circling the modern gray brick building with large windows, Elena came to a landing on the wide balcony outside the top floor of the penthouse. The sliding glass doors were closed. Beyond them was a lounge. A woman sat on a deep blue sofa reading some type of a document.

Elena's knock made her jump, the printed pages sliding to the floor.

Huge blue eyes stared at her in frozen silence before the woman flushed and scrambled up. Her mid-thigh-length black kimono was printed with a huge tropical bird on one side; it flapped around her legs as she slid open the door. Below the kimono, she wore a thin black slip from what looked like the same collection Elena had been intending to plunder before her world went to hell.

Despite the nightwear, however, the young woman was in full makeup, her eyelashes curled to within an inch of their lives, and her lips outlined plump and red. Door open, she twisted her hands together. "He isn't home," she whispered. "I think he's at the Tower."

"I've come to see you, China."

The other woman paled impossibly further under the creamy white skin so flawless it could've been that of the doll Piero had called her. The impression was solidified by the blunt fringe that framed her face, the rest of her thick hair cut in a short and silky bob with wispy edges that suited the softness of her features.

Her body was as sensually soft, with heavy breasts, and hips that curved. A Rubens painting come to life with a modern haircut and dark green nail polish on her toes. "Am I in trouble?" Her lower lip trembled, her eyes beginning to fill with tears.

Elena couldn't tell if any of it was real, needed more time to learn China's reactions. "I only want to ask you some questions about when you lived in the Quarter."

"I don't go there anymore. Hiraz doesn't like it." She hugged her arms around herself. "He's so nice to me. I don't want to lose him." Another tremor, perhaps an act, perhaps because Hiraz was cruel, or perhaps because she *was* afraid of losing her new life.

"I'll talk to Hiraz myself," Elena reassured her. "Trust me, he won't be angry at you for helping me."

China exhaled shakily but nodded. "He's real proud of working at the Tower." She waved at the sofa. "Would you like to take a seat?" The words came out a touch hesitant, as if she were parroting words she'd never actually spoken before.

Real, Elena decided at that instant, China's reactions were real. That of a girl who'd been pulled off a hard life on the streets and into a penthouse dream, but who wasn't sure quite how to behave in this rarefied environment. "How about we walk to the kitchen and you make me a cup of coffee?"

China's face glowed from within. "Oh, sure." Wiping off the remnants of her scared tears, she bustled to the kitchen. "I love coffee." She blushed and bit down on her lower lip as she cinched the kimono tighter. "Sorry about how I'm dressed. We had a late night."

"Perils of having a vampire boyfriend."

"Exactly." A dimpled smile. "But it's so *fun* going out with him at night. No one gives me disgusting looks or tries to grab me or even whistle at me, and I can have fun without worrying." She shivered, but this time it was accompanied by a delighted little smile. "Hiraz is scary, and that protects me."

"He is scary," Elena agreed, though Hiraz was tame in comparison to Dmitri and Venom. Of course, Tower-tame equaled deadly on the streets.

"He's so sweet to me, though," China said as she put together not only fresh coffee but a plate of small cakes from a white box on the counter. "He got me these cakes this morning because he knows how much I like them. I almost don't want to become a vampire because I won't be able to eat as many cakes."

"Have you been accepted?" Elena took a cake when China held out the plate.

"Yes, I got the acceptance letter a week ago." She drew in a deep breath. "I'm *so* scared of serving the angels," she confided, "but Hiraz asked Dmitri if he could see me during my time under Contract, and Dmitri said that we could even *live* together." The joyous words were whispered. "I only have to live in my angel's household for a while, until I can discipline what Hiraz calls the blood urge."

"Have you been assigned an angel?" Most vampires didn't know till after the transition, but Hiraz would've no doubt found out. And if Dmitri had assigned this gentle creature to Andreas, Elena would cut out his heart.

"Miuxu," China said. "Hiraz said she's kind?"

Catching the upward intonation, Elena nodded. "I like her a lot." At this rate, she really would have to start being nice to Dmitri.

"Oh, I'm so happy to hear that." China dimpled again. "Anyway, after my probation time, I can come home at the end of my shift, like with a regular job. Hiraz says that some vampires take longer than others to get control, so I shouldn't worry if I don't have it at once, but I don't think it will take me so long. I'm not . . . I don't wanna get away with anything. I just wanna be strong."

There it was, the fear that haunted this woman who had seen the horrors and ugliness of the world firsthand and yet contained within her an innocence that was a quiet rebellion.

China had steel in her, though many would never see it. Just like Beth.

Finishing off the cake, Elena took a sip of the coffee China held out. "It's difficult being human in a world full of immortals and near-immortals."

"Not for you." China's smile was deep and infused with New Yorker pride. "Even before you got wings. In the Quarter, folks used to talk about some of the vamps you hauled back and I'd wonder how you did it. Most of the ones I met before Hiraz could be real mean—and they weren't even a tiny bit as powerful as he is." A sniff. "He could squash them with his little finger."

Hiraz and China were starting to sound cute enough together that it threatened to puncture Elena's dark mood. "I have a feeling you'll make a wonderful vampire." As long as nothing went wrong in the process, she'd probably come out of it as sweet as she'd gone in. "Is it okay if I ask my questions?"

China nodded though her fingers were crushing her coffee cup. "I don't like to think about that time." A soft confession. "I got turned out on the streets at fourteen by my stepbrother. Fresh meat, you know." She shrugged, dipping her head so that her hair slid forward to hide her expression. "It was bad."

The simplicity of the description only made the horror of it worse. "You should be proud of coming out on the other side with your personality and your gentleness intact."

China's eyes were unbearably vulnerable when she raised her head. "When I couldn't take it anymore, I went inside my head, so I didn't have to be in my body."

Elena thought of a ten-year-old girl surrounded by the mutilated pieces of her sisters' bodies, of a teenager who dreamed of drowning in blood. "Sometimes, it's the only way to fight."

"He's not mean, my Hiraz," China whispered. "Tough,

but not mean." A hesitation. "He calls me by my real name. The one my mom gave me."

Wanting to kick herself, Elena said, "I'm sorry, I should have asked." Of course China was a working name, one likely chosen by the stepbrother—a moniker to advertise her looks. "I'd like to call you by that name, if you're happy to share it."

A trembling smile. "Jenessa. Jeni for short."

"Nice to meet you, Jeni."

The other woman laughed softly before taking a big gulp of her coffee and squaring her shoulders. "Okay, ask me."

When Elena led her back to the incident in question, Jenessa's eyes widened. "Yes, I remember! Oh, I remember everything!"

Startled, Elena put down her coffee. "Why was it such a memorable night for you?"

"Because that's when I met *him*." Smiles on top of smiles. "I was running and running, and I ran in front of his car and it nearly hit me before he managed to stop. I was so scared I couldn't run anymore and my heart was pounding and I thought for sure that he was going to smack me around for nearly putting a dent in his car."

Another gulp of coffee before she continued her rapid-fire story. "But he *didn't*. He asked me why I was crying, and when I told him, he put me in his car and we drove back to the apartment to check if Lucy was all right. But only Eric was there when we reached it, and he was unconscious. One of the neighbors said the man who'd beaten up Simon had taken Lucy with him."

Lucy.

Elena's blood buzzed. "Can you tell me about Lucy?"

Jenessa nodded. "We met on the street. We even shared a small apartment for a while after she first came to the Quarter. But . . . Lucy liked drugs." Her fingers clenched around the empty mug. "My stepbrother banned me from taking drugs when my skin started to attract customers with money, and after he was gone, I'd seen how bad it could get, and I stayed clean."

"But Lucy did drugs? Cocaine?"

Jenessa nodded, her hair a glossy shade of purplish black Holly would appreciate. "There was this one vampire who'd give her coke if she'd do stuff with him and his friend." She shuddered. "Both creeps. Both into sick stuff. I never went with them—my stepbrother got knifed in a fight when I was nineteen, and I had a few regulars who agreed to pay me twenty-five extra a month so I wouldn't have to work the streets and risk having my skin torn up."

A hard swallow. "I didn't know how to do anything else."

Jenessa had ducked her head through the entire latter part of her statement, shame thick in the words. Elena wanted to reach across and hug her, but after knowing Aodhan, she made no assumptions about touch. "You survived and your piece of shit stepbrother is dead. Makes you the smarter one I'd say."

Jenessa raised her head a fraction, looking at Elena through her bangs until she seemed to decide Elena meant it. "You want more coffee?" she asked with a hopeful smile that was a fragile construct.

"Sure." Elena saw Jenessa pull herself back together again as she poured. "You remember the name of the creeps who gave Lucy coke?"

"Nish and Terry," Jenessa said with a shudder. "Vamps. They liked to put things inside Lucy's body and record her being humiliated then put the videos online. It makes me sick that those videos are out there in the world."

Nishant Kumar and Terence Lee.

Elena's heartbeat rocketed, a sick feeling in her gut. "Did Nish and Terry pass Lucy on to Simon Blakely?"

40

"Lucy met him at Nish's." Sadness in her voice. "He treated her nicer than Nish and Terry."

Bastard had been playing games, the good-guy rescuer who got off on girls the other two had fundamentally damaged. "You liked him."

"Yes, he seemed okay. After hanging with us at a local diner a few times, he invited us to visit his apartment. I was careful not to go too much because I didn't want him starting to think he was my pimp, but his roommate, Eric, always had free coke for Lucy, so she went all the time."

Jenessa tightened the belt of her robe compulsively. "I didn't like her doing that, but I thought at least she was safer than she'd been with those sickos Nish and Terry. After a while, she and Simon hooked up and she moved in with him—he liked to have sex when she was high, but it was all normal, nothing weird, and Lucy liked being high, so . . . She let Eric do honey feeds from her sometimes, too, to thank him for the coke."

"Eric try to get it on with you when you visited her?"

"Eric?" A giggle. "No, he only liked guys. Mostly the big biker types with the beards and the chest hair and the leather."

That was a piece of information no one else had shared. It fitted in neatly with his wounds: hand cut off for offering Lucy drugs, but genitals left intact because he'd never abused her sexually. "You okay talking about the night Lucy's father came and got her?"

"Yes." Jenessa's hand shook as she topped up her coffee, but she walked into the past despite her fear. "It was cold that night, and I didn't have enough money to use the heating at my place." A haunted look beyond the balcony doors. "It'll be exactly one year in a week."

A shiver ran over Elena's skin, a hitch of memory she couldn't capture.

"So you came over to Simon and Eric's to hang out, get warm," she said past her frustration.

A jerky nod. "Even though Simon was a vampire, he usually had food in his apartment, and he didn't mind if I took it. Once in a while, he even put my favorite cookies in there."

Drugs for one, Elena realized, food for the other. Simon Blakely and his friend had been a slick operation. Lining up Jenessa for when they were tired of Lucy? Sex with a damaged young woman for Blakely; honey feeds for Acosta.

"When I got there," Jenessa said, "Eric had just had a honey feed from a boy who passed me on the stairs as I was coming up. Eric was wasted, told me Lucy and Simon were in the bedroom. I didn't bother them, just made myself microwave ramen then sat on the couch and watched a comedy show on TV."

"And Eric?"

"He sacked out on his mattress on the floor, kind of half watching, half sleeping like he did a lot after a honey feed. I'd almost finished my noodles when the front door smashed open, and this man came in yelling for Lucy. I thought for sure he'd hurt me, but he grabbed Eric around the throat and said, 'Where the fuck is my daughter?'"

Jenessa had unconsciously mimicked the intruder's deep growl.

"What happened next?"

"Eric had a baggie of coke on the coffee table, and I could tell it made the other man furious. His face went all red. The door to the bedroom opened right then and Lucy stumbled out dressed in just her panties and a tank top."

Jenessa tucked her hair behind her ears. "She was screaming at the man, saying she wished he was dead instead of her mom. I could tell she was high, but he ignored her to smash his fist into Simon's face." A wince. "I was frightened Simon would kill him, but Lucy's dad was fast and he had a weapon—a piece of heavy chain like people use on their biting dogs."

"Did Eric try to help?"

"He used so much that he couldn't move quick even on normal days. That night, he was half asleep. Lucy kept trying to jump on her dad, but he ignored her even when she was clinging to his back and clawing at his face. He never hurt her. I guess 'cause he was her dad and he loved her." A wistfulness to her. "My dad left me with my stepbrother and never, ever came back. But Lucy's dad came for her."

"Is that when you ran?"

"I was screaming at Lucy to come with me, but she wouldn't come—and one of the neighbors began yelling that she'd called the cops. That's when I ran." Her lower lip shook. "I never saw Lucy again."

"Her father never hurt her even when she was attacking him," Elena reminded the other woman.

Jenessa nodded, sinking her teeth into her lower lip again, her eyes wet. "Lucy had a dad who cared. Why didn't she just go home when it got awful on the streets? Why did she let Nish and Terry do those things to her?"

"Can you describe Lucy's father for me?"

"Dark eyes, dark hair—not black, brown like dark chocolate." Lines on her forehead. "Tall and strong." She held up a hand indicating the man had been several inches taller than Elena.

Jenessa couldn't, however, pinpoint his race. She'd been in shock and the scene had been chaotic. She thought he might've been white and tanned, but he could've also been a light-skinned member of multiple other races.

"It's strange," Jenessa murmured. "I think of him and he just kind of disappears. Like he was real good at being ordinary."

Elena's blood went cold. And she remembered what she hadn't before: roughly a year ago, she'd run into Archer and he'd had a number of bad gouges on his face. She'd commiserated with him about how vicious vampire claws could be, and he'd said, "I wish it were that simple, Ellie. My baby's gotten into drugs—but I've entered her into a resident rehab program. Maybe I'll get her back."

Nausea churned in her gut.

Archer's daughter had died of an overdose just under nine months ago. A daughter who'd had a dead mother. Archer had been called the phantom for his ability to hide in plain sight. He was also a good enough fighter to have demolished Blakely and Acosta, and smart enough to have remained unseen when he set the fire that took Kumar's and Lee's lives.

The broken blade. The mourner.

It all fit.

Elena shook her head, not ready to look at the final line of Cassandra's warning. She needed more information. She couldn't zero in on Archer when every piece of evidence they had said he was dead and buried. And when his daughter's name hadn't been Lucy. Samaria, that was it. Elena remembered thinking it was a pretty name when Archer mentioned it once.

After she left Jenessa, she updated Ashwini and Janvier then confirmed with Vivek that Hiraz was at the Tower. Landing on one of the balconies below Dmitri's floor, she tracked the vampire down to an office where he stood arguing with another vamp.

When Elena poked in her head and said, "Can I borrow Hiraz for a second?" the man on the other side of the argument said, "Take him. Keep him for all I care."

Hiraz narrowed his eyes at his enemy and pointed a finger. "I'll get you for this." Something in the threat said it was more for show than anything; the two were friends beneath it all.

Strange, but vampires and angels got like that. They lived long enough that they treasured their friendships, even when those friendships drove them crazy. Of course, Ransom often drove her nuts, and she'd be devastated if they stopped being friends, so maybe it wasn't just an immortal thing.

"My apologies for the language, Consort," Hiraz said to her in the hallway. Clean-shaven and dressed in a simple white shirt with black pants, his skin a light brown and his expertly cut hair black with red undertones, he had a sharp handsomeness.

"Trust me, I've heard far worse." Guild hunters weren't exactly blushing violets when it came to language. "Let's talk on the balcony." Once out in the crisp cold, she told him about her visit to Jenessa.

His shoulders stiffened. "She gets scared easily."

"Jeni's fine—we had cake and coffee and talked."

Lips curving, he inclined his head in her direction. "I should've remembered that you are not like other immortals." He slid his hands into the pockets of his pants while the chill wind rippled his shirt against the ridged planes of his body. "I'm overprotective, but I can't forget how she was when I first met her. So skinny that her bones stuck out, bruises on that beautiful skin, her eyes endless pools in her face."

"What happened after your visit to Acosta and Blakely's apartment to look for Lucy? How did Jeni end up with you?"

"I couldn't bear to just leave her there, especially when I saw the way a group of vampires in the street were watching her. Predators waiting to run down wounded prey." Jaw hard and muscles bunched, he stared sightlessly at the winter-kissed glitter of the city.

"I got her a hotel room of her own in my building, made sure she had food and warmth, then I went back out and taught those predators never to look at her that way again." Age in his voice now, power that was deadly music. "Next afternoon, when I dropped by to check on her, she opened the door dressed in her underwear. She was petrified of me but determined to pay back her 'debt.' She thought I'd hurt her if she didn't. Decided it was better to cooperate than try to run."

He shook his head, his jaw grinding. "You've met her— her sweetness and gentleness isn't a shell. It goes down to the bone, and the world taught this harmless, kind creature only abuse and fear. I told her to put on clothes; took her out for a meal." He swallowed hard. "After that . . . after that it became difficult not to see her every day, and slowly, she became mine."

"She's not your blood donor." Elena had wondered if part of Jenessa's attraction for Hiraz was the life-giving fluid that ran in her veins.

"No, she's my everything." Rough words. "I've got her into school, too—she's wanted to be a hairdresser since she was a kid, and you should see how happy she is when she comes home from her lessons." He pointed at his hair. "I'm a man who's had plain black hair for four hundred and fifty years, but how could I say no when she asked? She trims it every week, so it's always perfect."

It was ridiculous, Elena thought—she was a big, tough hunter who was about to lose her wings. But her heart went mushy at this happy ending for a girl from the streets and a vampire who'd been alone since she'd known him. "Tell me what you saw that night in the apartment when you went to find Lucy."

"A vampire was lying unconscious on the lounge sofa. Black bruise forming on one side of his face, more bruises around his throat. Jenessa identified him as Eric." Hiraz curled his lip as he spoke the name. "Apartment was destroyed—table overturned, chairs broken, holes in the walls, sprays of blood. One of the two bedrooms stunk of sex and blood, but aside from Eric the apartment was empty."

The vampire frowned. "I know Eric and his roommate recently got themselves murdered, but I didn't think to come to you with this. It was a year ago, and I figured an irate father dragging his daughter home from Blakely's wasn't exactly unusual. From what Jenessa's told me, the man was no prize."

With the data Hiraz'd had, Elena would've made the same call—but she still wished he'd passed on the information. "Jenessa didn't have Lucy's last name. You ever track her down?" Apparently the apartment the two women had rented together had been under Jenessa's name because Lucy didn't have a bank account—and Lucy had laughingly given a different last name each time Jenessa asked.

"I tried because Jenessa was worried about her friend," Hiraz said, "but Lucy disappeared. No body ever turned up, and Jenessa was adamant the father was careful not to hurt Lucy. I thought he took her home, maybe to a distant state. Is she—"

"I've got nothing on Lucy—she might not even be connected to what I'm investigating." Many pieces fit, but a couple of crucial ones didn't. "One more thing, you heard any rumors about a fire in the Quarter two months ago? Vics were Nishant Kumar and Terence Lee."

"Jenessa mentioned them after she read about the fire in the papers, said it was probably because of drugs. The two were dealers and suppliers." Even as he spoke, his expression altered, became thoughtful. "The picture in the paper wasn't that clear. You have a photograph of the two?"

Elena took out her phone and pulled up the images from the file Vivek had sent her. "You recognize them?"

A slow nod. "Saw their faces in photographs pinned to the wall of the lounge when I went into the apartment with Jenessa that night."

No surprise there—she already knew the four men were connected, but Hiraz wasn't finished. "One particular photograph stuck in my memory because it was about to fall off. Five men with a girl I think must've been Lucy. I didn't ask Jenessa at the time, but afterward when she described her friend—blonde hair, brown eyes, a mole at the corner of her left lip—it was a match.

"The only difference was that Lucy was healthy in that image while Jenessa described her friend as emaciated from drug use." He frowned, eyes narrowed. "I remember bottles behind the people in the image. Not only bottles of blood. Alcohol as well. A long black bar."

Heart kicking, Elena said, "Five men. Kumar, Lee, and . . ."

"Eric and his roommate, Simon, were in there." Hiraz's eyes met hers, his discomfort a stiffness in his words as he spoke. "The fifth man was your brother-in-law."

White owls settled all around them, their golden eyes watchful. And in Elena's head, the old voice sighed. *The broken blade draws near. The mourner walks on destiny's road. It is your time, child of mortals.*

41

Ignoring the chill on her skin and the ghost owls that watched her with unblinking focus, Elena used her phone to search for a photo of Archer's daughter. There'd been an obituary in the Guild newsletter, the text written by Archer. There it was . . . but the photo was a childhood one. Blonde hair, brown eyes, face angled so the left side of her mouth wasn't visible. Unsurprisingly, Hiraz couldn't identify the child as the adult woman whose image he'd seen. She shot a message to Sara to see if she had another photo, then read the obituary.

My baby girl was smart and funny and loved doughnuts so much she once ate six in a row. She shouldn't be gone. I'll miss you always.

Below that was a note asking people to donate to a scholarship set up in her name: The Samaria Candace Archer Scholarship. No way to get Lucy from that, so maybe she was wrong and none of this had anything to do with the murders. Or maybe it was like China and Jenessa. One woman. Two names.

With more questions than answers, she called Ashwini the instant Hiraz left to return to his duties. "You manage to dig up anything about Lucy?" The other couple hadn't had much time since her briefing, but Elena had just lost three more feathers, two of them primaries. She was on a strict deadline.

"Lucy's dead."

Elena's heart was ice, filled with thoughts of a young woman who'd passed away a year and a half after her mother. "When?"

"Exactly eight months and twenty-three days ago," Ashwini replied, and Elena felt the confirmation like a kick to the chest.

Picking up another feather she'd just shed, she stared at the fine filaments of inky black. "Where did you get your information?" There could be no crossed wires about this, no mistakes.

"Where I get all my weird information."

"I thought you glimpsed the future?"

"I see . . . someone standing at Lucy's grave—I got the date of death from the gravestone. What I see, the person—possibly people—at the grave, that hasn't happened yet."

Elena's fingers clenched on the feather. "What was the name on the headstone?"

"This isn't like high-resolution photography, Ellie. All I got was the date and the knowledge it was our girl in the ground." Ashwini carried on. "Janvier managed to dig up that she appeared on the streets maybe three months before her father found her. She was new, so our informants noticed—fresh meat."

The echo of Jeni's description of herself made the hairs prickle on the back of Elena's neck. Nothing unusual about that in a conversation with Ashwini—the other hunter had a way of existing just out of time.

"She was already experimenting with drugs by then, and word on the street is that Nishant Kumar supplied her to get her on camera." Edgy words. "One of our informants kept a clip from one of the recordings on his phone. He pirated it off a porn site. 'Degrading' is the word I'd use. Wasn't about the sex but about humiliation. Real hard-core, brutal humiliation. Janvier had to stop me from beheading our informant. Then he turned around and nearly tore off the fucker's head. Lost that informant for sure. Oh, well."

"Harrison was friends with these assholes." Elena kicked at the snow on the balcony, careful to do it away from the owls. "I have him in a photo with them and Lucy before she began to look like a junkie."

"I've got bubkes on your brother-in-law so far. Call you back if we unearth more."

Elena put away her phone and bent to pick up the three feathers she'd lost earlier. Walking through the phalanx of owls, she dropped those feathers plus the poor black one she'd crushed, over the edge of the balcony in her own personal good-bye. Two more lost primaries wouldn't ground her, but at the rate they were shedding, she'd lose her ability to fly by the end of the day.

Tiredness was already beginning to infiltrate her bones, her back aching. Mind strangely clear, she decided that if this was to be her last day with wings, she'd fly her heart out. She'd be careful, not fly alone and land the instant it became dangerous, but she'd wring every last drop of wonder out of her dream of flight.

Streamers of white over the back of her hand, her bones shoving up in jagged peaks against her skin. Elena pushed off the visible filaments and rubbed at her face to ensure nothing was sticking there. Her palms came away with fine white strands. "Great." She scowled at the owls. "Now I'm going to grow a beard?"

Spreading their wings, they flew off into the heavy gray-blue sky, fading into nothingness in front of her eyes as the spot on her chest, the dark mirror, began to pulse like a second heartbeat.

You could stop now, lower the chances of meeting the broken blade, the mourner.

Elena discarded that thought as soon as it arose. If she

flinched and left Beth and Maggie in danger, she'd die inside anyway. Elena Deveraux was no coward; she'd face her reckoning head-on. "Archangel," she murmured, searching the skies for him, though she'd sent him away herself.

A black fear crept insidiously through her veins.

"The last feather to fall," she reminded herself, glancing back. "Yep, got plenty yet." Spreading her wings, she prepared to take off.

Her phone rang.

It was Dmitri on the other end. "Harrison's awake. Talk to him before he starts thinking about trying to cover his ass."

"Have you heard from Raphael?"

"Geothermal field is unstable, but he's close to achieving containment."

"Casualties?"

"Ten dead, double that wounded. Without Raphael, it would've been in the hundreds."

Saddened at the loss of life but relieved her archangel was safe, Elena ran to the infirmary, found Nisia with her brother-in-law. The healer was bent over him, her attention on his no-longer-bandaged neck wound. It appeared a macabre mouth, the flesh red and wet, and the skin around it dark.

"How bad is it?" Harrison croaked, his gaze on Elena.

"You won't win any beauty contests," she said, "but you'll live."

Exhaling, her brother-in-law closed his eyes for a long moment before opening them again and saying, "I need to talk to her." Halting but determined words directed at Nisia.

The healer looked between the two of them. "Five minutes," she said firmly. "Talk fast."

Elena shut the door behind Nisia then came to sit on the chair beside Harrison's bed. "You heard her. We only have five minutes. You need to tell me what you're involved in, Harrison. No bullshit."

"Beth, she was here?" Dread skittered in his eyes. "I didn't imagine it? Maggie is safe?"

"Both Beth and Maggie are fine." It was obvious he

wouldn't be able to talk about anything until he was satisfied on that point. "Maggie never saw you like this—she thinks you're away for work."

Shuddering, Harrison croaked, "Eve? Is she okay?"

"Eve is tough." Though she had to like Harrison for being worried about her. "Does this have to do with a girl called Lucy?"

Harrison's pupils dilated, his breath escalating in speed. "I never hurt her," he said. "I never touched her, and—"

"This isn't about blame." Elena fought to keep her tone curt and businesslike. "I just want to protect Beth and Maggie." *And get justice for Lucy.* "Tell me all of it," she ordered Harrison. "If you love them, don't try to cover your ass, and just give it to me straight."

"I met Lucy in a bar," he rasped "It's not what you think. I wasn't on the prowl." A tremor of breath. "I was meeting friends for a drink and they were late and she came up and started talking to me. I told her I was married and in love with my wife and little girl, and she said I might be her perfect man."

Elena fed him chips of ice from the cup on the bedside table.

Melting the ice on his tongue, Harrison swallowed. "I laughed and flirted with her a little. I was flattered she'd hit on me but I never crossed any lines." Desperate eyes clinging to Elena's. "I knew I was going home to Beth and I wasn't going to fuck that up. Then Nishant and Terence arrived, and I introduced her to them. I was the reason she met them."

"That's it?"

"I literally said, 'Lucy, these are my friends Nish and Terry.' After, Nish bought her a drink, and the four of us chatted for a few minutes. Lucy was open about having a thing for vampires and wanting a vampire boyfriend." He licked his dry lips. "I never knew so many women were into that until I was Made."

Vamp groupies lived for the thrill of danger that came with fangs in the throat. "Was this bar known to be popular with vampires?"

Harrison nodded. "Najat's not a 'get drunk' bar. More a 'have a drink with friends after work' kind of place." He gratefully accepted more ice chips. "Eric and Simon came in about ten minutes after," he said when he could speak again.

"I didn't know them except in passing, but Nish and Terry did. All four were post-Contract and older, and I could tell Lucy was attracted to that. She asked the barmaid to take a photo of us all maybe half an hour later. Andreas called me in for some unexpected work right after, and I left the bar."

Another quick inhale. "I swear on Maggie's life that I didn't do anything but introduce Lucy to people I thought were friends. I knew they were into drugs, but I thought it was a hit now and then. Recreational. And Lucy was smart, nicely dressed, confident talking with them. I didn't worry she couldn't handle herself."

Elena believed him. If there was one thing she knew about her brother-in-law, it was that he loved Maggie. He wouldn't take her name lightly. And hell, if that was his connection to it all, it was too thin a thread to justify attempted murder. "You're sure this is linked to Lucy? Anything else that could've come back on you?"

"He whispered it in my ear after he cut my throat. 'For Lucy. Why should you have your Beth and Maggie when Lucy's gone? Think of them rotting in the earth as you die.'" Coughs shook his body.

Bones aching from deep within and her wings crushingly heavy on her back, Elena waited for him to find his breath again before she said, "Do you know Lucy's last name?"

But Harrison was lost in his own need to prove his innocence. "The next time I saw her was at a party they invited me to at Simon's—it was that weekend you and Beth and the others went out of town. I asked Jean-Baptiste and Majda to babysit Maggie so I could drop by the party for an hour."

It seemed a mirage now, those two days filled with laughter in a private hotel that provided spa treatments, manicures, mimosas, pretty much anything a bunch of women blowing off steam might need. "Go on," she nudged Harrison when he stopped.

"Lucy had tattoos all over, weighed half of what she did before, and that smile was gone. I asked Nish what the fuck was going on, and he called me a loser, said I needed to learn to have a good time. Terry was feeding off her at the time."

"Did you try to help her?" Elena asked.

"I told Lucy if she wanted out, I'd get her out." Shivers wracked his body. "I figured I could talk to you, and you'd make sure Nish and Terry didn't cause me trouble over losing Lucy."

Elena nodded.

"But she wouldn't come." Harrison's voice was anguished. "In spite of how Simon let Nish and Terry use her even after they got together, he had her convinced he loved her. I knew she'd die if I didn't get her out, that they'd use her up and break her, but she refused to come. I was desperate, so . . ."

The world hung in the air, a thin glass bauble.

"So I called her father," Harrison finished softly.

Elena went motionless. "You know the identity of Lucy's father?"

"She'd said a few things about him at the bar, kind of offhand, even a little angry—but I remembered, because I thought it must make for interesting family dynamics with her wanting a vampire boyfriend. I put the pieces together and tracked him down. He was out of his mind with worry. I told him where he could find her."

"You didn't wonder when Nishant Kumar and Terence Lee were murdered?"

"That was *ten* months after her father took her back. I stopped hanging with them after Lucy, but I heard they were mixed up in the designer-drug trade by then. I figured it must've been a gang hit."

Ten months was a long time between action and reaction. It spoke of patience, of justice served cold. "Did you ever hear from Lucy's father again?"

"He sent me a funeral card in the mail nine months ago," Harrison said, tears clogging his voice. "Lucy died. Drug overdose two months after she got out of rehab."

Wishing she were wrong about Lucy's identity and knowing she wasn't, Elena carried it through. "You go to her funeral?"

"No, I was in Alaska that week to gather data for a small business deal Andreas was considering, but I called with my condolences," Harrison said. "He thanked me for giving him three more months with his daughter, said she'd been his sweet girl again for weeks, that they'd cried together and figured out their problems."

Elena frowned. What could've pushed Lucy's father from gratitude to wanting to murder Harrison?

Then her brother-in-law said, "I told him I was so sorry I'd ever introduced Lucy to Nish and Terry."

The hammer fell. "What's her father's name, Harrison?" she asked on a whisper, because she knew and she wished she didn't. Hunting a friend was the worst thing that could be asked of a person. It was why Slayers walked the periphery of the world. It was why Archer had only become her friend after she was beyond the Guild's reach.

Her eyes stung.

42

Sara went silent on the other end of the line when Elena told her what Harrison had confirmed. "Archer's dead," her friend finally said.

"I sent Santiago a message before I called you. He's rechecking the file." She was so tired, her back screaming from the weight of her wings—and her mind reaching out to Raphael's only to hit a blank wall over and over again. "Lucy must've been her street name."

"No, that's what Archer called his wife. First name was Sabrina, so I always thought Lucy must be her second name."

A grieving daughter taking her mother's name to hold on to her? It made an awful, sad kind of sense. "There're no missing pieces, then, Sara, no facts that don't fit. It all leads back to Archer."

"It could be another one of us."

Sara's words were a punch to the solar plexus. "Was he close to anyone else in the Guild?" Elena asked, well able to see one hunter taking vengeance for another who hadn't been able to survive his grief.

"You know how it is with Slayers." Sara's voice was thick with withheld emotion. "He and Deacon went out for a beer now and then, and I invited him over for dinner as much as I could without it rubbing him the wrong way. I'd say we were his closest friends in the Guild."

Deacon was very much capable of taking vengeance on his friend's behalf, but he would've never slit Harrison's throat where Maggie could've found him. Deacon was father to a little girl of his own—more, the last time Elena had brought her niece over, he and Zoe had given an ecstatic Maggie the plastic tools Zoe had outgrown, spent long minutes showing her how to use them.

Maggie idolized her "big sister" Zoe.

Had Deacon been hunting Harrison, he'd have taken Harrison in some dark street where no children would stumble on his body.

"Since I know it wasn't you or Deacon, we're looking for a dead man," Elena said flatly, just as a message lit up her phone. "Hold on a sec. It's V."

I contacted Najat about security footage of the night Harrison says he met Lucy. It was a shot in the dark— nearly all businesses wipe footage after a couple of days. But you have the luck of the Irish, Ellie.

They had a big bar fight there the same night—it was hours later, but they had to keep the entire day's footage because one of the participants decided to sue the bar. Link will take you to it. It's cued to the right place, and I've speeded up a few sections so you can watch it quicker.

"Sara, I'll call you back."

"I'm going to call Santiago, ask him to pull up everything he has on Archer's death," her best friend said before hanging up.

Elena clicked on the link, and there was Harrison waiting at the bar, dressed in jeans and a casual navy shirt. Lucy walked into frame seconds later. She was wearing a cute sparkly dress of gold that came to her upper thighs, her hair healthy and shiny, and her body language welcoming. She could've been any young woman on a night out who'd spotted a man who interested her.

Elena saw Harrison flush at Lucy's greeting and get that look men got when they couldn't believe a pretty woman was hitting on them, but credit to her brother-in-law, he kept it to conversation. At one point, Lucy touched his arm, but he pulled off her hand in a gentle but firm way, and she actually saw his mouth form the words: *I love my wife.*

"Okay, Harrison. Many brownie points for you."

The rest was exactly what Harrison had described. The other men arriving. Conversation. Photos taken. Harrison leaving early.

On-screen, an unknown man bought Lucy a drink in fast-forward and she drifted away with him. Her flirting was . . . aggressive. Frantic in a way. It made Elena sad. Archer's beloved daughter was searching for a way to exorcise her grief, but she was doing it in all the wrong places and with all the wrong people.

Had it been a man like Hiraz Weir whom she'd run into that night . . . but this was the past. Not the future, subject to change.

Nishant Kumar eventually went over and lured Lucy back from her admirer. From that point on, she stayed with him, Acosta, Lee, and Blakely until all five walked out of the bar—with Lucy snuggled up against Kumar. She looked sober and conscious of her decision, her face set in deliberate lines. Elena slowed down the footage but saw no indication of coercion or drug use. Steady gait, sharp eyes, active in conversation with the men.

A message popped up on-screen: *I ran facial recognition on the rest of the footage for you. These five never come back.*

Shutting it down, Elena stared out at the city. It was all so pointless. Lucy had been grieving and going off the rails, even courting her hunter father's disapproval by trying to hook up with vampires, but she shouldn't have had to pay for that with her life.

A shadow against the wall, swinging so softly.

A single cherry red high-heel lying sideways on check-erboard tile.

A beloved life lost to grief.

Swallowing back the deluge of memory, Elena called Santiago, who managed to conference-call Sara so the three of them could talk at once. The detective had spent the time since Sara's initial call gathering his files. He had plenty for them, but the gist of it was that the body found in Archer's car had been too badly burned to offer viable DNA. However, it had been of the right height and ethnicity—as per the forensic anthropologist.

"Guild paid for the bone doc," Santiago added. "Her report made me feel better about closing the case despite the weird things I'd noticed."

"What?" Sara asked.

"It was a crash, no doubt about it," the detective said. "Car wrapped around the center of the gas station like a tin can. Limited skid marks, but there was a ton of rain that night, and it was possible the hunter skidded across the road and his brakes couldn't get enough traction."

Rasping sounds as he no doubt rubbed at his bristled jaw. "But here's the thing—that car went up like a tinderbox, rain or no rain. I had the fire guys look at it, and they said with the gas station going boom, there wasn't much they could do to find other accelerants if they'd been present. We did manage to discover that the vic was carrying burnables—possibly clothes in bags. Like he was going to donate them."

"Convenient," Elena murmured.

"Yeah," Santiago continued. "But, while suicide was an option because of the shit luck in his personal life, I had no reason to think 'body substitution.'"

Elena caught something in his voice. "You know what body."

"When Sara told me maybe Archer'd come back from the dead, I spent a coupla minutes looking up this odd case I remembered from back then. Two of the guys telling ghost stories in the squad room about how bodies had started to get up and walk away from the morgue and how maybe a sleep-deprived doctor had accidentally ruled a vampire dead."

"A body was lost from the morgue?" Sara swore under her breath.

"When I looked it up, what do you know—same ethnicity as Archer, same height, around the same weight even. Could've been the body in the car, but no way for us to know that. Your guy had no metal in his bones, and neither did this missing stiff—and here's the kicker, the morgue body was never recovered."

Elena had no uncertainties any longer when it came to the name of the assailant. Everything fit. And the wait for the right type of corpse would explain the delay between Lucy's death and the start of Archer's vengeful spree. The problem was they didn't know enough about Lucy's time on the streets to guess who he might go after next—and Beth and Maggie remained in his crosshairs. All a man of his training needed was a single slip in their protection, a single opportunity.

She, Sara, and Santiago hung up after deciding to activate their separate intelligence networks to be on alert for Archer's name and face. Elena told Jean-Baptiste and Beth who to watch for, and she warned Jenessa. In the grip of a fever of revenge, Archer might decide that she'd led his daughter into life as a prostitute. The young woman was in a hairdressing salon with her mentor, and Elena got that mentor to lock the door and close the salon by promising to cover her lost profits for the day.

Thankfully for Jenessa's dreams, her mentor appeared more excited at the intrigue than put out. Especially when she heard that her student lived with a senior Tower vampire and that he'd be by to pick her up.

Flaring out her increasingly heavy wings afterward, Elena decided to take flight. She didn't know where she was going, Archer a phantom who'd left no trail that Vivek could find, but she ached to fly. According to a message

Dmitri had sent her during the call with Sara and Santiago, Raphael was on his way back. Maybe she'd fly toward him as far as she could, and then she'd wait.

For one last flight with her archangel before her wings failed.

It wasn't to be.

The phone rang in her pocket. "Ellie?" Ashwini said on the other end. "We've got two more bodies."

So many owls surrounded her that Elena had to push through them to get to the dead, the birds' bodies soft and warm against her. She wondered if Cassandra was trying to help her cheat destiny. *Is this it? The broken blade? The mourner?*

No answer, but the owls didn't move. Elena continued on, her skin flushing hot then cold. Should she back off? Would that throw a spanner into the mechanics of destiny? Or would it alter the future in the worst way, leading to Beth's and Maggie's murders at Archer's hand?

No, she had to finish this, eliminate the threat. And it wasn't as if she was alone. Her three Legion shadows were waiting on the roof—even Archer couldn't take on four trained fighters at once. And while her wing muscles might be sluggish in responding to her commands, warning of imminent failure, she had plenty of feathers left. Nowhere close to losing her last one.

She reached the first of the dead.

The small, pudgy vampire had been killed in his combined convenience/pawn shop in a seedy corner of the Quarter and his body found behind the counter by a regular customer. It was a miracle the customer hadn't decided to rob the place. The corpse was so fresh that the blood was tacky rather than dry and encrusted.

"Spine bisected at the neck, hands cut off." Janvier rose from his crouch beside the dead vampire. "And we've got a connection to Lucy."

"How?"

"She pawned her jewelry here," Ashwini explained. "Was easy to check the records after you gave us her legal name." She pointed at a small laptop that sat open behind the grill that should've protected the shopkeeper from harm. "He demanded official IDs and recorded every transaction. Gave a fair price, far as I can tell."

The same records had probably led Archer to his door. "When did she pawn her things?"

"Roughly two weeks after she first met Kumar and crew."

A time when Lucy would've had access to other funds—she couldn't have drained her bank account dry that quickly. A memory flared at the thought, of Jenessa saying Lucy had no bank account. It hadn't struck Elena as odd at the time because Lucy had been on the streets working in a cash profession—and unlike Jenessa, she'd been an addict.

"She always gave me the rent money," Jenessa had said. "But anything else, she kept in a jar until she wanted to spend it. She didn't trust banks."

However, now that Elena knew Lucy's true identity, her cash existence took on another cast. As the daughter of the Slayer, she must've known her father might be able to track her if she accessed her accounts. "She made a choice to pawn her jewelry rather than go home or ask Archer for money."

Anger or wild grief, they would never know Lucy's motivations. "But it's a choice Archer will never accept." To do so would be to accept that Lucy had made conscious decisions along the way to her descent into darkness.

That didn't nullify her suffering or in any way excuse the abuse she'd endured—what Kumar and the others had done to her was unforgivable—but it also didn't mean that her every action had been coerced. Kumar and Lee'd had money. They'd had no reason to force Lucy to pawn her jewelry.

Also, she hadn't been a prisoner under the vampires' control—it had been very early on in her life in the Quarter, probably while Kumar and Lee were still grooming her. She'd shared an apartment with Jenessa at the time, been free to come and go as she pleased. Logic said she must've made the decision to come to this pawn shop on her own. "Who's the second victim?"

Ashwini's eyes flashed. "Owner's wife, I think. In the storeroom."

Elena followed Ash to the small doorway just as Santiago arrived. A woman's body lay crumpled inches from the door, her head separated from her neck. A gold wedding band twinkled on her left ring finger. "I don't have a scent. She's human."

Ashwini swore. "Why the hell would Archer kill her?"

"Probably 'cause she saw his face." Santiago pointed to a security mirror that would've given the woman a view out front even while she was in the storeroom. "He's got no reason to think he's already been made."

Simon Blakely, Eric Acosta, Nishant Kumar, Terence Lee, even Harrison, Elena could've allowed that Archer's vengeance had been justified. He'd skirted the line with Harrison, but in his grieving mind, Harrison could've been the reason behind all the others.

But these victims, especially the woman . . . they'd just been going about their lives, running a small business. Lucy had come to them, not the other way around. The owner hadn't even cheated her. Archer's lines had shifted, his justifications no longer explicable or excusable.

"Your boy's a loose cannon," Santiago rumbled in an unknowing echo of Elena's thoughts. "He's so angry he'll find reasons to keep killing."

"Yes." Drawing in a deep breath, Elena ignored the noxious scents that wanted to slide into her nostrils and focused on the iron richness of blood.

Sugared doughnuts and cold winter rain.

Vampires could have peculiar scents to her hunter-born nose, but this took the cake—or the doughnut, she thought with black humor. Returning to the body of the shopkeeper, she knelt, closed her eyes, then inhaled the scent directly from the gaping wound at the dead vampire's throat. His head was only attached to his body by a flap of skin at his nape.

Yes, he was the sugar and the doughnuts and the icy stab of rain against the skin.

Opening her eyes, she took in the violence around them. The sprays and smears of blood on the walls and on the floor. The footprints in blood that led to the back door. Archer hadn't run this time. No, his stride had been confident but unhurried.

Child of mortals. The broken blade is close. Your destiny nears.

Heart jerking at the distress in the old voice, Elena stared directly into the eyes of an owl as she said, "I can track him." Ashwini was a gifted tracker, but she couldn't pursue by scent; what she did took time and patience. They needed to move fast, follow the scent before it dissipated—and once and for all eliminate the threat to Beth and Maggie.

Archer was smart, had probably already thrown his bloody clothing in the trash. But given the recent nature of the kill, he was unlikely to have had enough time to shower. And it was *hard* to strip away every tiny speck of blood. Droplets got in hair, or in the inside shell of the ear, and his weapon would need careful cleaning to remove all traces.

No hunter would abandon a perfectly good weapon.

She began to move, the sword she'd grabbed from her and Raphael's Tower suite heavy in the sheath she wore down the center of her spine. She also had her crossbow as well as spare crossbow bolts in a flat sheath strapped to her thigh—plus a smaller number of bolts in a combined bolt-and-knife sheath worn on her left forearm. Those weren't her only weapons; going up against a Slayer would require everything she had.

Santiago and Janvier stayed with the body, while Ashwini ran with her, keeping watch and acting as her backup. The owls danced right in front of her face, their wings buffeting her, but she put her head down and kept running.

It was time to finish this.

43

"Scent's strong!" she called back to Ash.

Archer had more blood on him than she'd thought. He couldn't, however, be visibly bloody, or he'd have left a trail of horrified people behind him, at least one of whom would've called the cops.

No one had until she'd told Santiago of the find, so he was either wearing dark clothing that had absorbed the blood and he'd wiped his face clean, or he'd taken off his coat before the massacre, putting it back on afterward to hide the evidence of his crime. When her boot came down on something disgustingly squishy, she ignored it to carry on.

Her next step crunched a syringe.

The owls flew ahead of and around her . . . and her wings began to drag through the crap that littered the streets of the Quarter. No matter how hard she tried, she couldn't pull them back up. Tears clogged her throat. Her muscles were too weak. She wouldn't be soaring aloft on her own wings again.

"Ellie!"

"I know!" She didn't halt, even as feathers tore off her beautiful, powerful wings that were useless appendages now.

Vampires scuttled into hollows, and humans watched from the same. Many were junkies and homeless people, but she caught sight of the odd better-dressed individual stumbling home after a big night out at the clubs. That it was the middle of the day didn't matter—in the clubs, anytime was nighttime.

A homeless woman standing by the side of an alley grinned to reveal a toothless mouth, and pointed silently to the left.

Archer's scent was pungent in her nose.

Another homeless person screamed indignantly when she slammed by his hiding place. "Thief! Thief!" A piece of newspaper flew up in a small wind to flutter against the edge of her boot before it tore off to fly down the alley.

The wind was crisp and rising.

She didn't have to look up to know the clouds were moving in. It was obvious from the turgid gray light. Elena could track through snow, but depending on how much it snowed, it might become more difficult. And rain—rain was the worst. If Archer got a real drenching, she'd lose the trail. He wasn't a vampire himself, wouldn't regenerate the scent.

Exiting the narrow space, she found herself confronted by a street buzzing with traffic. She stepped out onto it and held out a hand. Cars screeched to a stop around her as she ran across the road. Then cameras flashed as quick-thinking people stuck their heads and arms out of car windows to take snapshots of her and Ash before they disappeared between the buildings on the other side.

If anyone had caught her dragging wings . . . Well, Dmitri would think of some explanation. A bad injury sustained during the hunt, maybe. As an angel-Made, humans, vampires, *and* angels expected her to be a little mortal. She was allowed to be flawed in a way Jessamy would never be. The Tower could use that to conceal what was happening to her until . . . until her wings were gone.

She blinked back her pain and thought of Raphael. And she knew one way to fuck with destiny would be to bring him in when events seemed to be conspiring to keep them apart. And if she died and she hadn't reached out to him . . .

I will become a monster without you.

She grabbed her phone to make a call as she ran. It was dead. "I don't fucking believe it!" She'd charged it this morning. "Goddamn Cascade!" Turning on her heel, she said. "I need your phone!"

Ashwini held it out. And a massive wind slammed into her hand. It grabbed the phone and crashed it against a neighboring wall. Into fucking pieces.

Shit!

Looked like the Cascade didn't want her to make the call. Teeth gritted, she ran and she thought. She couldn't send one of the Legion without leaving her and Ash vulnerable. Right now, the three flew escort above, a deadly squadron focused on keeping her alive.

There was one other way, she realized. One being in the world who could still hear her mental voice.

Send your owls to Raphael, she ordered the old voice in her head. *Tell him where I am and that I need help.*

I cannot interfere with what is written in—

Who made that fucking rule? Elena exited the narrow space to cross another road. *Do you like being helpless to stop what you see? Wouldn't the nightmares go away if you could use your sight to help save those who've never done you harm? Weren't your owls trying to stop me from chasing Archer?*

A long pause before the old voice stirred, rising to a brighter wakefulness. *You seek to fracture destiny, child of mortals.*

Seek. So she hadn't yet succeeded. It was getting difficult to run, her heart working brutally hard. She was now weaker than she'd been as a mortal. *So, how about it? How about taking control of what you see?*

No answer, but the owls in front of her faded with stark suddenness.

Elena bared her teeth as she pounded into another narrow space between buildings, an area littered with broken glass that bit at her badly damaged wings. "Screw the Cascade and its hard-on to shape our lives," she vowed. "We're going to write our own future."

It was darker here, especially with the clouds settling heavy and bloated with snow over the space. There were no windows looking down into it, and though it was tempting to call it an alleyway, it wasn't quite that narrow. Possibly a service entrance or a maintenance road. Running down it, she saw lingering piles of slushy, dirty snow on the sides.

The first snowflake hit her cheek. Others brushed cool over her wings as her feathers slipped away one after the other. Ignoring the fall and the awful loss that made her want to scream her grief, she continued to run, chasing a quarry who was strong and determined and mad with a darker, more horrifying grief.

Archer would never surrender. Not when he'd lost everyone who'd ever mattered to him. He had nothing for which to live. The only thing that remained was vengeance.

Coming to a corner, she hesitated, torn between two directions.

"He chucked his coat into the trash can," Ashwini pointed out, her breath jagged, the same as Elena's.

Spotting the black triangle of fabric hanging over the edge of the trash can on the right, Elena went left. The scent was weak here, far stronger in the direction of the trash can. She hesitated. "Check if he threw his sweater in there as well."

Ashwini ran over and dug in, lifting both pieces of clothing above her head. "Damn."

Pausing, Elena took a number of deep breaths in an attempt to make the right call.

"Hunter-angel!"

Flicking open her eyelashes, she saw a large man, his fat carried all over his stocky body and a bloody apron around his waist, leaning out the door of a butcher shop. "Crazy hombre who stripped off his clothes in the middle of win-

ter, he went that way." The butcher pointed left. "Had a
big-ass sword."

"Thank you!"

"Go get him! I got children! I don't want some whacked
asshole running around with a sword!" he called from behind her.

She caught the scent of sugared doughnuts and icy rain
on the air currents two minutes later. It was fresh, and it
was coming back to her from someone up ahead, though it
was far fainter than when they'd started. Most of the blood
must've got on his sweater, but Archer had enough on him
and his weapon that she could track it.

She pushed herself, aware she was slowing down. She
couldn't, however, tell Ashwini to go ahead. Archer could
turn at any point, and she didn't want the other hunter to get
ambushed alone. The Legion wouldn't leave Elena even if
she ordered it. Not now.

"Ellie, your wings are bleeding!" Ashwini said from beside her.

"I can't feel it." Couldn't feel any part of her wings.

The snow kept on falling, a soft whisper that covered the
dirt and the garbage and the stains of this dark corner of the
city.

"Ellie!" A shove that sent her to the left.

The bullet passed between her and Ash to slam into a
light pole. Ashwini couldn't have seen the bullet coming—
they didn't have a line of sight around the corner. *See?* she
said to Cassandra. *Foresight kicks ass when it's used to
change death to life.* She reached for the gun she'd shoved
into an ankle holster and strapped on at the last minute,
swung it up in a smooth motion, and pressed the trigger. It
jammed. Again and again.

No, goddamn it!

Three more shots aimed in their direction.

Two bodies falling from the sky, one slamming her in
the side as he went down. Jesus, Archer had hit two of the
Legion. Headshots. Having managed to keep her feet,
Elena reholstered her useless gun and fought the instinct

to stop. The Legion would regenerate, but it'd take several minutes.

She began to run again.

Archer had the instincts of a predator. Lose him now and she might never catch him again.

Another turn and she and Ashwini found themselves in an area of dead silence, a part of the Quarter that only came to life after dark. It looked to be the back of a row of restaurants and clubs, a single lane just big enough to retrieve the Dumpsters that lined the sides, a couple of them overflowing with garbage.

Elena stopped at the mouth of the accessway.

At least the cold weather meant there was no smell and no bugs. Only large clumps of dirty snow and ice pushed to the sides by the wind. A lot of it had collected against the dented and scratched trash containers.

The hulking objects provided plenty of hiding spaces, and the shadowy dimness fostered by the clouds didn't exactly help. Elena squinted past it all and saw the accessway came to an end at a brick wall about twenty yards forward. A bitch for the drivers of the trucks that collected the trash, but a perfect place for a Slayer armed with a sword to make his stand against a woman with useless wings. She'd be clumsy, unable to move as well in the comparatively tight space.

Fighting her primal need to assure Beth's and Maggie's safety herself, she said, "You have the lead," to Ash. "You want the sword?"

"No, I have my stars." Razor-sharp edges glinting in her hand, Ashwini moved forward with slow caution, using the nearest Dumpster for cover. Elena watched her back, her crossbow held at the ready as they crept down into the dark. The last remaining member of the Legion took position atop the wall at the end of this accessway.

It was inevitable they'd be exposed at certain points. Their target had hunkered down, while they had to keep on moving.

Ashwini angled her head toward a graffiti-splattered

door on the left. Elena turned that way at the same time, but they were both too late. The Slayer fired through the wood.

Boom!
Boom!
Boom!

Elena slammed back to the wall and out of the way, saw Ashwini move to do the same . . . But the other woman crumpled instead, blood blooming on the muddy snow.

44

"Ash!" Twisting to slam multiple crossbow bolts through the door in rapid progression, the powerful bolts splintering the door to find home on the other side, Elena ran to her fallen friend. The Legion fighter landed in front of them, a crossbow in his hand.

"He got me in the leg," Ashwini said with a painful wince. She had her hand clamped over the wound. "It's not a major artery. Prop me up behind the Dumpster and go after him—Archer's lost his fucking mind."

Elena hauled Ashwini to safety and made sure the other woman had her weapon. "See if you can hail down help." Even if Cassandra's owls had gone to Raphael, it had only been a short time ago. He was unlikely to make it here in the next few minutes—Elena wasn't going to count on the startling burst of speed that had brought him to her when she collapsed.

The Cascade was never that obliging.

"I know the people around here," Ashwini assured her

through a grimace, her hand continuing to clamp down on her wound. "No one will hurt me. Go."

Elena looked at the destroyed door and knew she couldn't fit through. Her wings were too wide. Then she realized . . . her wings were already dead. *Numb.* She was shedding feathers at a phenomenal rate. Several lay in the snow around them. She couldn't slice off the wings without causing open, bleeding wounds on her back, but she also no longer had to worry about damage.

"Elena." The Legion fighter moved in front of her. "You are wounded."

"This must be done—and you are my Legion."

"Yes." He turned. "I will go first."

"Agreed." The Legion could fight like berserkers.

She angled her body through the door after him. The jagged edges gouged into her abused wings, more feathers torn off to lie against the rucked-up snow outside. Inside, the closed restaurant smelled of garlic and tomatoes and cleaning solution.

Good to know they had excellent hygiene.

Too bad about the blood she'd streak on the floors as she walked through with her wings dragging behind her. She or the Guild would send the owners a check for the cleanup and the door.

Her stomach twisted on itself, hunger striking at the worst moment.

Ignoring it, she unsheathed her sword with soundless grace. She'd chosen a scabbard lined with softness for this very reason. No point getting that glorious unsheathing sound if it put you in the crosshairs. She padded across the large kitchen space . . . just as a door banged against a wall.

Her eyes snapped forward.

Shit!

This restaurant spanned not one but two properties. Archer had exited out a second door she'd assumed belonged to another restaurant. He was in the back accessway with Ashwini . . . and Elena didn't trust Archer to remember that Ash was a friend.

"Go! Go! Go!"

The Legion fighter rushed in Archer's wake, while she raced back the way she'd come. Dragging herself through the splintered doorway, she slammed her booted feet onto the ground before Archer was halfway down the access-way, Ash safely hidden by the bulk of a Dumpster to her back right. Elena was poised to move in an attempt to avoid bullets, but the former Slayer was already turning to shoot behind him.

Elena went to scream a warning, but the Legion fighter had learned from watching his brethren fall. He used his sword to deflect the bullets. Ducking, Elena realized she risked being hit by a deflection if she went any closer—and the fighter didn't need her help.

But she reached to reload her crossbow anyway. Her forearm sheath proved empty of bolts, so she went for the one on her thigh . . . to find it gone. Torn or fallen off at some point. Likely when the Legion fighter fell out of the sky and hit her on the side.

She still had knives—plenty of them—and the sword.

"Ash, you have a gun?"

"Yeah," Ashwini said, "but it's jammed."

Fucking Cascade. It was bullying hands on her back shoving her toward a destiny she DID NOT CHOOSE!

"Blade stars?"

"Here."

Elena took four stars from her friend and fellow hunter, and only then noticed Ashwini's paleness. "Ash?"

"Lost too much blood." Her lids lowered. "Vamp. Will survive. Janvier will have heard from stree . . ."

The world went silent, Archer out of bullets. For a sear-ing instant of relief, she thought this was it: Archer's end and the end of the prophecy. But she should've remembered he was a Slayer.

Throwing aside the gun, he used his other hand to re-lease a spin of razor-sharp blade stars even as the Legion fighter's sword whistled down toward Archer's neck. Two blade stars stuck in the Legion fighter's eyes, blinding him.

Ocular fluid ran down his cheeks.

Archer had his sword out and had beheaded the fighter before Elena could throw her own blade stars. Her vision had become blurry at the edges at the critical instant, refused to clear. But she stood facing Archer, not willing to let him escape.

"No spare gun?" she said, her chest heaving. All she had to do was keep him talking. The two Legion fighters who'd gone down first would soon appear. "Oversight, huh?"

Avoiding the knives she'd launched his way under the cover of conversation, Archer raised his sword. His brown hair was disordered, his upper body clad in a thick but ragged sweater he must've grabbed during his escape—maybe from that raving homeless man—and from his dark pants wafted the scent of sugared doughnuts and cold air.

Old blood invisible against the black.

His eyes were hyper-focused. "You're one of them now, Ellie," he said, dead calm. "You think immortal life gives you the right to treat mortals like disposable dolls."

"Not sure if you've noticed, Archer," Elena said, "but I'm not exactly immortal." Her wings were dragging weights at her back, and she could see streaks of blood on the sharp edges of the doorway into the restaurant.

"You'll heal." No anger in his tone, just that same inexorable calm as he moved his sword in a stance of readiness.

Elena brought up her own sword. She was better with a crossbow than a sword, but she was no novice swordswoman. The real problem was that Archer's sword was much heavier. Hers wouldn't last long against his, but it didn't need to last long. Elena wasn't here for a swordfight. She was here to end this however she could.

"It's over," she said to the seasoned hunter in front of her. "You know it's over. There's no way you can hide now."

"I'm not hiding," he said, his voice cold. "I'm hunting." He swung out with the sword.

Elena danced back . . . and almost tripped on a limp wing. Managing to catch herself at the last moment, she held her feet while blocking his blow. *Careful, Ellie,* she reminded herself as Archer moved back. *Use your knives and Ash's stars.*

She threw the first star . . . and a sudden wind ripped it off course. Skin cold, she realized it *would* be a swordfight.

Her opponent had the advantage of not just the tight space but a slightly longer reach. Elena threw knives and two of the remaining stars without warning. The wind interrupted again—but one knife got through.

Hissing at the pain, Archer ripped out the blade she'd embedded in his biceps and threw it aside, but he kept his distance from her. His eyes flicked to the Dumpster that hid Ashwini's body. "She's one of them, too," he said. "Vampire sympathizers don't deserve mercy."

"I'm not going to argue that Eric Acosta, Simon Blakely, Nishant Kumar, and Terence Lee didn't deserve their punishment."

Archer's eyes narrowed. "Then why are you standing in my way?"

"Because you're punishing people who did nothing wrong. Harrison didn't set Samaria up. He didn't bring her to the Quarter, didn't abuse her. As the pawn shop owners didn't steal her jewelry—she chose to pawn it for money."

Color flushed his cheeks, rage glittering in his eyes. "She would've *never* been in that position if it wasn't for the blood-sucking monsters who prey on girls like her. Monsters and their cattle who lead others to slaughter."

Elena realized with shock that he was talking about Jenessa, whose only crime had been in clinging to Samaria/Lucy as a friend. "Your rules are changing." Elena was having trouble moving, numbness at her toes and at the very tips of her hands. "You're going after people who never laid a finger on your daughter."

Archer lowered himself into a fighting stance. "I guess your brother-in-law sleeps well at night because he doesn't think feeding the monsters equals being a monster himself.

My girl, my sweet Samaria would still be alive and breathing instead of rotting in the ground if he'd driven her home that night!"

"She was an adult, Archer! Harrison couldn't drag her away from the bar!"

"You know nothing about her." Archer began to advance again, slashing out with his sword and moving at lethal speed. Elena should've backed off to give herself more room, but she couldn't do so without exposing Ashwini. Archer's sword, she knew, would slice through Ash's neck like a hot knife through butter.

She began throwing knives with one hand, peppering the air with metal, while she used the slender blade of her sword to slam up against his. The vibration rang down her quivering arm, but the weapon held.

A sudden assault she pulled out of nowhere as her heart strained. Archer lost enough ground to give her breathing room and hope that the other two Legion fighters were up and on their way. Elena capitalized on her advantage by spinning a blade star toward him. The wind changed its trajectory enough that the lethal edge just grazed the side of his neck.

Giving a bloodthirsty yell, Archer came at her, sword raised. The wind dropped to dead calm, giving him no resistance. Out of throwing knives and stars, Elena went to evade him, her intent to slide out her legs and trip him . . . but her body failed her. Something snapped in her leg, causing her to stumble clumsily . . . and Archer thrust his sword through her stomach.

She looked down at the razor-sharp metal buried in her abdomen, the point coming out her back, and she thought of her archangel. *No. Fuck destiny.* But her rebellious thoughts were hazy at the edges, her blood running down to pool in the dirty snow.

Archer drew back his sword.

As she crumpled to her knees in the cold, she saw that the sword was red.

45

ELENA!

Raphael didn't bother to waste words on the man whose sword dripped with Elena's blood. A single surge of power and that man was ash. Raphael cared nothing for who he was or his motivation in harming Elena. He cared only for the hunter with hair of near-white who knelt in the bloody snow, her hands clamped over the gushing wound in her stomach and her eyes watching him land.

A soft smile on her face when he reached her. "You are magnificent in flight." It was a whisper almost without sound. "Ash . . ."

"Help comes." He'd alerted Janvier and every other vampire and angel he trusted in the vicinity when the ghostly owls had appeared around him, warning him to go to Elena.

But no one had found his heart, his Elena, in time.

The owls had led him here on white wings while Raphael pushed his immortal body to the limit, his wings of white fire repudiating his attempts at preternatural speed.

He was sweat-soaked, his heartbeat a roar, but the owls were unchanged. They sat silent and solemn around Elena's mortally wounded body.

A motorcycle crashed to the road as Janvier ran down the dark lane to his wife.

"Your friend is safe," Raphael told his hunter, because he knew that mattered to her.

A sigh. "Sorry . . ." Blood coughed out of her mouth. "Had . . . so many feathers left . . . when I started. Thought . . . could fight fate."

Cradling her in his arms, his wings solid and aglow, Raphael lifted up into the air as two Legion fighters rose from the dead. He told them to stay with Janvier and Ashwini.

"Fuck fate," he said in response to her words. "We'll write our own future." And in that future, Raphael would not have a dead consort.

Child of the flames.

To be called a "child" by anyone but his mother was a strange thing for Raphael, but Cassandra was older than an Ancient. To her, he was barely formed. *Cassandra,* he said, *I thank you for the warning.*

It had not come soon enough, but he'd found Elena while she yet had life in her body. Now he flew his consort not to the Tower but to their home. He'd already ordered Nisia to meet him there. Elena would not want to be seen this way by those in the Tower. She was a warrior, her strength her armor.

Fate realigns. She must die for the other to live.

Jaw hard, Raphael landed on the snow outside their home.

"Raphael." Elena's voice, so thin now. "My wings . . ."

Raphael's skin burned with golden lightning. "They will heal." He'd fight the Cascade itself to make that happen.

"No." Shallow breaths, her hazy eyes finding his. "Cut them off. They're dead."

Rage tore through him because she was right; her wings were nothing but heavy protrusions pulling at her spine, limp and without strength. And yet, to strip his Elena of her wings? *"Hbeebti?"* It was a plea.

"I'm sorry, Archangel." Her body swaying into his. "Please."

She could've shot him again and again, and it would've hurt less.

He shifted her in his embrace so that she was "standing" against him. Her blood dripped to the snow. Barely able to see through his angry grief, he used his power to cleanly excise both wings from her back, searing the wound shut as he went. They fell bloody and broken to the snow.

A burst of power and her wings were ash.

He would not have Elena see her amputated wings. Cradling her against his chest again, he ran into the house.

Montgomery's face was a study in horror, but his butler snapped to action. "I will bring supplies to help with the wounds."

"Nisia comes!" Raphael rose up on his wings to the second floor and their bedroom. "Bring her the instant she lands."

A moment later, he lay his bleeding and badly wounded consort on the bed and he had a sudden panic. "I should've taken you to the human doctors."

Bloody fingers brushed his cheek. "No. Look."

Thick white filaments covered the back of her hand, and when he tore off her jacket and the top she wore underneath to reveal her brutal stomach injury, he found more of those delicate filaments crawling across her skin. He ripped them away in clumps, but they only regenerated. Like vines growing on her as soil.

"Cascade." Her voice like air, Elena put a bloody hand on his. "Not human thing."

Tearing his wrist open, Raphael went to drip his blood into her mouth. She didn't stop him, though she made a face, his hunter fierce and wild and laughing and his eternity. Her eyes blazed golden and he thought it would work . . . right as golden streamers of energy poured out of her stomach wound to sink back into him.

Her eyes dimmed, became mortal gray again.

"NO!" It was a roar of sound. "Why is your body rejecting my energy?"

"I'm mortal." Elena coughed up more blood.

It is time, child of flame. She must die for the other to live.

Raphael went to thrust Cassandra out of his mind—he was not Elena, who had no such ability. He was an *archangel*. But a fraction of sense shoved through the storm inside him. *Who is the other?* The one question Cassandra had not answered. *Will Elena live if I destroy the other?* Raphael didn't care if the other was a being capable of ending Lijuan herself; weighed against Elena's life, that unknown being had no value to him.

She is the other.

The words made no sense. "Cassandra says you are the other," he said to his consort.

The thunder of feet, Nisia running into the room to jump onto the bed beside Elena.

Raphael kept his hand cupped around the side of Elena's face as the healer attempted to seal the wound that had stained the bed a dark scarlet.

"I am the other," Elena repeated on a bloody whisper.

It is a time of change.

Hope burst open in Raphael's heart. *Is this just a stage in her development? Like the creatures that form a chrysalis then emerge?* That would explain the white filaments that were now spreading up her neck in fine tendrils, like living snowflakes. On her chest, the spot the Legion had called a mirror sat silent and dark beneath the thick covering of white.

Wrong, he thought, that was wrong. A mirror should not absorb all light, all energy.

Yes, said Cassandra's voice at the same instant. *But she will not wake. The other will wake.*

Raphael found patience he'd never known he possessed. *What will happen to my Elena?*

Memories, thoughts, laughter, tears, these will not survive. The other will be new. A birth.

Horror clawed at him. "Elena, you must listen." He kissed her, and when she opened her heavy lids, he told her Cassandra's words and saw the dawn of her own horror.

"Raphael."

"I remember, *hbeebti*. I remember."

I would rather die as Elena, than live as a shadow.

Words she'd said to him long ago, when he'd spoken about erasing her mind of certain memories.

Why? he asked Cassandra. *Why does the Cascade kill Elena? She is my heartbeat and the reason I can fight Lijuan.* Her mortality had helped create the wildfire that was the one weapon they knew worked against Lijuan.

Child of fire, child of love, you cannot carry enough of the wild, bright fire in your body to fight the nightmare that comes. A mirror is not enough this time. There must be a vessel.

His rage became ice. *I do not wish to be Lijuan who feeds from others, and I don't need anyone to turn my consort into an energy container. I need her.*

End her now or let the newborn vessel rise. That is the only choice.

"Sire." Nisia, always unflappable, was sobbing so hard she could barely speak. "I can't make her body heal itself." She raised bloody hands from Elena's wound. "My power is rejected."

"Go," Raphael ordered. "My consort and I have a decision to make."

Elena was barely clinging to consciousness, but she managed to meet his gaze. "Tell me."

So he did.

A faint smile. "A glorified gas tank?"

"This is no time for jokes, Guild Hunter." He went to cradle her into his arms, but her body was stiff with all the filaments blooming on her skin. A few thin tendrils crawled up her cheek. "We must find a third solution."

Elena's hand curled on the bed, a weak motion, her eyelids fluttering.

And Raphael's mind went cold in the way that had infuriated his consort. But now, in the horror, it allowed him to think with crystalline clarity. "Elena, I can take your memories, all of you." He'd never attempted such a wholesale gathering of memories, had only ever taken or erased discrete ones. "I'm awash in power. I can hold you inside me until your body returns." That was all the "newborn" would be—no mind, no heart, no soul.

Never his Elena.

"Trust me, Elena-mine," he begged. "I will not violate your mind. I will hold you safe deep inside me."

"Trust . . ." A breath. *"Always."*

But when he placed both hands around her head, those hands rippling with bolts of golden power, and tried to pull her into him, it failed. Over and over again. "NO." His voice boomed with a power that was useless here.

"Not even an archangel," Elena whispered as her lashes shut, "can carry two souls."

"I have no intention of surrendering you to the Cascade." He tore away the filaments blooming on her face, so he could see her. They bloomed again, and he tore them away again.

And again. And again.

Each time he did so, her face was thinner, her bones more prominent. Elena was being consumed. And all his power meant nothing. If the Cascade wished to turn him into a monster, it had chosen the perfect hell to break him. His skin burned with a glow that made Elena's hair appear like fire when he tore away the filaments with relentless focus.

"Knhebek, Raphael." Her breath rattled.

She was dying in his arms, her wings stolen, their future erased.

Throwing back his head, Raphael roared out his pain and his rage. When he could see again, focus again, he saw the Primary crouched on the balcony railing outside. Hundreds of the Legion were landing around him. "Why does the Cascade care if I have the power to battle Lijuan?" The Cascade wasn't a sentient being; it was a confluence of time and power that shaped immortals in strange, unexpected ways.

No answer from Cassandra.

But the Primary said, "It does not. It seeks only chaos. There is no chaos in one power."

"I will not be alive without you," Raphael said to his warrior. "I will be another form of the dead. I will care nothing for good or evil."

Elena's breath was so shallow now it was almost nonexistent, but she forced her eyes open with a will he'd loved from the first. "Stay . . ."—she coughed, blood flecking his tunic—"a little mortal, won't you, Archangel."

"You are my mortality." Cold and dark, Raphael's mind cut through the shadows to see each and every essential truth. His power was being rejected because he was too immortal in nature and Elena was mortal again. Until the filaments swallowed her whole and the transition began, she would stay mortal.

And his heart . . . his heart was a little bit mortal. *Had* to stay a little bit mortal for Cassandra's prophecy to come true when the world faced Lijuan once again. He must remain the archangel kissed by mortality—and it was around his heart with its touch of mortality that the wildfire crackled.

That heart was where his new golden energy was slowly being changed into more wildfire, powered by his will and refusal to be manipulated. His heart was the engine of change filtering the new energy into the most dangerous form possible. But the wildfire would've never been born without Elena.

It would be a risk. If he was wrong, Elena would die.

But if he did nothing, she would die.

Tearing off his tunic as her breath got shallower while she fought to the last to hold on to consciousness, he punched his hand through his ribcage with archangelic power to capture his beating heart. The agony was blinding, Elena's eyes suddenly wide in panic, but Raphael had a task to complete.

He dropped his heart to the bed, where it continued to pulse frantically. He had only moments—even an archangel could not function without a heart. It would take time to regenerate, and he needed to act before this heart was dead. Golden Cascade-born energy rippled through his heart, but hidden within was a near-uncontrollable and radiant white-gold flame . . . with iridescent edges of midnight and dawn.

The earliest, most primal form of wildfire.

Of Raphael and his consort.

"Your body cannot absorb a full archangelic heart," he managed to say even as his own body began to shut down. "But a small piece of one could give you power enough to resist the tyranny of the Cascade energies."

Distress in Elena's eyes, she went to reach out her hand . . . but that was when her chest shuddered in a last, gasping breath. The white filaments began to bloom rapidly over her body, ready to consume her and birth an abomination of his Elena.

Not hesitating, Raphael thrust his hand through her own ribcage and tore out her heart as the weak and failing organ riddled with white filaments gave its last beat. He used his power to incise out as large a piece of his own heart as he thought her body could bear, from the very core—the part with the most wildfire, and thrust it within the bloody cavity.

Wildfire exploded inside her chest, but his vision was fading, his body about to topple. As he fell, his gaze caught on Elena's vulnerable and soft mortal heart and he couldn't abandon it. He would protect it. Picking it up, he thrust it inside the hole where his heart should've been . . . and fell onto the bed, his wing heavy over Elena's body and his mouth full of blood.

46

Sire. You must wake.

The voice nudged at his consciousness again and again until Raphael stirred. *Jason?* Scents of old blood and absence in his breath, his chest a heavy ache.

Yes, it's Jason. You must wake.

Jason was not an angel to say such things without reason.

Shrugging off the heaviness of sleep, Raphael opened his eyes. His wing no longer lay over Elena's body. Where she'd been was an oval chrysalis. White filaments flowed out from the chrysalis like water, falling over the bed and spreading across the carpet.

When he rose, he had to tear himself from the strands that had flowed over him in his sleep. "Fight, hunter-mine," he said, not knowing if she could hear him . . . if she'd ever hear him again. "You have always written your own history. Now write ours."

Sire.

The sharp concern in Jason's voice got through this time. Reaching out his infinitely more powerful mind to catch the spymaster's faint whisper, Raphael said, *How far away are you?* Jason had to be incredibly distant for his voice to be so weak in Raphael's mind.

I am over the ocean. Perhaps two hours on the wing from Manhattan, his spymaster told him. *I took too long to leave—I could not go while there was no news of you or Elena. I intended to fly into Titus's territory first, pick up any news from there, then fly on to China.* Augmented by Raphael's archangelic strength, his voice came through strong and clear. *I have just seen what appears to be an army headed toward New York.*

Raphael looked down at his chest. The hole remained, though it was webbed over with wildfire. He hadn't finished healing, had only half a heart. It seemed appropriate that he would go into battle with only half a heart when he had no Elena by his side.

"I will keep the predators from the door," he promised her. "Just come back to me."

Leaving the bed, he washed off any dried blood then dressed in leathers of old and weathered bronze paired with worn-in boots. It wouldn't do to advertise that he was wounded. That done, he gripped two heavy swords and slid them into crisscrossed sheaths on his back. Archangels rarely fought sword-to-sword when it came to it, but Raphael wanted to be ready for anything.

How long did I sleep? he asked the Primary, for a number of the Legion sat on the balcony, watching through the glass doors.

Four days. We did not allow anyone to interrupt.

Raphael nodded. *Protect her. She is your only priority.*

He hauled open the doors.

Illium stood on the far edge, swords at the ready and his expression wearing death. When he saw Raphael, he shuddered, his eyes closing for a heartbeat before he raised his lashes again. "Ellie?"

"She fights," was all he said, and saw Illium's heart break in front of him. "Come. Jason says an army is heading toward the city." Chest aching, he lifted up into the air.

Do you believe Lijuan has woken? Raphael asked his spymaster as he and Illium flew seaward.

I cannot see her, but she could be hidden in the mass of the flyers.

I am coming out to you, Jason.

"Sire," Illium said across the icy winter air between them. "I have alerted the squadrons to join us."

"Stay with me. Tell the others to follow."

Illium was one of the fastest angels in the world, could keep pace with Raphael. He didn't have the endurance of an archangel, but he wouldn't need it for the distance in question. It still took him effort to stay with Raphael, was one of the few times Raphael had seen the blue-winged angel breathing heavily in flight, beads of sweat rolling down his temples.

They hit the water, New York disappearing rapidly behind them until it wasn't even a smudge on the horizon, but there was no sign of Jason or of the army he'd warned against.

Jason, where are you?

Heading in your direction. I flew back to see if I could discern anything further.

A risky move, but if anyone could do it, it was Jason. *Did you see Lijuan?*

No. Favashi is the archangel flying in the center.

Fly toward me as fast as you can, Jason. This is a battle of archangels.

Sire.

His chest straining from the force of the flight, Raphael told Illium what Jason had shared. The blue-winged angel swung down on an air current, riding it to conserve his energy, then swept back up. His wings glittered in the sunlight. The sluggish cloud cover had finally moved, and though the sea would be a chilling embrace for a fallen angel, no snow fell from the sky.

"Sire," Illium said aloud, the two of them close enough now that they could exchange words again. "What possible reason could Favashi have for mounting an assault against New York? You've always had a good relationship with her."

"She has no rational reason to come at me—and if her spymaster is even half as good as Jason, he must know that my territory is heavily guarded." Raphael didn't sit on his laurels; he'd learned from the last battle and fixed the holes in his defenses.

He'd also taken on more warriors. Many of them had been independents to whom he'd had Galen make a personal offer. He'd expected perhaps a quarter to respond—sometimes ennui got to even the best of men, and they felt no impetus to interact with the world. Most eventually slid into Sleep.

The response rate had been seventy-five percent.

It turned out that doing scandalous things like falling in love with a mortal then turning her into an angel, followed by defeating Lijuan in battle, had made New York something of a "fascinating hotspot" to immortals.

Elena's words.

That their city also had pretzel bars, coffee stations, even burger carts on rooftops—fly-throughs, as some clever human had nicknamed them—was seen as exotic and outlandish and worthy of a visit.

But if the old vampires and angels had originally come to satisfy their curiosity about Raphael's territory, they stayed because New York had seduced them. More, Elena had seduced them. She didn't even know she was doing it, but he'd seen the way the old ones watched her—as if she was a new and prized treasure, surprising and unexpected.

Three weeks before it all began to go wrong, he'd seen her offer to take a five-thousand-year-old female warrior to a dance club on a rooftop after the angel mused about not having danced for centuries. The warrior had returned luminous with a renewed sense of excitement about the world, her gaze holding a whisper of the youth she'd once been.

Elena woke people up with her raw zest for life, reminding them what it was to be alive. And now his hunter battled a foe that sought to erase her . . . and Raphael went into battle with her heart cradled inside his, the fragile light of mortality somehow not extinguished by the violent forces in his body.

I see Illium's wings.

Raphael spotted Jason at the same time that his spymaster's voice filled his mind. Jason's black wings were stark against the winter blue sky, his black clothing the same. *How far behind you are they?* An army could never move as fast as a strong lone warrior.

At least twenty minutes, Jason told him.

The three of them met above the ocean, nothing beneath them but waves that had begun to crash in a pattern that did not reflect the weather. First, he got numbers from Jason about the size of the army; then he asked if Favashi had brought her senior people. A single skilled and powerful fighter could do the same damage as a hundred unskilled warriors.

"That's the strange thing," Jason said. "From what I could see, all of those at the leading edge of the formation are Lijuan's people who stayed behind and joined Favashi's court."

"Impossible." Illium shook his head, the blue-tipped black strands of his hair whipping wildly in the wind that had begun to rise. "Favashi may have accepted those people into her court, but she wouldn't trust them, not enough for anything like this."

"I agree," Jason said, his power a quiet but potent darkness. "But that's what I saw."

None of this made any kind of sense.

"I'll go ahead," Raphael said to Jason and Illium. "Flank me, but stay back far enough that she can't eliminate you both with a single strike."

The two angels nodded.

And Raphael flew toward the approaching army as his grievously wounded heart struggled to beat.

The Legion

In the bedroom in the Enclave, the chrysalis lay unmoving. It was too small, the Legion thought, their bodies crouched all over the room. A chrysalis that size could not hold Elena.

There was no room for her wings. Her height.

Will she be born as a child? one part of their mind asked.

Conversation abounded in silence.

We do not know, was the consensus. *But the chrysalis is too small.*

47

The rising wind ripped at Raphael's hair as, ahead of them, a huge army took shape. But holding to archangelic expectation and the "rules" of war, Favashi broke off to fly directly toward him. Two others came with her, an echo of Illium and Jason.

The rest of her forces were too slow to keep up with Favashi and her seconds, and so when they met, it was as an even grouping.

"Favashi."

"Raphael."

His blood iced. Because that wasn't Favashi's voice. It held death and whispers and screams. It was the voice of an archangel who was meant to be lost in Sleep, far from the living world.

As for the rest of her . . . Those weren't Favashi's eyes either.

The former Archangel of Persia and current Archangel of China didn't have black eyes. Her eyes were a deep, rich brown.

"You are changed," he said to her.

"I am *more*." Favashi's voice was awash with screaming whispers, and when she raised her hand, it crackled out of existence. Not as smooth a shift as with Lijuan, but Favashi shouldn't have had such a power at all. The ability to go noncorporeal *was not hers*.

Favashi was rumored to have gained power over the winds during the Cascade—which might explain the howling gale that now surrounded them, but the rest . . . that belonged to the former Archangel of China.

Unless . . . "Did you gain this power in the last Cascade surge?"

Black lightning crackled from Favashi's fingertips in answer, the bolts screaming over Raphael's shoulder and past Jason, who'd dropped to avoid the strike. "A demonstration only," she said in the aftermath, as the black energy that "smelled" of Lijuan smashed into the ocean and disappeared. "I am a power now, and you will bow down before me."

Raphael missed Elena with a ferocious need at that instant. She would've said something about "Her Creepiness" coming back from the dead, and inside, he would've found amusement even during the prelude to war.

Sire, can archangels be possessed? Illium's voice, so different from Elena's, and yet the question was one Elena might well have asked—there was a reason the two had become such friends.

Raphael thought of how he'd battled to hold Elena's memories, her essence, inside himself only to fail. And he thought of Holly Chang, who'd been haunted by an energy that should've ended with Uram. *Lijuan was no ordinary archangel—and we do not know how the Cascade twists the rules of life and death and Sleep.*

Ignoring the pain in his chest, his heart with its mortal core straining to support his archangelic body, he coaxed a ball of wildfire to his hand, the colors swirling brilliant white-gold with deep edges of midnight and dawn. His

Elena, inside him. "We have had this battle before," he said softly. "You lost."

The words should've made no sense to Favashi, who had never faced Raphael in battle, but she screeched and unleashed another bolt at him. This time it was aimed directly at his heart—and it seemed to him that Favashi flinched . . . just before he intercepted it with wildfire and it dissipated into nothing.

He had more wildfire inside him, all that had been generated before he tore out his heart, but he was too drained to rule it to his will. If he drew much more, he risked it going wild—his half-regenerated heart with its mortal core couldn't take the strain of access and control.

To win this battle, he would need to fight with cutting intelligence.

Suddenly Favashi was throwing the black lightning from every fingertip, her assault so vicious that her own guard fell back, unable to break through the hail of black to safely get to Jason or Illium.

Both members of his Seven dropped to a much lower altitude. Raphael meanwhile was avoiding the strikes but not attempting to neutralize all of them. He caught only the ones at risk of hitting his body or his wings. And still, he was nearly at his limit, his heart about to fail.

Sire, the squadrons near, Illium informed him. *But Favashi's army will arrive first.*

Raphael avoided another bolt—and realized Favashi was wavering, her targets off. It was just as well, because his heart was beginning to miss beats. He avoided Favashi's last bolts before they fizzled out to nothing.

Across from him, the Archangel of China swayed in the air and her eyes cleared for a second to reveal the deep brown with which he was familiar. "Raphael." It came out a whisper. "You must not let her take me."

Streaks of black snaked up her eyes again.

Raphael surged forward. Favashi's attendants tried to stop him, but Jason and Illium had already intercepted the

two. The strike of sword against sword rang out across the
air as the four fighters clashed.

"Give the order," Raphael said to Favashi when they
were only a hairsbreadth apart. "*Quickly*, while you can."

Favashi curled her fingers into her palms, squeezed her
eyes shut, and said nothing. But the two angels who'd been
fighting with Illium and Jason fell back. One said, "My
lady?"

Whatever message Favashi gave them, they flew off toward the rest of her army . . . Which began to turn as one.

"I am not a mortal to be taken," Favashi gritted out. "I
am not a beast to be broken." Each word was red with
power and anger and rage. "I am an *archangel*."

The black crackled over her irises again. As it had once
attempted to blind Raphael. "Is it a part of Lijuan?" Uram
had left behind an echo of energy, but his victim, Holly, had
been young and a multitude of times weaker than Favashi.

"It feels like an infection. A virulent one designed to
crawl into archangelic bones." She shivered hard, streaks of
black racing through the aged ivory of her wings before
they began to retract, as if she was fighting a battle within.

"I do not think it can take you, Raphael. You beat her.
That's why, when it pushed me to battle madness, I fought
to take the battle to you." Her eyes landed on the wildfire
that danced on Raphael's fingertips. "This death is buried
in China. Send no one there. Not one of us. It is made for
us." Her back arched, a scream pouring out of her mouth
and it was a scream of violence, of madness.

Raphael placed his hand directly on Favashi's heart, his
palm burning with the last whispers of wildfire he could
coax to do his will. Instead of fighting what might be a killing blow, Favashi gripped his wrist, holding him to her.

And the wildfire punched into her.

The black disappeared from her wings under a searing
edge of wildfire, the screaming madness stopped, and when
she looked at him again, her eyes were that familiar rich
brown. "I cannot know if it has been destroyed. I was too
long in that place."

What had Lijuan become that she'd been able to leave behind a virus that attacked an archangel? Even Charisemnon's disease-causing abilities didn't dare reach for the Cadre.

"I can't keep pushing wildfire into you," he told Favashi. "If you are infected with a death born of Lijuan, the wildfire will eventually kill you."

Favashi's head jerked, a sudden faraway look on her face. "There is another kind of fire in your territory. It calls to me."

In front of Raphael, her face began to lose its softness, until her bones shoved out against her skin, her collarbones appearing as suddenly, her arms no longer smooth but jagged with bones. She was being consumed as Elena had been consumed.

"It has taken all my energy to fight this," she rasped, no fat on her bones now, her skin holding together bones and muscle and tendon alone. "I feel your wildfire eating away at it, but I must . . ." She crumpled.

Raphael caught her skeletal form and, after confirming her army was fading into the distance, flew directly toward the only fire in his land that could've spoken to Favashi. Illium fell in with him, while Jason broke off to take control of the squadrons that had responded to Illium's command.

As per the plan Raphael had put in place for just such a contingency, New York's forces would now spread outward, a constant watch on all their borders until Jason's spies reported that Favashi's army had landed in China.

The journey to the sinkhole at the foot of the Catskills was again a hard one for Illium. Despite his exhaustion and faltering heart, Raphael gave no quarter, needed to be back with Elena. The blue-winged angel was dripping with sweat by the time they arrived.

Ah, you have come.

"To the edge, Bluebell—this is a matter between an archangel and an Ancient among Ancients."

Illium's expression held rebellion, but he gave a curt nod and went to hover at the very edge of the sinkhole.

The lava began to bubble and spread in a pattern that formed a whirlpool at its very center. Elena would've found it astonishing, he thought. She'd also have wondered what kind of insanity they'd be facing now.

Zombies, Archangel. Fire-breathing ones.

Yes, she'd have muttered that while staying courageously by his side.

But it wasn't a zombie that emerged out of the flames. It was a woman formed of fire. When the glowing magma dropped away to rejoin the swirl that was the sinkhole, he saw an angel clad in a long gown of palest green that was like air given form; it both clung and fell away from the lush curves of her body. Her hair was a tumble of lilac and her eyes empty, bleeding orbs. Dark red tears ran down her cheeks, her skin a pitiless white canvas for the brutality of it. Her wings, in contrast, were a violet so deep it was blue.

Reaching Raphael with soft beats of her wings, she looked at him with those sightless eyes. "You have half a heart." A pause, a frown. "And you have two hearts. Yet you are not whole."

"I won't be whole until my Elena wakes." An absolute truth. "What do you see?"

"The future has warped." A bloody tear dropping to stain her gown. "I see . . . nothing. I see a million possibilities. I see chaos and horror. I see hope and life. I see everything that could be."

We battled destiny and changed time, Elena-mine. The future was now theirs to shape.

Cassandra touched his face with fingers that bore nails encrusted with blood. "Ambrosia will flow and a mortal will be made an angel when an archangel loves true." She spoke the words in a singsong voice. "That is what I saw and that is what I wrote and that was a future born."

"Elena is the first angel-Made." That was the answer to why there were no records, no road map to follow; the legend of ambrosia had been born of a prophecy spoken by an angel so old she was legend.

Cassandra held out her arms. "This child of kin's blood-line is mine. In this moment, and in this time, she is mine."

Raphael gave her Favashi because there was no other choice and because Favashi had spoken of this place. "When will she return?"

"Madness is coming. Life is coming. Wonder is coming. Death is coming. The future warps again and again." Tired-ness, such aching tiredness. "I try so hard to Sleep, but even in my Sleep, I dream. I see." A pause. "I helped your love, this prophecy-of-mine, alter time. A new dawn not yet seen, not yet known."

She hugged Favashi's frail body close. "Fire cleanses. I knew fire would be needed. On this day and in this time, fire would be needed. For you alone cannot fight what she has become. The Cadre alone cannot fight the evil that Sleeps."

Cassandra pressed a kiss to Favashi's brow. "Archangel of Death. Goddess of Nightmare. Wraith without a shadow. Rise, rise, rise into your Reign of Death. For your end will come. Your end will come. At the hands of the new and of the old. An Archangel kissed by mortality. A silver-winged Sleeper who wakes before his Sleep is done. The broken dream with eyes of fire. Shatter. Shatter. Shatter."

More bloody tears. "This was to be. Death, endless death, followed by victory. But you and the fragile, courageous prophecy-of-mine have rewritten destiny, erased the future to be. Time warps and changes. Only one constant remains. The Sleeper, the Wraith, the Goddess. She will rise and she will be monstrous."

Cassandra began to lower herself into the lava. She was a being of liquid fire again before she reached the molten core, Favashi invisible against her.

The sinkhole began to close over in front of their eyes.

Two minutes after the encounter with an Ancient out of angelic myth, there was nothing there, no sign a sinkhole had ever existed. The earth was not bare. Grass grew, peb-bles rolled around on it, and the wind swirled snow against the barrier of the fence.

Elena would not be pleased to have missed such a sight.

Inside his chest, his heart gave a sluggish beat. *Come, Illium. You must watch for my fall today.*

The blue-winged angel flew below him all the way home.

But even safely landed, Raphael could not yet rest. First, he must warn the Cadre about China. He called an urgent meeting using a signal that was never to be ignored. Their faces appeared one after the other on the screen in his study, cold and immortal and altered with Cascade-born power.

Only Michaela, strikingly beautiful and deeply manipulative, was different. She appeared . . . faded, tired.

Raphael described only what had happened to Favashi, shared only what Cassandra had said about Lijuan being a monstrous world-destroying force when she next woke. Too big for even the Cadre.

It was Caliane who broke the silence that had fallen after his short, curt report. "I would ask if you dreamed this, my son, but I know you are too practical and pragmatic a warrior to create fantasies—and I saw Favashi's strangeness firsthand a month earlier, when I flew to offer her counsel."

Neha was the next to speak. "So did I," said the Archangel of India, her sari a yellow that made her skin shimmer with light. "I wanted to brush it off as arrogance, but there was a falseness to her presence, as if a shadow lay atop it."

Raphael conserved his energy and let the ensuing discussion flow at its own pace until Titus said, "China is not safe."

All the Cadre nodded as one.

Even Charisemnon's expression was black. Archangels, after all, were not supposed to be prey. Such a line had never before been crossed in their histories.

"It cannot be left unguarded." Alexander's silver eyes were a painful echo of the ring of silver around Elena's irises. "We saw what happened in the short period that Lijuan was missing. We cannot know how long Favashi will be gone."

"She was adamant that whatever it is that Lijuan left behind in her territory, it affects only archangels," Raphael pointed out. "Favashi has a number of strong men and women loyal to her who can run things in the interim. There are also enough of us that we can rotate through China to ensure no one in her territory forgets the Cadre exists even if they do not have a resident archangel."

A cycle of flights was swiftly worked out. None of them would land in China, but an archangel didn't need to land to make his or her power felt. Raphael, Astaad—Archangel of the Pacific Isles—and a number of others would stay in Japan when it came time for their turn at policing Favashi's territory in her absence.

Caliane was considered neutral ground. She wasn't neutral, of course, would always fight in Raphael's corner. But she also wouldn't take it amiss if an archangel guested in her territory—perhaps it was because of her love for Nadiel, but Raphael's mother could tolerate the presence of another archangel close by for relatively long periods.

It was also agreed that none of them would use an archangel's absence from his or her own territory to attempt to gain a foothold in that territory. The rest of the Cadre would unite against any such attempt, no matter friendships or alliances. This was a thing about controlling vampires; the Cadre would not let the world drown in bloodlust regardless of their other enmities.

Neha volunteered to take extra shifts. "It will be less of a distance for me, and seeing me will remind them that an archangel resides within easy reach."

Caliane also volunteered to do extra shifts. "Five years," his mother said afterward. "If Favashi yet Sleeps, then we must make a long-term plan."

"It is settled," said the Cadre, and the meeting was over.

His wound bleeding under his leathers, Raphael staggered up the steps. Such a wound needed the deep recovery of *anshara*, not a battle against another archangel.

Sire. Sire. Sire. The Legion's voices filled his head as he entered the room. *The chrysalis is too small.* Dismay in every word. *Where will her wings grow?*

Hand pressed to his heart, Raphael crashed onto the bed and onto the silken filaments that flowed from the chrysalis that *was* too small to hold his hunter's tall body and extra-ordinary wings. His own wing fell across the chrysalis and his heart, it stopped.

The Legion

The Primary watched Raphael's blood seep from his body in a direct line to the chrysalis, where it was absorbed without a trace. The filaments from Elena's chrysalis spread over him, cocooning him in a delicate blanket.

The Legion sat. They held guard.

Time passed.

Others loyal to the *aeclari* came to the place where they slept, but they did not disturb the sleeping pair. The one the Legion thought of as the Blade entered only once, to ensure his archangel lived.

He told the Legion that the archangel was not in *anshara,* the deep healing sleep that also allowed reason. Raphael's sleep was beyond that. He didn't breathe. His heart didn't beat. But he lived, his hair midnight under the filaments of white and his skin cracked with gold.

Of Elena, no one knew. The chrysalis was opaque to the healer who had watched Elena become an angel, and he left with sorrow deep grooves in his face.

The one she called Bluebell stood often on the balcony, a silent sentinel.

A warrior child came to the house once. She demanded to see her sister, but the Legion knew this Elena would never permit. They were not mortal, but they had been enough in the mortal world to understand what it was to protect a young heart. But they did not have to tell the warrior child she could not see Elena.

The one called Montgomery, who often asked the Legion if they needed food or drink, did the task with a quiet voice, and gentle arms that held the warrior child close when she cried. But it was the Blade who spoke to the others, for they came to the Tower in search of Elena. Sara, the friend of Elena's heart who spoke for all the other hunter warriors. Jeffrey, the father who was not a father. And Beth, a sister so scared of the Tower, but who came asking after Elena.

Others did not come, but the Legion heard the Storm with black wings talking to the Blade and they knew the Cadre watched New York. Where was Raphael? they asked. Where was his consort? When the one who had sent disease to the *aeclari*'s city thought to grasp at this land, the archangel who laughed and made women smile massed his forces on the diseased archangel's border and peace held.

The Mother came. She fought with the Blade to see her son. The Blade would not move. "You are an archangel," he told her when she threatened his life, "but he is my liege. I cannot allow you to pass."

The Mother was very strong, but she was not mad. Not in this life. She fought bitterly, but she did not destroy. And she made it clear to the others of the Cadre that if they came for New York, they would come for her. The General who had once been the Mother's sent his birds of prey and his wild cats to the city in a silent symbol of allegiance.

And the peace held.

When the Queen, who mourned her daughter and looked at Raphael with hate but also sometimes with sorrow, told the Blade of the continuing strangeness in the land of the giver of death who Slept, he told her he would tell his sire. He said nothing about when, and she did not ask.

And the peace held.

Quakes ravaged the lands of the archangel who was of water and islands. Such things should not be, but they were. Ice furies hit the lands of the archangel of sunlight and silver. Heat scalded the mountainous territory of the archangel of beauty. And deep inside the territory of the giver of death who Slept, there was a growing hollowness, thousands gone without a trace.

But the peace, it held.

Those of the house of the *aeclari* accepted the Legion's right to guard the sleeping place, their activity muted and near-silent. Without the archangel and his consort, they moved like automatons deprived of their reason for being.

The Legion saw all of this. They were seven hundred and seventy-seven, and they could not all stand sentinel while the *aeclari* slept; they did many tasks and the knowledge was shared. But always, their core watched and held guard. This was their truth. This was their existence.

The chrysalis grew. Too slow. Too small. Still too small.

The Legion did not move.

They listened for the restarting of an archangelic heart.

They waited for the chrysalis to open.

They watched.

48

"Shh, my darling, shh."

Raphael had not stood in this verdant field far from civilization for . . . a long time. He had been a boy when he
fell. When his mother crashed him to the earth. His blood
had been rubies on the pure green of the grass, each fila-
ment so perfectly designed, each dewdrop a diamond.

And his bones, they'd been in so many pieces he could
not even crawl.

He'd lain in the field as the seasons turned. He'd watched
an insect labor across the earth. And he'd listened to the
birds sing. They had brought him berries, those birds,
thinking him a fledgling fallen out of the nest. There he'd
lain with his broken wings spread out on the grass while it
grew around him, over him.

Wildflowers had bloomed in his blood.

He'd been haunted by the memory of his mother's delicate feet walking away. Her bare soles stepping on the grass
bejeweled with his blood while the white of her gown flickered at her ankles.

"Eyes a blue as pure as the heart of the sun. Hair the heart of midnight. My son who is her mirror."

On this field, he'd been a broken mirror.

Raphael frowned as the birds fell silent. "Mirror," he spoke aloud into the silence of this field where his mother had left him.

Aeclari are mirrors.

The mirror is not enough.

Sounds clashed into the peace of this place out of time and he knew he dreamed. And he thought of the last time he'd lived this memory. Elena had invaded his dream then. She'd found him in the stygian darkness of the sea, too, when the Legion drew him into their domain.

Sounds shattered the silence once more, sword against sword, a desperate battle.

"A little help here, Archangel." The voice was faint, but he'd know it even were it soundless.

His consort was invading his dream again.

Though he knew it was only his mind attempting to find hers and filling in the emptiness with illusion, Raphael withdrew his swords from the crisscrossed sheaths on his back and stepped forward out of the grass and into a deep gray nothingness that reminded him of the darkness below the ocean.

He'd lit it with wildfire then, creating a small sun.

Coaxing newborn flickers of wildfire from his body, he threw it up into the gray. It cut light across the world. And he was spinning before he'd consciously processed what he'd seen, his back slamming up hard against Elena's.

He lifted his swords to block the strike of an assailant that had no face.

"What took you so long, Archangel?" Elena called back.

"I'm growing my heart around yours," he answered even as he spun to help her block the advance of three bloodlust-driven vampires with hooked claws. "I'll keep your heart safe, but it's too mortal for an archangel. I must grow an immortal one around it."

Breath hard, Elena said, "That's super-weird, because I

have the most *ginormous* heart inside my chest. I'm getting used to it, though." Her back slammed against his again, the ridged scars where he'd amputated her wings apparent to him even through her clothing and his. "The Cascade fucking took my fucking wings!" Each word accompanied by a throwing blade finding its mark.

Raphael's body stirred, his blood wildfire. "Am I in your dream, Elena, or are you in mine?" She felt real, not an illusion. When his skin brushed hers, when his wing moved across her body, when her voice reached him, it all felt *right*.

"No idea." A possessive kiss when she faced him again, the rawly physical act erasing any notion of dreams and illusions.

Her eyes melted to silver, inhuman in their beauty. "I remember now, Archangel." Twisting out, she blocked another attack, as he did the same.

When they came together again, she was breathless. "You shouldn't have given me your heart. You shouldn't have taken mine—it was fully mortal with a side of Cascade weirdness."

"A thank-you would be nice." He beheaded a horde of reborn with rotting limbs. "It's not every day a man gives you his heart."

"What did I say about the jokes?" She poked him gently with the hilt of her sword before they were deluged by opponents.

In a small moment of peace: "Raphael, how long can we keep this up?"

"Not long," he said, able to see the green of the grass beyond the gray. He could step out and be back on that field so brilliant and bright and bloody. "Can you see the field?"

"What field? The one you dream?"

"Yes."

"Nope."

"Then I am in your dream." If his mortal consort had once invaded his dream, could he not invade hers? She'd anchored him in the dreams, in the bloodstorm that had sought to turn him into a cold, heartless being of pure power.

Hauling Elena against him, he sheathed one sword and gripped the side of her neck. "Elena-mine, as you were my anchor, now I am yours."

Her hand rose to his cheek, her sword falling to her side even as the wildfire light began to fade and the darkness crept closer, ready to consume her. Behind him, the green of the field grew brighter.

"I'm so tired, Archangel," said his wild and beautiful Elena who didn't know the meaning of giving up. "We really need to wake up."

He resisted. "The chrysalis is too small."

"No wings? Or are we talking even more missing limbs?" She pressed her fingers to his lips. "We'll find out soon enough." A sigh before she came into his arms.

Around them, the gray raged, reaching out grasping tendrils toward her. And he knew . . . he had to wake them up before the Cascade got what it wanted and consumed her. Even Elena could not battle forever. "How do I wake us?"

"Remember the bloodstorm," she said, her eyes closed and her sword dropping to the floor as her strength deserted her.

His mind bled with thoughts of the sky that had boiled crimson, the rain like shards of ice. He'd given up the dark and old power that wanted to fill him to the brim because that same power would kill Elena with its coldness.

He'd ejected it from his body, waking himself back to reality.

Today, it was golden lightning become wildfire that filled his veins. A power he could control. A power he could use and that didn't use him. But—"No power is worth you, Elena-mine. I would give up immortality for a single mortal lifetime with you."

"See you on the other side, Archangel."

Her words were yet sounds being formed when he released every drop of the wildfire that was so bright and so beautiful and of them. And because his heart was more than a touch mortal, he told that energy to go to ground. Not to turn the sky into an inferno that erased hundreds of angels from existence, but to sear itself into the earth.

It was eerie, how he saw white owls in silhouette in the burn of light, watching with eyes of gold.

Cassandra! What do you see!

The future aligns. Paths are chosen. Death comes. A voice so very languid, falling into a deep Sleep. *Such death, child of flames. Goddess of Nightmare. Wraith without a shadow. Rising into her Reign of Death.*

Do you see her end? he asked as the wildfire light spread and spread and spread.

I see . . . Sleep heavy in every word.

Cassandra! The light was almost to the edge, Elena motionless in his arms. *What do you see!*

Wings of silver. Wings of blue. Mortal heart. Broken dreams. Shatter. Shatter. Shatter. A sundering. A grave. One last sigh of a being slipping into the Sleep of immortals. *I see the end. I see . . .*

Raphael came awake with the side of his face on dirt so hot it glowed, his rest prematurely ended, and his new heart not yet ready. It had, he realized, broken under the weight of the violent energy release and exposed the small mortal heart within. That small heart had exploded from the pressure.

Fragments swam in his blood, weaving their way through his entire system. A system devoid of wildfire. Devoid too of the golden lightning. Uncaring of the loss and of the agony in his chest, he opened his eyes . . . and looked into those of liquid silver.

If you haven't tried Nalini Singh's bestselling Psy-Changeling series, dive in with *Silver Silence*, available now from Berkley!

1

To be a Mercant is to be a shadow that moves with will, with intelligence, with pitiless precision.

—*Ena Mercant (circa 2057)*

Silver Mercant believed in control. It was what made her so good at what she did—she was never caught by surprise. She prepared for everything. Unfortunately, it was impossible to prepare for the heavily muscled man standing at her apartment door.

"How did you get in?" she asked in Russian, making sure to stand front and center in the doorway so he wouldn't forget this was her territory.

Bears had a habit of just pushing everything out of their way.

This bear shrugged his broad shoulders where he leaned

up against the side of her doorjamb. "I asked nicely," he replied in the same language.

"I live in the most secure building in central Moscow." Silver stared at that square-jawed face with its honey-dark skin. It wasn't a tan. Valentin Nikolaev retained the shade in winter, got darker in summer. "And," she added, "building security is made up of former soldiers who don't understand the word 'nice.'" One of those soldiers was a Mercant. No one talked their way past a Mercant.

Except for this man. This wasn't the first time he'd appeared on her doorstep on the thirty-fourth floor of this building.

"I have a special charm," Valentin responded, his big body blocking out the light and his deep smile settling into familiar grooves in his cheeks, his hair an inky black that was so messy she wondered if he even owned a comb. That hair appeared as if it might have a silken texture, in stark contrast to the harsh angles of his face.

No part of him was tense, his body as lazy limbed as a cat's.

She knew he was trying to appear harmless, but she wasn't an idiot. Despite her offensive and defensive training, the alpha of the StoneWater clan could crush her like a bug, physically speaking. He had too much brawn, too much strength for her to beat him without a weapon. So it was good that Silver's mind was a ruthless weapon.

"Why did you need to see me at seven in the morning?" she asked, because it was clear he wasn't going to tell her how he kept getting past her security.

He extended a hand on which sat a data crystal. "The clan promised EmNet a breakdown of the small incidents we've handled over the past three months."

Those "small incidents" were times when Psy, humans, or non-clan changelings needed assistance in the area controlled by StoneWater—or elsewhere, when members of the bear clan were close enough to help. As the director of the worldwide Emergency Response Network run under the aegis of the Trinity Accord, Silver was the one who coordinated all available resources—and in this part of the world, that included the StoneWater bears.

Of course, she had no ability to order them to do anything—trying that on a predatory changeling was an exercise in abject failure. But she could ask. So far, the bears had always come through. The data crystal would tell her how many clan members and/or other resources had been required to manage each instance; it would help her fine-tune her requests in the future.

She took the crystal, not bothering to ask why the alpha of the clan had turned up to personally deliver the data.

Valentin liked to do things his way.

"Why does Selenka let you get away with breaching her territory?" The BlackEdge wolves had control over this part of Moscow when it came to changeling access. The city was split evenly between the wolf pack and the bear clan, with the rest of their respective territories heading outward from that central dividing line.

This apartment building fell in the wolf half.

Valentin smiled, night-dark eyes alight in a way she couldn't describe. "StoneWater and BlackEdge are friends now."

If Silver had felt emotion, she may have made a face of sheer disbelief. The two most powerful packs in Russia had a working relationship and no longer clashed in violent confrontations, but they were *not* friends. "I see," she said, refusing to look away from those onyx eyes.

Predatory changelings sometimes took a lack of eye contact as submissive behavior, even when interacting with non-changelings. Bears *definitely* took it as submissive behavior. They weren't exactly subtle about it, either. In fact, bears were the least subtle of the changelings she'd met through her work as Kaleb Krychek's senior aide, and as the head of EmNet.

"What do you see, Starlight?" Valentin asked in his deep rumble of a voice that spoke of the animal that lived under his skin.

Silver refused to react to the name he insisted on calling her. When she'd pointed out he was being discourteous by not using her actual name, he'd told her to call him her *medvezhonok*, her teddy bear, that he wouldn't mind. It was difficult to have a rational conversation with a man who seemed impossible to insult or freeze out.

Bears.

She'd heard Selenka Durev say that through tightly clenched teeth on more than one occasion. While Silver's conditioning under the Silence Protocol remained pristine, her mind clear of all emotion, in the time she'd known Valentin, she'd come to understand the wolf alpha's reaction. "Thank you for the data," she said to him now. "Next time, you might wish to consider an invention we in the civilized world call e-mail."

His laugh was so big it filled the air, filled the entire space of her apartment.

The thought made no sense, yet it appeared like clockwork when Valentin laughed in her vicinity. She'd told herself multiple times that she worked for the most powerful man in the world; Valentin was only a changeling alpha. Unfortunately, it appeared changeling alphas had their own potent brand of charisma. And this bear alpha had a surfeit of it.

"Have you thought about my offer?" he asked, the laughter still in his eyes.

"The answer remains the same," Silver said as a burn spread through her chest. "I do not wish to go have ice cream with you."

"It's really good ice cream." Smile disappearing, Valentin suddenly shifted fully upright from his leaning position against the doorjamb, the size and muscle of him dangerously apparent. "You doing okay?"

"Quite fine," Silver said, even as the burn morphed into a jagged spike. Something was wrong. She had to contact—

Her brain shorted out. She was aware of her body beginning to spasm, her lungs gasping for air as her legs crumpled, but she couldn't get her telepathic "muscles" to work, couldn't contact her family or Kaleb for an emergency teleport.

M oving far faster than most people expected bear change-lings to move, Valentin caught Silver's slender body before she'd done much more than sway on those ice-pick heels she liked to wear. He knew it wasn't the heels that were toppling her; Silver was never in any danger on those heels. The woman walked on them like he walked on his "bigfoot-sized" feet, as described by one of his three older sisters.

"I've got you, Starlight," he said, scooping her up in his arms and walking into her apartment.

He'd been trying to get in for ten long months, ever since he first met Ms. Silver Mercant. But he'd never expected it to be because she was convulsing in his arms. Placing her on the dark gray of the sofa, he turned her onto her side and gripped her jaw to keep her head from jerking too hard. At least she was breathing, though the sound was ragged.

With his other hand, he grabbed his phone, went to call Kaleb Krychek. The viciously powerful telekinetic could get her to help far faster than any ambulance. But Silver's body was spasming too violently for him to both hold the phone and keep her from hurting herself. Swearing under his breath, he dropped the phone and placed his other hand on her hip, holding her in place.

"Not how I wanted to put my hands on you, *moyo sol-nyshko*." He kept talking so she'd know she wasn't alone, but his blood was chilling with every second that passed. It was going on too long.

Deciding to risk it, he released her hip and, snatching up his phone, managed to make the call. "Silver's apartment," he said to the pitiless son of a bitch who was Silver's boss. "Medical emergency."

He dropped the phone as Silver jerked again. "Hold on, Starlight," he ordered in his most obnoxiously alpha voice, trying to keep her body from wrenching painfully at the same time. If Silver was going to respond to anything, it would be to the idea that he'd dared give her an order. "You're tougher than this."

Her eyes, that glorious silver, met his, the pupils huge . . . right before her body went limp.

Kaleb appeared in the room at the same instant, the Psy male dressed in a flawless black-on-black suit. "What happened?" he asked, his voice as cold as midnight on the steppes.

"Get her to a doctor," Valentin growled, the sound coming from the human male's vocal cords but carrying the bear's rage. "Tell them it was poison."

Kaleb was smart enough not to waste time questioning him. He simply teleported out, taking Silver with him. Teeth gritted at the fact she was out of his sight, Valentin got up and, going into Silver's kitchen, began to pull out anything that could be food. Psy had strange ideas of food—meal bars and nutrient mixes. The only surprise in Silver's cupboard was a block of fine dark chocolate.

Wondering if he'd discovered a secret about the most fascinating woman he'd ever met, a secret he could use to sneak past her defenses—no, he had no shame whatsoever when it came to Silver Mercant—he turned over the block and found a small card still attached to it. The writing was in English. It said: *Thank you for your assistance, Ms. Mercant. I hope you enjoy this small taste of our family business. ~Rico Cavalier*

His bear rumbled inside his chest.

This was the kind of gift a man gave a woman he was interested in—but it looked like this Rico had struck out if the chocolate was sitting in the back of what passed for Silver's pantry.

Good. Otherwise, I'd have had to pound the fool into dust.

The only one courting Starlight was going to be Valentin.

Having collected all possible food items, including some bland-looking "cake" from the cooler that was probably a nutrient-dense protein supplement, he began to go through them. Changelings had the sharpest noses of the three races.

Bears had the sharpest noses among changelings.

Nothing would escape him now that he'd pinpointed the poisonous scent from the millions of others in the air at any one time: the exemplar had come from Silver, her body screaming a warning to his senses as the poison went active.

"Hungry, Alpha Nikolaev?"

He didn't start at Krychek's midnight voice, having scented the cardinal telekinetic's return to the room. Thankfully for his nose, Kaleb didn't have the astringent metallic scent that some Psy did, the ones who were so deep in the emotionless regime they called Silence that Valentin didn't think anything would get them out.

It was as if they'd cut out their hearts and souls.

Silver was pure ice, but she didn't have that metallic scent, either. It gave him hope. As did the faint touch of fire he kept picking up around her, a hidden sunshine that flickered against his skin. Valentin was determined to seduce Silver's hidden wildness out into the light. Who better than an uncivilized bear, after all?

"How is she?" he asked, looking Krychek in the eye.

The telekinetic's gaze was the eerie white stars on black that denoted the strongest among the Psy race, difficult to read even if it hadn't been Kaleb Krychek—a man Valentin respected for his relentless will but mostly for his unexpected capacity for loyalty.

StoneWater did its research on possible business partners. Valentin, a young second to Zoya at the time Krychek first appeared on StoneWater's radar, was the one who'd dug into the Psy male. And what he'd discovered about Krychek was that if you didn't betray him, he wouldn't betray you.

Valentin could work with a man like that.

Especially since Krychek had had the good sense to employ Silver.

The words the telekinetic spoke were toneless. "The medics are working on stabilizing her."

Valentin's gut clenched.

A deep rumbling building in his chest, he held out a barely used jar of nutrient mix. "This has the same toxic scent as what I scented on her—get it tested. I'm going to finish checking the other items."

Kaleb left at once, no doubt aware that, to treat Silver effectively, the medics needed to know the type of poison she'd ingested. Because while Valentin could tell something was toxic, he couldn't separate out individual poisonous scents—not when he'd never made it a point to learn those gradations.

He saw the half-full glass on the counter, realized he'd interrupted Silver at breakfast. He didn't need to lift the glass to his nose to scent the toxins swirling in the coffee-colored liquid. If he'd been here, he would've smashed that glass out of her hand before a drop touched her lips.

Jaw grinding, he handed the glass to Krychek when the other man returned. The third time Krychek came back, Valentin had found a second contaminated jar of nutrient mix. "It was the third from the front on the right-hand side," he said, knowing the location of the poisoned jars might be important. "The nutrient bars were clean." He'd ruthlessly opened each and every packet, exposing them to the air and to his nose. "Silver's going to be mad I trashed her kitchen."

Kaleb took the jar, examined the label, then teleported out with it. When he returned, he said, "That was ordinary nutrient mix available at any Psy grocer."

"You thinking product tampering?"

"It's a possibility—those of my race are not universally liked."

That was a vast understatement. Many of the Psy might be attempting to regain their emotions after more than a hundred years of training themselves to feel nothing, but their previous rulers had done massive damage, killed and tortured and created a deep vein of ill will.

Both humans and changelings had long memories.

"The other option is an assassination attempt." Krychek's cardinal eyes took in the mess Valentin had made of the food. "I trust in your sense of smell, but I'll get everything tested regardless."

Valentin felt no insult. This wasn't about pride. It was about Silver's life. "Do it. Now tell me where she is."

Kaleb slipped his hands into the pockets of his pants. "Silver hasn't mentioned a friendship."

"I'm working on it." Had been doing so since the day he'd walked scowling into a meeting and come face-to-face with a woman who made him think of hidden fire and cold, distant, searingly brilliant starlight. And, let's be honest: skin privileges. *Naked* skin privileges. Wild-monkey skin privileges. He couldn't be around Silver and not have his body react. Her own body, it was slender, but with *all* the right curves. And she was *tough*, tough as a female bear out for blood.

Never once had she backed down against his deliberate provocation.

His bear liked that. A lot.

Enough to throw her over his shoulder and carry her off to his lair if only she wouldn't fry his brains for daring. He was tempted to chance it anyway. He had a hard head, could probably take it so long as she wasn't trying to kill him.

That mind of hers . . . He'd never met its like. Silver Mercant forgot nothing, and she had a steely presence that made even rowdy bears sit up and take notice. Woman like that, she'd make one hell of a mate. Too bad she refused to even consider the idea: Silver wasn't budging on the whole emotionless Silence thing.

"My people chose Silence for a reason," she'd said to him three visits earlier. "While parts of that reasoning have proven false enough to topple Silence for many, other parts still apply. I am and always will be Silent. That means I will never be ready to 'run off' and experience 'shenanigans' with you."

No matter. Valentin had a plan.

Because she damn well was going to survive. "Don't even try to stop me from seeing her, Krychek," he said to the cardinal, who still hadn't spilled Silver's location. "I'm bigger and meaner than you."

Krychek raised an eyebrow. "Bigger, yes. Meaner? Let's leave that an open question. However, since she's alive because of you, I think you can be trusted with her whereabouts." He told Valentin the name of the hospital.

It happened to be a short ten-minute run from here. Normally, Valentin would've covered that distance without hesitation—his bear would've barely stretched out by the time he reached the hospital. He could do vehicles, but he didn't really like them. They were all too damn small as far as he was concerned. But this wasn't a normal day. "Can I hitch a ride?"

The other man didn't say anything, but less than a second later, Valentin found himself standing in an antiseptic white corridor, the floor beneath his feet a chilly gray-blue. The chairs on one side were attached to the wall, the seat cushions darkest navy. On the right of the chairs was a door inset with a small square of glass.

Beyond that glass lay an operating theatre where white-garbed doctors and nurses worked with frantic efficiency to stabilize Silver. He couldn't see her, but regardless of the powerful hospital smells in the air, sharp and biting, he could scent the ice-cold starlight and secret fire of her.

"I thought you'd take her to a private clinic." This public hospital was an excellent one, but Silver was critical to the fragile balance of their fractured world—and Krychek could teleport anywhere in the blink of an eye.

"The lead doctor working on her is one of the world's foremost specialists in toxins and poisons and their impact on the Psy body."

"You download that information from the psychic network you're all part of?"

Krychek nodded.

"Useful." Valentin couldn't imagine a life in which his mind was connected to a limitless vastness that included millions of strangers, but as a bear whose clan was his heartbeat, he could understand it. "You didn't leave her here alone." Krychek had been delayed returning to him the first time around. Long enough to bring in someone to watch over Silver.

"No, he didn't." The woman who'd spoken had just walked over from where she'd been getting a glass of water not far down the corridor. Her language of choice was English, and she had a scent that was almost no scent. But to a bear, everyone had a scent, and she hadn't quite managed to erase every thread of hers. The subtle memory of soap, the natural body scent that was uniquely hers, a touch of roses.

He didn't have to ask her identity; this woman was Silver in fifty years. Her hair pure white and her eyes the same as his Starlight's, her facial bones fine, she was clearly a Mercant. And, if the rumors Valentin's third-eldest sister had heard were true, then she was probably *the* Mercant.

He took a chance. "Grandmother Mercant," he said in the same language she'd used, inclining his head slightly in acknowledgment of another alpha.

Silver's grandmother didn't display any surprise at his greeting, so regal, she clearly took it as her due that she'd be recognized—this despite the fact the head of the Mercant family preferred to stay firmly out of the limelight. Yes, the Mercant women were as tough as steel.

More than tough enough to handle bears.

"You have me at a disadvantage," was her polite but in no way warm response.

"Valentin Nikolaev," he said. "Alpha of the StoneWater clan."

"He was with Silver when she collapsed."

Grandmother Mercant's eyes bored into Valentin's on the heels of Krychek's words. "If my granddaughter survives, it'll be because of your quick actions." She shifted her attention to the cardinal who was the third point in their triangle. "Any response from the lab?"

"No," Krychek said, then paused. "I have the report. I'm sending it through."

Beyond the square of glass, Valentin saw a doctor lift up her head. She nodded once toward the window to acknowledge the telepathic message before beginning to issue orders to her staff.

Minutes turned to an hour, more.

Still, they waited.

The Human Patriot

He didn't consider himself a bad man. He wasn't in any way like the other self-centered bastards in the Consortium. They wanted to sow division and foster chaos because it would be better for their bottom line. He was disgusted by their greed, had accepted the Consortium's overture only because he intended to use the group to achieve his aims, aims formed of conscience and hope and love for his people.

To him, the Consortium was a tool to help him mount a righteous revolution. Yes, he made ruthless decisions when called for, but that was in business. In life, in politics, he acted on the conviction of his heart, and that heart was telling him the Trinity Accord would lead to the destruction of all that he held dear.

His beloved children, his accomplished and beautiful wife, they'd all be destroyed by this "proto-Federation" agreement being touted as a force for unity. Psy, humans, changelings, people of all three races would be equal, all have a say in the direction of the world.

"Bullshit."

He closed his hand into a tight fist on the aged cherry-wood of his desk, the top inlaid with fine gold and semiprecious stones. It was a status symbol, this desk. Worth hundreds of times the yearly income of the common man on the street, it reminded him every day of what he'd achieved through determined intelligence . . . and the genetic luck of the draw.

Without the natural shield that protected his mind, he would long ago have become another casualty of Psy arrogance, another human psychically raped and violated by the emotionless, soulless bastards, his ideas and his freedom stolen.

His eyes went to the photo of his wife on his desk. So *much* light in her eyes. That had been before. She still laughed, she still loved, but she hadn't been the same since that horrific day when she'd come up with an invention a Psy coveted. The monster had stripped her clean before the man who loved her to the core of his being could find a way to protect her.

She no longer created, knowing it could be taken from her at any instant.

But they were supposed to believe the Psy were turning over a new leaf, that they'd suddenly begun to respect the sanctity of the human mind?

Throwing down the pen he'd picked up to sign a contract, he rose to his feet and, stepping out onto the balcony attached to his home study, looked down at the cool paradise of their white-tiled courtyard with its fountain in the center. His children's laughter drifted up from below, their small bodies hidden by the black plum trees that hung heavy with fruit.

"Papa! Papa!" His boy ran out from under the trees, held up a toy truck. "Come play!"

He smiled, his heart so full he could hardly bear it. "In a moment," he called down. "Let Papa finish his work first. We'll play afterward."

Happy with the promise, the boy returned to his play while a little girl jumped into the fountain in laughing delight. Wild, his daughter was, and the apple of his eye. How could it be otherwise when she was so like her mother? And his son, oh, he loved his son, too.

So much.

Enough to fight for a future where they wouldn't be used and discarded. Because if his informant was right, the Psy race desperately needed to harness human minds for some reason the informant hadn't yet been able to unearth. And whenever the Psy needed something from humans, the powerful psychic race just took it.

No more.

If that meant he had to become a monster himself, had to circumvent loyalties and buy betrayal, even order the death of a brilliant woman who—on the surface—appeared to have no bias in sending aid to various humanitarian crises around the world, so be it.

Silver Mercant and EmNet were one of the foundation stones on which Trinity was built. But that foundation stone was set to break, alongside several others.

Soon.